GOD'S DICE

To Sandy

R. Roy Lutz

"Randy"

ISBN-10: 0692767150
ISBN-13: 978-0692767153

To my loving wife Chris,
who never stopped believing.

PREFACE

Before writing *God's Dice,* I had been pondering how the seemingly random events in my life had lead to the many unexpected ups, downs and u-turns that my life had taken. I realized that, if I traced back the chain of events that resulted in each major life change, it had often started with one trivial decision, made on a whim, which seemed inconsequential at the time, with no hint of its long term repercussions.

At about this same time, I was working with developmentally disabled adults. I had previously worked in photography, electronic design, marketing, computer repair, and in auto manufacturing. Nothing in my education or in my experience would have hinted that social work was a possible career option. I was amazed that, despite my background, I would now somehow find myself helping mentally impaired adults learn to live independent lives. I had not *consciously* chosen this career path. Had it been my fate, written in stone by God, or had it been simply the result of my own choices?

I was particularly intrigued by the autistic adults that I was privileged to work with. Although none were savant, the autistic people I met and worked with were all extraordinary individuals in their own way.

I read up on autism spectrum disorders and the associated savant abilities that accompany 20% of cases. My curiosity exposed me to various theories about the possible causes of autism. I was especially interested in the rare cases of delayed onset autism and of the even rarer cases of suddenly acquired savant abilities in adults.

The question of fate and the mysteries of autism form the foundation of this possible, albeit improbable, story about how ordinary people try to change the roll of *God's Dice.*

I use the term *ordinary people,* but nobody is truly ordinary. We are all unique in our own way. I have attempted to capture that uniqueness in my characters. And, this is why I wrote each chapter as a character's first-person account.

God's Dice is not a story about events, as much as a story about the people living those events.

–R. Roy Lutz

ACKNOWLEDGMENTS

I wish to thank the following people for their enthusiastic support, and for their critical beta reader reviews of this novel. Their timely and helpful input was invaluable: Mireille Hatchell, Irma Polster, Claire Mattson, Donald Solari, Charlie Shumila, Aurelia L. Scorgie, Janet Lutz; Sandra Azelton, Freda Thompson.

Also, the members of the following writers groups contributed many useful suggestions and much needed feedback: Clearwater Writers Meet-Up, Palm Harbor School of the Novel, Palm Harbor Sci-Fi & Fantasy Writers Meet-Up.

Lastly, I must give a special thanks to my wife Chris, who has been my most steadfast cheerleader. Without her constant support and encouragement, this novel would not exist.

"God does not play dice with His universe."

Albert Einstein

CHAPTER 1
HECK

The bear was only a hundred and fifty feet away.

I first noticed him coming around a patch of fireweed, moving toward the camp. I recognized the one-thousand-pound Kodiak grizzly bear at once. Tom and I had seen him in the area a few days ago. We had named this one Limpy because he had an injured left-front paw that produced a pronounced limp.

Tom had researched Kodiak bears in preparation for his planned National Geographic article. Tom said he was somewhat underweight for a male Kodiak bear of his apparent age, and for this time of year. He guessed that the bear had probably weighed three-hundred pounds more last year at this time. The injury was likely hindering his hunting and fishing effectiveness.

I wished Tom was here now, but he'd gone 'shooting' some two hours ago.

I froze. "And, what are you up to, big guy?" I whispered to myself.

When Limpy saw me, he stopped and sniffed the air several times.

"There's no food here, buddy." I said a little louder.

Tom and I had been meticulous about sealing food in bear-proof containers, and burying waste well away from our tent. The bears that we had encountered so far were either indifferent to our presence, or more often, were cautiously wary and kept their distance. I assumed that Limpy's arrival was accidental, and that he'd turn away when he realized there were humans around.

Limpy sniffed the air again and seemed to make a decision. He took a tentative limping step in my direction. Despite our precautions, he smelled something that said *food,* and that something was apparently me.

I had fried bacon yesterday morning. We had buried the grease and washed the pan, but I had been wearing the same parka. *The splatter?*

"Okay, so you're gonna be a bad boy." *Time to make some noise.* I kept a Beretta 9mm semi-automatic pistol loaded and ready for just this kind of contingency, but I had left it in the tent, some thirty feet away. I knew the Beretta had little chance of stopping a big grizzly. I was only hoping to scare him off with it.

Tom had the Remington bolt-action thirty-aught-six rifle that we had brought for more serious situations. At least that was the plan, but Tom and the rifle were not here at the moment.

Limpy took another couple steps toward me. I knew better than to try and run from a grizzly. I kept my face toward him and backed slowly away toward the tent.

Looks like that "stalking behavior" *you told me about, Tom. He must be a hungry camper. Beckman steak on the menu?* This thought held no humor. I could feel my heart pumping.

Tom had left just before daybreak so he could try to get some silhouette photos of bears he had seen congregating for the last couple days by the river only a half a mile away. He took two cameras, a walkie-talkie, and the 30-06. He should have been back a half-hour ago.

That's it, the walkie. I hope Tom's still on channel five. I slowly pulled the walkie-talkie from my parka vest pocket while continuing to back toward the tent.

I pushed the talk button and said, "Tom, are you there?" I waited. No response.

"Tom, I think I need the rifle." I tried again, a little more demanding this time.

The radio crackled with Tom's tinny but distinctive voice. "Jesus, Heck, this better be good. I'm getting some great shots here. What the hell did you say you needed?" Tom did not like to be interrupted when he was focused on his work or "in the zone" as he called it.

"Bring the rifle. Limpy's in the camp." I tried to keep the quaver out of my voice but I knew I had failed.

"Did you try to scare him off?" Tom would have heard the shots.

Limpy moved more boldly toward me. Less than thirty feet separated us.

"Ah… No. Ah… Just get back here. Hurry!" My voice was as unsteady as my legs. I glanced over my shoulder. I was still twenty feet from the tent.

"On my way." Tom's clipped response told me that he understood the urgency of my situation and would get here as fast as he could. I hoped it would be fast enough.

Please hurry Tom.

I was only fifteen feet from the tent, but Limpy had closed the distance between us. He was less than twenty feet from me. From this close distance, he was a jaw-dropping monster.

I could see the severity of the injury to Limpy's paw. It was swollen a great deal, and pus oozed from between the first and second toes. Apparently, he had received a cut of some kind and it had gone septic. Limpy barely let that paw touch the ground as he limped along.

He must be in constant pain. It was a death sentence. I felt a momentary pang of sympathy for him. *Just tryin' to stay alive, huh big guy?* My sympathy turned to terror when he bared his teeth and gave a low growl.

I had left the tent door unzipped. The pistol was on the foot of my sleeping bag just inside. When it was finally within reach, I stooped and slid my hand inside the tent with only a quick glance to verify that the 9mm was still where I had left it.

This movement apparently confused the animal. He stopped his advance for a second. It was enough time for me to retrieve the weapon, rack a round into the chamber, and flick off the safety.

I stood up and continued to back slowly away from the looming beast. He continued his advance, now just fifteen feet away. The breeze had shifted. I caught a whiff of his musty stench.

I glanced behind me and saw that I was nearing a long log that lay near the fire pit. We had used it alternately as a bench and as a chopping block. Stepping over it backwards, or negotiating my way around it, would be awkward. I decided I needed to stand my ground here before I was cornered.

"That's close enough." My voice was more commanding than I felt.

I raised the Berretta over my head, pointed it at the sky, and pulled the trigger. The resulting crack seemed louder than I remembered.

I thought Limpy would bolt, and run away. Instead, he let out a startled roar and lunged at me. He covered the space between us in an instant. Before I could react, the beast was on me.

It felt like I had been hit by a truck. His charge threw me backward onto the rocky ground.

The first swipe of his massive right paw landed just behind my left shoulder. The impact was horrific, rippling through my whole body. It might have ended there except for the heavy parka I was wearing. The thick canvas material of the parka was shredded from my shoulder to my elbow, leaving a deep gash along my arm that immediately sprayed blood.

Somehow, I still clutched the Berretta in my right hand. I swung the pistol up and squeezed the trigger. Too soon. The bullet went wide to the right.

His roar spilled saliva, and hot putrid breath onto my face. As his wide-open jaws descended, I squeezed the trigger again. This time the bullet found flesh, but only his left ear. It was enough to make him spin his head to the left, to fend off the unseen attacker.

Seeing nothing, Limpy whirled back at me and swung again with that deadly right paw. This time the blow landed below my left armpit, instantly splintering ribs and knocking the last bit of air out of my lungs. Only the walkie-talkie that I had stowed in the left vest pocket prevented his claws from gouging a hole in my chest. The left half of my parka was ripped away like so much tissue paper.

I clinched the handgrip on the gun in reflex to the blow. The gun discharged again. At this range, it was hard to miss. The slug sunk deep into Limpy's infected left foreleg. He gave no indication that he even noticed this new injury.

I struggled to suck air in, but nothing happened. I felt oddly disconnected from my body. My vision blurred. I was passing out.

The grizzly continued his assault, now inflicting damage with his right hind foot. With one quick kick, his claws ripped across my left thigh. I felt the bone break with a dull snap, and four parallel slashes rip through my flesh.

I watched everything slow to an impossible crawl. As my consciousness faded, I became a disconnected spectator to a slow motion horror movie, like the playback from a high speed camera.

There was pain, but it seemed to float in the air like a mist. I could not identify where it came from, nor even be sure that it was mine.

Despite my lack of any movement, the pitiless predator continued his attack. He began another slow-motion swipe at my head. I knew it would be the last.

If he had stopped then, I would have given no further resistance. The prize was his. He could eat. He could live. *Good for him,* I thought, strangely empathetic for the wellbeing of my murderer. I accepted my imminent death.

Time all but stopped.

I'm going to die, I thought matter-of-factly. There was no fear at this thought. There was only calm, a calm that defied the chaos that I was fully aware surrounded me.

The clawed catcher's mitt of a paw was closer, bigger.

I can live. Playfully, I tried out this new thought. I let the thought flutter like a butterfly aimlessly across my mind. A curious awareness coalesced out of the fog that was now the remaining essence of my being.

Life or death, it was a choice. I understood that I could choose to live…or not. The option of dying did not frighten me. Instead, it tempted me. A sense of fulfillment and oneness with the universe beckoned seductively.

No, not now. Not just yet. There's more, more to do. I thought. Exactly what the "more" was I didn't know, but I knew it was somehow, in some way, *important.*

Then, I will live. I made this decision casually, as one might select a yellow jellybean rather than an orange one.

The gun. I thought. *What gun? Why is that important?* I struggled to link one thought to the next. *Life. Gun. Trigger. Finger. Move.* I wasn't sure if my finger got the message. I did not hear the shot as my index finger, now disconnected from my consciousness, flinched on the trigger. But I was not concerned. I knew it was done. I knew, with absolute certainty, I would live.

My last dispassionate vision in that silent, high-definition, ultra-slow motion movie was of a giant maw agape inches from my face; saliva dripping translucent strands; the giant paw moving ever so slowly toward me; Limpy's tongue and cheeks silently undulating from the power of his roar; teeth, white, yellow and orange, like Halloween corn candies; eyes, black pools amid blazing halos of primeval rage.

The massive paw swung ever closer; dirty cracked paw pads, fur projecting from between the toes.

A tuft of fur floated toward my face, like a feather. *Strange.*

Limpy's paw touched my left ear.

My universe instantly went black. Only the tiniest speck of my existence remained—an infinitely small, perfectly black shadow, floating in a limitless ocean of nothingness.

Peace.

CHAPTER 2
RAY

I loved her. Mostly, I loved how she loved me.

Her love was complete and unquestioning. It was a love that was innocent without being naïve. It was a love of total faith in me. She knew all of my faults, and loved me despite them. She could always see the best in me, even when I was at my worst. And through her eyes, she made me see the best in myself. She made me ignore my own tarnished self-image and see the shining reflection of the man I wanted to be, but had never believed that I could be.

She was young, but not too young to understand that the ugliness of the world is often veiled in false beauty. She was wise in the subtleties of the human heart. She could see lies and she could smell deceit.

She was beautiful, not in big and obvious ways, but a thousand small ways. Her voice was clear but soft and never harsh. It caressed my ears like a cool breeze on hot summer's day. Her hair was a non-descript light brownish color that seemed to dance across her face with a joyful exuberance for the woman it was privileged to adorn.

She was slim, but not painfully so. Her long legs complimented her slender arms. Every part of her body flowed effortlessly into the next, creating a joyous harmony of skin, and muscle, and bone that was hard to define, but just as hard to deny.

Her eyes constantly smiled, even when her mouth did not. Her lips only revealed the smile that was always impishly hiding just beneath the surface. A simple grin could light my day. But her full smile was like the first warm rays of dawn after a long cold night. It made my heart glow with a light I had not known existed before we met.

Her gentle touch conveyed all the love she felt for me. Even in casual moments, her touch clearly proclaimed, *"I love this man with all of my heart. He is the most precious thing in my life."*

I loved the love she gave me that I knew I could never fully deserve. I could only try to live up the perfect man she believed I was. With time, perhaps I could become that man.

###

I had been gazing out of the window watching the Japanese shoreline disappear slowly thousands of feet below us. My reverie was interrupted by Julia's enthusiastic, "Aaaaachoooo!"

I turned to her as she reached for a tissue from her purse. "Wow! Where did that come from?" I said.

"I don't know, Ray. Maybe I picked up a bug somewhere." She sniffed. "I have that funny feeling in my nose like I did when I got that cold last Christmas."

I leaned over and gave her a kiss playfully on the lips before she was even done with the tissue. "Share and share alike. Isn't that the deal?" I said with a chuckle.

"Ha, ha. You won't be laughing when we're both stuck in bed all day with a cold." She said with a smile as she pushed me away.

"Hmm. Let me think about that." I pretended to be in deep concentration for a moment. "Both of us in bed all day, you say? Sounds pretty good to me." I quickly planted another kiss squarely on her lips before she was able to dodge it.

We both laughed as I gently squeezed her hand in both of mine. I could feel the warmth of her love radiate through the whole of my being.

After a moment of silence, I said softly, "Forever, babe."

"Forever." She repeated, as our eyes met and we gave each other that now familiar look that only we understood.

How I loved this woman. I had tried to tell her on several occasions the true depth of my love, but I had never been able to exactly find the words. Maybe there were no words for my feelings for her. It didn't matter, she knew.

I married Julia in June, just three months ago. Our religious convictions would not allow us to simply live together until the wedding. We decided on getting married sooner than we originally planned and have a mini-honeymoon, rather than waiting to get married later just for the sake of the bigger *official* honeymoon trip to Japan.

A weekend at a romantic secluded lodge near Snoqualmie Falls in the foothills East of Seattle would serve as our June mini-honeymoon.

The official honeymoon trip to Japan could wait a couple months. We had finally saved enough for the trip by last August. The off-season airline ticket rates to Japan were cheaper for September, so we decided not to wait any longer than we had to, and go then.

Since our first opportunity in June to fully express our love for each other, I knew we had made the right choice. I often vividly recalled our wedding night. After our first feverish, and slightly clumsy, sexual session, we had cuddled naked under a blanket in front of the fireplace in our luxury room, just talking and kissing for hours.

Every moment since then, she had fulfilled my every dream, and not just in the bedroom. It was as if we had always been together. Her thoughts were my thoughts. Her feelings were my feelings. After the first night, when we made love, it was like her body was my body, and mine was hers. And now, my life was her life. I couldn't imagine it ever being any other way.

This two-week trip to Japan had been worth the wait. The trip had been all we had hoped for and more. But mostly, spending time together without the mundane day-to-day chores to attend to, nothing but time to enjoy each other's company, this was shear bliss. I was still basking in the afterglow of our adventures together in Japan.

It was forty minutes since United flight 876 had left the terminal at Tokyo's Narita Airport. I checked my watch, 5:45 p.m. *Still on Japanese time,* I thought. *Hum, might as well reset it now.* I manipulated the watch-stem as I did the mental calculations. *Let's see, 18 hours back would make it 11:45 p.m. in Seattle. We should be able to get out of Sea-Tac airport by about 9:00 a.m. Just in time for a little breakfast, and maybe a little nap to resynchronize our biological clocks.*

A barely perceptible smile invaded the corners of my mouth. The vision of a little late morning bed time with Julia was one I savored as I returned my gaze to the window. The last hazy wisp of the Japanese shoreline had faded into the endless blue expanse of the Pacific Ocean.

###

"Ray, I'm getting dizzy and I can't breathe." Julia said weakly as the wheels touched the runway. I carefully brushed an errant lock of her long brown hair from her flushed face.

"Hang in there, sweetheart. We're on the ground now. This is some nasty bug you gave me. I'm getting chills, my face feels hot, and I wish I had a couple aspirin. Looks like we're going to be keeping that bed warm for the next few days, huh?" I tried to sound cheerful, but I knew my voice betrayed my concern and worry for her.

"I'll be fine. I just need to get some fresh air and soak in a hot bath for a while." I wasn't buying it and she knew it.

This looks bad, really bad. If I could just get her away from all these other sickies, she'd be fine.

"Look sweetie, let's forget about the luggage for now. I'll get a cab to take us to the emergency room. That way we can get some prescriptions for some good drugs right away. We'll have them called in and pick them up on our way home."

"But I'm going to need some of my things in my suitcase." She said.

"I'll call Ken and get him to come down and pick up the bags for us."

"Okay…I guess. I think he'll be willing to do that for us." She was probably hoping he'd be awake when I called.

"He better! It's about time your slacker brother pays us back a favor or two. That reminds me, he still owes us that fifty bucks too."

"Ray, I told you not to call him that. He's just having a hard time finding a good job."

"Yeah, that's what you've been telling me for the last year. Ya know, if he didn't sleep in 'til noon every day, he might actually be able to find a good job. I bet he'll still be in bed when I call."

"If he is, just tell Mom to kick his butt out of bed. You know Mom, she's always up by six. I know he'll do it, if Mom tells him too."

"Okay then, we won't worry about the bags. We just have to worry about getting you home and in bed." I gently brushed the hair from her forehead with my fingertips.

"I told you, I'll be fine. You don't have to worry about me." Julia tried to put a lilt in her voice for my sake, but it was overruled by the wheezing sound she made.

CHAPTER 3
ANNA

I keyed the microphone on the intercom as the plane turned off of runway 34R onto the taxiway. "This is Anna Grant, your senior flight attendant. On behalf of United Airlines and the crew of Flight 876, I would like to welcome you to Seattle/Tacoma International Airport. We are ten minutes ahead of our scheduled landing time."

I paused. *Keep it light and positive,* I told myself. "Unfortunately, we will not be going directly to the gate. Because of the numerous passengers that have become ill, we have been instructed to wait temporarily in a holding area, until medical assistance can be arranged.

"Although we do not know for certain how long this will take, we are hopeful the delay will be short. We will keep you informed as we get any further information. In the meantime, we ask for your patience and we wish to thank you again for flying United Airlines."

They're not ready for the word "quarantine," *not yet. No need to get them all upset about it. Maybe it won't be that bad. There's nothing we can do about it anyway, and they'll find out soon enough. Besides, my first job now is to keep them calm.*

As I expected, my announcement was met with a round of groans from all the well passengers, and even from many of the sick ones. *Resignation. That's the reaction I was hoping for,* I thought, as I made my way to the front of plane. *I know they don't like the delay, but they're not angry and there's no sign of panic.*

I muffled a sneeze in my handkerchief before I knocked on the cockpit door and cracked it open a couple inches.

Mark McKenzie, sitting in the left seat, glanced over his shoulder and then quickly back to the controls as they rolled down toward the end of the taxiway. "C'mon in Anna, and close da door."

I had known Mark for most of the twenty-five years we had both been with the company. We were both getting close to retirement, and we both knew that calm professionalism was the only way to handle a stressful situation. That bit of wisdom had been earned the hard way from having seen it all and done it all during our many years in the air.

"That was jis' right, Anna, jis' enough, but not too much. Yer good!" He chuckled. Mark had mentioned once that he had grown up in Amarillo, Texas, but that had been forty years ago. In spite of the years, his Texas accent still leaked out at times when he was under stress or just plain ticked off. I had heard Mark's *Amarillo* drawl before and read this situation as mostly the later, just plain ticked off.

"I wanted to see if they've told you anything more about how they want us to handle this. Are they going to quarantine us or not?" I said calmly. I normally didn't take this kind of casual tone with the cockpit crew. But in this case, I knew Mark's style. I knew he liked to keep things loose when the going got tough. It kept people calm and focused on their job. Also I wanted Mark to know I was just as calm as he was and in control of the passenger situation.

"It's soundin' like they're keepin' that option open. If they do, is there anythin' more you're gonna need to take kir of da passengers?"

"Yes, we're going to need some detailed direction for starters. It's not something I get to deal with every day, you know."

"Unless you're real lucky." Mark chuckled.

"I know what the book says, but the book is pretty short on specifics."

"I know. That's because it's The Centers for Disease Control that calls the shots."

"So, what do they say?" I asked.

"Good question! I've already ask'et twice, and I'm still waitin' fur'in answer."

The co-pilot, Bob Donahue, chimed in as he turned to look at me over his left shoulder. "I don't think they *know* how they're going to handle it yet. I suppose they'll figure it out eventually."

"Well you see, i's like this. I'm jes' the bus driva he'ya. They tell me to par'kit over yonder in da back forty, so that's jes' what I'm gonna do." Mark chuckled again.

Yes, definitely a little ticked off, Anna thought. "But in the meantime we're the ones that have to deal with 215 passengers."

Bob cracked a big grin, " 'We?' I think that's *your* job, Anna, isn't it? Like Mark says, we're just the bus drivers up here. But then, that's why you get paid the big bucks. Isn't that right Mark?"

We all laughed. "Anna, you jes' let me know how it's goin' in the back seat, an' we'll keep shakin' their cage over at the CDC."

"Okay guys, I guess we'll do whatever we've got to do. Don't have too much fun up here. I'll let you know how they're handling it in back."

As I turned to leave, Mark said with a smirk, "Oh an' Anna, I'd lik'a cup'a coffee when you git a minute."

I would have gotten it for him if I had thought he was serious. I could tell by the smirk that it was just Mark's way telling me he knew how busy I was, and that he had confidence that I could handle it. I said sarcastically, "Sure. No problem. I'll get right on that for you. How about a little snack to go with that, too?"

Mark chuckled again, seeing that I'd gotten the message. I turned and slipped out the cabin door.

My smile dropped off my face the second the cockpit door closed behind me. After a long flight, I was tired. This was not going to be a picnic. Even if everything went smoothly, I was still going to have to go through at least a few days of quarantine related hassles, before my life could return to normal.

I sneezed again into my handkerchief, and I felt a heaviness in my lungs that wasn't there a half hour ago. *Oh yeah, there's that too.*

CHAPTER 4
SAL

My desk phone rang. I was only a little annoyed by the interruption. "Hello, this is Dr. Salinger." I wanted to finish up that stack of routine paperwork so that I could work on something more interesting.

"Ma'am, Dr. Edelman would like to see you in his office." It was Rose. I would have known who was calling, if I had bothered to look at the phone console display.

"Right now?"

"Yes. He said to tell you it's important."

"Did he say what it's about?"

"Ah, no ma'am." Rose probably knew what it was about, but she also knew 'her place.'

"Okay. Thanks Rose. I'm on my way." I had worked with Rose for three years now. I knew that when Rose hedged on a question, it meant that she knew more than she wanted to say.

I glanced at a small mirror I keep by my desk and gave my long blonde hair a quick brush, then I grabbed a notebook and a pen and headed down the hall.

Is it good, or bad? I thought I heard a positive note in Rose's voice. Maybe it wasn't bad, but the urgency couldn't be good.

As I passed Rose's desk, she said, "You can go right in. He's waiting for you."

Yes, there was just a hint of a smile there, I thought as I entered the Director's office, *but something else too.*

I had been working with the Centers for Disease Control and Prevention, Epidemiology Program Office (EPO) since I got out of school. It was my first and only paid job.

I was proud to graduate third in my class. I got my Doctorate degree in Health Sciences, with a major in Epidemiology from Harvard Medical School. It had only been a few years, but it seemed long ago.

Dr. Edelman thought he saw something special in my sparse resume and had taken the time to actually read my doctoral thesis on *Genetic Immunity to Viral Pathogens in Rats.*

He later told me that he was impressed by my attention to detail and my solid analytical approach. I think the fact that I looked a lot like his daughter might have had something to do with it too. In any case, he had a generous offer waiting for me when I graduated.

Even though the door was open, I knocked before entering.

"Oh, Dr. Salinger. Close the door and have a seat." *No hint.* He waited for me to settle into my seat.

"Dr. Salinger, you've been with the CDC here in EPO for, what is it, almost three years?

"Yes, that's right, Dr. Edelman." I sat up straight and proper in my chair.

He shook his head, paused and leaned closer. "Ah, look can we drop the Dr. thing? I know your business card says *Dr.* Sally S. Salinger, but you've been here long enough. You can call me Albert. I've heard some of your friends call you Sal. Do you mind if I call you Sal?"

Where had he heard me called, Sal? There were only a couple of people in the Center that were on a first name basis with the Director of Epidemiology Program Office. And, only my close friends called me Sal. But at work, I preferred using the Dr. title. I thought it was more professional, but more importantly, it kept a certain emotional distance between me and my coworkers. I felt more comfortable that way.

I've learned that being too open and friendly, with a figure like mine, is too often misunderstood by male coworkers, and only serves to make me appear less competent. At least, that's how it felt to me.

I wasn't worried that Dr. Edelman would get the wrong idea or get funny with me. He was mostly bald, twenty years older than me, happily married with grandkids, and as straight laced as they come. But still, men are men, and I think it's always better to keep a little professional distance. But, how could I say "no?'

"Ah, sure. That's fine, D…Albert." I felt uncomfortable using his first name, but what could I do? I just wanted him get to the reason he called me in.

"Thank you Sal." He paused looking out the window and pulling on his left earlobe as he collected his thoughts. The ear thing was his trademark idiosyncrasy, and the gist for more than a little good-humored mockery behind his back around the office.

I had too much respect for the man, and I considered it unprofessional to engage in this kind of office wit. But still, I had to suppress an urge to smirk.

"We've got two big problems. First, I just got a call from Seattle International Airport. United Airlines just landed a 767-400 full of a lot of sick people."

"Is it the food?"

"No, that's what I asked. There's no apparent connection there. The symptoms are primarily respiratory, but there are other symptoms too. It looks like it might be something airborne."

"How many are we talking about?"

"It could be a couple hundred."

"Wow!" It was not a very professional remark, I noted to myself, but "Wow" was how I felt.

"Now, here's what I'm worried about. Nobody was sick when they left Tokyo six hours ago, now more than half the people on the plane are showing mild to severe symptoms. That means this thing, whatever it is, has an extremely short incubation period. You know what that means." He said.

"We could have a serious outbreak on our hands if we don't seal that plane up." I felt my heart rate increase.

"Exactly right, quarantine, which brings me to my second problem." He looked at me squarely in the eyes. He took a breath and let it out slowly through his nose holding his gaze on me.

I was afraid to say anything. *Where was this going?* I could only guess.

"I don't have anyone who's experienced with this kind of outbreak, and who's available to head up the field team to coordinate the quarantine, and to do the follow-up investigation. Bill Forbes is working to isolate the source of those three new cases of small pox from Uganda. Adrian Feldman has been tied up with tracking down that new strain of malaria that's been popping up in Florida. And then, there's Joyce Farley who just had a baby last week. They would have been my first three choices."

He let that sink in for a moment.

"Sal, you're a big girl. I don't have time to beat around the bush. There's no one outside this office going to hear this."

Not good.

He continued, "Every review you've had since you started here has been outstanding." He picked up and dropped a thick file folder that I just noticed had been sitting on his desk. "You work hard. You're professional. You're thorough. You're eager to take on new responsibilities. You work well in a team environment. And, you're as smart as they come. You've got a real knack for asking the right questions.

"Sal, I'd like to give you this assignment. I know you want it, and I know you'd do your best. I'm just not sure your best is going to be good enough for this. I don't think you have what it takes to lead a team." He intentionally dropped that in my lap like a three-day-old mackerel and waited for my response.

It took me a few seconds. "I don't understand." I did understand, but I wanted to make him say it.

"Sal, you're great at doing what you're told. But, can you tell other people what to do, and will they do it? I need someone who has some leadership abilities. Nothing in your background demonstrates that. I can't afford to have a team running off in all directions without strong leadership, not on this one. It's too important."

Okay, I guess I asked for it.

He continued. "If this isn't handled right, we could have one hell of an outbreak. Too much has got to get done, it's got to get done right, and there's not a lot of time to do it. And, as good as you are, you can't do it all yourself. You have to be able to delegate the work and make sure it gets done. You haven't had to do that before.

"I had planned to give you a less important assignment with a small team just to get your feet wet, and to see how you handled it. I think this one might be just too much, too soon for you"

He leaned back in his chair and waited to see how I would respond.

I fought back the urge to get misty eyed. I couldn't understand why he was treating me like this. I needed to get control of my emotions before I said something I would regret. He was deliberately attacking me, challenging my abilities. *Why? He knows my work has always been flawless and always on time. Why doesn't he appreciate that? Why is he treating me like a little girl? Why did he bring me into his office, just to tell me I can't do the job?*

I thought of all the times, men mostly, but older women too, had *assumed* I couldn't do something because I was just a little blonde girl. I had hoped those days were over. I thought I had proven myself. Now this.

Part of me wanted to tell him that he was a sexist pig, that it was unfair, that I would just quit if he thought I wasn't good enough. But a bigger part of me, knew he was right. People *did* tend to discount my ability because of my age and appearance. It *was* hard for me to get people to take me seriously, to follow my lead, to give me the respect I knew I deserved. Then why was he even talking to me about it? A test?

I remembered what my daddy said when I was struggling with how to handle the break up with my first high school boyfriend, "Sally Sue, it's always best to be direct and honest. Say what you mean, and mean what you say.'

"Dr… ah, Albert, don't take this the wrong way, but look at me." He looked puzzled.

"If you had never seen me, or that file there before today, what would you see?" I said.

He waited to make sure I really wanted to get an answer. "Honestly?"

"Yes, honestly please. Of course, it stays in this office."

He raised one eye and pulled on his left earlobe. "Okay." He looked me over as if trying to see me for the first time.

"In my younger days I probably would have been looking at more than I am now." He smiled. I didn't.

"I see a young lady who takes herself seriously, someone who is professional and shows it, someone who, except for the hair, reminds me of my daughter, Marie, before she married and had little Joseph."

"Thanks, but I know what most people see. They see a little blonde girl who doesn't look like she's old enough, or experienced enough, or smart enough to be capable of much more than keeping a bed warm at night."

He started to raise his hand to object. I stopped him. "No, no, that's okay. I'm used to it. The point is that I *do* know how people see me. And, I *am* smart enough to know that it can be a real problem. Hell, I've only been dealing with it my whole life. Believe me, I've learned a trick or two about dealing with pea-brains. You've seen me at work. You can't name one person who I've worked with, who doesn't respect my abilities."

I couldn't stop now. I took a deep breath. "You're right to be concerned about my ability to lead a team. To be honest, if I were you, I think I would have the same concerns. But you called me in here because, number one, your 'A-Team' is out of town, and number two, you *have* looked at that file, and you *do* know that I'm one of, if not *the* best you've got."

He smiled and leaned back while I took a much needed breath. That old leather swivel chair of his squeaked in protest. *He's enjoying this.* At that moment, I thought I saw a glimpse of my daddy in that smile.

He crossed his arms and let me continue. "What you don't see in that file is that I really want this assignment, probably more than you know. I know it's a big bite. I know the leadership thing might be more of a challenge for me because of my looks, but I think I'm ready for it. I've worked very hard, *and* I deserve it."

"Are you done?" He was still smiling.

"Yes. Well, one more thing. Whether I'm the lead on this or not, I definitely want to be involved in whatever way I can." *It never hurts to hedge your bets.*

He swiveled his chair to the side while he looked out the widow and tugged at his ear. He shook his head once, chuckled and turned back to face me. "Well, I guess that's what I wanted to hear. I needed you to convince me that *you* are convinced that you can do the job. If you can handle your team the way you just handled me, I think you'll do okay." He stood up and extended his hand across his desk.

"The job's yours." He said.

I let out the breath I just realized I had been holding. I could hardly contain my excitement. I stood too quickly and took his hand. "Thank you!" I wanted to say more. I wanted to give him a hug, but this was not the time to act like a simpering toady, or worse, a girl.

"Just remember, Sal, you're not the only one with a boss looking over your shoulder. Keep me up to date. And, make me look good."

"I will." I locked my gaze with his for a moment to let him know that I meant it.

As I left Dr. Edelman's office, Rose saw the glow on my face. She smiled broadly and gave a knowing wink.

"Hold all my calls, Rose. I'll be in my office. It's going to get real busy. I just need a few minutes of quiet time now."

CHAPTER 5
TOM

I had run about fifty yards when I heard the first shot. It echoed back and forth between the hills. If I had not known where the camp was, I would have found it hard to determine where the shot had come from.

The camp was less than a half a mile away, a distance I could sprint in less than four minutes on level ground with jogging shoes. But, this was far from being level ground, and I was wearing heavy hiking boots. I knew I would be lucky to get there in less than ten minutes.

The second shot came a second later, then a third, and a fourth. There was a longer pause and then I heard the fifth and final shot. I still had the walkie-talkie in my hand as I ran. I keyed the talk button. "Heck! Heck, are you there?"

No answer.

I hoped Heck was just too busy with the grizzly to answer. *The bear is probably hightailing it right now,* I thought. The thought also occurred to me that he might even be running in my direction. It would be wise to make some noise to let any bear know I was there, to prevent a surprise meeting.

"Hey, Heck! Here I come... I'm on my way... Heck..."

After running a few more minutes, I tried the walkie again, "Heck, come in. I'm just around the hill. Can you hear me?"

No answer.

Now I was getting even more afraid for Heck. This gave me a surge of adrenaline that spurred me to an even faster pace. There was no good reason that Heck would not be answering now, if he had succeeded in scaring the bear off. *Maybe he didn't scare him off. Maybe.* I didn't want to think about the maybes. I forced myself to be focused on the path in front of me, on the next bush to skirt around, on the next rock to sidestep.

"Hold on Heck!"

Eight and a half minutes after I had begun my run, I rounded the last clump of bushes, bringing the campsite into view. At first I didn't see Heck. I stopped, catching my breath.

"Heck?" There was no sound except my own labored breathing. Not even the birds were chirping, as was usual for late morning. I unslung the rifle and worked the bolt to make sure there was a round ready in the chamber.

"Heck?" I slowly walked into the camp. A foot emerged into my field of view about 12 feet behind the tent.

"Jesus, Heck!" I began to run toward him, then stopped short as the rest of the scene was revealed. There was blood everywhere. Heck was a mass of red. He lay in a large puddle of blood. But it was the sight of a very large grizzly lying a few feet away that made me stop in my tracks.

The bear was lying on his side in an even larger pool of blood. He didn't seem to be moving. The monster looked menacing, even lying perfectly still. I raised the rifle to my shoulder and aimed at his head.

I was about to pull the trigger, but something told me I didn't have to. He was dead. I poked him in the butt a few times with the barrel of the rifle just to make sure.

When there was no response, I dropped the rifle and went to Heck's side. "Heck!" *He can't be dead!* "Heck!"

I quickly surveyed the damage to his body. I could not recognize my friend's familiar face. It was covered in blood. His left ear was torn. A six-inch flap of skin from his jaw and cheek lay over his left eye.

"Oh God!" Blood flowed freely from Heck's right thigh.

His clothes were in ribbons. Blood oozed from the left side of Heck's chest. But, his chest was moving slightly. "You're alive!"

I removed the Beretta from Heck's right hand, being careful his finger was free of the trigger guard, and then checked his pulse at his carotid artery. It was weak, but it was there. *Thank God!*

I was overjoyed that Heck was alive, but at the same time, I was almost paralyzed with fear at the knowledge that he might not be alive for long, if I didn't do something, and do it quickly. *Do something! Do something, stupid!*

I didn't know where to start. "Okay, stop the bleeding!" The leg seemed to be bleeding the worst. I tried to find the wound, but the blood soaked tattered remains of Heck's pants hampered my search. I pulled my Swiss Army knife from my pocket and cut away most of the right pant leg from the pocket down. A secondary artery had been ripped open. If it had been the femoral artery, Heck might have been dead already. As it was, he was losing a lot of blood. I used the pieces of Heck's pants to make a crude pressure bandage. I tied a tourniquet above the worst part of the wound. When I pressed the bandage down on the cut, I felt bone grinding. It wasn't until then that I noticed Heck's leg lying at an odd angle. I was careful not to move it any more than I had to.

The bleeding from his leg at least was stopped.

I ran back to the tent to get the first aid kit and some additional articles of clothing to use as bandages. I spotted a water canteen on my way out of the tent and grabbed it too.

When I returned, I dumped the contents of the first aid kit on the ground. I quickly scanned the articles. The only things I could identify, that had any immediate value, were the rolls of gauze and the Insti-Ice packets. I activated four of the ice packs and set them aside.

I turned my attention to Heck's horribly mutilated face. The most shocking wound was the flap of skin that had been torn away and laid over Heck's left eye. I could hardly bear to look at it. I fought back the urge to vomit. There was dirt and grass contaminating the open flesh. I opened the canteen and poured water over his face and ear until most of the blood and dirt had been washed away. I gently picked up the flap of skin and placed it back where it belonged. There was little I could do about the ear.

Next, I wrapped four layers of gauze around Heck's head, being careful to leave openings for his mouth, nose, and eyes. I then placed two ice packs over the area and wrapped the gauze around his head several more times and tied it off.

"Hold on, buddy." I was shaking, partly because of the exertion of my long run, but also because of my fear that Heck was going to die. If he died, I would have to blame myself, first because it was my idea to take Heck along on the trip, and second because I didn't save him.

As I worked, some of my fear began to subside. It gave me the illusion that I had things under some control, but I knew it was only an illusion. We were in the middle of nowhere. Heck could die at any minute. Heck's life was in my hands. *This is payback time buddy. I owe you this one.*

Heck's chest wounds were another matter. There didn't seem to be a whole lot of bleeding, but there might be internal injuries. I tore open his vest and shirt. Once I washed off most of the blood, I could see extensive bruising all across the left side of his chest.

The cuts on his chest were relatively minor. The walkie had taken much of the blow. It was scattered in pieces at Heck's side. I noticed that the left side of his chest did not seem to rise as high as the right, when he took a breath. I figured there were probably broken ribs and maybe a collapsed lung. I decided on a loose bandage so as not to inhibit his breathing and a couple ice packs to limit the swelling.

I worked steadily on each of Heck's wounds. I was satisfied that Heck was not going to die, at least for the moment. I wrapped him in an emergency thermal blanket and wrapped a sleeping bag over that. I was afraid to move him.

When I was done, I sat back and took a drink of water from the canteen. It was almost empty now. Mid-swallow, I coughed and bolted to my feet. "You idiot!"

In all the excitement, I had forgotten the satellite phone we had rented from the outfitter in Anchorage. National Geographic had recommended that we bring one, but the cost to buy one was more than I wanted to spend. Besides, I figured the chance that we'd actually need to use it, was slim. I had decided against it.

I had already spent more than I wanted on optional equipment, like the GPS, which I thought was necessary in order to log the positions and movements of the Kodiak grizzlies we sighted and photographed.

But when we met Pete Putnam, owner of Outland Outfitters, he suggested that we just *rent* a sat-phone from him. It was a new service he had recently started to offer, and he was anxious to start showing a return on his investment. The rate wasn't too steep for a one-month rental, but there was a sizable deposit. I was not too anxious about spending the extra cash, but Heck thought it was a good idea and offered to split the rental cost and front the deposit money.

I had put Pete Putnam's business card in my billfold, so he was the first person I called.

"Outland Outfitters." The voice sounded familiar.

"Hello, is this Pete Putnam?" I spoke louder than normal, for no particular reason.

"Speaking. What can I do for you?" Pete had told me that he was a thirty-two year resident of Alaska, and that he knew people, or he knew people who knew people, who could do or get whatever anyone needed for life in the wilderness. I hoped it was more than a brag.

"This is Tom Birch. I rented one of your satellite phones. My partner's been attacked by a bear."

"Did you scare him away?" Pete was used to city folk from the lower forty-eight defining any menacing act by a bear as an "attack."

"No, listen, the bear's dead, but Heck is hurt real bad. I think I stopped the bleeding, but I don't…"

"Bleeding? Did the bear bite him? How bad is it?"

"I don't know. He's unconscious. He's lost a lot of blood. I think I stopped the bleeding, but I think he has some broken bones too, his leg, maybe some ribs."

"Christ! Where are you?"

"On Kodiak Island, near the Karluk River, about eight miles downriver from Karluk Lake. I don't know how much time…"

"Sounds like you're going to need an airlift. Give me your GPS location and I'll call the Kodiak Coast Guard station."

It took me a minute to find the GPS and give him the coordinates. "How long will it take?"

"I don't know. If you don't hear from the Coast Guard or me within fifteen minutes, call me back. In the meantime, keep him warm. If he wakes up, keep him from moving around too much."

"Okay. Just hurry."

I disconnected the call and checked on Heck's condition. He seemed the same, terrible, but still alive. *I'm sorry Heck. Please hang in there. I'm going to get you out of this.* I had to get him out of this.

Twenty-five minutes later, I heard the first faint sounds of helicopter rotors coming from behind the hills to the Northeast. It seemed like an eternity to me.

They loaded us into the helicopter, and were off the ground in minutes.

I noticed Heck move. His eyes fluttered. I unbuckled my seatbelt and moved to his side.

The Coast Guard helicopter headed North as it left our disheveled camp behind. Then, when it had crossed the first high ridge and had gained altitude, it turned to the Northeast. A shaft of bright morning sunlight flooded through the starboard window and fell across Heck's bloodied and bandaged face.

"I'm here Heck. You're going to be okay." I took Heck's hand and hovered over Heck's face. I spoke loudly over the sound of the wind and the rotor blades.

Heck's face winced, as if in pain, and his hand clinched mine. His eyes fluttered and opened for a second, then closed and his muscles relaxed again.

"We're taking you to a hospital." I said to Heck.

When I saw that there was no response, I turned to the crewman who was busy taking Heck's blood pressure. "Is he okay?" I spoke into the microphone on the military headset I had been instructed to put on.

"Sir, I need you to buckle in." Lt. Tito Brown pointed to the jump seat I had just left. Ignoring the pleading look on my face, Lt. Brown turned his attention back to Heck.

He pulled one of his eyelids open for a second then turned back to me. "He's unconscious, sir. His blood pressure is good though, and his pulse is steady. I think he'll make it." I did not hide my relief.

"We've radioed Kodiak Island Hospital. They'll be ready for him. It should only be about fifteen or twenty minutes."

"Did you tell them about his face?"

"Yes sir. They'll probably need to get him into Anchorage for more treatment, but right now we need to get him stabilized." He pointed insistently again at the jump seat. "Now, would you please buckle in sir?" The tone Lt. Brown used told me that it was *not* a request.

I returned to my seat. I watched the lieutenant as he went about his work. He first affixed an oxygen mask over Heck's nose and mouth. He then set up a saline drip, and finally checked his thigh for bleeding, insuring that circulation was maintained into the lower part of his leg.

I felt a wave of relief flow over me as I watched. Lt. Brown obviously knew what he was doing. He was in control. He had said Heck would be okay, and he looked like he should know. I realized, for the first time since I had gotten the call from Heck on the walkie, that I was totally exhausted.

I let my arms fall to my sides and leaned my head back against the wall. My thoughts turned to my memories of Heck since we had met as kids, and to my memory of eight years ago on Mt. Rainer, when our situation had been reversed.

My foot still ached sometimes to remind me how lucky I was to be alive. Heck had done what the park rangers called "impossible" to save my life that day.

The Coast Guard helicopter was just about to land in Kodiak. I looked over at Heck. *We're just about there. Hold on.* One side of the clear plastic oxygen mask over Heck's mouth had turned red.

"There's blood… on his mouth!"

"What?" Lt. Brown looked twice before he saw it. The mask was obscuring the view from his angle. He removed the mask to inspect closer.

"I think he's got a punctured lung!" He said this to the pilot. After further inspection he said, "He's stopped breathing! Tell the hospital. I'm starting CPR."

"He's not breathing?" I felt helpless. Lt. Brown was ignoring me. He was busy saving Heck's life. *Don't die on me Heck! Oh God, don't die!*

The helicopter skids hit the pavement with an unexpected jolt. I could see attendants running toward us with a gurney.

CHAPTER 6
ANNA

"May I have your attention please?" I released the talk button on the mike long enough to cough before continuing. My voice was weak and rough.

"Several ambulances will be here in a few minutes." I stopped again to cough. My head was throbbing, like the worst hangover I ever had. I could have let the number two attendant handle this, probably should have. But it was *my* job, and as long as I *could* do it, I *would* do it.

"The people with the worst symptoms, those people we already moved to the business class section, you should all have a letter "A" on your arm. You will be taken first by ambulance to Harborview Medical Center in Seattle. They have an isolation ward set up." I coughed unexpectedly and forgot to release the talk button.

"Excuse me. I'm not doing too well myself. I guess I'll be going along with some of you to the hospital." I thought of putting a smile in my voice, but thought better of it. No one, least of all me, was in the mood to hear an artificially cheerful voice. I was feeling weak and dizzy, but I mustered the strength to continue.

"The rest of you will be taken to two areas they have set up here at the airport. If you have only mild symptoms, you will go into Area B. If you have no symptoms at all you will go to Area C. You should all have a piece of tape that one of the doctors put on your left arm, with a letter A, B, or C."

I had to cough. The pain felt like I was hitting myself in the head with a hammer every time I coughed.

"They are setting up phone lines so that you can call your friends and relatives, if you don't have a cell phone. If you have small children, you will need to stay with them." I felt dizzy. I leaned against the wall to stabilize myself.

"The CDC has not told us how long it will be necessary for you to remain in isolation or when the quarantine will be lifted. They will have more information for you after you get to the isolation areas." I was racked with a particularly strong fit of coughing.

Just one more thing. "I'm as anxious as any of you to get off this plane, even if it is to go to the hospital. It'll be just a few more minutes now.

"You have all been very helpful and understanding. Thank you very much. And a special thanks to Dr. Malone and Dr. Winston, and to the other people with medical experience who were able to help. We were very lucky to have all of you aboard."

The passengers had indeed been very helpful, more than I might have expected. It had been two hours since we had landed. At first everyone was grumpy and complaining.

Their schedules were being altered. Their lives were being interrupted. Why did they have to put up with such an inconvenience? But once the passengers had been told the flight had been quarantined, and began to understand the seriousness of the situation, the grumbling and complaining had stopped. Many of the people with mild or no symptoms volunteered to help with those who were in worse condition.

It was a little unusual to have such a large number of passengers on board with medical experience. There were two doctors, along with one veterinarian, three nurses, a pharmacist, and several other people with some level of medical training. I quickly organized them into an efficient team. The other passengers were reassured when they saw that something was being done, that someone seemed to know what they were doing, and that things were under control.

I succeeded on my second try to hang the microphone back in its cradle. I walked down the aisle toward the cockpit, steadying myself on the seat backs as I walked. It seemed like an awfully long way. I felt wobbly and concentrated on carefully placing each step.

I had done a good job, and I knew it. But, I was not feeling proud at this moment, just relieved. Pride was an emotion I rarely allowed myself, and now was definitely not one of those occasions.

I had kept a bad situation from getting much worse. I had maintained control and order in the face of potential chaos. That was my job. I had done it as well as anyone could, and in a few minutes it would be up to someone else to take over.

I surveyed the passengers on either side of the aisle as I walked. We decided to put the sickest passengers in business class to make caring for them easier, and to make them more comfortable. The business class section was surprisingly quiet. There was some coughing and sneezing, but there was little talking; and what talking there was, was subdued.

It reminded me of a funeral parlor. I was shocked that my mind would betray me with such a vulgar image. Like an unwelcome fly come to share my picnic watermelon, I quickly waved it out of my mind.

I opened the door to the cockpit without knocking. "Just wanted to say goodbye before they haul me away." I coughed.

Mark and Bob turned to look at me over their shoulders. Mark said, "Hey Anna. You don't sound too good. Are you going to make it." Mark and Bob had been helping out with the passengers for much of the time since they had parked and shut down the engines. Now that things seemed to be under control, they were taking a break. Neither of them was showing any symptoms, not even a sniffle.

"Yeah, I'm okay." I coughed again. "It's just this cough, my head feels like it's going to explode, and things are spinning around on me a little. Other than that, I guess I'm doing great." I tried on a smile to see if it would fit, but abandoned the effort immediately.

"Why don't you just sit down and relax until the ambulances get here." Mark sounded worried and studied me closely. I noted that I hadn't heard his Texas twang since they officially declared the flight quarantined.

"Yeah, look Anna, you've done all you can do." Bob echoed Mark's concern.

"And Anna, I'm sorry you're sick, but I just want to say, I'm sure glad you were aboard. If you hadn't organized all the volunteers back there, things might be a lot worse."

Coming from Mark, I knew it was a sincere compliment. If I hadn't been feeling so woozy, I might have allowed myself to enjoy a second or two of pride. I managed a half smile to acknowledge the compliment.

Mark continued. "I know you have family in Seattle, but I'm going to personally make sure they take care of you at the hospital."

"Thanks Mark. Really, I'll be fine. Don't worry about…me!" I felt the cockpit start moving around me. I grabbed the door-frame to keep from falling.

"Here, let me help you." Mark stood up and stumbled to get around his seat.

Mark's voice had taken on an odd muffled echo quality. "Okay. I just need to sit … down." I turned to leave the cockpit as Mark grabbed my right arm.

Mark guided me out of the doorway. He could see that I was having a hard time moving my feet. "Bob!"

Bob had been watching and was already getting up to lend a hand. Before he could reach us, I stumbled, then collapsed onto the floor.

Mark was not in position to be able to completely catch my fall, but he was able to slow it enough to keep my head from hitting the floor.

"Anna! Anna, are you okay?" Of course, I wasn't okay. He just wanted to see if I was able to respond.

I could see Mark talking, but his face was spinning around. His words were somehow disconnected from the movement of his lips, like a poorly dubbed foreign movie. I knew I should say something. "I think… I…" *What was I trying to say?*

The pain in my head was all I could think about now. It felt as if my head was being stepped on by an elephant. At any moment it certainly would be crushed. Mark's face was getting dark. *What happened to the lights?* I tried to open my eyes wider with no effect. Mark's voice and all the sounds around me had blended into one continuous ringing. *The pain!*

Then, the pain stopped. The ringing stopped. It was quiet, and dark, and peaceful.

CHAPTER 7
SAL

I needed to collect my thoughts and get my head in gear for what I knew would be a hectic next several days. I wasn't sure if I was excited or scared to death.

I closed the door to my office and plopped into my chair. "Okay Blondie Girl, time to get down to business. Don't blow it!" I said aloud.

Now was the last chance I'd have to take a deep breath, organize my thoughts and formulate my plans. This was the opportunity I'd been waiting for. I didn't want to screw it up. *Relax. Breathe. Think.*

I had found it helpful, in times like this, to let my thoughts wander for a minute, to clear my mind.

Sometimes it's easier to find something when you're not looking for it. My daddy was full of little truisms like this. They would often come back to me at times when I was under stress. His words, and the memory of his voice saying them, had a calming effect on me.

It had always been *Daddy*. Most of the people I grew up with in Eastern Tennessee used *daddy*, not *dad*, including all of the adults. When I moved away from home, I'd often get funny looks if I used *daddy*, so I tried to avoid using the word at work.

I'm on a first name basis with Dr. Edelman, Albert. Now, that is something I'm going to have to get used to.

I remembered how thrilled I was after, I received my doctorate, to finally be called *Dr.* Salinger. I refused to allow anyone to call me Sally Sue, except my daddy.

I hated that name when I was growing up. But when I became old enough to change it, I didn't because I knew my daddy loved it, and me. He always used the whole thing, Sally Sue, never just Sally, although he had sometimes called me his little Blondie Girl when I was small.

Now days, my close friends just called me Sal. To everyone else, it had been Dr. Salinger, thank you.

Back in school the kids would make fun of my name, especially the boys, and would tease me about my premature development. By eighth grade I was five-foot-three, one-hundred-ten pounds, and well-proportioned.

The popular girls didn't talk to me much. I was never really allowed into their tight circle of friendships. Having long naturally blond hair and a figure like a Barbie doll didn't help. I considered cutting my hair short, but again, my daddy liked it long, so I left it long.

Partly to prove I was more than my funny name and my overdeveloped body, I excelled academically. This also served to make Daddy proud of me. He would brag about me to everyone we knew. Making Daddy happy was worth any amount of ridicule the kids at school could dish out.

I wondered why, just now, that I couldn't stop thinking about him. He had been dead for two years. At least he had lived long enough to see me receive my doctorate before his heart gave out. I owed him so much. At least seeing me graduate, was some small payment for all he had given me.

He never remarried after Momma died. I knew it was because of me. If only I could talk to him now. He always knew just what to say to calm me down and put my thoughts on track.

Here I am. Eight years of the best education money can buy. Three years on the job working for just this kind of assignment. People are depending on me; and I'm daydreaming about dear old Daddy! Okay, let's get to it. I won't let you down Daddy.

With that thought, I picked up the phone and started pulling my field team together, giving out assignments, getting travel and equipment logistics in order.

Rose poked her head into my office. "Excuse me ma'am, here's that fax from Sea-Tac International with the status summary on the condition of the passengers and crew on United Flight 876. I know you wanted to see it right away."

Rose was at least five years older than me, and I have always felt uncomfortable being addressed as 'ma'am.' I had known Rose since I started work at The Center, but we only talked a little about our personal lives. That seemed to be the way we both liked it.

I would have preferred to address her as Ms. Washington, but Rose wouldn't allow it. I thought that she felt that it would make her forget herself, and become too 'uppity,' as she called it. I concluded that she wanted to remember who she was, and where she came from.

Rose had worked as an Administrative Assistant with the CDC for six years. In bits and pieces, I had learned some things about Rose that gave me a lot of respect for her.

Her husband, Carlton, had been killed in a drive-by shooting. He wasn't the intended target, but he was standing a little too close to the gang-banger who was. She could have gone on Welfare and ADC, like so many other single mothers in the neighborhood. But, she told me that she wanted to be better than her 'crack-head momma.'

She confided to me once that she couldn't bear the thought of her kids growing up like she had, living on handouts and seeing a constant stream of 'boyfriends' come and go.

She moved out of the neighborhood, got a job waiting tables at Denny's, and took classes at the community college. It took two years of hard work before she landed an entry-level job at the CDC. The word 'Senior' had been recently added to her title, along with a respectable raise.

She obviously loved her ten-year-old son Lamar and twelve-year-old daughter Jewel. She mentioned them often. From what I gathered, she held them to some pretty high standards when it came to homework, chores, and especially 'respect.'

I respected Rose for her dedication and efficiency, but I also liked her personally. I think the feeling was mutual. Even though our life experiences and backgrounds were radically different, I felt that we shared a deep professional pride and a positive can-do attitude that we could admire in each other.

"Thank you, Rose." I said as I took the fax.

"I'll let you know if anything else comes in." Rose was off on another chore.

Okay, what have we got? I studied the one-page fax. My mouth unconsciously opened slightly as I scanned the numbers.

'Time: 09:15 PST
215 Passengers
6 Crew
63 Mild symptoms: Light coughing, Sneezing.
11 Moderate symptoms: Chills, Moderate coughing, Mild headache.
17 Severe symptoms: Flushed face (hot to the touch), Strong headache, Vomiting, Heavy coughing (labored breathing), Dizziness.'

I started to read some of the details.

'…Symptoms were first reported onboard approximately 12:00 PST…'

That's less than an hour after takeoff. This report was already an hour and half old. Wow! This thing moves extremely fast. This situation was going to need some quick action on my part.

I continued reading from the fax:

'There are two passengers who reported having symptoms prior to boarding: Thao Dang Jung, 20 y.o. female, and Hero Onisaki, 48 y.o. male.

Ms. Jung is a student at the University of Washington in Seattle, and was returning from a visit to her family who live on a farm near Bangkok. She had originally boarded United Airlines Flight 838 from Bangkok, departing at 5:55 a.m. ICT and arriving at Tokyo Narita Airport at 2:35 p.m. JST.

> *She then boarded United Flight 876, which departed on time at 5:10 p.m. JST.*
>
> *Mr. Onisaki is traveling on business for the Mitsubishi Corporation. His home is in Tokyo. He is married with two children. He had booked a connecting flight to Denver. He has made three other international trips in the last thirty days, Hong Kong, Singapore, and the most recent was to Sydney, Australia.'*

Time for action, little Blondie Girl. I picked up my phone and buzzed Rose. When she picked up I said, "Rose I'm going to need your help. I need to get ahold of a lot of people, and I don't have time to send out letters or even faxes. I have to make a lot of person-to-person calls. I don't even know the names of some of the people I have to talk to, and some of them might be hard to track down. I'll give you a list. Can you help me get people on the phone while I talk to the others?"

"Yes Ma'am. You give me a list, and I'll get right on it." Rose seemed excited to be involved. I knew she wanted to see me do well with my first important assignment.

An hour later I had contacted most of my field team, SeaTac airport security, Harborview Hospital in Seattle, and the heads of the World Health Organization in Japan and Thailand. The wheels were definitely moving. Containment was my number one priority. Everything had to be coordinated before I left.

I had debated staying at The Center in Atlanta. I had many more people and resources at my disposal in Atlanta that I wouldn't have easy access to in Seattle. I thought of what Dr. Edelman (Albert) had said about delegating. And then, I thought of my daddy telling me, "If you want something done right, do it yourself." It was Daddy who finally won my internal debate. I would be on a flight to Seattle that afternoon.

CHAPTER 8
RAY

I was unaware of all the commotion that was going on around us. My attention was focused on Julia. I had heard the announcement, and I was relieved that Julia would soon be cared for properly. Along with many others, now seated in business class, we had both gotten much worse in the last two hours. But, I was only concerned about Julia.

"How ya doin', hon?" I said as I gently kissed Julia's forehead.

"I think I'm going to throw up again."

"Can you make it to the restroom, or do you want a bag?"

"Maybe if I sip on the water some more, it will calm my stomach down."

I handed her the water. "How's your head?"

"It's pounding. Those aspirin didn't do anything. I guess they didn't get a chance. Probably what made me throw up."

"I didn't throw up, but they didn't do me any good either. I've got the worst headache since the morning after my bachelor party." I said.

"Ray, I'm getting really dizzy. I keep seeing these flashing lights." She sneezed and then coughed. As she did so, she grabbed her head and moaned.

"I'll go find one of the doctors, and see if they can do anything to help."

I started to get up, but Julia grabbed my arm. "Wait. Just hold me for a minute." Her voice was weak and wispy.

"But the doctor…"

"Just for a minute. I'm scared."

I put my arm behind her head and pulled her close. I was scared too, and I was feeling almost as bad as her, but I wanted to be strong for her. I wanted her to believe everything would be okay, that I would make it okay. I wanted to believe it myself. All I could think of to say was the one thought that I was able to sustain over the throbbing pain behind my eyes. "I love you, Julia."

Something seeped into my tone that made her turn to look me in the eyes. "Forever."

I couldn't tell, by the way she said it, whether it was a statement or a question. "Forever?'

"Ray, tell me again what we're going to do." She leaned back and closed her eyes. Her voice was even more wispy.

I knew what she was referring to. I wondered why she would bring that up now. She did not seem as lucid as she had been only moments before. *Anything to make her feel better.*

"Well first, there's the kids." I began. "We'll have to start working on that one really hard." I managed a chuckle even though my head was a dark cloud, complete with thunder and lightning.

"Then the house. We'll get a nice big lakefront house over in Medina, I think maybe that one we saw with the indoor/outdoor heated pool. We'll work hard, raise the kids and retire. Of course by the time we retire, we'll be rich and have half a dozen grandkids."

"What about the rest of it?" She sounded like she was fading off to sleep. I wanted her to sleep. I wanted her suffering to stop.

It took me a second to remember. "Oh, that's right. We're going to 'make the world a better place.' " I tried to say it with some degree of conviction for her benefit. It still sounded silly to me, but I knew it wasn't silly to her.

"I love you, honey." It was less than a whisper.

A verse from the Bible popped into my head as they often did.

Many are the plans in the mind of man, but it is the purpose of the Lord that will stand. Proverbs 19:21.

###

My Baptist parents insisted on a family reading from the Bible *every* night after dinner, from a very early age. They made it a game. I would be rewarded with candy and toys for memorizing verses. Later, I did it just for the praise that they would give me.

It was a game with very little religious meaning to me at the time, but one that I was very good at it. I must have been only seven or eight when I could recite complete chapters. I remembered giving demonstrations at church every Sunday, and getting a lot of hugs and pats on my head. My parents were very proud of me, and that was the reason I did it.

The game continued into my teen years, until my parents were killed in a car accident. After that, my heart was no longer in it. I considered myself a true believer, but not an evangelical. I had felt no special calling to 'spread the Word.' I quit the church and went to a secular college, not the seminary school my parents had hoped for.

The Bible was forever a part of my brain now, regardless of how it had gotten there. Even if I wanted to forget it, I couldn't. Verses continually popped into my head at odd moments. Sometimes they were a comfort and an inspiration. But usually, they were just Bible trivia.

###

What was the *purpose of the Lord?* I wondered. I hoped it would be as we had planned.

I held her for a moment longer while I silently said a prayer, *Please God, let her be okay. If I have to die to take her place, let it be. Please God take away her pain and let her be okay. Amen.*

"I'm going to find that doctor now, hon." She did not answer. I gently laid her head back on the seat so as not to wake her. Her skin was glowing red. I noticed I had a wet spot on my sleeve from the back of her neck.

As I stood up, I had to support myself with both hands. The airplane cabin spun around. I waited a moment until the spinning slowed a bit.

I turned down the aisle and met Dr. Stanley Malone coming back up from the coach section. He had been introduced over the intercom earlier. I learned later that Dr. Malone was still an intern serving his residency at Harborview Medical Center in Seattle. Apparently, he had started medical school late, and the prematurely receding hairline made him look much more seasoned than he was. His presence gave me hope.

"Doctor, can you look at my wife again. She's worse. She's really hot. I'm worried."

"Mr. Miller, you shouldn't be walking around. You said your wife is…" He suddenly focused his attention behind me. "Oh, shit!" He said under his breath as he darted around me heading for the cockpit door where the head flight attendant had just collapsed.

I turned to see what was happening behind me. My vision was blurred and things kept moving, making it hard to focus. For a second I thought the stewardess looked like Julia. My heart stopped at the thought of her passed out on the floor. I stumbled back to our seats, only a couple steps away.

Julia appeared to be still sleeping, but now I knew she wasn't.

"Julia. Julia!" I dipped my fingers in the water glass and patted her gently on the cheek. "Wake up sweetheart. Julia. Julia." *She must be just sleeping.* I put my ear by her mouth. I could hear her softly breathing, although there was a slight wheezing sound. *Thank you God!*

I shook her shoulders, a little more insistent now. "Julia, wake up." I pulled open one of her eyes. I had seen someone do this on TV once. I wasn't sure what I was supposed to see, and felt a little foolish. The pupil was almost as big as the iris. *That's not right!* It just looked unnatural.

"Doctor, she's not waking up!" I called over to Dr. Malone.

He looked up from Anna only long enough to say. "I'll be with you in a minute."

He obviously didn't understand. She needed him now! "Doctor, please. Something is wrong with her!"

"What's the problem?" Dr. Winston Hadley, the other physician onboard had just come up from coach to oversee moving the "A" passengers into the ambulances. He had developed a slight cough and was running a little temperature, but was otherwise feeling well.

"It's my wife Julia, she's not waking up." I relaxed a little when I saw the gray hair around his temples and Dr. Hadley's general air of confidence.

"Let's see." He felt her forehead and cheek, and poked his fingers into her neck next to her throat. He then produced a small penlight out of his shirt pocket and pulled her eyelid back, just as I had done a moment before.

"See." I felt vindicated that I had at least looked in the right place, even though I still wasn't sure what the doctor was looking for.

Dr. Hadley pointed the light at her eye, then away, then back again. "We need to get her to the hospital right away."

"What's wrong? Is she okay? Can you do something?" I was pleading. My head was a balloon that had been over inflated and was about to burst. Everything turned around and around.

"Yes, she'll be okay." Dr. Hadley dunked a napkin into the half-full water glass, patted her face and forehead with it, and then gave it to me. "Just try to keep her cool. I'll be back in a minute."

The airplane door had opened, and the first of the stretchers was being brought in. Dr. Hadley wanted to make sure they took the worst patients first.

I saw the Doctor walk away, but it was hard for my eyes to follow the movement. Instead, I looked down at Julia. She would be okay. The doctor said she would be okay.

I tried to focus on her face. *It's getting dark. Did a light burn out?* Her face was hard to see. My head felt like it was double its normal size. *Oh God, the pain!* Florescent colors splashed across my eyes. Sounds were muted. *She'll be okay. God will protect her.* It was the only thought that I had. I clung to it like a life preserver in a stormy sea.

She'll be okay. I held onto that thought with all my will. It was like holding the hand of God himself. I saw its warm glow like a golden star of hope, it comforted me and I would *not* let go.

My hand fell from Julia's face and I heard the wet napkin flop onto the floor, but I couldn't stop it.

Why did they turn out the lights?

CHAPTER 9
SAL

I took another sip of my iced tea. The pastrami-on-rye, I had eaten for lunch an hour ago, was now churning in my stomach. The tea felt cool going down, but the fire would be back in a minute or two. I needed to take an antacid. *Maybe Rose has some I can borrow.*

I knew the pastrami wasn't the real cause of my excess stomach acid, it was the preliminary case review meeting with Dr. Edelman and the rest of the eight-member review panel scheduled for 2:00, just twenty-five minutes from now.

It had been three months since the Bangkok Encephalitis, or as the press had tagged it, the Bangkok Flu, had infected Flight 876. Much study of the virus had been conducted since, and was continuing, but the nature of the virus was still not well understood.

Although the outbreak on Flight 876 had been *mostly* contained successfully, the fact that it was an airborne virus with an incredibly short incubation period, not to mention the severe and unique symptoms, made it the subject of much discussion and debate in medical and scientific circles. Further studies were now underway.

My job today was to layout the state of the investigation to date, the origin, pathology and treatment of the disease, as well as to delineate steps that had been taken for its containment and prevention.

I had been putting in twelve to fourteen hour days. I knew I could have, and probably should have, delegated much more of the work than I had. I was physically drained, and mentally exhausted. I knew I needed to take a break.

I knew that my presentation today would not only be a summary of events of the outbreak, but would essentially be a report card on my own performance in handling the case. I felt like I deserved only a C- at best.

The part of my 'report card' presentation I was dreading most was my discussion on the one new case that was discovered in Florida two weeks after the original outbreak. It was the only case I knew could have, and should have been prevented.

It was a small oversight on my part, one that I knew most people would not hold me directly accountable for, but I felt that I had failed to live up to my own standards. A man had almost died because of a mistake I had made.

I could have easily covered it up or shifted the blame, but that was not how my daddy had raised me. I had resolved that today was the day I would officially take full responsibility for my indiscretion. It was the way Daddy would have wanted it. I might lose my job, but it was the right thing to do.

I wished again that Daddy was still around to give me guidance at times like this, when things were tough or confusing, the way he always had when I was growing up. It seemed like such a long time since I was small enough to cuddle up in his strong arms.

I always felt so safe and protected. I hadn't felt that way in years, but the memory remained. I nurtured that memory, trying to bring the feeling back to life. I closed my eyes and willed my mind to create an image of my daddy, the way he looked when I was a girl, the way he smiled at me as he reached down to pick me up. I wanted so much to be that little girl again, if only for a moment.

After I left home for school, I was only able to visit home a few times each year. And when I started work at the CDC, the visits were even more infrequent. I promised myself that I would take some time for an extended visit, maybe next year.

Now that Daddy was dead, I always regretted not making more time to spend with him. I imagined all the memories of him that might have been created, if I had just taken the time. I would have to live without those memories now. There always seems to be plenty of time for 'later' until there isn't any more 'later.'

My phone rang. I was startled to find myself back in the present. I glanced at the clock as I reached for the phone. "Dr. Salinger."

It was Rose. "Ma'am, your meeting is in five minutes. You asked me to remind you."

"Thanks Rose. I was just…ah, working on something. Are all the handouts ready in the conference room?"

"Yes, ma'am."

"And my slides and…"

"Yes, ma'am. All your presentation materials are ready to go. Also, I got fresh coffee and ice water. I think you're all set." I didn't have to tell Rose how important this review meeting was for me.

"Thank you Rose. I'm on my way now." Rose was usually efficient and helpful, but I knew she had put in a little special effort for me. I made a mental note to thank her in a more material way. *Maybe some flowers, or at least a card. Something.*

I knew most of the members of the review board, but there were a couple of new faces. Dr. Edelman had wanted a broad spectrum of medical and scientific disciplines represented.

After introductions were made, the coffee and water poured, handouts distributed, everyone settled in and looked expectantly to me to begin my presentation.

I had planned to begin with an overview of the chronology of the outbreak, but I thought I should make a couple informal comments first, before I got into the specifics of the case.

"I want to thank you all for taking part in this review. I want to specifically thank a couple of you who have provided help and guidance over the last couple of months. Although I am relatively new with the CDC and the EPO, I believe this is an extremely unusual outbreak case.

"I know some of you are already up to speed with most of the information I am going to present today. For you, I think I may have some new information that will help fill in the gaps. For the rest of you, I would like you to pay particular attention to differences between this and other outbreaks we have encountered. The implications of these differences have been the subject of much debate by many scientists and medical clinicians.

"There's been a lot of speculation by the press too. I have included, with your handouts, a copy of the press release package we plan to distribute later today. We have tried to stick to only the facts of the outbreak, and the underlying disease, without any speculation on their possible implications."

Okay Blondie Girl. I took a deep breath and pulled up my first slide. "The outbreak began three months ago with the first reported symptoms on United Flight 876 from Tokyo to Seattle around midnight Pacific Standard Time, September 9th.

"By the time the plane landed shortly before 9:00am, 91 passengers and crew of the 221 souls onboard were presenting with mild to severe symptoms. The flight was directed to park away from the main terminal and the aircraft was put under quarantine."

I noticed a few raised eyebrows at the 91 number. *Good, that got their attention.* "By 11:00am the most seriously affected passengers and crew were taken off the plane. Two isolation areas were set up at the airport and an isolation ward was set up at Harborview Hospital in Seattle.

"Fortunately, the hospital was about to open a new burn ward. They were just waiting for completion of the therapy bath facilities. Of course, we didn't need that, but the special antiseptic air filtration systems that had been installed made it an ideal isolation ward for the worst cases. There were 17 patients with serious enough symptoms to be taken to the hospital.

"74 passengers and crew who had only mild to moderate symptoms were isolated in one of the temporary areas set up at the airport. The other 130 passengers and crew with no reported symptoms were isolated in a second area.

"Within 24 hours all but two of the non-symptomatic passengers and crew were released to home isolation for a period of one week. No new cases have been reported in this group to date.

"Also within 24 hours all of the mild to moderate patients, plus the two who had developed symptoms from the non-symptomatic group, were transported to the Harborview isolation ward for further observation and treatment.

"The aircraft itself was sanitized per standard procedures similar to those used before for cruise ship outbreaks. The aircraft was returned to service on September 22nd.

"By September 16th, one week after the outbreak, all of the 74 patients who initially presented only mild to moderate symptoms had recovered and were released to home isolation for a period of one week. Interestingly, none of this group presented with any of the more serious symptoms.

"Unfortunately, of the 17 severe patients, 15 had died by this time, and two became comatose. Upon investigation of the patients' medical histories, it was found that patients who fully recovered had been previously exposed to the H5N1 virus, and those who died, or had become comatose, had not. This is a hopeful note, because it points the way to a possible vaccine.

"On September 30th, another case was reported in Tampa, Florida. Mr. Leonard Atkins, a maintenance technician for United, apparently contracted the disease while working on part of the ventilation system on the same Boeing 767-400 aircraft that was involved in the Seattle outbreak. Mr. Atkins also became comatose." My voice broke slightly. I hoped no one noticed. I took a sip of water. *I'm sorry, Mr. Atkins.*

"This patient was isolated, and the plane's ventilation system was thoroughly sanitized. There have been no other reported cases since."

That wasn't too hard, but that's not the end of it. I wanted to stop my prepared presentation and lay out my part in this last case, but that wouldn't be professional. My confession could wait a few minutes.

"During the last month there has been a very interesting development in the three comatose cases. They have all recovered from their comatose state, but are displaying various autistic-like symptoms, and even some savant abilities. I've include specifics of each case in your packets.

"Historical cases of Acquired Savant Syndrome are very rare. The couple of cases we know about have been the result of some type of brain injury. Some children have experienced the regressive-onset type of autism at an early age, but it has never been seen in adults, and also not as a result of disease.

"Two of the three cases appear to be quite severe. Interaction with others is minimal. They become agitated when they are touched or are forced to interact with others in any way. They mostly sit and rock themselves all day. The third case is capable of greater social interaction and verbal abilities, but has both physical and psychological abnormalities. There have been some signs that their conditions may be improving somewhat, but the prognosis is that a full recovery is very unlikely.

"Obviously, there has been some level of neurologic damage or at least an alteration in normal brain function. I'll get into what we know about the pathophysiology of this disease in a moment. It may explain how the autistic-like condition of these patients could have been acquired through a viral invasion."

I could see I had their full attention. Those who had been taking notes, stopped and listened intently.

"Before I get into the odd symptoms manifested by this virus, I think it will be helpful to first look at its origins.

"We conducted a detailed survey of everyone onboard Flight 876. From that survey, we narrowed it down to two candidates as the original carriers of the virus. The first was Hero Onisaki, a 48-year-old businessman residing in Tokyo. Although he was one of only two passengers reporting any flu-like symptoms upon boarding, he was quickly ruled out. It appears he simply had a bad cold that had nothing to do with our virus.

"The other passenger who was presenting symptoms upon boarding Flight 876 we now believe to be the original carrier of the *so called* Bangkok Virus. This person then spread it to the other passengers.

"Ms. Thao Dang Jung, a student at the University of Washington in Seattle, was returning from a visit with her family who live on a small farm on the outskirts of Bangkok, Thailand. During her two-week visit she became ill and was diagnosed with acute herpes virus type 1 encephalitis. The diagnosis was at first confused because the virus unusually manifested as aseptic meningitis. She was treated in Bankok and seemed to be recovering when she returned to Seattle.

Also, some days before she left Bangkok, three other family members had contracted what is believed to be influenza A strain H5N1, avian flu, or a variation. As you know, avian flu is rare in humans. But the fact that they did get the disease is significant because what we are calling the Bangkok Virus has characteristics of this virus as well.

The Bangkok Virus has been isolated from serum samples collected from infected Flight 876 patients, and it has been genetically sequenced. The results of the gene study show that it was a hybrid virus composed of genes from both the encephalitis and the influenza viruses."

I paused to let that sink in. I watched their eyes as the significance of this settled into their awareness.

"This is not being released to the press until we can confirm these results, but it is now being hypothesized by some that Ms. Jung also contracted the Avian flu during her visit home, probably from direct contact to poultry raised on the farm, and the two viruses genetically merged to become the Bangkok Virus. The mechanism that would allow this to happen is only hypothetical at this time. There has never been a documented case like this one.

"Fortunately, the marriage of these two viruses seems to be an unstable one. It appears that the virus only was able to survive one generation. No one with a documented secondary contact with victims of the disease has become infected. In other words, only people who had direct contact with Ms. Jung, or breathed the same air as her, contracted the virus. The only exception is Mr. Atkins, but even there, he had contact with the airplane's ventilation system, not another patient.

"Also, the World Health Organization has reported no other cases either in Bangkok or Tokyo, or anywhere else. It appears now that the virus was born inside Ms. Jung sometime after she boarded Flight 876, gestated there, spread primarily by air through the ventilation system on the airplane, infected secondary victims and did its damage, but that's where it seems to have died. Or at least, that's where we were able to stop it.

"Before I get into the pathophysiology of the virus, are there any questions on what I've covered so far?" Everyone looked at their handouts and notes, and looked back at me expectantly.

After a few seconds, when it appeared there were not going to be any questions, Dr. Edelman, who was sitting closest to me, raised his hand and said, "Is there any research, or at least speculation, on why some of the characteristics of this new virus are so different from either Avian Influenza or herpes virus type-1 encephalitis? For example, neither of these viruses has been historically spread through airborne micro particles. Also, neither has shown such a short incubation period."

I was hoping someone would ask a question. "That's a very good question. No, there is no research that has been completed yet. However, the working hypothesis at this time is that the merging of genetic material that occurred to form this new virus was not simply the addition of genetic material from two different viruses. It appears that it was combined in a much more complicated way.

"For example, in human genetics, two parents who have no musical talent can have a child that is a musical prodigy. The parents may have recessive genes with traits that are only expressed when combined with other inherited recessive genes in the offspring. Or, different traits from the parents, that are seemingly unrelated, may randomly combine to produce a new capability in the child that was not present in either parent.

In my musical prodigy example, one parent may have good hand-eye coordination, but have stubby fingers, while the other parent has poor hand/eye coordination, but has long fingers. If the child inherits the best of both, he is then able to become a virtuoso on the piano. Of course human genetic dynamics are much more complex than for a virus, but the principle is still valid."

Dr. Edelman shook his head. "But, viruses don't reproduce sexually like humans. They reproduce asexually by using the biochemistry of a host cell to manufacture copies of viral RNA, which are released to infect other host cells. How could this mechanism allow for what is essentially sexual-like reproduction?"

"We're getting into an area in which I have little expertise, but it's an interesting question, and one that I asked myself. I can only pass along what information I've come across on the subject.

"First of all, you know that bioengineers have been successfully inserting foreign genes into the DNA of plants and bacteria using viral agents for some time now. They attach the desired gene to a virus, and let the virus invade the nucleus of the host cell, inserting the new gene into the DNA sequence.

In these cases, the result is a genetically altered cell that is then able to reproduce in the normal way. This is how we get pest-resistant corn, for example, and how pharmaceutical companies use altered strains of bacteria to artificially reproduce various enzymes and complex compounds for medicine.

"So, we know that viruses have the ability, not only to use the host cell's biochemistry to reproduce its own genetic material, but in so doing, to also alter the host's genetic material. If the host is not destroyed in the process, an altered host is able to reproduce a new strain of corn or bacteria or whatever.

"In our case, the working hypothesis is that the two viruses invaded the same cell at the same time and inserted their genetic material into the host cell, as they normally would. This would normally switch on the cell's biochemistry to begin producing copies of the virus. But in this case, instead of producing copies of each virus separately, the two viruses somehow accidentally inserted their genetic material into each other's RNA, producing a completely new RNA strand.

"There's probably about a one-in-a-trillion chance of this happening. But once it did occur, the host cell began to churn out copies of the new virus, thus infecting other host cells in the normal way.

"Some scientists have speculated that the evolution of sexual reproduction on Earth may have originally occurred in a similar random accident." I wasn't sure if there was anyone at the table that might take offense at the suggestion that a literal interpretation of Biblical Genesis might not be the whole story. Just in case, I added, "Of course, others disagree."

"Hypothetically, this kind of thing might have happened quite often during the history of life on Earth. But either the resulting viruses have been inferior and have not reproduced, or it may in fact be one mechanism that viruses have used in the past to mutate into new forms.

"For this discussion however, it doesn't matter how it happened. If the genetic sequencing results are confirmed, the fact that it *did* happen is all that matters for now."

Dr. Edelman raised his eyebrows and pulled on his left earlobe. Some of the others were scribbling notes, apparently this was a topic they wanted to look into later.

I waited a couple seconds to see if anyone had a follow up question. "Thank you for that question, Dr Edelman. I wasn't going to get into hypothetical issues, but I think this subject is very interesting, and it might help you better to understand the dynamics of this disease."

I pulled up my next display titled, "Pathophysiology" and continued with my prepared material. "The Bankok Virus, as with other viral encephalitides, traverses the blood-brain barrier to infect the brain parenchyma, clinically manifesting as viral encephalitis. It may also infect the leptomeninges, resulting in aseptic meningitis. And, it may also infect pulmonary tissues, resulting in severe respiratory distress.

"The more severely affected patients presented symptoms of both encephalitis and influenza: headache, mental confusion, tremors, stiff neck, extremity weakness, high fever, runny nose, muscle aches, nausea, vomiting, diarrhea, and in the worst cases, coma.

"Lab studies show the similarities and differences with other encephalitis and influenza viruses:

"Leukopenia, borderline/low normal white blood cell count.

"Mild elevations of serum glutamic-pyruvic transaminase.

"Positive enzyme immunoassay with plaque reduction neutralization test.

"Highly elevated acute titer.

"Exhibits CT scan or MRI abnormalities in one or both temporal lobes, as well as EEG with unilateral focal electrical abnormalities in the temporal lobes.

"Cerebrospinal fluid reveals moderate pleocytosis with a lyphocytic predominance.

"And, this is particularly significant. Brain biopsy findings from deceased patients exhibit diffuse encephalitis as you might expect, but also there is an elevated neural density, about 10% more brain cells than normal. A closer look at the brains of these patients shows new micro-folds in the cerebral cortex and in the temporal lobes."

I brought up a slide showing a normal brain compared to a Bangkok Virus victim's brain. "As you can see, the Bangkok Virus brain has these small additional creases or folds, here and here. It looks as though their brains grew and these new folds were created to accommodate the growth. Of course, such an invasive analysis of our living patients is not possible.

"Brain cell growth is consistent with the onset of autistic symptoms. It has been shown that excessive brain growth in infants during their first year may be predictive of autism. There is a study I included in your packets.

"During the early stage of development, infant brain cells begin developing in proportion to the baby's first experiences. The brain cells normally develop in pace with the growth of the baby's experience.

"But, too-rapid growth during this period is thought to produce too much neural noise that overwhelms the infant's ability to make sense of its world and it withdraws. In other words, their brain is allowing them to perceive and experience more information from the world than they are able to process and to understand. 'Perceptive overload' is what one researcher has called it.

"This appears to be similar to what happened with our Bangkok virus victims who have recently come out of their comatose state. But the difference is, that in infants, brain growth stops very early in their development. In our virus victims, somehow the virus triggered their neural growth to be switched back on for a time.

"This is all preliminary of course, but we are hopeful that this information will help in treatment and in diagnosis, should there be any future outbreaks."

The rest of the presentation was straight forward. I outlined measures that had been put in place to prevent the spread of the virus, and future steps that were planned.

Here it is. I took a deep breath. Everyone thought my presentation was about to end when I pulled up my last display. "Failures." I read the title.

"Even though this outbreak was quickly controlled, I believe the investigation and follow up measures could have and should have been handled better."

Everyone seemed to stop breathing. They were not expecting this at all, none less than Dr. Edelman. I caught his eye for a moment. He looked at me with a combination of surprise and disappointment.

I wished I was anywhere but there, right then. I wished I didn't have to do this. But I told myself it has to be done. *Be true to yourself.*

"There were several minor oversights and omission. I've listed them for you. But there was one serious error that I take personal responsibility for. I failed…" My voice quavered. "…to specify and emphasize that the airline should sanitize the ventilation system on Flight 876. I knew the pathogen was airborne."

Dr. Edelman abruptly stood up and held out his hand palm-out toward me like a traffic cop's signal to stop. "Wait just a minute. You can't blame yourself. It was the airline who dropped the ball."

I avoided his eyes and turned my head from side to side. "In the instructions the airline received, I essentially copied the procedures that have been used in the past with gastrointestinal outbreaks on cruise ships. In most ways the situation is the same. But the cruise ship outbreaks were from pathogens that were spread primarily by contact with contaminated surfaces. They were not airborne. I should have emphasized sanitizing the airplane's ventilation system."

"Dr. Salinger, I think you're way off base. I think everyone here would agree that you did an outstanding job." He glanced around the table. Everyone was nodding their agreement.

I didn't know what I had expected, but this wasn't it. I continued to proclaim my guilt. "Because of my oversight, one additional victim contracted the virus and is now possibly debilitated for life. And worse, it was sheer luck that even more victims did not contract the disease because of my negligence."

"I think you are through with your presentation. Thank you." Dr. Edelman's voice was abrupt and stern. He was now glaring at me. "I'd like to talk with the panel members for a moment."

He was deliberately controlling the tone in his voice. This was as close to displaying anger that I had ever seen him. "I will see you in my office in fifteen minutes."

I realized I was being told to leave the room. There was nothing more for me to say. The other panel members didn't know what to say, so they remained silent as they watched me pick up my notebook and walk to the door.

I tried to maintain as much dignity as possible. I refused to allow them to see me break. I could feel every eye burning a hole through my back as I opened the door.

I closed the door behind me, and immediately broke into tears.

I ran the short distance to my office. I passed Rose in the hall. Rose instinctively knew this was not the time to say anything to me. Something had gone very wrong, that's all she needed to know for now. She'd find out the details later. She always did.

I closed the door to my office and collapsed into my chair. I grabbed a handful of tissues, buried my face in them, and let the flood gates open. I had worked so hard on this case over the past three months. I was exhausted, much more than I had realized. For the first time in years I let the tears flow and made no attempt to stop them.

I cried because this might be the end of my career. I cried because all my work would be for nothing. I cried because my daddy would be so disappointed in me. And then, I cried because I realized I was all alone. Daddy was gone. There was no one's shoulder I could cry on. I had friends, but there was no one who *really* cared, not the way Daddy had cared, not the way I dreamed someone else would someday care. But it *was* just a dream.

CHAPTER 10
HECK

I saw an eagle flying toward me. The brilliant sun was directly behind him creating a silhouette image surrounded by a halo.

As it approached, I could hear the flapping of its wings. Thwop, thwop, thwop. It became larger with every flap. It was huge, as big as a man. It was a man, or at least it had a man's head. It was Tom! Tom, the eagle-man, landed beside me.

He looked scared. He was trying to tell me something. I could not hear the words. Tom was screaming at me. Why couldn't I hear what Tom was saying? Tom tried to grab my arm, but he could not grip with only feathers for hands. Tom wanted me to go somewhere. Tom's mouth was moving, but there was no sound. There was no air coming out. Tom was not breathing.

Then I was the eagle looking down at myself. I saw myself sleeping peacefully. I had to wake myself up. I tried to yell, but no sound came out. There was no air in my lungs to make the sound. The terrible feeling of being suffocated was overwhelming me. I had to wake myself up.

I no longer had wings. I had hands, but my fingers had huge claws. I reached down to slap my own face. I had to wake up! The claws ripped my face open, but it wasn't my face anymore. It was Tom's face. "No, no, I didn't mean it Tom." I tried to yell, but my lips moved with no sound.

Tom was awake now. He was talking to me. His voice was calm, but it sounded like a woman's voice. Tom didn't make any sense. "…a few minutes… landing… Seattle-Tacoma… that your seatbacks and tray tables are in their upright and locked positions."

I opened my eyes. The plane had turned onto its final landing approach, and sun was now streaming into the window beside me. I blinked a few times, squinting against the sun, and took a deep breath. The air from the ventilator jet felt clean and satisfying as I filled my lungs. I was awake. I was alive.

The dream was similar to the dreams I had had all too often over the last months since the attack. The feeling of suffocating had haunted my sleep, but the dreams were becoming less frequent now.

I would have preferred to sleep a lot less, but the drugs made me drowsy much of the time, and the docs and the nurses kept telling me, "You need to rest, Dr. Beckman." As I recovered and wanted to become more active, this repeated admonition from the hospital staff began to sound like some kind of bizarre cult mantra. I was tired of resting. I resolved to stop taking the drugs.

There was still pain. But, sometimes I liked to feel the pain. It reminded me that I was alive. I could get around pretty well now with the help of crutches, but I still became winded very quickly. The ordeal had left my body weak, although I had become a little stronger in the last few weeks. I knew it would be a lot of work and a lot of pain to get my body back to where it had been, but I couldn't wait to get to the gym.

It was a rare sunny day for late November in Seattle. I looked out the window to see the late morning sun sparkling off of Elliot Bay. The Space Needle and the rest of the familiar Seattle skyline looked like a picture post card. The city seemed to be welcoming me back. *Home.*

East of the narrow isthmus that was downtown Seattle, I could see Lake Washington and Mercer Island. I couldn't make out the building, but I knew Tyler was there somewhere on the north end of the island. *Where the heart is. Where had I heard that phrase?*

It had been three months since I had been home. Christmas was only a few weeks away. My thoughts of past Christmases at home gave me a warm feeling inside. I could see Wendy gleefully opening gifts while I held baby Tyler on our last idyllic Christmas morning together.

Two months later, Tyler would be diagnosed with autism, and everything would change. I was forced to remember that "home" didn't mean what it once had, and that Christmas would never be the same. This would not be a family Christmas.

Tom was waiting to meet me, as I hobbled on crutches past the security gate at the exit from the tram.

"Hey Heck!" Tom was afraid I might try to do the hug thing, and he extended his hand instead to discourage it.

"Hey Tom!" I fumbled with the crutches and shoulder bag to free my right hand. I pretended I was just going to shake his hand, then I pulled him in and gave him a big manly hug.

"You've learned how to use those things pretty good in the last two weeks. Let me take that." Tom snatched up my shoulder bag. I didn't object.

"Can we sit down for a minute?" Tom noticed I was breathing hard and sweating.

"Sure." Tom tried not to be too obvious as he assessed my condition. I looked better than I did the last time he saw me, only two weeks ago, but I still had that withered, gaunt look that I could tell was painful for Tom see.

The surgeons had worked a miracle on my facial injuries. They sewed the ear back together; and with a little reconstructive surgery, it looked almost like the other one. They were able to repair the flap of skin that had been ripped loose. The careful stitching had paid off there too. After the swelling had gone down and the stitches removed, I was left with only a jagged red line that ran from behind my left eye to below my jaw. In time, the doctors said the scar would be barely noticeable, but when the stitches were removed, I had decided to let my beard grow out to conceal the worst of it.

"Whew!" I plopped awkwardly into a seat. "That was a bit of a walk from the gate. I just need to catch my breath for a minute."

"That's okay. They won't have your bags ready for a few minutes anyway. Ya know, you *could* have asked for a wheelchair."

"Yeah. But, I figured there must be some little old lady somewhere that needed a wheelchair worse than me."

"Well, all you need is a polka-dot dress and gray wig, and I think you could pass for a little old lady." He grinned the biggest Tom Birch patented grin he could muster and chuckled. I know he felt good to have me back, but this was as close as Tom was going to come to saying so.

"I would huh?" I wiped the sweat off my forehead with the back of my hand. "Well, you don't look like you've been spending much time at the gym either."

"I'll meet you on the court anytime you think you're ready."

"So, you think you're good enough to take on a man with crutches on the racquetball ball court? Big man. I'll bet you've been challenging little girls to arm wrestle with you too." I was glad to be with the same old Tom I knew and loved, not the worried, guilt ridden Tom I had seen when he came to visit me at the hospital in Anchorage.

"That's right. But they weren't *little* girls, and I wasn't 'arm wrestling' with 'em. But I *pinned* 'em all right." He snickered.

"So *that's* what you call exercise these days? I gotta get you down to the gym and get you back in shape." I was looking forward to the familiar faces, sounds and even the funky smells of the gym.

"Any time." Tom said with a serious tone in his voice. I was back, at least back in Seattle. Tom was eager do whatever he could to help me get all the way back to my old self.

That was an open question. Was my 'old self' was ever coming back?

I stood up slowly and stiffly. "Okay, let's get the bags. Hey, you know what I'd like?"

"What?"

"I'd like a big bloody piece of prime rib and a cold beer. Wudaya say, I'm buyin'?"

"Sounds great, except I'm buyin', and I'm taking you to your favorite place."

I thought for a moment. "Seacrest Landing Restaurant?"

"Yup! That's the one I had in mind." Tom said.

Alki Point is on the other side of Elliot Bay overlooking downtown Seattle. The Seacrest Landing Restaurant had large picture windows and was ideally located to give the best views of the city.

And, they had great steaks, something I hadn't tasted in months. Hospital food did not compare, in fact it only barely fit within the technical definition of 'food.'

"You're on! But I want to see Tyler after, and I need to call the University too."

On the drive into town from the airport, I was somehow amazed at how everything was the same. I don't exactly know why, but I expected things to be different. Every landmark was just as I remembered seeing it months ago. Maybe I had changed.

We didn't talk much in the car before we arrived at the restaurant. When there is a lot to be said, sometimes it's best said in silence.

I stared out the window as I sipped my beer. The waitress at Seacrest had just taken our lunch order. It felt great to be back on familiar ground, but it was familiar in an unfamiliar way. I would have been content to do nothing for the next hour but sit and stare out the window at the Seattle skyline across Elliot Bay.

Tom cleared his throat. He was never as comfortable with silence as I was. "You know, I wanted to spend more time up in Anchorage while you were in the hospital."

I continued looking out the window. "You stayed there for a whole month. And, you were at the hospital every day."

"Well yeah, but I probably could have taken some more time off, and…"

"And, you would have missed the deadline for the National Geographic project. Then, you'd be even more broke than you are now for spending all that extra money on room and board in Anchorage."

I turned back from the window to look at Tom. "Not to mention coming back up for two weeks, just to help me get things squared away for the trip home."

"I wasn't sure when, or even if, they were going to let you go." He said.

"I've been trying to get out of there for the last month. They just kept telling me, 'Not yet. We'll see how you're doing next week.' They said they were worried about the lung."

"I know, but I think it was the nurses. I saw the way they looked at you. They just couldn't stand to let a handsome stud like you go." He laughed.

It was at least partly true. The nursing staff all liked me, and maybe some, in more than a casual way. I always said please and thank you. Even when I was still suffering severe pain, I would often make small complimentary comments about their hair, perfume, or changes in their uniform. I never said anything inappropriate or obtrusive, just a friendly observation from time to time. It's a wise habit to always be nice to waitresses and nurses.

Sometimes the nurses would drop by my room, when things were slow, just to talk. From these conversations, I got to know most of them fairly well. They told me about their families, their kids, their husbands or boyfriends.

I listened much more than I talked. I've always been able to make people comfortable and draw them out. I didn't want to talk much about my life anyway, especially about Tyler and my breakup with Wendy.

The nurses on duty at the time, remembered my arrival at Providence Alaska Medical Center the day after I was attacked. I had been transported in the hospital's LifeGuard helicopter from Kodiak Island.

Doctors at the Kodiak Island Medical Center had performed CPR, given me oxygen and stopped the external bleeding, but they knew they were not equipped to deal with a patient as severely injured as I was. They worked throughout that first night to get me stabilized enough for the half hour helicopter flight to Anchorage.

One of my doctors told me that all of the staff admired my will to recover. I had arrived on the brink of death. Most of the doctors and nurses thought I would not survive. But I regained consciousness on the third day, and stubbornly continued to fight my way back from then on.

The head nurse told me after a few weeks that I had "some kind of inner strength" that set me apart from the other patients who were under her care. I don't know about that, I just wanted to get the hell out of that place.

All the nurses made it a point to stop by on my last day to wish me well and to say a special goodbye. They were of course happy that I had healed enough to leave, but a few hinted that they did not want to see me go.

I said to Tom, "Maybe so. There *were* a couple of cute ones. But, if it hadn't been for the collapsed lung and that damn pneumonia, I would have been out of there a lot sooner, cute nurses or not." Memories of gasping for breath suddenly rushed back.

My left lung had not functioned for most of the first two weeks I was in the hospital. The puncture, a byproduct of the four broken ribs, had filled the lung with blood. Emergency surgery stopped the internal bleeding and realigned the broken ribs. A second operation a few days later was required to drain the lung and allow it to re-inflate. However, before it could heal completely, pneumonia set in, and a week later, the lung collapsed a second time. The doctors then waited another two weeks to let the antibiotics deal with the pneumonia before performing a third and final operation to again drain and re-inflate the lung.

Tom must have noticed the odd look that had just flashed across my face. "How are those ribs doing?"

"They still hurt, but only when I breathe." I tried to smile. "No big deal. I can live with it."

It *was* a big deal. It still hurt a lot. It had been over 12 hours since I last took a Vicodin. Right now I was questioning my decision to go cold turkey off the drugs.

I changed the subject. "It's the leg that I've got to work on."

"Isn't the bone healed?"

"It is, mostly. But I haven't used the muscles in two months. I wasn't able to do much exercise because of the lung thing, even after I got the cast off. The muscles and tendons have all atrophied. It hurts like hell when I try to use it to actually walk. I need to stretch it out and get it limbered up."

I could see the pain on Tom's face from discussing my injuries. I needed to get off this subject. "So, how's the National Geographic project coming?"

Tom's smile snapped back onto his face. "Done! The final draft of the text was approved last week. I'm still working with the editors on the images we're going to use. But other than that, it's done!"

"I've never seen those pictures. I'd really like to see the ones you took when you went back to the camp to get all the gear."

"Well, okay. I did take a few shots of the camp, but it wasn't a pretty scene. I just wanted to get our stuff and get out of there."

"Was all your film okay?"

"Yeah, everything was in cans except for the roll I was shooting. It got wet from the camera being left out in the rain. I could have saved it though, if I had thought to put it in an opaque bottle of water to keep it wet, but I let it dry out and it glued itself together on the roll." Tom shrugged.

"Too bad. Hey, I heard they have these newfangled cameras that don't use film." I said teasingly.

"Someday, maybe." Tom smiled. We had had the film vs. digital debate before. "But, it's okay. I already had everything I needed for the project. Those were just some more creative shots I was trying to get."

"What about…" I felt strange talking about it. "You said Limpy was dead when you found me. Was he still…there?"

"I told you that Pete Putnam helped me arrange for the helicopter to take me out there."

"Yeah?"

"Well, it was part of my deal with Pete, to keep the cost down, I told him he could keep the bear."

"*Keep* the bear? Why would he want a dead bear?" I hadn't wanted to think much about poor Limpy until now.

"Of course the meat was no good, most people don't like bear meat anyway. He wanted the fur. He had to get a special permit."

"What permit?"

"Ordinarily, the State of Alaska would issue a hunting license."

"We weren't *hunting*."

"I know. That's why he needed a permit. If an animal is killed accidentally, the State allows people to use what they can. They figure it's better than letting road-kill animals just lay there on the roadside, for example, or paying a disposal service to pick them up. Anyway, this qualified as an accident."

"Okay, so he got a permit. How did he get that bear on the helicopter?"

"He didn't, at least not the whole bear."

"Huh?"

"He skinned him while we were there."

"Holy crap! You didn't tell me that. I thought… Well, I don't know what I thought, but..."

"I didn't think you'd mind. I mean after all…"

"What did you do with… the rest of him?"

"Pete helped me bury him. Nature would have taken care of him eventually, but I convinced Pete to help me."

"That ground was pretty rocky. That must have been a job."

"We did the best we could, but we weren't able to bury him very deep. Besides the smell was getting pretty bad. He'd been dead for four days. We just wanted to get it done and leave."

"Jeez! I don't think I needed to hear that." I was sorry now that I'd brought it up.

"That's why I *didn't* tell you, but you asked."

"Okay, fine. Let's drop it."

"Just one more thing." Tom reached into his pocket and pulled out a small plastic bag with something that looked like a mangled penny, only it was larger than a single penny. "I debated telling you about this, but I thought you should have it."

"What the hell is that?"

"It's the bullet."

"*The* bullet?"

"It's the one that killed Limpy. Pete found it in Limpy's throat. He said it had cut through his windpipe and his carotid artery."

Tom dropped the bag into my hand. I was speechless.

Tom continued. "The only other bullet holes were in his left ear and in his left forearm, but of course those wouldn't have killed him."

"Why is it all flattened out like that?"

"Good question. I asked Pete the same thing. He said a metal jacketed bullet like this, that didn't hit a bone, should be mostly intact. He couldn't figure out why it flattened out the way it did, maybe a ricochet, but in any case he said it was a lucky thing."

"Why lucky?" I turned the deformed bullet over in my hand. It reminded me of a miniature jagged circular saw blade. It was about the diameter of a quarter with pieces of copper metal jacket sticking out of the lead core at odd angles.

"Pete said that the bullet, flattened out the way it is, made a much wider cut than it would have otherwise. And, if it had hit on the flat side, it probably wouldn't even have penetrated the fur. But it entered edge-on, clipped off a chunk of fur, and cut an inch-wide gash into his throat. Pete said if the bullet hadn't been flattened out, it might have missed both the windpipe and/or the carotid artery. Limpy might just have lived long enough to finish you off."

"Okay, but then, how *did* it get flattened out?"

Tom gave me a knowing smile. "I didn't have a clue, not until I got home and was unpacking the gear." Tom paused.

"And…" Somehow I had an odd feeling that this was important in a way I couldn't quite put my finger on yet.

"And, I pulled out the hatchet we were using to chop firewood, the one we left stuck in that log by the campfire. I thought it was odd that the hatchet was beside the log and not stuck in it, where we had left it. But, I didn't give it a second thought at the time.

When I took a close look at the head of the hatchet, the blade had a slight dent on one side with copper colored smudges around it. I'll show it to you sometime."

"So?"

"So, it didn't have that when we bought it before the trip. *Somebody* shot it with a copper jacketed bullet. *You* must have shot it with the Beretta."

"You think that this is the same bullet?"

"Well, it fit's, doesn't it? What do you think?"

My conscious mind was struggling to deny the obvious, and it was losing. "I'm thinking…" My conscious mind gave up and acknowledged what my subconscious mind already knew. "I'm thinking, 'What if the bullet had missed the hatchet?' " I had a flash of memory, *It's done. I will live.*

"Then, I don't think we'd be talking about it right now."

I couldn't take my eyes off the bullet. The waitress brought our meals, but I barely looked up. I no longer had an appetite.

Tom had taken two bites of his prime rib before he noticed that I hadn't started eating yet.

"Eat up Heck. It's great." He mumbled through a mouthful of half-chewed meat.

I continued to stare at the bullet. *How could something so small, so seemingly insignificant, at the same time be so important?* There was something more I was not seeing, some hidden meaning begging to be revealed.

As I looked at the bullet, memories of that day began to return. Images flitted across my mind's eye. Then I knew what it was, the thing I had hidden from myself, the thing that both amazed and terrified me.

"Tom…" I paused. I had to put it into words. Somehow, it wouldn't be real until my voice brought it into the physical world.

"Yeah?" The prime rib was exceptional, and Tom was definitely enjoying it.

"Tom, I never told you this." I forced the words out. "I remember the attack, the whole thing."

The changed tone in my voice made Tom stop chewing. He waited for me to continue.

After several seconds, I said. "I knew I was going to live." I felt like I was listening to someone else talking. "Huh. Sounds kinda' ridiculous doesn't it?" Tom remained motionless.

I continued. "Tom, I had a choice! Funny, huh?"

After I offered no immediate explanation, Tom said, "You had a choice of what?"

"I had a choice to live or die!" I looked back directly into Tom's eyes.

Tom's eyes widened, but he just looked at me.

I wanted Tom to understand. "I remember while Limpy was trying to kill me. First, I thought I was going to die. Then, I just… I don't know. I just somehow *knew* I could live… or die. It was like I had a choice. I wasn't afraid of dying. I actually wanted to die. It would have been easy. I remember thinking, *No, I should live.*

"When I decided, something told me to pull the trigger one more time. I didn't even know for sure if I did it. I just remember *knowing* I would be okay, that I would live." A pained look crept onto my face and was reflected back to me in Tom's.

"Heck, you *did* live. It's okay. You're okay now." Tom had never seen me upset like this, and I could tell it was scaring him.

"You don't understand, Tom. I thought it was all a delusion. I was half unconscious anyway. Who knows what kind of crazy stuff could be going on in my head at a time like that, right?"

"That's right. You were probably just thinking crazy stuff, but you're okay now." Tom wanted me to be okay, but his worried gaze said that he knew I wasn't okay.

"That's just it. Tom, I was *not* imagining it! This bullet is the bullet I knew I should fire if I wanted to live." I could feel my face become even more gaunt and withered than before.

"But, I didn't want to live! I *almost* decided to die. I don't even know why I chose to live. It just seemed to be the right thing to do."

Tom could see my pain, confusion and fear all written on my face. "Tom, I decided my life on a *whim!* That's all it was, just a *whim!*"

Was it just a whim for Dad too? A tear began to form at the corner of my right eye. I blinked and fought back the tear, and took a ragged breath. I could see how I was affecting Tom, and I fought to compose myself.

"Look Heck, let me take you home. You look exhausted."

I was exhausted. It hadn't occurred to me until Tom said it, but my body and mind were spent. Maybe it was the beer. I hadn't had a beer in over three months. "But, the…" I looked down at my untouched plate.

"I'll have them put it in a box. We'll take it home. You can eat it later."

"Okay. I'm sorry. I…" I could not object. The need for sleep was becoming overpowering now. Tom waved over the waitress. I could only sit there limply, while the perplexed waitress boxed up my untouched prime rib.

Tom helped me to the car, and watched me fall asleep almost as soon as he closed my car door.

As I closed my eyes, I thought, *It was only a whim! Why did I choose to live? How did I know? There has to be a reason I decided to live.* My rational thought processes were becoming blurred, giving way to the logic of pure feeling.

There, beyond the realm of rationality, I began to feel the peaceful warmth of simply knowing. The feeling spread through my body like a drug, relaxing and soothing me. Questions of "why" and "how" no longer seemed relevant. *It is what it is, because it is.*

A sense of purpose enveloped me as I fell asleep. I did not know what the purpose was, I just *felt* it, somewhere. It didn't matter what or when or how. I *knew.* I did not understand, but just knowing was enough for now.

The soft glow of purpose followed me into the mists of sleep. It was a deep and peaceful sleep, like the sleep of a baby, safe in his mother's arms.

I did not dream.

CHAPTER 11
RAY

I sat rocking myself in a corner of the dayroom at The Mercer Residential Rehabilitation Institute. A casual observer would have thought that I was oblivious to the world. There was no indication that I was aware of anything going on around me.

I didn't have to be an expert on autism to understand that a lack of awareness of the world was not my problem. It was my initial inability to deal with all the sensory input bombarding all of my senses. Like many people with "normal" autism, my rocking, and other repetitive actions, was a way to limit my awareness and to help focus my attention away from the outside world.

But no one understood exactly how acutely aware I was of the world around me. I was only beginning to understand.

I was thinking, remembering. Thinking was like breathing to me now. It was automatic. It was an intensity of thought I had not known before. I could not stop it, any more than I could stop breathing. I didn't sleep. I didn't need to. What a waste of time. I no longer had an "off" switch, and I no longer needed one, or wanted one.

When I awoke from my coma, it was a rebirth. I was like a baby coming out of a warm, dark, never changing womb where muffled sounds are the only sensory input. And then I was thrust into a world of intense sound, light, touch, smell, and even taste.

When a normal baby is born, brain growth and awareness are kept in pace with the ability to process and comprehend sensory inputs. When I was reborn, it felt like I was forced to drink the full volume of water coming from a fire hose.

This Bible passage popped into my head as I remembered my ordeal. *"Do not marvel that I have said to you, 'You must be born again.' " John 5:7.*

Unlike a baby, I was fully self-aware. And instead of finding myself in a world of normal awareness, I was suddenly overwhelmed with an awareness that was a thousand times what my brain had been capable of processing before the coma.

All five of my senses were more intense than before. I read somewhere that ninety percent of what is inaccurately called "sensory ability" is actually the ability of the brain and nervous system to receive, process, and interpret incoming sensory information. I was experiencing a phenomenal increase in my brain and nervous system's processing capacity. All five of my sensory abilities were heightened beyond what I was sure any human had ever experienced.

My consciousness was inundated with an explosion of amplified sensory input. I now understand that profusion of sensory information had always been there. But like all humans, I had simply been *unaware* of it until the moment of my rebirth.

I had no way of processing or understanding all of the new information flooding into my brain. My world had grown from the relative size and complexity of a golf ball to the size and complexity of the whole planet and everything in it. It overwhelmed me. It consumed me like the fires of hell. It was far beyond white hot.

I remember once jumping into an overly hot Jacuzzi. It took my body several minutes for my nerve endings to adjust to the new reality of the heat before I was able to tolerable it. But unlike hot water, I was thrown into a world that felt like the surface of the sun. It seared my very soul. And unlike hot water, my consciousness could not adjust to the new reality of my sensory awareness, not for some time.

I guess I did what most newborn babies do. I screamed. And, I writhed in agony. And, I continued to scream and writhe until I was tied down and sedated.

The drugs lowered my awareness to a somewhat more tolerable level. But at first, even with the drugs, just being conscious was impossible for me to handle. They gave me more until I was blissfully unconscious.

Upon becoming conscious again, I would close my eyes as tightly as I could. I would cover my ears and hum loudly. I found that by making a repetitive noise or motion it helped to focus my attention, to screen out some of the chaos.

The drugs gave me some control, but they also blurred everything. It was an acceptable tradeoff at the time. I can never forget the scorching blaze of awareness I had experienced upon my first awakening. The thought of having to face it again without the drugs, terrified me at first.

I knew I could not do it alone. I felt so very alone, and I desperately needed someone to help me. But there was no one. I prayed to God.

He did not answer. *My God, my God, why have you forsaken me? Why are you so far from saving me, the words of my groaning? Psalm 22:1.*

According to Matthew 27:46, Jesus on the cross asked the same question of God, "Eli, Eli, Lema Sabachthani?" A Roman spear in his side was God's short answer then.

Or maybe, God's silence *was* His answer. Was He laughing at my pain? What sin had I committed to justify my sentence to this blast-furnace corner of hell?

I felt like a gnat flailing alone against the typhoon of awareness that was ripping my mind to shreds. I could not possibly face it by myself.

Then I thought of Julia. Her radiant image glowed before me, soothing me.

They say it was three weeks after I first awoke from the coma that I spoke my first intelligible word, "Julia." My voice was a mere rasp from weeks of screaming, but in my mind her name chimed like a silver bell in a dark forest.

Just by saying her name, I was comforted, calmed. Julia was helping! She had heard my cries.

I said her name over and over again. "Julia! Julia! Julia! Julia! Julia! Julia!" As I did, her face became clearer in my mind. And the stronger the memory, the more I was able to focus my mind.

I said her name louder and louder until it was a scream, a chant. "JULIA! JULIA! JULIA! JULIA!" The clutter of sensory input became more organized, the hurricane winds of awareness steadied. I gained more control of my thoughts. "JULIA! JULIA! JULIA! JULIA!" I rejoiced.

I clung to my love for her, for Julia my savior. My love for her was better than the drugs they gave me every two hours. My love for Julia brought my world into focus.

I was amazed! I could direct my attention and focus on specific senses, separating one from another. Out of the unbearable chaos, there was now some degree of order, there was love.

I wanted to see her face again. I desperately needed to see her face. My cries for Julia became a question. "JULIA? JULIA? JULIA? JULIA? JULIA? JULIA?"

Barbara Wilson was on duty that night when I discovered Julia would be my savior. I remember seeing her badge. Why do I remember that so clearly? When she heard my screams for Julia, she ran into my room. I was tossing from side to side on my bed in time with my chanting for Julia. She called an orderly, but before one could get there, she threw herself across my bed in an attempt to pin me down. She was afraid I was going to fall off my bed.

I remember I grabbed her by the shoulders and screamed in her face, "JULIA?" But she was not Julia. It was only the frightened face of nurse Wilson.

"Ray, calm down. Ray! It'll be okay, Ray." She said. But, I continued to toss and turn while still calling for Julia. The sound and motion were one.

I think she wanted to give me a sedative shot, but she wanted to tie me down first.

She told me. "Ray, listen to me! Ray, Julia is gone!"

What did she say? She's gone where? Surely, not far. "JULIA? JULIA?" I pleaded.

"Ray, Julia died! She's dead!" I stopped moving. *Dead.* The word landed like a blow from a sledge hammer, but it stunned me in a way that no sledge hammer could.

Scott Babcock. The image of his badge seems burned in my memory. He was an orderly–big guy, built like a linebacker.

He jumped on top of me. He was hurting me.

"Hold him down while I give him a shot." Wilson got off of me.

I tried to lift him off but couldn't at first. "Jesus, he's strong!" He said.

"Hold on! Just a second!" She was getting the syringe ready. I stopped struggling. I gave up. *Why fight,* I thought.

The sting of the needle coincided with the sting of my realization that Julia was gone, really gone. *Dead.* I understood.

Julia is dead. Julia is dead. Julia is dead. I repeated the thought just as I had chanted Julia's name. The control I had gained over my awareness was dying too.

Julia's name gave me an overpowering feeling of love. Now, the thought of her death filled me with despair. Then, with anger. I thought about her death more, and the anger turned to rage. *How? Why?*

I felt the rage grow inside me. And as it did, my control over my awareness returned, and grew. The rage for Julia's death gave me even more control than had my love for her. I felt a new power.

I was amazed at the almost instantaneous transition. Even in death, Julia could still save me! She was now the source of my righteous rage. Now I could harness the furious typhoon in my mind.

Wilson depressed the plunger on the syringe. I felt the drug flow into my vein. It didn't matter. I focused on my newly found rage. Julia was dead, but she could still help me make the world controllable. She gave me a tool to cope, a weapon to wield, a weapon to wield against the world. She was at my side again.

Julia, help me make the world a better place.

I felt the power surge inside me. *Focus, brain, nerve, muscle.* I threw Babcock's two-hundred-eighty-six pounds ten feet across the room. He hit wall and flopped unconscious onto the floor, spilling a trash can as he fell. I felt bad about the trash can. Someone would have to clean that up.

Wilson looked stunned, like I had thrown *her* across the room. I wouldn't do that. I remember her frightened, bewildered stare.

I relaxed back onto my bed holding her eye, and saw the totality of her for the first time. I smiled. I liked her. She did look a little like Julia after all.

I saw the question on her face. "A better place." I said as clearly as I could.

Then the drug touched my brain and my eye lids got heavy and fell shut. I cuddled into sleep, like I remembered Julia and me spooning together during those lazy Sunday afternoon naps. She was with me again.

My last thought was, *'If you lie down, you will not be afraid; when you lie down, your sleep will be sweet.' Proverbs 3:24.*

CHAPTER 12
TOM

I watched Heck sleep in the car on the drive to his place from Seacrest Landing. Heck was not the same. That was obvious. Maybe it was temporary. Heck was certainly a long way from being fully recovered. I thought, *it's my turn buddy.* It had been eight years ago when I signed that unwritten promissory note. As I saw it, the debt was now due and payable.

###

We had planned a weekend climb of Mt. Rainier.

I had talked Heck into putting an ad in the Date Mart dating section of the paper. As a new professor at the University of Washington's psychology department, and with his looks, he was "a babe magnet." The new BMW convertible didn't hurt either.

He had gotten a lot of responses and photos from single women around the Seattle area. The women he had arranged to meet thus far had been a mix of everything from simply "not my type" to "really weird."

He was discouraged, and he was worn out from playing the dating game. It was a game he was not very comfortable with, and one he thought he was not very good at either.

On the Friday before the weekend of our planned trip, the weather turned bad and we postponed it until the following weekend. With nothing to do for that weekend and with my encouragement, Heck decided to contact "just one more" of the women who had responded to his personal ad. Her name was Wendy.

He told me all about her. She was smart and confident without being arrogant, and she had a subtle understated sexiness that Heck found attractive. She had a stable job as a Product Manager for a high tech company on the Eastside, and she had a comfortable independent life with many friends and activities, and no kids. A big plus for Heck was that she showed none of that neediness that he had seen with many of the women he had dated. This flaw, more than any other, had been a serious turnoff for Heck.

Heck and Wendy hit it off immediately. By the following weekend, Heck was trying to back out of our trip to Mt. Rainier so that he could spend more time with his new flame, Wendy. I was having none of it. So, we packed up our stuff and left Seattle on Saturday morning at 6:00 a.m.

It was early June and there was still a lot of snow on the mountain. At 14,410 feet, Mt. Rainier is the highest peak in Washington State. Like Mt. St. Helens, Mt. Rainier is also a volcanic mountain. But unlike Mt. St. Helens, Mt. Rainier has not erupted for a very long time, although the geologist still considered it an active volcano.

As long as the weather is good, Mt. Rainier is one of the easier mountains to climb. Every year, hundreds of people simply walk to the summit, as long as they are in reasonably good health, anyone can climb the mountain. Aside from the thin air at that altitude, it's a fairly easy climb if you pace yourself. And other than maybe a pair of crampons, very little technical climbing equipment is really needed if you stick to the trails.

But the mountain can be dangerous. Bad weather is the biggest hazard. But many have also died, or have been seriously injured, when they ventured away from the safety of the trail. Most people plan on spending one night on the mountain, and warm winter overnight gear is always recommended, regardless of the time of year.

Heck and I were prepared. It was a sunny day, and there were several other people on the trail that weekend. In a way, it was the good weather that led to my accident. I remember the air was cool in the shadows, but the sun was warm. There was a stiff breeze. Some clouds were moving in from the Northwest, but they were still far off on the horizon.

We both loved the mountain air. There's something about the wilderness that always seemed to put me in touch with myself.

Heck had reason to be feeling good about himself. He had a great position at the university. He was making great money at last after years of being a poor student. And, he had met a woman that he said might just be the one.

I had brought along my camera equipment; two cameras, a Nikon 35mm and a Bronica 645 format, along with a tote bag filled with several lenses, a mini-tripod, film, and various other photographic gadgets and supplies. As a professional photographer, the clear mountain air and spectacular views were irresistible. I was counting the dollars that my Rainier photos would bring in. Back then I made my living primarily by selling framed prints of my work down at the Pike Place Market. I had tried doing wedding photography to pay the bills, but gave it up when I discovered that trees and rocks and birds were a lot less demanding, and a lot less emotional, than new brides and their mothers.

We had planned to summit on the first day, come back down and spend the night at a lower altitude, and then finish the decent the next day. We figured we could get back to Seattle Sunday evening early enough for dinner.

Heck knew I would be taking a lot of pictures, but he didn't think it would put us as far behind schedule as it did. I didn't want to miss anything, and I had plenty of film.

Heck kept bugging me about needing to get moving if we were going to make the summit before dark. I promised I'd hurry. I made up some excuses to keep him off my back. I told him the snow was throwing off my exposure meter and that I needed to bracket my shots to make sure I got it right. Of course, it was all bull. Amateurs have to do that, but I get it right the first time, because you never know if you'll get a second shot.

Heck would always relent in the end. "Fine. Get your shot. Then we've got to move."

A conversation similar to this took place several times during the late morning and early afternoon. We finally made Camp Muir at 3:30 p.m.

I told Heck that there was still plenty of light and that we could make the summit before dark. I was feeling a little guilty for all the delays I had caused.

Heck agreed that we could make the summit before dark, but we could never make it back down to camp before dark. He was right of course. And I definitely didn't want to have to spend a night on the peak. It could get bitterly cold and windy on the peak even in summer.

I used a four letter word and kicked a rock as a kind of an apology. We agreed that we'd get to bed early and head for the peak at first light. Heck pulled off his pack and dumped it on the ground and let out a sigh. There really wasn't much choice.

Since we weren't going to summit, we had a little time to kill. Heck made me promise to get all my shots that day, and keep my cameras packed up *all day* the next day. I told him it was deal.

I gave Heck my patented grin, the one that says, *I may be a pain in the butt, but you gotta love me anyway.* It seemed to work with my girlfriends. Heck just shook his head and turned away so that I couldn't see him smile. I chuckled to myself.

The next day we made the summit by noon, even though we both had woke up that morning with hangover-like altitude headaches. Despite my promise, I had to get a few shots from the top. Since we were a little ahead of schedule, Heck only made a feeble protest.

It was after 1:00 p.m. by time we started back down the mountain. By 2:00 we had made our way a good distance down the mountain. We hadn't seen anyone on the trail since the summit. The other climbers had started down earlier, or were taking the alternate route down the North side of the mountain.

We stopped for a break. I wanted to get a shot or two from a dramatic cliff a hundred yards or so off the trail. We were making good time, so Heck was content to munch on a granola bar and wait for me.

My memory of the rest of that day is foggy at best. Much later, I would force Heck to tell me the whole story. I wouldn't let him skim over any details.

He said he was chewing on a granola bar, staring off at the horizon when something changed. He told me that he wasn't sure if he had heard something or just sensed it, but he said he knew something was just wrong.

He called out for me several times. When I didn't answer, I guess he was getting a little pissed. He picked up his gear and walk in the direction I had gone.

He spotted my tripod with the Nikon mounted on in, but didn't see me. He walked over to the tripod and scanned the area, and called again.

He said he knew he should be pissed, but something didn't feel right. He noticed that I had mounted a radio controlled shutter release on the camera, a little gadget that I sometimes used to get distant self-portrait shots. I think I must have been trying to get a shot of myself on the cliff to show the scale of the scene.

Heck looked through my camera viewfinder and saw an outcropping of rock hanging over a cliff, but he didn't see me. He stepped in front of the camera so that he could see further down the cliff. He spotted my red windbreaker fifty feet below the rock outcropping. I wasn't moving.

There was no way Heck could get to me quickly, short of jumping off the cliff himself. He could go for help, but that might take several hours. He didn't want to do the safe thing.

Heck studied the terrain, looking for an option. After several seconds, he saw a way to get to me. If he backtracked and came down around the far end of the cliff where the incline was not so steep, he could climb partially back up the cliff from below to my location.

Heck tried to move as fast as he could, but it took him about fifteen minutes. He kept glancing over at my location, but he didn't see any movement since he had first spotted me. I might have been dead for all Heck knew. He said he was scared that he wouldn't get to me in time.

When Heck reached me, he immediately saw that my left foot was bent sideways at almost a ninety-degree angle.

He yelled at me, but I did not respond. He checked my pulse at the carotid artery as he had been taught in that first aid class he had taken a few months before. I guess my neck felt cold to the touch. At first he thought I was dead, but he was able to find a faint pulse.

He saw the cut on my head. It wasn't deep and did not appear serious at first until he noticed the extensive swelling and bruising under my hair. He knew that a concussion could be deadly if not treated quickly.

We were miles from help. Heck was forced to make a decision. He could leave me and go for help and then come back, and probably find me dead. Or, he could stay with me and probably watch me die.

Heck did not accept either alternative. He fashioned a sling out of his and my jackets. With some difficulty, he lifted my 160 pounds onto his back and secured the sling. Heck didn't know if he could carry me all the way down the mountain. He didn't know if anyone could do it. But, he was damn sure going to try.

He explained to a reporter later, "I didn't have a choice."

As the sun dipped low in the West and the clouds began to move in over the mountain, Heck was met by a park ranger as he staggered down the trail about a mile from the Paradise Visitor Center. The park ranger overtook him as he was coming down the trial. He had been checking Camp Muir and would have been down sooner, but had stayed to clean up some litter left by a careless camper.

Heck had followed the Nisqually Glacier down most of the way. He had not been able to pick up the trail until he was much closer to Paradise. There was no way he could carry me back up the way he had come, so Heck was forced to negotiate his way without the benefit of a nicely maintained trail.

The park ranger had a radio. He contacted the ranger station, and the people there arranged for an airlift. Along with Heck's heroic efforts, the airlift saved my life, a fact that I am reminded of every time I make a payment on the bill the park service sent me for their services.

I did have a concussion, and a serious one. A hole had been quickly drilled in my skull upon my arrival at the emergency room to relieve the pressure and prevent brain damage. The doctors told Heck that I would not have survived the night without treatment.

One hour after the airlift helicopter picked up Heck and I, it began to rain on the mountain. The rain turned to snow as the temperatures dropped unseasonably low. In the snow and darkness, an air rescue would have been impossible. If Heck had chosen to stay with me and waited for rescue, we would have been stranded at a high altitude on the mountainside, and would have probably both died of hypothermia before we could be rescued.

I almost lost my foot. The ankle had multiple fractures. The blood vessels were badly damaged by the foot flopping around while Heck carried me down the mountain. Heck hadn't thought to put a splint on it, and because of this oversight, I might have lost my foot, and I might have been crippled for life.

It did not appear at first that the foot could be saved, but the decision did not have to be made until I regained consciousness a day later. I pleaded with the doctor to keep the foot. Yes, I knew the risk, that it could become infected, that it may not have any feeling, that I may never be able to walk on it, and that it might have to be amputated anyway, if it didn't heal right. They let me have my way, at least for the time being.

No one blamed Heck for the condition of my foot, in fact the papers treated him like a hero, and no one agreed with them more than me. Heck apologized to me several times for the foot. He felt terrible that he had been so stupid to not secure it. It just hadn't occurred to him. At the time Heck was focused on just getting me down that mountain.

I surprised all the doctors as well as Heck. Not only did the ankle heal without infection, it healed without losing feeling and was almost completely functional within six months. The doctors attributed my successful recovery to my diligent, if very painful, physical therapy. Heck kidded me that I wouldn't have done all the therapy, if I hadn't had all of my girlfriends around giving me sympathy and encouragement.

What I didn't tell Heck was that I worked hard to recover full use of my foot because I owed it to him. Heck had done something almost super human. He had carried 160 pounds of dead weight over seven miles of some of the roughest terrain Mt. Rainier has to offer. I knew that if I had been on the mountain with anyone else, I would be dead now. The least I could do was keep Heck from feeling guilty about my damn foot.

###

When I got back to the apartment, I helped get Heck's groggy and limping body from the car to his bed. I helped him pull off his shoes and returned to my car to get his luggage. It was still early, but by the time I returned, Heck was out for the night.

I decided to stick around at Heck's place. I didn't think Heck would really need any help during the night, but then who knows.

I cracked a long forgotten beer in the back of Heck's refrigerator and turned on Heck's TV. I took a swig of beer, and then thought better of it, twisted the cap back on the bottle, and stuck it back in the fridge. It was going to be a long night. I didn't want to fall asleep too soon, or too deeply.

I thought of how I'd heard of new mothers waking in the middle of the night to check on their baby *to see if he is still breathing. A mother's worry is sorta like a friend's worry I guess.* I thought with a smile.

I kicked off my shoes and settled in.

CHAPTER 13
RAY

The all-encompassing love I felt for Julia, and the resulting intense rage I felt at her death, had saved my sanity. Julia had saved me.

Hatred stirs up strife, but love covers all offenses. Proverbs 10:12.

Did my intense love "cover" my "offense" of intense hatred? I had no doubt that this had saved me. Was this then the answer from God to my prayer of salvation? It must be. Maybe God was smiling on me, not laughing at me. Why then, had He killed Julia?

Incrementally, over the next few weeks, my conscious awareness became able to process more and more sensory input. I did not feel the need for further violent outbursts except when I was touched. The hospital staff now took precautions. Rocking and humming helped to focus and distract my mind. As long as no one touched me, I could keep myself under control.

Anger is my friend, I thought. It gives me control and power. It was the power to destroy those who were responsible for Julia's death. This is why I nurtured my rage, and as it grew, control over my world grew.

With greater control, I became aware of the intoxicating sense of power that came with it. It was an unfamiliar feeling that I found irresistible. The rage that had saved my sanity had now become the center of my soul. Living without it was inconceivable. My increased sensory awareness was only the raw material. My rage was what gave it form, and what gave it purpose.

Dr. Janet Martin entered the dayroom holding the hand of a blond, green-eyed eight-year-old boy bobbing his head from side to side.

"Tyler, I want you to meet someone new." She led him over to the far corner of the room where I sat in a straight-backed chair rocking.

She told me that I had made "progress," as she called it, over the last week. She said that she wanted this kid, Tyler, to spend a little time with me so that maybe he could learn something from me. Maybe. Why not? I was curious. Maybe I could learn something too. I didn't object.

"Ray, I have someone I want you to meet." I turned my head slightly to look at Dr. Martin but said nothing and continued rocking.

"This is Tyler. Tyler, this is Ray." We looked at each other briefly without speaking.

"Ray, Tyler has been with us for a long time. He likes to color pictures." I turned back and continued my rocking.

"Tyler, Ray is new here, so you can show him where everything is."

At the words "color pictures" Tyler had already headed off toward the shelf where the crayons and drawing paper were stored.

"Color, color, color." Tyler sang gleefully continuing to bob his head back and forth.

"That's it Tyler, you can show Ray how to color." Then to me, "If he bothers you, I can take him to the other side of the room." She turned to go help get Tyler set up to color.

"Okay." I said without looking at Dr Martin and without breaking the rhythm of my rocking.

She seemed surprised when I spoke. She had heard me talk only once since I had gotten there, but it was only a couple of words and was not directed at her. I responded appropriately when talked to or given instructions, so I knew that she knew I understood speech.

She stopped and turned back to me. "Thank you, Ray. I know you two will get along just fine." She smiled broadly.

I sensed Dr. Martin as she helped Tyler get set up with his colors at a table behind my left shoulder. I heard Tyler start a circular pattern. It was a red crayon, a familiar smell. He continued the circular pattern with the same crayon until it was worn down to its paper wrapper. Then, he traded it in for a new crayon from the box. I smelled blue as he started again.

I don't think he cared about the color, nor did I. It was all about the motion of the coloring. Yes, the motion, circles and circles, and circles. It was soothing, even to listen to the sound.

"Color, color, color, color." Tyler resumed his gleeful chant.

"Now, stay on the paper Tyler. Show Ray how well you can color." I was sure that, to her, I appeared to be paying no attention to Tyler.

"Blue." I said. My voice felt like breaking glass in my throat. It sounded like finger nails on a chalk board.

It was worth the pain to sense the subtle change in Dr. Martin's demeanor. Her shoulders tightened as she looked at Tyler's artwork. I knew that she knew that I had not looked at Tyler and his coloring since he had started.

"That's right Ray. Tyler is using a blue crayon." Her voice contained micro tremors. Not many, but I knew what she must be thinking. Maybe eventually I would be able know exactly what she was thinking.

I allowed the hint of a smile to flicker across my face.

She turned back to Tyler. "That's very pretty. We'll have to show that to your father when he comes."

I overheard Dr. Martin talking with one of the nurses a few weeks ago. She would have liked to be able to say "mother" also, but she said that Tyler had not seen his mother in two years. Tyler had never shown any indication, even to me, that he remembered anything about his mother.

Buried, I concluded. I know that I too could forget about the pain. I could bury Julia in my mind. But I would never do that. It would be like killing her all over again.

Sometimes we measure success in baby steps. I had heard Dr. Martin say this once to a staff person, but I was no longer a baby. My steps were becoming longer.

To those who by patience in well-doing seek for glory and honor and immortality, he will give eternal life. Romans 2:7'

I continued sitting with my back turned away from Tyler, some four or five feet away. Dr. Martin had left us now.

Seventy-six, seventy-seven, seventy-eight, seventy-nine… I counted to myself in sync with Tyler's rhythmic circular motion. It soothed my mind. *Eighty, eighty-one, paper, eighty-two, paper, eighty-three, paper. Stop. Smell, red, no, magenta. One, two, three, four…*

CHAPTER 14
JAN

I remembered the words that my first psychology professor had said to me many years ago. "Sometimes we measure success in baby steps."

My looks were important to me, but not an obsession. The book said my BMI was too high. So what if I had a few extra pounds on my hips. At fifty-eight years old, I had worked over thirty years as a psychiatrist. I had worked with some of the most difficult cases over the years.

Many of the colleagues that I had worked with early in my career had long since given up working directly with the tough cases, and had moved into less demanding areas, but not me. I loved the challenge. And even though it was no longer necessary, in my position as Director, I insisted on keeping in direct contact with my patients at the Institute. It kept me from turning into a bureaucrat.

Ten years ago my husband David, a successful heart surgeon, died ironically of a massive heart attack. We had been on a cruise to the Bahamas to celebrate our thirtieth wedding anniversary when it happened.

We had first visited the islands in 1960 for a short three-day honeymoon just after we both had finished medical school. From the time we returned from our honeymoon, and started our residence training, we seemed to be always on the go, taking off precious little time for ourselves.

The Bahamas trip was to be a much needed respite for us. If we had stayed at home and just enjoyed some "quiet time" together, as David had wanted, I might have been able to get him to a properly equipped hospital in time to save his life.

My feelings of guilt for talking him into the Bahamas trip lasted only about thirty seconds. While I grieved for his loss, I was never one to hold on to the past or to carry regrets into the future.

I combined our joint savings and investments, with his life insurance money. Then, I sold our ridiculously large waterfront home on the south side of Mercer Island, and I moved into a much smaller, but still very comfortable, upscale condominium on the north end of the island.

David had always taken care of the money. When I finally had to face the finances, I was surprised to discover that I was a multi-millionaire. But instead of spending the money on luxuries I didn't need, I founded the Mercer Residential Rehabilitation Institute.

I had underestimated the amount of money and expertise it actually took to launch such a venture. I was able to obtain additional State and Federal grant money after construction was underway to fill the money gap. And my many friends and contacts in the medical industry, contributed much-needed know-how to get the fifty-bed facility up and running.

Since then, the facility had doubled in size, and had earned a reputation of having some of the best psychiatric professionals in the Seattle area on staff. The care provided by the Institute was considered the best in the state, possibly the best on the West coast.

Not to brag, but this was in no small part due to my tireless efforts and unflinching commitment to excellence. I typically worked ten or twelve hours a day and I had not taken a vacation in the ten years since we opened the doors.

The Institute provided both long-term care and rehabilitation services. I took personal pride in how many patients the Institute had been able to return to productive lives in the community.

But the services of the Institute did not come cheap. Those who could afford it, or had insurance to cover the expense were charged a premium rate. However, I set up a fund to take care of special pro-bono patients. These patients were selected on the basis of need and challenge. If the case was tough, and the need was great, the Mercer Residential Rehabilitation Institute would excuse the bill.

The Institute was my whole life now. David and I had never had children. The Institute was my baby, and I treated it like any mother would treat her child.

CHAPTER 15
HECK

Dr. Janet Martin, or Jan, as her very close friends were allowed to call her, hadn't seen me in months. I had told her the whole story about the bear attack and my surgeries and recovery. She told me she was afraid she might not recognize me.

She reminded me that "Tyler looks so much like you." She said it was those "penetrating" green eyes as she described them. I had assured her that at least that part had not changed.

I had called her from the hospital in Anchorage just two days ago. I said I'd be back in town the next day and would call when I got in. When she did not hear from me, she called my home number that morning. There was no answer, but she had left a message. She seemed anxious to see me.

Our relationship had become more than just a professional one over the last couple years since Tyler came to the Institute. I know she respected my professional skills as a behavioral psychologist, and for the help I had provided for patients at the Institute, but she said she admired my "commitment" to Tyler too. I told her it wasn't a matter of commitment. He was my son, and that was all there was to it.

Jan and I hit it off immediately when we first met. Twenty years my senior, she was always a professional, but she exuded a sort of motherly warmth to everyone around her.

Mincing words was not a talent that came naturally to her. She told me once, out of the blue, that I was "confident" yet "humble," like her late husband David, and that I reminded her of him. I took issue with both these words, but she just shrugged off my objections. In that knowing motherly tone she often used, she simultaneously declared the matter settled and ended any further discussion.

She had never said as much, but I got the impression that she had grown to think of me as the son she and David never had, and therefore Tyler was like a grandson of sorts. It was good for Tyler.

Despite Tyler's occasional violent and self-destructive outbursts, he was a sweet child in his own way, and she made sure he was treated with the love and nurturing he needed.

###

It was Tyler's violent, self-destructive outbursts that had originally motivated me to bring him to the Institute. When Jan had first seen him, his head was still bandaged from an incident at the daycare that had occurred the week before.

It was not the first time Tyler had tried to hurt himself, but there had always been someone around to stop him. This time he was at the daycare center. They were understaffed that day because two people were out with the flu.

Colds and flu were an accepted, if bothersome, occupational hazard of working closely with children. I had overheard one of the staff jokingly call the kids under her care, "Those little germ bags." I didn't say anything. It was said in jest after all, but it was also true.

A nineteen-year-old girl named Mindy had the misfortune of being the one caregiver left in charge of watching all of the children in the playroom that day. She had only been working on the job for a little over a month. She viewed it as her first step in fulfilling her dream of becoming an elementary school teacher.

She had left the room *for just a minute* to relieve herself in the restroom. In the short time she was out of the room, Tyler had pried a small mirror off of the wall, broken it, and began repeatedly smashing his head into the shards of glass on the floor.

When Mindy returned, Tyler was splashing his head into what was now a pool of blood. He had already splattered blood onto several of the other nearby children. It would have been a shocking scene for anyone, but it was more than the nineteen-year-old Mindy could handle. She just stood in the doorway trembling and screaming at the top of her lungs.

The owner of the daycare, Marta Velazquez, was preparing lunch in the kitchen when she heard Mindy's ear-piercing scream. When she got to the playroom, it took her only seconds to evaluate the situation and to jump into action. With no help from the hysterical Mindy, she grabbed Tyler, assessed the damage, tied a damp towel around his head to stop the bleeding, called 911, calmed down Tyler, and the other ten confused and crying children. She had even cleaned up most of the blood by the time the ambulance arrived.

Marta called Wendy first. "Mrs. Beckman, there was an accident and Tyler hurt himself."

"What?"

"He cut his head. I called an ambulance to take him to the hospital."

"Was it that bad? Did he have to go to the hospital?"

"Yes ma'am. It was bleeding pretty bad. I think he'll need a few stitches. They're taking him to Harborview."

"Is *someone* going with him to the hospital?"

"They said his parents needed to be there before they can treat him." Mart explained.

"Shit, Marta I'm in an important meeting!"

Marta expected worry, even anger, but not this. "I'm sorry Mrs. Beckman, but…"

"Sorry! I've got a *real* job here! I've got a new product launch in just three friggin' days! Can't you understand? I can't just take off any time I feel like it! That's why I pay *you* to take care of him! Damn it!" Marta could hear Wendy's frustrated huff of a sigh, and knew there was nothing more she could say that wouldn't make it worse. She remained silent while Wendy decided what to do.

"Okay, look, I *cannot* handle this today! Why did you call *me* anyway? Why didn't you call Heck?" Her frustration had turned to open anger. "That's it! I don't care! I am *not* going to deal with it! Call Heck! Tell *him* to handle it! I've got better things to do today than deal with that damn… kid!" Wendy slammed down the phone without waiting for a response.

I was in the middle of a lecture when I got the call on my cell phone. I usually turned it off before a lecture, but I had forgotten. Normally, I let whomever called leave a message. When I saw that the call was from *Little Ones Playland*, something told me it was important. I excused myself, stepped into the hall and pushed the send button.

"Hello, Marta?"

"Dr. Beckman, there's been an accident. Tyler cut his head."

"Is he okay? How bad is it?" I was worried, but the tone in her voice said "serious", but not "drastic."

"I think he's okay, but it was bleeding pretty bad so I called an ambulance to take him to the hospital. He may need a couple of stitches."

"Okay, okay, good. Which hospital?"

"Harborview. They said a parent has to be there before they can treat him."

"Okay. Thanks. I'm on my way now." I told myself Tyler would be okay. I felt a wave of guilt welling up from my stomach. I had to admit to myself that I knew this was going to happen eventually.

"Oh wait, Marta, is Wendy going to meet me at the hospital?"

There was a pause. "No. She… ah, couldn't get away?"

"What?"

Marta couldn't keep her indignation to herself any longer. "She said she's got better things to do than deal '*with that damn kid.*' " Marta, a mother of six grown children, couldn't imagine a mother not rushing to her child when he's hurt.

I was stunned and embarrassed. I couldn't believe it. "No, wait a minute Marta. She said she had 'better things to do?' " I had to admit to myself that I *could* believe it.

"Yes sir." Her tone said that she regretted opening her mouth. "I'm sorry Dr. Beckman. I shouldn't have…"

"No, that's okay Marta. I'll *talk* to her later." It wasn't the first time Wendy had behaved this way toward Tyler. It had been the subject of many heated arguments over the last few months. But this! This was just too much! I was resolved that I was not going to let her get away with it, not this time.

I put my anger at Wendy on a back burner. I had to get to Tyler now. I gave my lecture notes to my teaching assistant and thanked him for taking over the class.

I was heading for the door when I remembered the BMW was at the garage getting a brake job today. Tom had agreed to give me a ride over there later that afternoon to pick it up. *My son is going to the hospital and I don't have a Goddamn car!*

I flipped open my cell phone, scrolled down to the third name on my phonebook list, and pushed the send button.

"Hey bud. Wa'sup!" It was Tom.

"Tom, Tyler's had an accident! I need to get to Harborview! Can you pick me up now?" I think my voice said everything Tom needed to know. I was more than anxious.

Tom was in the middle of an outdoor shoot over at Gas Works Park on Lake Union, but there was no hint of hesitation in his voice. "I'm on my way. I'll tell the model to take off for the day. I can be there in five minutes. Where you gonna be?"

"Pick me up on Pacific in front of University Hospital. That'll be quicker than coming on campus. It'll just take me a couple minutes to run over there."

The cuts on Tyler's forehead did require a few stitches, but it was not as serious as it first appeared. The hospital kept him overnight for observation anyway. I stayed with Tyler until he fell asleep. Wendy did not show up, or even call.

I waited at home for Wendy to come in. I didn't know what I would say to her exactly. We had had the same argument before. I would accuse her of not caring about Tyler, and treating him like he was not much more than a pet dog. She would accuse me of trying to control her life, that I didn't want her to have a career, and that she wasn't going to be a barefoot and pregnant nanny to a bunch of screaming kids.

When we first married, there was talk of having at least two children. We were so happy when Tyler was born. I was excited that he was a boy, so that I could pass on my family's male middle name, Clinton, to the next generation.

And even after Tyler was born, Wendy remained positive about having more kids. But when Tyler did not develop, and was eventually diagnosed with autism, Wendy's attitude toward having kids and a family changed dramatically.

Wendy had always been a high achiever. I suspected that she thought of herself as a failure with Tyler, and that she wanted to distance herself from anything connected with that failure, including me.

I told her my analysis during one of our arguments over Tyler. She exploded with fierce denial, accusing me of psychoanalyzing her like one of my "lab rats." I realized then that my analysis was probably true, but I also knew there was nothing I could do about it.

As a psychologist, I understood that true change can only come from within. She had to willingly admit she had a problem and sincerely want to change it. Any efforts on my part to force the issue would only be counterproductive.

At one point, I thought things were getting better between us. She seemed to be coping with Tyler better and was treating him with a little more affection. It was almost like the old days before Tyler was born. Tyler reminded me more and more of Nan these days, but I didn't mention that to Wendy.

Buoyed by the feeling that things were going to work out, I casually mentioned one evening over dinner that maybe we should think about having another child like we had planned. I quickly realized that I had been deluding myself. Things were not working out.

She not only didn't want to talk about it, she didn't even want to think about it. Her improved attitude was apparently only due to her temporary ability to sweep her "failure" under her conscious rug. Talking about kids only served to throw it back in her face.

I loved Tyler despite his less than perfect condition, and I wanted more kids. I wanted a happy family. Wendy did not want anything to do with kids or family. She had her career, something she could excel at. Eventually, it was all she wanted. Our relationship went steadily downhill after that.

When Wendy finally arrived home the night of the accident at 1:30 a.m., I could tell immediately that she had been drinking and partying.

Before I could ask the question she said, “I know, I know, I’m late. Stan took us all out for a pre-launch dinner meeting, and we all stayed for a few drinks.”

Stanley Malone was Wendy’s boss. I met him once. A self-absorbed ass, was my immediate assessment. He came off as one of those arrogant guys who look in the mirror a lot, and like to surround themselves with “yes” men, and women. Wendy said he was “going places” in the company, whatever that meant.

Her hair was in tangles and her clothes were disheveled. “I hope you had a good time.” I said sarcastically.

In her condition, the sarcasm went completely over her head. “Yeah, I did.” She said with a giggle. “Charlie and Martin sang karaoke. They’re real hams. You know Pam, she tried to dance on the table and almost broke her neck.” The giggles turned to a full laugh. “Oh, and me and Stan won the fifties dance contest, see!” She pulled a three-inch plastic trophy out of her purse.

I just stared at her, waiting for her to land back on Earth.

“What?” She finally noticed I was not enjoying her story.

“Don’t you want to know about Tyler?” My tone had the intended effect of pouring ice water over her head. She had obviously completely forgotten about the call from Marta.

“Oh. Yeah. How’s Tyler?” She was immediately sober, but only a little embarrassed for not making at least the pretense of caring about Tyler’s condition.

"What do you care?" I knew I should wait until morning when she was sober and I was rested, but my anger wouldn't wait.

"Don't start with me Heck! I have commitments at work. People depend on me. I can't just leave work anytime I want!"

"What about the people in your family that depend on you? What about your commitment to Tyler? He does have *two* parents you know." I knew what her answer would be.

"There you go again! Don't try to pull that guilt trip shit on me! You still think I should be some kind of cookie-baking, barefoot, baby maker!"

"I never said…"

"Yes you did! Didn't you say you wanted another baby? When am I supposed to get time to deliver a baby, let alone take care of it after it's born? Am I supposed to just quit my job?"

"Of course not, but…"

"But nothing! I'm *not* going to be your little baby maker! That's all you think I am. Get it through your head, I've already got a job. If you want more kids, you're just going to have to find yourself another incubator!" Then she sardonically added, "If you haven't already." We hadn't had sex for five months, but having an affair had never entered my mind. Although, I suspected that it had probably entered hers.

"You know that's bull! All I ever wanted was for us to have a happy family. I *thought* that's what you wanted too."

"Family? We don't have a *real* family! I don't feel like I'm part of any *family!* I'm just the one who has to live with a shrink and a retard!"

I didn't think it was possible for Wendy to shock me. I was wrong. I'm sure my mouth dropped open. Wendy knew my hot buttons, and she knew that one was the biggest.

"Aw shit! Don't look at me like that! That's what he is, a goddamn retard! There, I said it! He's six years old and he can't even dress himself. He only knows about six words! He can barely feed himself! Hell, he can't even wipe his own butt! Is that what I'm supposed to do with my life? Sit at home and wiping the little retard's butt?

"And you want *another* one? How about a girl this time? We can name her *Nancy*." That was a very low blow. I would have preferred a kick to the balls, and she knew it.

She plopped into a kitchen chair and began to sob. Her tears had always melted my heart, but not this time. I raised the ante. "We are a family, *if* that's what *you* want it to be."

She stopped sobbing and looked squarely at me. "Then, I guess I *don't* want it." She had called my bluff. We both always had that trump card. She chose to play hers, now.

It was not what I really wanted nor expected from her.

Maybe it was the alcohol. I gave her an out. "Wendy, I know you're tired. It's late. Let's talk about it in the morning."

She didn't take it. "No Heck! We will *not* talk about it in the morning, because I won't *be here* in the morning!" She stood up, grabbed her purse, and started for the door.

"Where are you going?"

"Don't worry about me, Heck. I'll find *someplace.*" Her voice was cold and determined.

I watched her transform into a complete stranger before my eyes. I could no longer recognize the woman I had married. Something indefinable about her had changed.

Maybe it was just the way I saw her. But, the Wendy I once knew was gone.

She paused and turned back as she opened the door. "I'll turn the porch light off. I won't be needing it tonight." She said with a little grin. The knife was already protruding from my chest, but she couldn't resist giving it a little twist on her way out.

I was going to try to stop her. I was going to say I was sorry, even if I wasn't. Then I remembered that I hadn't told her about Tyler's condition. She hadn't asked about him again either. She really *didn't* care. As the door slammed behind her, I knew that I didn't *really* care about her anymore either. I made no attempt to stop her.

Wendy came back the next day while I was out getting Tyler from the hospital. She packed up all her clothes and personal items. She left town the following day on a two-week product introduction tour around the country. I didn't hear from her for several weeks.

I learned through a mutual acquaintance that she had moved in with Stan. I had suspected there was something between them from things she had said about him, and the way she had said them. It was probably a smoldering chemistry thing that had lay dormant waiting for an ignition source. I figured it was for the best, for both her and me.

I made a half-hearted gesture at reconciliation, but Wendy would have none of it. We eventually sold the Bellevue house and split the proceeds. I moved into a small rental house in the Montlake area near the UW campus.

It was a while before we finalized the divorce though. For my part, I just didn't want to think about it. Call it avoidance. For Wendy's part, she was just too busy to be bothered.

###

When I first came to the Mercer Residential Rehabilitation Institute, I had come to the conclusion that I needed help with Tyler. I had to acknowledge that Tyler's development was going to be limited. I needed a safe, positive environment where Tyler's development would be nurtured to his fullest potential. An at-home caregiver was an option, but I wanted Tyler to have interaction with other children and adults.

It was obvious to me, and to Marta Velasquez, that Little Ones Playland was not the place for Tyler. Marta was apologetic, but told me that she could no longer take care of Tyler. I understood her position. She had to think of the other children, not to mention legal and licensing issues.

Some of the other parents had been understandably very upset when their children were return to them that day with blood on their clothes. And to add to Marta's concerns, she was now even more short-staffed. Mindy had quit and taken a job at a convenience store, her teaching career now in question.

Dr. Janet Martin was sympathetic to my situation, and she could understand my sense of guilt for even considering putting Tyler in an "Institution," but the kind of care Tyler needed was beyond what the insurance would cover. I made a better than average salary at the University, but I was not going to be able to make up the difference.

Wendy could have helped, but she didn't even want to talk about it. I considered forcing the issue in court, but I had no desire to have any contact with her. I knew she felt the same. Tyler, and her marriage to me, was a part of

Wendy's life she simply wanted to forget. I was content to let her have her way.

Dr. Martin and I talked about it for some time before we arrived at a solution. I would donate ten hours per week working with patients at the Institute, to make up the difference between what the insurance would cover. Plus, I would be welcome to spend whatever additional time I could, working with Tyler onsite. It was also agreed that I would take Tyler home at least one weekend per month. Instead, I took him home almost every weekend.

It was an arrangement that worked out better than we had expected. I think I'm a better than average therapist. I was able to help many of the more difficult patients to gain skills that gave them a more independent life. In addition, I threw myself into studying all the research being done on autism. I became the Institute's de facto resident expert on Autistic Spectrum Disorders.

###

It was partly because of my success working with autistic patients that had prompted Harborview to recommend that Ray be transferred to the Mercer Island facility.

Accepting Ray was definitely a challenge for the Institute. Janet had never dealt with a patient quite like Ray. It was exactly because of the challenge that Janet had accepted him, that and the fact that she knew I would be returning from Alaska soon. She told me that she needed her "autism expert" back, and the sooner the better.

Ray was proving to be a more intriguing case than she expected. She said he seemed to have skills that she had never seen in an autistic patient.

She said I would understand when I met him. But I didn't understand, not at first.

CHAPTER 16
SAL

It took me several minutes to compose myself. I used the small mirror by my desk to freshen my makeup. *You're a big girl now, time to act like one.*

I finished my makeup, then stopped and took a long look at myself in the mirror. I tried to look beyond the image. *Who am I?*

I was certainly not the same girl I was when I left Tennessee. I wasn't even the same woman I knew just three months ago, before I was assigned to the Bangkok Virus case. I felt like I was losing touch with who I really was. I did not quite recognize the woman staring back at me from the mirror.

My close inspection revealed a couple tiny lines at the corners of my eyes and between my eyebrows. I hadn't noticed them before. *When did that happen?* They contributed to a general drained look around my eyes and mouth. I realized again how truly exhausted I was. I had to admit to myself that I had been working too hard. I needed a break. I needed to find myself again.

It was time. I got up from my desk and headed toward Dr. Edelman's office. It felt somehow strange walking down the familiar hallway, perhaps for the last time. I imagined what it would be like to never see it again. The thought did not frighten me the way I thought it should.

Rose looked at me with an odd expression as I approached Dr. Edelman's office. "He's waiting for you, Sal. Go right in." There was a softer tone in her voice than usual. It was the first time Rose had ever called me Sal. *Huh. What's that about?*

"Thanks Rose." I had thanked Rose for many things, many times, but this time was different. It might be the last time. I locked eyes with her for a moment and made sure there was sincerity in my voice.

As I opened the door to Dr. Edelman's office and stepped in, I felt like I did the first time I took a ride on a roller coaster.

"Come in Sal. Close the door. Have a seat." His tone was flat. No hint of what, if any, feelings he had.

I sat down without saying anything. There was an unexpected composure that came over me as I settled into the chair. *What will be, will be.* I decided to let him speak first.

Dr. Edelman crossed his arms and leaned his elbows onto his desk as he studied me. It was a full minute before he spoke. He did not pull on his left earlobe.

"Sal…I was going to be very angry with you." He paused to collect his thoughts.

"Don't get me wrong. I *am* very angry with you, but for a different reason than what you might think." His gaze was penetrating.

"I talked with the rest of the panel. Do you want to hear what they said?"

"Okay." I did *not* want to hear it, but what else could I say?

"They all agreed that you have handled this case as well, or better, than anyone else could have, and I agree." He paused to let that sink in. I waited for the rest.

"But that's not all they said." He paused again. "They said that assigning this case to you was a mistake." He paused. His pregnant pauses were wearing away at my composure. "Do you know why they feel that way?"

"Because I screwed up?"

"No, damn it!" He slammed his fist down on his desk, rattling a paperclip holder close to the impact point. "You did *not* screw up!"

"But I…" My composure was now completely gone.

"You did not double check the work of one of your team members." He pointed his finger at me. "That's right, I checked. You did not *personally* send out those decontamination instructions to the airline."

"But I was responsible." I was not going to let him shift the blame.

"That's right. You were responsible. A simple mistake was made. So what!"

"So what? A man is in a coma because…"

"A man is in a coma because he caught a disease. It was *not* your fault! Shit happens! Call it bad luck. Call it fate. Call it whatever you want, but it was not your fault."

He slumped back in his chair with a sigh. "And that's exactly why you should not have been put in charge of this case. You took it too personally.

"Look at yourself. You've probably lost ten or twenty pounds in the last few months. That might be good if you had extra to loose in the first place. You're exhausted. I'll bet you haven't gotten a full night's sleep in months either, have you?"

It was true. I did not confirm it in words, but I lowered my eyes.

His tone softened to one that I imagined that he had used with his own daughter, Marie, when she was growing up. "No one ever expected perfection, certainly not me. The only one who did was *you.*

"Don't you understand? The only thing that hasn't been *perfect* about the job you've done is your *unrealistic* expectation of perfection. Did you ever consider that exhausting yourself, in the name of perfection, is likely to *cause* you to make mistakes?"

"I just wanted to do my best." I fought the tears welling up in my eyes.

"And you did. But you're no good to me, or to the CDC, if you can't keep the job in perspective."

He shook his head. "You're what, twenty-eight, twenty-nine? You haven't had a vacation in two years. When was the last time you went to a movie? When was the last time you went out on the town and partied with your friends? How many friends do you have? When was the last time you went out on a date?

"I know you love your career, but have you thought about having a family someday? What I'm saying is, there is more to life than your job and the CDC."

This was not at all what I had expected him to say, but it was true. I didn't really have a life outside of work. I was afraid if I spoke, my voice would start the tears that were about to run down my cheeks and take my freshly applied mascara with them.

He continued. "You know I expect dedication from the people in this department. But dedication does not mean burning yourself out on your first case. I need you ready to go for the next case and for the case after that.

"You are a valuable resource to the CDC. You are not easily replaced. When you push yourself the way you have, to the point of exhaustion, you compromise that resource, and you therefore jeopardize the mission of the CDC."

We both said nothing for a minute, each with our own thoughts. I saw the truth of what he said. I had never thought that trying too hard could be a fault, but I could see that I had somehow succeeded in making it one.

I watched Dr. Edelman, trying to gage his mood. He looked regretful. I wondered if maybe he thought he had laid it on a little too heavy.

"Sal, what do you really want to do? Do you really want a career at the CDC?"

"Yes, I do. Do I still have one?"

"I'm going to leave that up to you. Are you willing to do whatever it takes to have a successful career here?"

"Of course. What do you mean?"

"Sal, you need to take some time off, at least a month. You've got plenty of vacation time saved up." I noticed he had started pulling on his left earlobe.

"But I have more work to do on the case."

"Don't worry about it. There's nothing left to do that other team members can't handle."

"I know I need to take a break, but a whole month? Are you serious?"

He let out a sigh. "I'll tell you how serious I am. If I see you back here, let's say before Groundhog Day, I'll have to fire you."

"Okay…" *He's serious.*

To soften the sting, he quickly added, "Sal, you're too good to lose. I want you here. But you're no good to me the way you are. I want you to sleep in for a few weeks. I want you to eat some healthy food and put on a few pounds. Go to a few movies. Party a little. Go on a couple of dates. There must be plenty of guys waiting in line." He chuckled.

"You know how much I love this job." I lowered my eyes wondering if I could remember how to do those things again. "If that's what you think I need to do."

"It'll be okay, Sal. You can do it. You have to do it. Just take it easy and think about what we've talked about."

"Well then, I guess I'm going to get some rest, whether I like it or not."

"I think you *might* actually like it. Oh, and if I don't talk to you before then, merry Christmas!"

"Thank you Dr. Ed… Albert. You too. I'm sorry. I know you don't need to deal with this kind of... well, I really do appreciate the… I mean, I guess I didn't realize…"

"It's okay. It's my job. I had a boss who had to give me a little kick in the pants once. I'm glad he did." He shook his head to dismiss the subject.

"Anyway, we don't need to talk about it anymore. Now, get out of here and have some fun! That's an order."

I gave Rose a little smile as I left Dr. Edelman's office to let her know that everything was okay. Rose reciprocated.

Back in my office, I proceeded to organize my files and write a couple notes to my co-workers who would need to take over some of my unfinished work while I was gone.

What am I going to do with myself? I hadn't had that much free time since those long lazy summers when I was still in grade school. I remembered spending time with Becky down at the lake. Or sometimes, we would play dolls all afternoon under the big oak tree in Becky's back yard. My life was so much simpler then, at least simpler in some ways.

The image of Gary Boyle briefly flashed into my consciousness. He was seventeen years old leaning against the brick wall outside Ferguson's Restaurant. Green eyes. Smiling.

I had had a shake with Gary at Ferguson's once on a summer night many years ago. My stomach knotted up. *I screwed up.*

I shook my head, and the memory dissipated as quickly as it had come.

I picked up my phone and dialed the number I had memorized twenty years ago.

"Hello." The voice was a woman's, and it didn't sound like the one I expected. Maybe I dialed the wrong number.

"May I speak to Ben Donaldson?" I said formally.

"Yes. Who's calling, please?" The replied was just as formal.

Then I recognized the voice. "Becky? Is that you?"

"Yes…Sal! Your voice sounds funny. I didn't know it was you."

"I didn't expect you to be there. Aren't you supposed to be in Florida?"

"I was. I flew in last week. I'm gonna spend Christmas with the folks this year."

"Well that's why I was calling. I've got some time off, and I haven't been down in a while. So, I just thought…Ah, but you and Chuck are there too. I thought I should call your daddy first. I mean, is there enough room?"

"Oh yeah, I didn't tell you. Chuck and I are separated."

"What!" They were such a happy couple. *I am out of the loop.*

"It's been over a month now. I'll tell you all about it when you get here." She didn't sound very broken up.

"Are you okay? Do you need to spend some time with your momma and daddy; I mean without me around to complicate your life even more?" I wanted to get a better feel for what was going on with her emotionally.

"Don't be ridiculous! Oh wow! This is great!" I could hear Becky turn away from the phone and yell. "Hey Momma, Daddy, it's Sal. She's coming down!" There were faint voices in the background, but I couldn't understand what was being said.

Becky turned back to the phone. "Can you stay over Christmas? When are you coming? We can pick you up at the airport. Are you coming alone? You can bring someone, you know. I mean, if there is someone. Is there someone?"

Whatever was going on with her separation with Chuck, she seemed to be handling it. But, I knew there was more to that story. We had some serious catching up to do. We would most likely be spending some time shedding tears on each other's shoulder.

I laughed out loud. "No, I don't have a *someone*." It felt good to hear Becky's voice. Becky always had a tendency to run off at the mouth when she got excited. "Hold on there. I haven't even made any travel plans yet. Give me a couple days at least."

Becky had turned away from the phone again. "She's coming in two days!"

"I said a *couple* days. I don't know when I can get a flight. I'll call you when I do. And, I'll let you know if I meet *someone* in the next couple of days. Maybe I can pick *someone* up at the airport." I laughed, but Becky didn't get a chance to respond.

Uncle Ben was next to Becky now. He said, "Let me talk to her." as he grabbed the phone. "Sally Sue, you get on that airplane and get your little butt down here." His excitement was not disguised by his commanding tone.

Aunt Claire was next to him. She raised her voice so that it would carry the extra foot to the receiver. "Honey, we'd love to have you. Come as soon as you can."

"As soon as I can, I promise Uncle Ben. I can't wait to see you and Aunt Clair!" They weren't my biological Aunt and Uncle, but I thought of them that way. They were part of my family, and always had been for as long as I could remember.

" 'Can't wait,' she says? It's been almost two years that you *did* wait, young lady!"

"I know. I'm sorry. I've been busy. But I promise I'll make it up to you. By the time I leave, you'll be sick of having me around."

"Now, you stay as long as you want, sweetie. You know you're welcome anytime. And it'll be good for Becky to see you too." His tone was much softer. I took that as an indication that there was more going on with Becky than he wanted to reveal over the phone.

Becky grabbed the phone back. "Mom's still got the Barbie stuff. She says it's packed away, somewhere. We can play dolls just like we used to!" She giggled just like she used to.

"And maybe we can go skating on the lake, if the ice is thick enough! Oh my God, I can't wait! This is going to be a great Christmas!"

It was going to be a great Christmas, I told myself, when they finally let me off the phone. Just hearing their voices gave me a surge of renewed energy. They were my family. I almost forgot what that meant, and how it felt.

And Christmas at the Donaldson's had always been so wonderful. I could already smell Aunt Clair's pies baking, above the faint aroma of fresh pine pitch from the Christmas tree and, wood smoke from that giant fieldstone fireplace.

Yes, I did indeed need this time off. My body needed it. My mind needed it. I needed to simply rest. I needed to catch up on the months of shorted sleep. I thought of how wonderful it would be to snuggle under one of Aunt Clair's handmade quilts and fall into a deep, blissful sleep. *Ah, sleep, like a…like a… coma.*

The guilt was still there. It would not go away. I did not want it to. It was my fault. I would not deny it, despite what Dr. Edelman said.

CHAPTER 17
HECK

I woke up suddenly. Something had woke me, but I didn't know exactly what it was. A sound? I listened. There were noises coming from the kitchen. Someone was moving around.

I looked around the room. I was home, in my own bed! After months in the hospital, the familiar surroundings of my bedroom seemed somehow foreign now. *How…* Then I remembered Tom taking me home and putting me to bed after leaving the restaurant. *Tom. It must be Tom in the other room.*

"Tom?"

I heard footsteps coming down the hallway. A head poked through the bedroom doorway. "Hey! Welcome back to the land of the living!" It was Tom.

"What time is it?" Bright light was coming through the window.

"And, good morning to you too. Past my lunch time. I figured you'd be up pretty soon, so I went down and picked us up some burgers. I just got back."

"Lunch time? What happened to breakfast?"

"You snooze, you lose. It's past one now."

"One? Holy cow! You should have woke me up."

"I figured you needed your beauty rest. Besides, you didn't miss much for breakfast. Ya know, you need to do some serious grocery shopping. I had to scrounge around just to find a couple of old dried up frozen waffles. That, and some black coffee is not exactly what I'd call a gourmet breakfast. I'm starved!"

"Coffee. That sounds good." I tried to rub the sleep out of my eyes, and my mind. *Why didn't he eat at home?* "Hey, did you stay over here last night?"

"Yeah. I crashed on the couch."

"Why did you…"

"You were acting a little weird. I just thought I should keep an eye on you."

I remembered the episode at Seacrest Landing. The deep sense of undefined purpose still resonated within me, but now was not the time to talk about it. "Yeah, okay. I guess I *was* acting a little weird. Just overtired I guess. But, you didn't need to babysit me."

"Yeah, well, anyway, I'm gonna dig into those burgers. Gonna join me?"

"Okay. Give me a minute." I struggled to get to my feet and hobble into the bathroom to relieve myself and splash a little cold water on my face.

When I got to the kitchen, Tom was stirring instant coffee into two cups of microwaved hot water. "Oh, someone called earlier."

"Who?"

"I didn't answer it. I didn't think they would be calling for me, and I didn't want to wake you up. If it was important, I figured they'd leave a message."

"It's probably the Institute. I told Jan Martin I'd call her when I got in." I picked up my cordless phone and sat it on the table next to my coffee before I sat down.

I took a sip of my coffee before keying in the number for the answering service. There were two messages. The first was from two days ago.

"Heck, this is Wendy. I have some papers you need to sign. Can we meet somewhere? Call me."

"Oh crap!" *That's all I need.*

Tom raised his eyebrows in a question mark.

I deleted the message and listened to the second one left that morning. It was from Jan as I had expected, wanting to know when I'd be coming. She wanted me to meet a new patient. I deleted that message too and hung up.

I tried to avoid answering the unspoken question from Tom. "I need to call Jan at the Institute. She needs my help with a new patient. I really want to see Tyler too."

Tom waited a second to see if I was going to say more. When I didn't, Tom said, "That doesn't sound like an 'Oh crap' message to me."

Seeing that my ploy had failed, I grinned at Tom. "It was Wendy. She wants to meet me. She says she has some *papers* I need to sign."

"Oh crap!" Tom deliberately mimicked my tone.

"I guess it's time we settled things, but I don't know if I'm up to it."

Tom saw the stressed look on my face with the mention of Wendy's name. "What the hell, let her stew for a day or two 'til you get your life back on track. She can wait."

"Sounds good to me." I didn't want to even think about Wendy, not yet anyway.

"Now, where's those burgers." I said.

"Comin' up." Tom unpacked and distributed the contents of the drive-thru bag.

"Are you going to be able to drive?" Tom said before taking his first bite of burger.

"Oh, thanks for reminding me. I'm going to need to get a rental. I need an automatic. I don't think my left leg can handle the clutch on the Bimmer yet."

"My Mustang is an automatic. Why don't we just trade for a while?"

"Now there's an idea." It hadn't occurred to me, but it made sense.

"If, you think you can handle a *high performance* car." I said, as I feigned a worried look.

"What? You mean that little German go-cart?" Tom scoffed. "The question is, can *you* handle a car with some real American-made balls under the hood?"

We both laughed thru mouthfuls of ground beef. The conversation lagged as we dug into our feast of burgers. They weren't anything all that special, but my taste buds were lighting up like forth-of-July sparklers. Ah, the simple pleasure of familiar food, denied for a time.

It was good to just sit around and BS with Tom. We hadn't had a chance to do it much since the Kodiak trip. The night before we left was the last time I could recall.

Like now, we'd sometimes get onto a subject that challenged Tom's manhood, or that Tom felt was a manhood issue.

I was aware of Tom's tendency to underrate himself and his need to have a steady supply of positive input. He tended to be sensitive about anything he thought was criticism. This was one of the reasons I thought Tom kept a steady stream of new girlfriends flowing in and out of his life. He'd always dump them before they could get to know him well enough to see his perceived faults.

His unshaved boyish looks and his general bad-boy demeanor, along with his quick smile and generous sense of humor made him a target for women, especially younger women. He never was without a date on a Saturday night, but I knew him well enough to know that Tom thought it was just an act. He went out of his way to make sure women didn't see through to what he thought was the *real Tom.*

I could not avoid letting my psychologist training kick in from time to time. But Tom didn't want to hear it, so I usually kept my psycho-analysis to myself.

###

We had been discussing our racket ball abilities that night before we left for Kodiak. I said, "What can I say? Some of us got muscle, and some of us got speed." Tom winced a little as he twisted the cap off his beer.

Unlike Tom, I never felt like I had to work very hard at looking athletic. I had been told that this made me attractive to women, but I never really gave it much thought. *What you see is what you get, ya know.*

"Yeah, I got the muscle, maybe more muscle than brains to let you talk me into this. You're just taking me along so I can be your pack mule, right?"

"Well, duh! It ain't 'cause you got that psycho-PhD thing, now is it?"

"What? You mean I don't get to psycho-analyze the grizzlies?" I chuckled as I tipped the bottle to my mouth.

"If you think you can get 'em to lay on a couch for you, you're welcome to try." I glanced at my watch, 10:30 p.m. We'd been packing all evening and we were both getting a little punchy.

"Okay, explain this to me again. I get to lug around your stuff for a month, for free mind you, while big-ass bears are nipping at my butt; and you get to wander around smelling the flowers and taking pretty pictures?"

I had never thought photography could ever turn into a real job for Tom. But he had proved me wrong over the last few years. Tom had won several awards and photo contests, and had sold his work to several publications. This was to be his second assignment with National Geographic. The first was *Eagles of the San Juans,* a study of the birds of prey living on the San Juan Islands archipelago. The editors liked his work so much, that they chose one of his photos for the cover, a bald eagle frozen in a head-on view, just as it was snatching a fish from the water.

But, I still liked to tease Tom about his "artsy" profession.

"Yup, that's the deal. And, you can thank me anytime for giving you the privilege." We both laughed and sipped lazily on our beers.

I thought of another time. "Remember our first camping trip together?"

"Yeah, seems like a million years ago. Those were the days, huh?"

"We must have been about ten. That was the year after you moved into the neighborhood. Christ, that was twenty-five years ago." I shook my head at the thought.

"You and me and Billy Olsen stayed up the whole night before, just too excited to sleep."

"At least we get to drink beer to help us sleep this time."

"In that case, I think I might need a couple more."

"Yeah, me too."

We both sucked down a little more beer and let the silence linger. With old friends, sometimes silence was the best way to say the kinds of things a guy might find hard to say to another guy.

I knew that Tom didn't need me to tag along on this trip. I knew Tom was doing it just to get my mind off all the turmoil in my life right then. And there was a lot of turmoil too. My professional training prevented me from hiding my feelings from myself. I knew all the tricks. I had tried them all. And, I knew I couldn't hide it from Tom either. He knew me too well.

Tom had seen me in pain before. The year before I earned my undergraduate degree from Cornell, my mother was diagnosed with pancreatic cancer. She died just three months later. I was not with her when she died. Then, just six months later, my father committed suicide.

I was never really able to shake the guilt of not being with Mom when she died. It was a long trip to Seattle from Ithaca, New York. When I got the word that she was close to death, I was unable to make it back in time. At least, that's what I told myself.

I was away at school when my father died too. This time the guilt reached deeper. I was close to earning my MA in psychology. I was too distracted, and I had failed to recognize my own father's severe depression. Maybe I didn't want to see it.

I told myself I should have taken time off from school to spend with Dad. I can't count the times I wished I had. Partly out of regret, I transferred back to the University of Washington to finish my post-graduate studies and complete my PhD.

Dad had not left a suicide note. This made it worse. It left me with a nagging doubt about the reason my Dad decided to end his life. I knew my Dad had been very dependent on Mom, and was very distraught about her loss. But then, I thought Dad might have also felt deserted by his only son when I left to go back to school. I would never be sure.

I didn't actually see it, but visions of Dad's death haunted me for years. Dad had taken a whole bottle of sleeping pills, closed the garage door, started the car, opened the car windows, and simply went to sleep forever. A neighbor found him the next morning when he noticed smoke seeping under the garage door and went to investigate.

Through it all, Tom was there to offer what support he could, but only time could ease the pain. And maybe, the guilt.

Now, the situation with Wendy and Tyler brought up old memories, old doubts, and even older regrets.

Like the one about my sister, Nan. It happened when I was fourteen. Tom was there. He probably wanted to forget about it too.

I didn't actually avoid the subject. It just never came up, and Tom wasn't going to bring it up.

Of course, we didn't exactly talk about stuff like that anyway. "That's just not what real men do." Tom would say. No, the macho man Tom Birch would never talk to me about his own feelings, and he certainly wasn't going to voluntarily talk about mine. But, I left that door open a crack every now and then.

I looked Tom deliberately in the eye and said, "You know, I *have* always wanted to go on a trip like this. I just never had the time, or the money, or a good excuse, until now. Thanks buddy!"

I knew the serious tone in my voice might make Tom a little uncomfortable. This was about as close to the *warm and fuzzes*, as he called it, that Tom wanted to get.

Tom smiled uncomfortably, and then tried to pull the conversation back into his comfort zone. With a chuckle, he said, "I'll bill you later."

It was not a coincidence that Tom had chosen those words. I had used these same words a few years ago, when Tom had had a good reason to thank me. It was the only way Tom knew how to say, "Just a little payback, pal."

###

It was nearly 3:30 by the time I was able to get down to the Institute.

Jan got up from her desk and greeted me with a big smile as I came in. "Heck, it's great to see you!"

"Well, there's not much to see." I met her open-armed invitation half way around her desk. She had always been a *hugger.* "It's good to be back, Jan."

"You look great." She stepped back to get a better look at me. "Well, you could use a few pounds, and that beard will take some getting used to, but you look a lot better than you made it sound."

"I'm a little worse for wear, but you should see the other guy." I mustered an artificial chuckle.

"You're limping. How's your leg?" She sounded like a mommy ready to *kiss it and make it better.*

"It'll be fine. Just need a little exercise. So, what's been happening *here?*" I was uncomfortable talking about my physical ailments.

"I told you about the new patient that was transferred here last week from Harborview."

"Yes, but you didn't tell me much about him."

"Raymond Miller is his name. He's twenty-five. He appears to be autistic. He shows all the symptoms, but I've never seen a case quite like this."

"What's so different about him?"

"First of all, how he got to be autistic is pretty unusual."

"He wasn't that way from childhood?"

"No. He was not autistic until he came out of a coma four weeks ago."

"A coma? That is strange."

"Yes. Do you remember hearing anything last September about a flu outbreak onboard an airliner from Tokyo that landed here at SeaTac?"

"Ah, no. I, ah, wasn't able to read the paper much last fall, or watch TV for that matter."

"That's right. I'm sorry. Of course, you were in the hospital in Anchorage."

"Wait a minute. I think I do remember a follow up story on the news. I think it was sometime in October, that's when they let me be awake long enough to watch TV. It was about a CDC report. I think they said something about it coming from Bangkok?"

"That's right."

"I didn't think much about it at the time. Didn't the CDC say there were no new cases? I thought that was the end of it?"

"As far as the outbreak, it was. But, Ray was one of the victims. He and his wife and several other people lapsed into comas. They had a special isolation ward set up over at Harborview. Most of the people who were comatose, died, including Ray's wife Julia. The only other coma case to survive at Harborview was a flight attendant."

"Okay, I'll bite. What about the other person?

"I don't know a lot. Harborview sent me some information on her. Hmm, I had that right here." She shuffled through the papers on her desk.

"Okay, here it is." She scanned down the sheet. "Anna Grant. Fifty-five years old. She came out of her coma about a week after Ray did, and she's displaying some of the same behaviors Ray did."

"Now that's really interesting!"

"Yeah. I thought so too. They sent me some information on her because they're considering sending her here.

Between you and I, I think they're waiting to see what we can do with Ray first. And that's where you come in."

"Great! Sounds like it's right up my alley."

"I agree. I know you want to spend some time with Tyler, and I know you're still recuperating, so I don't expect you to be able to work a lot with Ray right away."

"Well, here's some good news. I called the Dean before I came over here. After talking about it, he decided that I should stay on short-term disability and take off the winter semester. I didn't argue with him. I should have plenty of time to work with Mr. Miller and get in some time at the gym too."

"That's great. When do you want to start?"

"I think I'd like to at least meet him right now, before I go see Tyler. But first, what else can you tell me about his behavior?

"When he got here, he was heavily sedated and in restraints. He seemed to be just angry at the world. But after a couple of days, he seemed to be calmed down enough to lower his meds. He is feeding himself now. He puts a ton of salt on everything, including desert. For the last couple days he has dressed himself too. I'll warn you, he does *not* like to be touched."

"That might be why he's dressing himself."

"Maybe. He's not very talkative though. He responds well to verbal instructions. He seems to understand everything you say. He said two words this morning when I was with him in the dayroom."

"What did he say?"

"He said 'okay' when I was telling him that I could move Tyler if he bothered him."

"You put Tyler with him?"

"I didn't think it would hurt. I wanted to see how they might relate, if at all. Mostly, I think they just ignored each other."

"What was the other word?"

"That puzzled me a little. He said 'blue.' The part that puzzled me was that Tyler was coloring with a blue crayon at the time."

"So?"

"I'm sure he wasn't able to see the crayon Tyler was using, unless he's got eyes in the back of his head"

"A coincidence? Was he even talking about the crayon?"

"I don't know for sure, but I got the feeling that he knew what he was talking about."

"Hmm. Well, I can't wait to meet him. Let's go."

Jan picked up the clipboard with Ray's file attached and handed it to me as she got up. "This is everything we've got on him. You'll probably want to look it over when you get a chance."

"Thanks. Yes, I will." I thumbed opened the cover of the file as Jan and I started down the long main hallway toward the residence section.

We walked slowly because of my limp. I tried to minimize it for Jan's sake without much success. Mostly to distract attention away from the limp, I said, "So, there were only two people who were affected like this by the disease?"

"No. I said there were only two people at Harborview. There is another one in Florida that's still in a coma."

"Florida? I thought it was just that one flight into Seattle."

"It was. A maintenance guy was working on the same plane a week later at Tampa International. I guess they didn't clean it up good enough." She pointed to the file in my hand. "I downloaded the CDC report last night. It's in there. I thought you might like to look at it. Interesting stuff when you get past the medical and bureaucratic jargon."

We walked slowly while I flipped through the file.

"There's a phone number for the CDC. It's for a Dr. Salinger who wrote the report. Maybe I'll give him a call, if I have any questions."

"Good idea. But I think he's a she. I saw her first name somewhere else in the report. Sally, I think."

"Here we are." Jan knocked on the open door, and led the way into Ray's room.

Ray sat in a chair next to his bed rocking and looking toward the window.

"Ray, this is Dr. Hector Beckman. He's going to be working with you."

I automatically reached out my hand, then immediately pulled it back when I remembered Jan's warning about physical contact. I turned the reach into a wave and said, "Hi! I'm happy to meet you. You can call me Heck. Dr. Martin tells me you've been doing very well. I'm going to try to help you, if I can. Dr. Martin says you've met Tyler. He's my son. He stays here too."

Ray continued to rock. He had not taken his eyes off the window. I looked questioningly at Jan.

"That's okay Ray, you don't have to talk to us if you don't want. We just wanted to say 'hi' before Dr. Beckman goes down to see Tyler."

Heck added, "That's right Ray, I'll be back tomorrow to see you."

"Have a good night Ray." Jan began to turn towards the door to leave.

"Hurt." Ray said.

They both stopped and turned back to Ray. "Did you say you 'hurt,' Ray?"

Both Jan and I waited, but Ray did not respond. I flipped open Ray's file to the daily log section. I thought I should make a note about this. I searched for a pen. All I had was the cheap green plastic retractable pen I had pick from a box full of 'Mercer Residential Rehabilitation Institute' imprinted pens at the front desk. I tried it. I was not surprised that it didn't work.

Jan noticed my problem with the pen and gave me hers and said, "Ray, what did you mean by 'hurt?' " Jan was concerned that Ray might be in pain. There was still no response.

I had dropped the useless green pen on Ray's nightstand to free my hand in order to take Jan's more functional offering. As I started to write, I had an idea.

"Ray, were you talking about me, about my hurt leg?" I hadn't tried to hide my limp when I came into the room, although I hadn't noticed Ray looking at my leg.

"Ribs." He paused, then, "One, two, three, four. One, two, three, four." He counted with a singsong voice.

Jan and I looked at each other in surprise. Jan said to me, "I don't understand. Do your ribs hurt?"

"No they don't, not much, not anymore." I scrunched up my eyebrows. "But, I did have *four* broken ribs. One of 'em punctured my lung."

"Really?" Jan said. Then, to Ray she said, "Are you talking about Dr. Beckman's ribs, Ray?"

There was no response from Ray. We stayed a minute more to make sure Ray didn't have anything else to say, then we said our goodbyes a second time and left. There was no change in Ray's expression, in his rocking, nor had anything else about him changed from when we had first entered the room.

When we were about forty yards down the long hallway, and had passed through double swinging fire doors, Jan said softly as if she didn't want anyone to overhear, "How do you think he did that?"

"Did what?" I copied Jan's soft tone.

"How did he know about your ribs?"

"I'm not sure he did. I mean, I was just guessing that he was even talking about me."

Jan considered what I said. "Yeah, you're right. But… I don't know, something about him just gives me the creeps."

"The creeps? Hmm, is that your *medical* diagnosis?" I said tongue-in-cheek.

"Ha, ha." She said with some emphasis, recognizing my sarcasm. "Heck, I mean it though, there's just something very, ah, well… very *different* about him."

"Maybe so. I know I'm going to want to spend a lot of time with him up front, just to try to figure out what's going on in his head."

"When you figure it out, let me know. I don't expect you'll be able to do much with him right away. Just do your best."

"You know I will." My serious expression was replaced with a broad smile. "Now, let's go see *the kid!*"

CHAPTER 18
SAL

It was a relatively short flight from Atlanta to Knoxville. I took the early flight so that I would have most of my first day to catch up and settle in with Becky and her momma and daddy.

Being a weekday flight, there were only a few passengers, mostly business. This meant that there were not any bored and fussy children. I could enjoy the uninterrupted silence, and be alone with my thoughts.

I was going home, back to my roots, to the place where my heart still lived.

###

My daddy had told me most of the stories that I remembered about the old days on the farm, but other friends and relatives had filled in the gaps over the years while I was growing up.

My daddy, Samuel Steven Salinger, or Sam to his friends, was 'just a Tennessee dirt farmer, at least that's what he always called himself. I really don't remember seeing him do much farming though. But I was assured that, for many years he had been just that, a farmer.

At first, he had helped his grandfather and his father work their one-hundred-sixty-acre family farm. My Great Granddaddy died when Daddy was still a child. Then, when Daddy was twenty-five his father died too, and he inherited the farm.

That same year he married my momma, Elizabeth Ann Perkins (Lizy), and a year later to the day, I was born.

It was good rich land, but with increasing expenses and weak crop prices, one-hundred-sixty acres was barely enough to pay the bills and still have enough left over for next year's seed. Daddy said he made ends meet by doing repair work on his neighbor's farm equipment.

He had a real knack for quickly finding the problem and fixing it cheaply. He was also good at making bailing wire work when there wasn't any money for new parts. Most times, if it was a friend, he didn't charge anything for labor. But even when he didn't charge, there would eventually be a favor repaid down the road, or often the pick from a new litter of pigs.

There was one story Daddy didn't tell me. I got it from uncle Dean at a family gathering. Once, when he was just twelve years old, Granddaddy Salinger caught him lying about finishing his chores so that he could go play with his friends. When confronted, Daddy tried to get out of it by lying even more. Granddaddy glared down at him with a disappointed look intended to make Daddy feel like he was nothing more than the dirt under his feet.

He expected to be punished, maybe a *whoopin'*, but what he got was much worse. Granddaddy simply said, "Sammy, a man is only as good as his word." Then, he just turned his back and walked away. I know that Daddy loved and respected Granddaddy more than anyone. The whoopin' would have been easier for him to take.

I guess Daddy felt like hiding under a cow pie. From then on Daddy never told another lie, or even stretched the truth a little, that I ever heard about at least. Not that he never got into trouble, teenage boys being what they are, but he always admitted his guilt and owned up to his responsibility to make it right. Since then, I heard this story several times from other sources.

Daddy carried this same ethic for honesty into his business dealings. His dead-on accurate repair estimates and timely completion of the work, quickly earned him a reputation for square dealing. He soon had more work than he could handle.

1979 marked the year when his income from the farm was less than his income from repair work. Although, Daddy put in many more hours in the field than he did in the garage.

Grain prices dropped that year. A lot of farmers were having a hard time then, including the Salinger's.

When the freeway went through in the sixties, they had put an exit at the corner of the Salinger property. It was the only freeway exit within twenty miles in either direction. Some of his repair customers, from time to time, would ask if they could park their equipment on his land near the freeway exit so they could put a For Sale sign on it and generate some extra cash to get them through until next season. This was a lean time for many, and a lot of used equipment found its way to "The Exit" as it was called.

After seeing how fast his neighbor's equipment sold he got the idea that his land near the exit might be used for a better purpose than just growing corn. After a little research, he was convinced the location was ideal for a farm equipment dealership, and that he was the man that could make it work.

For six months he spent every spare minute working on getting the dealership started. He first had to petition the county and get the zoning changed to allow commercial use. It was obvious to everyone that "The Exit" could and should become a commercial hub for the area. But, the wheels of government can move at a glacial pace. Fortunately, Daddy had some friends on the zoning board that pushed through the zoning change in record time.

Daddy hocked everything he and Momma owned, and with the help of some friends, a one-hundred-thousand-dollar SBA loan, and a lot of advice from the John Deere people, *Salinger's Agricultural Equipment Sales and Service* opened its doors on April 1, 1980.

That first year was insanely successful for the new business. Grain prices were up again, and Sammy's reputation had spread to farmers hundreds of miles away. The more business he got the stronger his reputation grew, as one farmer told another farmer who told yet another farmer.

They were able to pay off over fifty percent of their debt that first year, and at the same time make some much needed and overdue home improvements to the seventy-five-year-old family farmhouse.

Life was good for our family then. After years of struggling and pinching pennies Momma and Daddy could relax and enjoy their life together without worrying about making ends meet. Momma kept the books and looked after me and the house, while Daddy ran the business.

There was no time for working the land anymore. But rather than let it lay fallow, Daddy leased it out to neighbors who were glad be able to plant a few more acres at a generously low lease rate.

On June 10, 1981, Momma caught a cold. The cold got worse. After three days, she was wheezing and having trouble breathing. Daddy took her to the hospital in Knoxville. It was an hour drive. Lenoir City was closer, but the facilities in Knoxville were better. Daddy insisted on the best for Momma. They left me with the Donaldson's.

The doctors said Momma had pneumonia. They pumped her full of antibiotics and put her on oxygen, but it was too late. She died on June 15th at 4:13am with Daddy at her side. I was just four.

From what I heard later, Daddy struggled to get through the ordeal of making funeral arrangements and hosting out-of-town relatives. Daddy told me later that I was his "savior" because he needed to be strong for me.

I didn't really understand what had happened. Daddy said he watched me play as if nothing was wrong, and realized that he had never paid enough attention to me before.

It had always been Momma's job to take care of me. I guess Daddy began to see me differently. I had Momma's blue eyes and Momma's naturally blonde hair, but Daddy hadn't noticed before, that I had Momma's smile too.

Daddy couldn't explain to me what had happened to Momma. He just told me that Momma had *gone away*. I remember thinking, *What does that mean? Of course, she would come back*. I could see no reason not to be happy and play like I always had.

It was years later, on my seventh birthday, when I finally understood what it meant that my Momma was gone forever. Putting on that pretty dress for the party brought back memories of Momma. I could not stop crying and I clung to Daddy the whole day. We didn't have to talk about it. He understood.

I remember bits and pieces from Momma's funeral. I was all dressed up in my prettiest dress, the one that Daddy said made me look like a princess. Surely, this was a day to be happy, like it always had been when I wore my special princess dress.

During the funeral service, I was bored and fidgety as usual. Daddy sat me on his lap to keep me from moving around too much. I was paying no attention to the pastor who had begun to ramble a bit, just as he often did with his sleepy Sunday morning sermons.

Daddy told me only the year before he died that he wasn't able to look at the open casket, so he turned and looked at me instead. He said when my eyes met his, and I smiled at him, for a second he said he saw Momma looking back at him. It was the same smile Momma always used to calm him down when he was tired or frustrated. Momma would say, "It'll be okay, hon." And give him that smile, and it *would* be okay.

He told me that it was at that moment that it all became clear to him. I remember him crying, but he said it was because of the joy in realizing that his life now had a greater purpose, raising me. He said he could hear Momma telling him, "It'll be okay, hon."

I can't remember much from that day, but I remember Daddy crying. I only saw him cry on one other occasion, at my doctoral graduation ceremony.

After the ceremony, he hugged me, and told me, "You did it! That's my little Blondie Girl. I'm so proud of you honey." He hadn't called me that nickname in years, and it was the last time I ever hear him say it.

A year after Momma died, Daddy sold half of his, now thriving business, to his long time friend and neighbor Ben Donaldson. It was "Uncle" Ben and "Aunt" Claire that looked after me during Mom's hospitalization and funeral.

Their daughter, Rebecca, (Becky) was a year younger than me. We often played together. The Donaldson's had been there to help with the difficult, but inevitable, adjustments that had to be made in Daddy's life during the months after Momma's funeral.

Uncle Ben couldn't make his farm pay the bills anymore, and had decided to sell out. With the proceeds of the sale of land and equipment, he hoped to be able to settle in the city and get a regular job. He tried to put up a positive front to Daddy, his long-time friend, but it was obvious that Ben didn't want to leave the life and people he'd always known and loved. So, Daddy made him an offer he couldn't refuse. He made him a full partner in the dealership.

It was what everyone called a "sweetheart deal," and no one knew it more than Uncle Ben. He was eternally grateful to Daddy. Ben loved farming and he loved farmers. He was honest and hardworking, the rest Daddy figured he could learn.

Now that Ben would be there to help manage the business, Daddy could spend a lot more time doing what he loved most, taking care of, and being with, *the light of his life,* as he sometimes called me.

Daddy put the money he got from Uncle Ben into an annuity for my education. Each month thereafter, Daddy added a little more, whatever he could spare.

The Regan years were good for investors. By the time I was ready for college, the annuity was able to pay eighty-thousand-dollars per year for the eight years I was in school. That sounded like a lot in the 1982, but by 1995, the cost of higher education at an Ivy League school, had gotten much higher. As frugal as I tried to be, with tuition, books, fees, and just basic living expenses, there was never much left over, but it was enough.

They buried Daddy next to Momma in the small cemetery next to the church in town.

Heart attack, they said.

I was amazed to see the hundreds of people who turned out for the funeral. I knew he was well liked and respected by many people in the area, but I was never really aware of how many lives my daddy had touched. Dozens of people rose to speak in tribute to the man they called a good friend. Many I had never met.

Jimmy Johnson was one of the many who spoke. He told of how Daddy had loaned him a brand new tractor when his own ancient machine had blown its engine, and just when it was needed the most, at harvest time. Jimmy didn't have the money to get it fixed until after the harvest, and even if he had, it would have taken weeks to send for the long out-of-production parts to make the repairs.

Daddy didn't know the Johnsons that well, but he had heard from other farmers that this was a make-or-break season for them. If they didn't make a profit on this year's crop, the bank was going to have to take over the farm.

Seeing the situation that confronted Jimmy and his family, Daddy pulled the keys to a band new top-of-the-line John Deere, handed them to Jimmy and said, "Don't worry about it. Just bring it back when you're done. In the meantime, I'll get the parts for that old workhorse there and get it back in the field for you."

Jimmy had protested, "But I can't pay you right now."

Daddy said, "Don't worry about it. You can make it up whenever things loosen up for you."

There was never anything in writing. Daddy liked to do business on a handshake with his friends. Jimmy said he was surprised and humbled to be considered a friend by a man he had hardly known until then.

Three weeks later Daddy personally delivered the repaired tractor. But instead of taking back the new one he had loaned Jimmy, he pitched in and helped Jimmy clean up the last of his harvest. With two tractors working, the job was done in half the time. The day after they finished, a big storm hit the area. The heavy rain and winds would have destroyed much of Jimmy's crops.

Daddy would only accept payment for the cost of the parts. When Jimmy tried to pay him for his labor and something for the use of the new John Deere too, Daddy said, "Ya know Jimmy, I've had a pretty good year. Why don't you just keep it and get something nice for the wife and kids this Christmas. I promise, I'll charge you full price next time." He smiled and slapped Jimmy on the back, and that was the end of it.

Daddy never mentioned what he had done for the Johnson family, but Jimmy never forgot it. He was a loyal customer from then on, and recommended Daddy to everyone he knew.

Uncle Ben was not able to speak at the funeral, even though he had so much he wanted to say. He had lost a life-long friend he thought of as a brother, not to mention one hell of a business partner. But for most of that day, his face, like mine, was buried in a handkerchief. Aunt Claire and Becky tried to console him and me as best they could.

The Donaldson's were always thought of as part of the family when Daddy was alive. Now they were my only real family. I stayed with them during the funeral. But I hadn't been around much since.

I was away for college, and then after I graduated, I moved to Atlanta for work. Becky married and moved away with her husband to St. Petersburg, Florida.

Daddy's will was read two weeks after the funeral. It had always been agreed that the surviving partner would get the other's share of the business. It had been written into the partnership agreement, but it was reiterated in the will to forestall any possible probate problems.

I got the remainder of Daddy's estate. I decided to sell everything. I briefly considered keeping the farm, but living in, or even visiting the house where I had grown up, was just too painful for me. Even though it was a place that held so many fond memories for me, it was also a place where my daddy would never be again. Besides, it wasn't practical with my Atlanta job.

Daddy left me a short hand-written note attached to his will. The attorney said the will had been updated and the letter attached only one month before Daddy's death.

To my darling daughter,

Honey, if you are reading this, it is because I have gone to be with your mother.

I have tried to do the best I could to bring you up, and to help you through school so that you could have a good start in life. I know that I did not always succeed in being both mother and father for you. Maybe I should have remarried.

But despite my shortcomings in parenting, you have grown up to become a beautiful, intelligent, and simply amazing woman. I could not be more proud of you, and I know your mother is proud of you too.

I wish I could be there when you get married. I know you feel that love has betrayed you and will not come again, but be patient. The right man will come along, I promise you, and you will know when it's right. When you meet him, do not be afraid to give your love freely. Remember, the price for receiving love is giving love.

I wish I could be there to see my grandchildren. I know you will make a wonderful mother.

There will be difficult times, but you are strong. With patience and determination, I'm sure you'll come through the bad times even stronger.

Be true to yourself. Respect yourself, and others will respect you. Trust yourself, and others will trust you. Always do what you know in your heart is right.

Remember that life is a gift, happiness is a choice, and tomorrow is a promise.
I Love You!
Your Daddy

I kept the note in a special envelope in the drawer of my nightstand. I liked to read it occasionally before I went to sleep on nights when something troubled me. It seemed to help me sleep better. I had never been able to get through it without shedding a few tears, maybe I never would.

There were only a few small debts to be paid off on Daddy's estate. When all the sales commissions and taxes were paid, I was left with a little over six-hundred-thousand dollars. I put the money into high-yield long-term CD's and promptly forgot about it.

I know that Daddy would have wanted me to use the money to have a better life, but the thought of somehow benefiting in any way from my daddy's death made me feel a little nauseous. Besides, my job with the CDC provided for a comfortable enough lifestyle.

###

I woke up when the wheels hit the runway with a thump. I didn't realize that I had dozed off.

I maneuvered my two heavy carry-on bags through the throng of people leaving the security demarcation point at Knoxville's McGhee Tyson Airport.

Where are they? I figured they'd be right there waiting for me, but I didn't see them in the milling crowd. I wondered, *did they get the right flight number and the right time?*

I should have dug out my cell phone before I got off the plane. I switched it off and threw it in my carry-on when I boarded the plane earlier. It was probably buried somewhere. Uncle Ben and Aunt Claire didn't own a cell phone, but Becky did. I should try to find mine, and call her.

I thought maybe I should take a minute first and duck into the nearest lady's restroom. It would be a long ride back. Uncle Ben was like most men. He had a ten-gallon bladder, and he didn't like to stop once he got on the road.

I spotted the restroom sign and started walking toward it, just as Becky and Aunt Claire were coming out of the restroom exit doorway. I was only a few feet away when they noticed me.

Becky's eyes popped open wide as she ran over and threw herself at me. "Sal!"

I dropped my bags and we had a big long hug. "Becky!"

Aunt Claire was only a step behind. "Oh Sal, I'm so happy to see you." She joined us in a three-way hug.

Becky started crying. This of course made me start crying. Aunt Claire just laughed. Then we all laughed. Words were not needed or possible for a minute. God, it was so good to see them!

"Where's Uncle Ben?"

"Right here!" He was behind me. I had been focused on Becky and Aunt Clair, and I hadn't notice him waiting for them across the hallway. I turned, and he caught me in a hug that lifted me off my feet. It had always been his way of hugging me. I remember when I was little he would end his hugs by lifting me onto his shoulder. I was half expecting him to give it a try. But I was not so little any more, and he was not so young.

"Uncle Ben! I didn't see you."

"Sweetie, you sure are a sight for sore eyes." Uncle Ben was never at a loss for an old cliché. "I still have a hard time believin' you're all growed up. And a doctor now too!"

"Well, not a medical doctor. I just play with germs."

"That sounds disgusting." Aunt Claire said, and quickly added, "But, I'm sure it's not as bad as it sounds."

Becky chimed in, "Have you found any good bugs lately?" She was making a reference to our childhood pursuit of bug collecting. We used to make a pretty good bug hunting team as kids, to the chagrin of Aunt Clair.

"Have you heard about the Bangkok Virus?" Okay, so I wanted to brag a little.

"Yeah, I think I remember something on the news, that airplane in Seattle. A bunch of people died, right?" Becky was always up on the news. She prided herself on knowing what was going on in the world. Not so, Uncle Ben and Aunt Clair.

"No?" They both shook their heads. They recently broke down and got basic cable, but hardly ever watched *the tube*. Their TV was an ancient twenty-one inch, in a real-wood floor cabinet, one of the last. It had a bleeding-color picture and an equally ancient five-pound remote, one of the first.

They got the Sunday edition of the newspaper, but seldom spent more than a few seconds scanning the front page before going to the crossword page.

"That was my case. They put me in charge of researching it, and making sure it didn't spread." That last part stuck in the back of my throat. I suddenly didn't feel like bragging anymore.

"Well, you can tell us all about it in the car. Let's get your bags." Thank you, Uncle Ben, for changing the subject. He was clearly on a mission to get out of the airport and get home. It would be a long ride.

Being with them, made me feel like I was home again. Uncle Ben and Aunt Claire had gotten noticeably older since I had seen them last, but Becky hadn't aged a day. She still had that same naturally curly strawberry blonde hair, with those same matching freckles sprinkled generously across her cheeks. She hated the freckles when she was a teen. I was glad when she finally stopped trying to cover them up.

I better make that restroom stop now, while I've got the chance, I thought. I smiled at the memory of countless other road trips, and the exasperated refrain of Uncle Ben, or Daddy, or other assorted male drivers saying, "Why didn't you go before we left!?" or "Didn't you just go!?" They never got an answer that satisfied them, so why did they keep asking?

They were never going to get it. And despite his age, Uncle Ben still didn't get it. But he would soon find out, that with three women in the car on an hour and a half trip, we would *positively* be making an unscheduled stop, maybe two.

I could already hear the inevitable question, the inevitable unsatisfying answer, the exasperation, and finally, the resignation.

The thought occurred to me that sometimes, life's predictability in the small and mundane things can be comforting, and even beautiful in a way. We remember the big things, but the true essence of life is in the little ordinary things we usually forget. In the end, the seconds count more than the years.

CHAPTER 19
RAY

I continued rocking after Heck and Jan had left the room. They thought I had a speech impediment. Not exactly, I was just not ready to hear my own voice yet. It was too distracting. It was hard for me to think and talk at the same time. *One thing at a time. It will come. Focus.*

I picked up the green Institute pen Dr. Beckman had left on my nightstand. I studied it for a moment. I returned my gaze toward the window and began to twiddle the pen back and forth rapidly between a right thumb and forefinger. *Calm my thoughts. Focus. Listen.*

"The creeps. The creeps. The creeps." I whispered softly to myself in sync with my rocking.

###

"I'm here to see Ray Miller." Someone said. I cocked my ear in the direction of the main entrance to the Institute.

I was becoming very adept now at focusing my attention. From the myriad of voices and sounds coming from all directions into my expanded auditory awareness, I picked out a voice that I had not heard in months, not since the *before* time.

"Ray Miller? Oh yes, MILLER, Raymond Steven. Let me see." Sue flipped through the three-ring binder she kept next to the telephone switchboard until she found the page with Ray's name.

"I need some ID, and you need to fill out the sign-in form. I'll get you a visitor badge." I heard Ken put down the box he was carrying with an exaggerated sigh, then scribbling on a clipboard.

"Thanks! Here's your badge. He's in room 148, in the South wing, but he may be in the Dayroom right now, or maybe in the Rec room. I'm not sure. I can get a staff person to help you find him, if you'd like sir."

I had heard Susan Williams mention to another visitor that she had been working as a receptionist for the Institute for only three months. I had monitored her progress in remembering the names of all the staff and residents. She was struggling.

"That would be great. Thank you. I've got some of his things. I really don't want to carry this box any further than I have to." He said the last few words with a little grunt to emphasis the weight of the two-foot square box he was carrying.

Ken had always been painfully slim. He was now in his early twenty's. I knew he must be wearing his tattered jeans and that well-worn leather jacket of his over a t-shirt, probably that old faded black Pearl Jam t-shirt.

Dr. Martin stopped on her way to the Day Room. She had heard my name mentioned. "I believe Ray *is* in his room right now. I saw him there just a little while ago. I'd be glad to take you down there."

"Oh, okay. Thank you." Ken said.

"We have a dolly for that. Sue, do you want to get the dolly out of the supply room, please?"

"Sure." I heard Sue go into the small room behind the reception desk.

"I'm sorry, I'm Dr. Janet Martin. I was just going to get some things ready for our Christmas party tomorrow night, but that can wait."

"My name is Ken Perkins. I'm Ray's brother-in-law. I talked to you earlier on the phone." I could hear him shift the weight of the box to his left arm so that he could partially extend his right hand to Jan.

She shook his hand quickly, allowing his hand to resume holding the box. "I recognize your voice. I'm happy to meet you. You're the first visitor Ray has had since he's been here."

Sue brought the hand dolly around from behind the desk. Ken set the box down hard on it. *Weakling.*

"Then, Julia was your sister. Is that right?" Jan said as Ken took the dolly. They started walking the seventy-five yards down two corridors to where my room was located.

"Yeah, that's right." He added, "I guess I should have brought this stuff over sooner, but... I didn't feel right going over to her place. I mean, all of her stuff is still there." His voice trailed off.

"I'm sorry for your loss." *Was she really?* "You know, I had a real hard time going through all of my husband's things after he died too."

I heard Ken nod his head. I could almost see it. "You must have been very close. Do you have any other brothers or sisters?"

"No, it was just us two. She was three years older than me. Mom said she wanted more kids, but Dad died when I was three, and Mom never remarried. So, I guess it's just me and Mom now." He tried to lighten his voice to demonstrate that he was handling it okay. What Dr. Martin didn't say told me that she didn't buy it. Neither did I.

I liked Dr. Martin. I was learning things from her. Dr. Martin knew that, for some people, the anonymity of talking to a complete stranger often gave them the freedom to more easily express their true feelings. She was trying to draw Ken out a little while they walked. She probably figured that she might be able to learn a little more about my life.

"It's good that your Mom has you to take care of her now." It was a good educated guess.

If he had been closer, I could have smelled his embarrassment. "Ah, yeah… It's her arthritis. She can't get around too good. Julia used to help her out. But when she married Ray, she didn't have time anymore." His voice revealed that he was struggling to hide his feeling. "I *had* to move back in. You know, someone had to be around." He paused.

Dr. Martin said nothing. She was waiting to hear what he really *wanted* to say. Ken continued, "I'm working at 7-Eleven now, part-time. But they said they might put me on full-time next month. I put in my application at Wal-Mart last week too. They've been hiring, ya know." Was that a forced smile? I couldn't see it, but I knew it.

I was sure that Dr. Martin had guessed what I already knew. Ken needed a place to live, more than his mother needed someone to help her out at home. "I'm sure she's very glad to have you there to help her. It must be hard working and taking care of your Mom too." She must have thought that Ken was in need of a little positive reinforcement. *All he needs is a good kick in the butt.*

"It's no problem." There was a note of pride in his voice. She was maneuvering him to where she wanted him.

"I understand that Ray doesn't have any other relatives in Seattle. There are a couple of aunts and uncles in Boston, but you and your Mom are the only people he has out here." She was laying a little guilt on him and seeing what reaction she got. *Good for her.*

"Yeah, I guess." Another pause. She waited.

"Okay. Yeah, that's the other reason I didn't come to visit sooner." He struggled to say the words. "I don't think Ray likes me much. I mean, I don't think he did before at least. He says I'm a 'slacker.' " He chuckled uncomfortably. *Damn straight,* Slacker *is right.*

"What does that mean?" *Now she's getting to the heart of it.*

Ken took a deep breath and let it out. "I don't know." He did know. "I guess I'm not ambitious enough for him." He paused. She waited. "He always says, 'There's just two kinds of people, doers and slackers. Doers do something with their life, and slackers just slide through life.' " Ken tried to imitate an authoritative, know-it-all voice to portray my words.

Jan let that go without comment. She didn't need to ask the obvious question. After a moment, he answered it. "I don't know. I guess maybe he's right. He didn't drop out of college like I did. He made the big bucks. I get minimum wage." *You got that right, Slacker.*

His chin was on his chest. He must be studying the carpet weave. "He's one of those guys, ya know, one of those nose-to-the-grindstone types. He always does the right thing. Mom says he reminds her of Dad." That was *not* something that his mom ever said about Ken. "But he's...different now, right?" *Different? Yeah, better.*

"They said it was a miracle that he even came out of that coma. Only a couple people did." She was searching for words. "It affected his brain. We don't know exactly how yet. He was barely talking when he first got here. But now, he's communicating much more. He understands everything. He's not mentally impaired exactly, at least, not as far as we can tell.

"But don't expect him to be like he was before. He may not have anything to say at all today. Oh and, he doesn't like to be touched. Other than that, he's made big progress over the last few weeks. We have great hopes that he might eventually make a full recovery."

"Well, I was just going to drop this stuff off. Ah, so, I probably won't be staying long." I could tell that she had scared the slacker. *It doesn't take much.*

"I'm sure he'll be happy to see you." She *hoped* I would be happy to see him. That's why she had so quickly volunteered to escort Ken to my room.

"What did you bring him?" She asked.

"Just some of his personal things, some clothes, some pictures, a CD player, and some CD's. When I called, they said I should get some of his casual clothes: jeans, flannel shirts, that kind of stuff."

"That's great! It'll be good for him to be able to wear his own clothes and to have some of his familiar things around."

I had heard the entire conversation between Ken and Dr. Martin. I followed their progress down the hallway. I heard much more than just their words.

As they got closer, I detected other things about them, things that no one would believe I could possibly know. I could hear Ken's arms rubbing against the side of the jacket as he walked, same old jacket. A new leather jacket, or a cloth jacket, would have sounded different.

The lace on Ken's left boot was untied. I could hear the ends of the laces as they slapped against the side of the boot. If it had been a shoe, I would have been able to hear the loose laces hitting the floor too. I did not know exactly why I knew it was Ken's left boot and not the right one that had become untied. Why I knew, did not concern me. It was enough that I simply knew.

Dr. Martin was wearing a lab coat with two pens in the pocket, one metal, and one plastic. And there was a slip of paper in that pocket too. She wore a skirt with pantyhose, not slacks. I had seen her earlier, so I already knew what her outer layer of clothing looked like. The new auditory information only confirmed what I had seen.

But, what others could not see was that Dr. Martin was wearing cotton panties under the pantyhose. They were definitely not made out of a synthetic material. The sound of nylon rubbing against cotton is unmistakable. *She could stand a little pubic trim too.* I mused at the thought.

All this, and more, detailed and intimate information about Dr. Martin and Ken entered my awareness as they drew near my room. I concentrated, wanting to know all I could, testing myself.

It wasn't just curiosity that drove my desire to know more. It was the feeling of power that came over me when I focused my mind. A vibrant world of previously unimaginable detail exploded into my awareness. What had once filled me with terror, now filled me with awe and the feeling of unlimited power. The feeling was intoxicating, and I knew it was growing.

Dr. Martin peeked her head into the open doorway while she rapped on the door jam at the same time. "Ray, you have a visitor."

Ken stepped into the doorway. "Hey, Ray!" I was sitting in a chair next to my bed.

I did not say anything, but shifted my gaze into Ken's eyes. Same old Ken, timid, a wilted presence, like a three-day-old cut flower.

After a second, Ken decided to take my direct stare as an acknowledgement of his presence. "I brought some of your things." He wheeled the dolly and box into the room.

I immediately noticed the slightly dilated blood vessels in the whites of Ken's eyes. His body glowed with a new kind of light I had learned was heat. I could see Ken's body temperature was about one-half of a degree above normal. And his breath, the mint toothpaste he had used earlier could not disguise the distinctive smell of alcohol. A breathalyzer would have detected a .003 alcohol level. But I didn't need a breathalyzer to know that Ken had been out partying last night.

"Slacker." I said flatly.

Ken wasn't sure how to respond. Good. He chuckled nervously. "Yup, same old Ray. You can call me 'Slacker' if you want." Ken's smile was artificial. "How they been treatin' you here?"

"Marion?" There was deliberately no inflection in my voice to indicate that it was a question or a statement.

Ken decided it must be a question. "Mom's fine. She doesn't get out much. It hurts her too much to walk very far."

Dr. Martin seemed impressed. This was starting to look like an actual conversation. She was probably thinking that it might be another step forward for me. She didn't say anything that might interrupt the flow.

"Job?" Again, this was without inflection. Inflection is work. More fun to keep him guessing anyway.

"No. Well, yes. I'm working at 7-Eleven. But it's just part-time right now." Ken was uncomfortable, and apparently wanted to change the subject. He should. Slacker.

"Here, look what I brought you." He dragged the box over in front of me and unfolded the lid.

Ken began unloading the contents of the box onto the bed. "I got your jeans. And, here's some of your shirts. I just grabbed a few things. I can go back and get some more stuff too, if you want."

Ken got to the bottom of the clothing and started pulling out the hard items he had packed first. "I got your portable CD player and some of your CD's. Oh, and I thought you might like a few pictures."

Ken reached into the bottom of the box and brought out the expensive 8x10 carved wood frame with our wedding portrait mounted in it, and laid it on the bed. I stood up immediately, stepped to the bed and picked up the picture with both hands. It was a precious jewel. I had almost forgotten it. I suppose I should have said "thank you" to Ken, but I think he got the message.

My memory of Julia was photographic. I could remember every line of her face, every blemish, the smallest imperfection. But this was a real photo, one that I could see with my eyes, and one that held such powerful memories for me. I turned and sat slowly onto the bed while continuing to let my eyes devour the image. It felt like a drink of cool water after being thirsty for days in the desert.

"I can bring in your wedding album if you want." Ken could see the affect the portrait was having on me. I glanced at him and nodded affirmatively.

I said nothing. My eyes were riveted to the image of Julia and me on the happiest day of my life. I felt like if I concentrated on it enough, it might come to life. Maybe I could will that one happy instant of time back into reality. My stare burned into the image with all of the intensity my being could produce. But that glorious moment, refused to be resurrected.

Only this lifeless piece of colored paper, and my memory was all that remained. I knew that I could never change that reality. A pain stabbed deep within me, from a place I could not define. A tear trickled down my left cheek.

I saw that Dr. Martin noticed the tear. She must have understood that this was a critical moment for me, and not a good time for me to have to deal with anything or anyone other than my own feelings. "Ken, I think Ray might be a little tired. Why don't we let him rest. I'm sure when you come back the next time he'll want to talk to you some more."

Ken looked confused. I guess I didn't look "tired" to him. But even he could see that something had changed. "Sure. Okay. No problem. Ah, look Ray, I'll bring some more of your stuff next time, okay?"

I did not move nor speak, but now the tears were streaming from both eyes. I had not cried for Julia since I had come to the Institute. It was overdue.

Ken and Dr. Martin made a quick exit. When they were fifty feet down the hall, Dr. Martin said, "I'm sorry to cut your visit short. I just thought he needed to be alone for a while. I think that picture brought back some very painful memories for him."

"No problem. I understand. Whatever you think."

"If you want, you can come back tomorrow evening. We're having our Christmas party. Family members are always welcome to come. I think he'll be better by then."

"Ah, yeah, thanks, but I have plans. I'll try to come by next week though."

"Any time is fine. We don't really have visiting hours here you know." Dr. Martin should know that Ken would not be back next week or probably the week after, maybe longer, maybe never. *Slacker.*

I tried to focus on them as they walked away from my room. But my mind refused to obey me. I continued to stare at the portrait of Julia and me, my dear, sweet, loving Julia.

They killed her.

The rage began to return. With it, my mind cleared, and I was able to focus again. I listened again to Ken and Dr. Martin. I followed them to the front entrance. I heard Dr. Martin putting the dolly away. I followed Ken's footsteps as he left the building and walked to his car. I could hear him get in, close the car door, and start the engine. That old Chevy Citation still had that same rough idle. Ken had still not replaced the plugs like I had told him to months ago. *Slacker.*

My attention was broken when a portly man wearing coveralls walked into my room. I hadn't noticed him coming. Too much focus on Ken had distracted me. It was Ted Wheatly, the janitor. "Hi Ray. Just need to get your trash. Say, what ya got there?"

Ted talked incessantly about anything and everything. I had unwillingly learned that he had been a janitor at the Institute since it had opened. He was well into his sixties. He had never had any other type of job. He prided himself at remembering everyone's name. He was an affable man, if not terribly bright.

Because of his jovial nature and sheer size, he had been elected a few years ago to dress up as Santa for the annual Christmas party. It was a roll he greatly enjoyed, and told everybody about it, over and over. It had become a tradition. Ted was looking forward to tomorrow tonight, and was in an especially good mood, not that I had ever seen him in a bad mood.

I turned to look at him. He was looking at the picture. "Julia." I said. It was the one word that summed up everything, the picture, my feelings, my entire life.

"Oh, so that's Julia. Let me have a look." If Ted had not been in such a good mood he might have simply emptied the trash and left. Instead, he sat down next to me and put his arm around my shoulder.

The sensory input of Ted's hand on my shoulder was like a jolt of electricity. It was unbearable. I swung around violently, twisting away from Ted's all-too friendly touch. The wedding portrait flew from his hands, hitting the corner of the nightstand, and shattering the glass.

"Oh, oh, I'm sorry! Oh, oh, I'll get that!" He jumped up and away from me as if I was on fire.

I stared at the picture frame lying face down on the floor surrounded by splinters of glass. *Julia!* I could not move. I could not breathe.

Ted skirted around me and bent down to pick up the picture. He kept his distance while he did so. "Oh, okay, it's okay, see. I can put a new piece of glass in there."

I had not seen the photo yet. I followed Ted with my eyes as he took the picture to the large trash basket on his cart and picked off the remaining shards of glass. "See, it's okay. I'll get a new piece of glass." But he didn't show me. He laid the picture face-down on the other side of the bed while he quickly swept up the glass on the floor.

The frame was intact, and the photo was mostly unharmed, except for an inch-long, quarter-inch wide gash that scraped off the color emulsion layer of the paper. The gash went directly across Julia's face. Almost a third of her face, including one eye, was now missing. I hadn't seen it yet, but I knew.

Ted was apparently hoping I would not notice the gash. I continued looking at the back of the picture frame. I knew.

"I've got to go now." Ted said quickly. The rage inside of me began to build, but I did not act on it, not yet.

I turned my full gaze toward Ted. My mind was now on full focus. I sucked in every scrap of information about Ted that I could. I could see the femur that Ted had broken as a child. I could hear the small aortic valve defect that caused a slight heart murmur. Ted's pulse had increase by fifteen beats per minute since he had entered my room. I knew the brand of the underarm deodorant Ted used, and that he had eaten eggs and bacon for breakfast. Just now, I could smell Ted's nervousness in the changing pheromone signature in his sweat.

I was sure Ted could feel my stare penetrate through his body. Ted had worked around some pretty hostile patients before, or so he had said. But my eyes now made him tremble. I could feel his trembling through air vibrations. It felt good.

Ted quickly pushed his cart down the hallway. He was out of sight, but I sensed him glance over his shoulder several times as he walked. I followed him with my mind. He was afraid of me. *Good.*

I continued to focus on Ted as he walked away. It was interesting that I could have such an effect on someone just by focusing my mind on them.

Julia!

I retrieved the picture frame and held it for a second. I turned it over slowly. I saw the damage that I knew was there, and I stopped breathing. The cut across Julia's pictured face felt like a cut across my own face.

It was more than just a picture. To me, it *was* Julia. Light had once reflected off her real face to form the image. It was her essence that was etched into the photographic paper. It *was* Julia. And Julia, or at least a part of her, had been killed again.

Since indeed God considers it just to repay with affliction those who afflict you. 2nd Thessalonians 1:6.

He will pay. The rage surged inside of me. I felt the power surge with it. It filled me. I drank it in. *They killed my Julia!*

CHAPTER 20
BECKY

Sal and I were sitting cross-legged in our pajamas in the "guest" bedroom. The room had once been mine. But when I left two years ago to live in St. Petersburg with Chuck, Daddy had swapped the queen-size bed with two twin beds to make room for more guests, which they never got.

Momma then completely changed the décor of the room, so that it now reminded me of the beach house we had once rented on a vacation trip to Myrtle Beach. Momma explained that she had always wanted to live by the ocean, and this was as close as she figured she'd ever get.

Barbie doll clothes lay scattered all over our beds and several pieces had spilled onto the floor. Some things never change. There was even that iconic black and white swim suit that came with that slightly used hand-me-down Barbie I got from an aunt, probably worth a chunk of money now.

We decided to dress the dolls up in formal wear. Finding all the accessories, scrambled together in the huge box Momma had pulled out of the attic, was a challenge.

We had gone to bed early to "play dolls" in my old room, partly to allow Momma and Daddy to go to bed early. It had been a long day for them, and it showed. They weren't "spring chickens" any more, as Daddy liked to say.

As we completed dressing our respective Barbie dolls, the conversation turned from doll talk to current events.

"Okay Becky, tell me. What's going on with Chuck?" She asked.

I had never hidden anything from her, and Sal wasn't going to let me start now. We knew each other's closest secrets. It was this core of absolute trust that had always been the foundation of our friendship.

I glanced at her then looked down. At the end of a deep breath and a long sigh I said, "I guess it's me. You know, I've always wanted kids. I though he did too. But it's been over two years now. I guess I've been pushing him."

"I was wondering what you two were waiting for. I thought there might be a physical problem, and I didn't want to pry." Friends don't *pry*. They talk to each other. *Why didn't I call her?*

"No, nothing physical, as far as I know. He says he's not ready, and just doesn't want to talk about it. You know Sal, we haven't had sex in months. I think he's afraid I'll get pregnant. I'm taking the pill, but I don't think he trusts me." My voice showed my feeling of betrayal, and tears began to form at the corners of my eyes.

"Oh Becky, I'm so sorry." She crossed over and sat next to me on my bed. She wanted to fix me, if she could.

"Did you see a marriage counselor?" She asked as she put her arm around me.

Her act of consolation put me over the edge. I leaned onto her shoulder and began to sob. "No. He won't do it." I took a ragged breath. "I think he's seeing someone." I wasn't sure if she could understand me through my sobs.

"No! Are you sure?" She said incredulously.

"I don't know. Maybe it's just me. He stays out late. He says it's work, but he never had to work late before." My every other word was broken with a sob.

"Oh Becky, it'll be okay." How could she know if it would be "okay?"

She began to cry with me, and she rocked me from side to side. I had been holding back the tears for too long. I needed to let them out. I needed her to be here for me. I should have asked her to come much sooner.

She was my best friend. She has her own problems, but I should have called her anyway. I should have told her.

She continued to hold me and rock me until we both could catch our breath. We didn't talk for a few minutes. There was nothing to say. I just needed her there, by my side. She gave me time to get it out, time to breathe, time to put it all in some kind of perspective.

After several minutes, I took a deep breath to let her know, *Okay, I'm ready to face it now.*

I sat up and looked at her. "Sal, I was the one who left. He wouldn't talk to me. I felt like a roommate, not a wife. I couldn't take it anymore.

"I blew up at him. I accused him of cheating, you know, just to get him to deny it. I didn't believe it. But Sal, he didn't deny it! He just said, 'If you feel that way, I don't think we should be living together.' It was like he had rehearsed it.

"He wasn't even angry or upset. He sat there with his arms crossed like it was a done deal, waiting for me to respond. Well, you know me Sal, that just pissed me off more. I told him I was going to leave in the morning to stay with Momma and Daddy. He said, 'Okay.' No objections, no talking about it, nothin', just 'Okay.' "

"Have you talked to him since?" That's Sal, always looking for a ray of hope.

"No. I thought he would call to apologize, or something! You'd think he could at least call to say, 'Hi, how'a ya doin.' Or even 'Go to hell!' would be better than *nothing.*"

"So, have you called him?" She knew the answer.

"Hell no! His girlfriend would probably answer anyway." It was more about my pride.

"Well, of course he's in the wrong, and he's the one who should make the first move and apologize. But, maybe you should give him a chance. Send up a weather balloon. If he doesn't want to get back together, well, then you'll know. You can deal with it and go on. What do you have to lose?" She wanted me to stop blaming myself. But she was right, I needed to remove any doubts.

"Yeah, well, I guess, maybe. But it's up to him. I'm not going to kiss his butt!"

"You don't have to kiss his butt. Just show him your butt, and let *him* do the kissin'. Don't you want to know where you stand?"

I managed a smile. "Okay, I'll call him tomorrow. Thank you Sal." I hugged her to say, *Okay, that's settled.*

We were quiet, letting our thoughts settle down, like snowflakes in a snow globe.

I broke the silence with a small giggle.

"What?"

"I was just thinking. Momma is going to kill me. Look at this mess. Remember, Momma was always yelling at me to pick up my room when I was a little girl." I giggled again. It felt good to be home, where even the people who yell at you, love you.

"Well then, little girl, maybe we should pick it up before your momma sees it, and makes you do the dishes, or an even worse chore." She returned the giggle.

We began loading doll clothes and accessories back into the big box. As we finished the pickup, I said, "Now you."

"Now me what?" She knew 'what.'

"Now it's your turn. Let's hear it, guy problems, work problems, *girl* problems. You know what I mean." I re-crossed my legs and gave her an expectant look.

"Okay. We'll I'm not married, and I don't have a boyfriend. Bruce is long gone."

"Whatever happened to Mr. Carson, anyway?" I had refused to use his first name since they broke up. One does not refer to an enemy by his first name, unless it's an appropriate nickname like, Butthead, Dip Shit, or Ass Hole. I had used them all, but reserved the more formal "Mr." for when I was in a charitable mood.

"I haven't heard anything from, or about Bruce for a couple years now, and I'm happy about that. It wasn't all his fault you know." I could see that the memory of their breakup still brought some pain. Betrayal, yes. Guilt, maybe, but I couldn't justify any other emotion that she should have.

"I hope Mr. Dip Shit is in a hospital somewhere. Karma's a bitch!" Still formal, but not quite as charitable.

"I really don't care. Maybe he got married. Maybe he won the lottery. That was then, and this is now. I've move on." Has she? I gave her a skeptical look.

"So anyway, I don't have any guy problems now. Or, maybe I should say that *that* is the *only* guy problem I have right now.

"And yes, I am a girl, so I have *those* problems too, but nothing that every other woman doesn't have to deal with.

"So, that leaves work problems." I said. She took a cleansing breath. I could see she had been holding something in. Who's ear would be more understanding than mine?

"Well, you know, work is work. It's been exhausting these past few months."

"You said you were working on that Bangkok virus thing. Isn't that closed now?

"Yes and no. We haven't had any new cases. Of course, we're still tracking the survivors. We're watching for any new cases. And there's still ongoing research."

"So then, the heavy work is done and your boss gave you some well-deserved time off. What's the problem? Is there a problem?" I knew she wouldn't have brought it up, if something wasn't bothering her.

"Okay. I screwed up. I overlooked something. Maybe I was overtired."

"Hey, no one is perfect. It can't be that bad." I shrugged my shoulders.

"It was pretty bad. It caused an unnecessary exposure to the virus, and an unnecessary victim."

"How bad is *pretty bad?* Did anyone die?"

"No, he didn't die. It was a United Airlines maintenance worker in Tampa. He was working on the same airplane. I didn't order the correct procedures for decontaminating the plane. He was exposed. He contracted the virus, and went into a coma, like the other survivors. There's brain damage, and it's all my fault!" She blinked trying to hold back the tears.

"Wait a minute, you weren't fired so there must be more to the story. What did your boss say about it?" Sal always had taken minor failures too seriously.

"He was pretty pissed off, but not because of my screw up. He thinks I did a *wonderful* job. He was mad because I tried to take the blame. He said that it wasn't my fault, that it was a simple oversight that could have happened to anybody.

"That's just BS! It was an oversight that *I* made! It was *my* damn *simple oversight* that caused *brain damage! Simple,* my ass! It's not like he caught a friggin' cold for God's sake! He'll be disabled for the *rest of his life."* I had never heard her use the real "F" word, and she apparently wasn't going to start now, but I think she wanted to.

A tear slid down her left cheek. Another followed close behind on the right. I uncrossed my legs so that I could scoot closer and wrap my arm around her shoulder.

"I know you think you should be perfect, but you're not. Hell, nobody can be perfect all the time. I agree with your boss. It was a mistake, yes, but don't beat yourself up over it forever."

"But, it's a life that will never be…" I interrupted her.

"That's right! And how many *other* lives did you *save* by being there? It's easy to count your failures, but you need to count your successes too. Could anyone else have done a better job? Really? And, what other *oversights* would someone else have made? Sal, give yourself some credit. You did your best, and your best is better that just about anybody's."

She shook her head in protest, but I was not slowing down now.

"And the game's not over. You're still on the case. When you get back you can redouble your efforts and end up with an *almost* perfect score.

"Look, it's like when we used to go bowling on Saturdays. Let's say you've got a score of two-sixty-nine in the ninth frame, not that *you* ever got a score that high." She let a little smile sneak out. We had been competitive, but always supportive of each other, something guys seem to have a hard time with.

I continued with my pep talk. "Do you give up and throw gutter balls because a perfect game is no longer possible? No! You do your best to roll a turkey in the tenth frame! And you end the game with a two-ninety-nine. Not perfect, but not all that bad either, huh? You just need a rest like your boss says."

There was truth in what I was saying, and she had to see it. "Yeah, I guess." She had given up the argument, not that she accepted what I was saying, just that she didn't want to dispute it anymore.

I was rubbing and patting her back like you might to calm a baby. It was working.

"But what can I do now? There must be something. Dr. Edelman said he didn't want to see me back until February." The gears in her head were turning. I'd seen that look before.

"What if I didn't actually go back *there?* Maybe I can do some work "off the clock.' There must be some things I can do without actually going back to the office. I have my security codes. I could login to the system long distance." She was talking to herself.

"You were ordered to relax. I think you should do it."

She was still talking to herself. "If Dr. Edelman found out that I was working, in the office or not, he would probably follow through with his threat to fire me. I need someone on the inside who will help me cover my tracks. But, who is in a position to be helpful, who would also be willing to do me a big favor? Rose!"

"Huh, Rose who?"

"Rose is our Sec…. Administrative Assistant. I'm sure she will help me out if I ask her."

"Help you what?" I was skeptical.

She summarized her plan. I agreed to go along with her ploy, if she didn't tell Momma and Daddy, and if she promised not to overdo it.

I could see how excited she had suddenly become, and I didn't want to throw cold water on her.

We finished picking up the Barbie things, and when to bed. It *had* been a long day.

The next morning after breakfast, Sal reminded me about calling Chuck.

"Oh, yeah. I forgot about that." I hadn't forgotten about it at all.

"Just get it over with." Pushy, pushy. She knew when I needed a push.

"Okay. But only if you'll come with me into town later to do some shopping."

"Fine. But we'll have to stop for lunch at Ferguson's. I used to love their shakes."

"Ooh! That sounds great." I picked up the cordless phone. "I'll call him from my room. This shouldn't take long."

Sal started picking up the breakfast dishes while I went upstairs. Momma and Daddy had been up early and had already eaten. Momma had already rinsed and stacked their breakfast dishes in the sink.

I would have probably left them for Momma, but I figured Sal would beat her to them before Momma could object.

I made the call.

Three minutes later I was slowly coming back down the stairs. Sal knew there was a problem when she saw the stunned look that must have been on my face.

"What's wrong? What did he say?"

"A woman answered the phone." I said flatly.

"*Who* answered the phone?"

"That's what I asked. She said she was Alex, and she wanted to know who *I* was!" I couldn't believe it. "I told her I was Chuck's wife."

Sal held her breath. She knew what was coming.

"Sal, she laughed! She said, 'Oh, you must be Becky. Well, Chucky is still sleeping, and I'm not going to wake him up for *you. If* he wants to talk to you, he'll call you back later.' She said, 'You should check your mail box sweetie. I think his lawyer sent you something.' "

"Lawyer? Something? What?"

"She wouldn't say. She just said, 'Maybe you should have called him sooner.' and she hung up."

She knew what the "something" was, and so did I. Sal knew there was nothing she could say, she just hugged me.

I didn't cry. I didn't even talk. Of course, Momma and Daddy did what they could. But their hugs and condolences were met with a blank stare. I sat on the couch, motionless and silent. I had suffered a mortal blow. I was numb. I was contemplating whether I would survive it. I was doubtful.

At a quarter after one o'clock that afternoon, the mailman knocked on the door with a registered letter, asking for my signature. I walked to the door like a condemned person on her way to the gallows. I signed for the letter, and turned and walked back to the living room without taking it. Momma took the letter from the mailman for me.

It was a thick full sized envelope, sealed with extra packing tape. It sat on the couch next to me all afternoon. I didn't open it, or even look at it.

Sal sat with me in silence until dinner. I just shook my head when they asked if I wanted to eat. *What's the point?*

In the kitchen, I heard Momma say to Sal, "Don't worry Sal. She'll be okay. Just leave her to her thoughts. It's the way she handles things. Remember when Robbie got hit by a car? She wouldn't talk about it for weeks." Do I "handle" things, or do I just bury them, like Robbie.

Robbie was my pet beagle I had gotten him for my 10th birthday. I had been asking for a puppy for months.

The dog was a nuisance most of the time, but I loved him anyway. We were buddies, and he loved me too. He would follow me everywhere.

One day he followed Sal and I to the creek. There was a small bridge where the creek crossed under the road. We were under the bridge catching crawdads. Robbie was darting back and forth across the road above, wanting to be part of the action without getting wet.

There were never many cars on that narrow tar and gravel road. But on that day, a pickup truck driver was taking a shortcut to the main road, and he was in a hurry. He glanced away from the road for a second.

Robbie was dead instantly. The truck had crushed his head. The driver stopped and was apologetic, but anxious to be on his way. It wasn't his fault, it wasn't his dog, and he didn't have the time or the desire to be interrogated by upset parents.

I picked up Robbie's crumpled body as I watched the man drive off. I cradled Robbie in my arms for the entire half-mile walk back home. I cried all the way. I was covered in blood by the time we got home.

Daddy buried Robbie in a simple grave he dug out by the barn. The gravesite was never marked. I didn't want to remember where he was buried.

I never owned another pet. I tried. I failed to take care of him. I wouldn't make that mistake again.

Sal escorted me to bed early. I went fast to sleep without saying "good night." There was no tossing and turning. I don't think I moved all night.

The next morning, I was up early and in the shower. It was over. I had tried. I had failed to save my marriage. It was dead and as good as buried. I wouldn't make that mistake again.

I came out of the bathroom wrapping a towel around my head just as Sal's feet were patting the floor next to her bed trying to locate her slippers.

"Good morning." I said.

"Good morning." Sal replied cautiously.

"I guess I should open the letter from Butthead." Chuck had officially lost his first name. I was back in the real world. I grinned to let Sal know I was okay.

I grabbed the envelope and ripped it open. I quickly scanned the boiler plate divorce papers. There was a cover letter that I read more carefully.

"Oh great! The Ass Wipe put all my stuff in a storage locker that will expire in two weeks. If I don't go out there and get it, or pay to extend the storage, it's gone."

"Is there anyone out there who can pack it up and ship it for you?"

"No, just some relatives of his. I wouldn't ask them for snot!"

"Well if you want to go, you know I'll go with you. As a matter of fact, I have some work related business out there. You know that Bangkok virus victim I told you about who lives in Tampa? I want to look in on him."

"Oh yeah. Sure. Sounds good to me. I just want to get all this stuff taken care of, and get that sleaze bag out of my life as quick as I can. Can you believe that slut has already moved in with him!"

"No, I can't believe it." Sal shook her head. "Well, I'll help you. Whatever I can do."

CHAPTER 21
HECK

"Good morning, Ray." I said as I poked my head into the open door of Ray's room.

"No cane." Ray said with his back still to the door looking toward the window. It was not what I expected, if I expected anything.

"Yeah, I decided to see if I could get around without it today." It was an observation that anyone might have made, but I was disconcerted at how Ray was able to make these kinds of observations without doing any noticeable observing.

In the last two weeks since I had first met Ray, he had made significant progress. Ray had stopped rocking himself as often, but continued to twiddle a pen between his thumb and forefinger. I recognized it as the non-functioning green plastic Institute pen I had inadvertently left in his room two weeks ago. It seemed to be Ray's favorite for some reason.

At first, Ray had hardly responded to me, but Ray had become much more talkative over the last week. I was hopeful that Ray's new willingness to communicate would help me to get a better understanding of how to help him progress even faster. It was exciting to work with a patient that showed measurable improvement over weeks, instead of years.

I had suspected that Ray's hearing was acute, and I arranged for a hearing specialist to come in and test it yesterday. I was more than a little surprised when the test revealed that Ray's hearing was even more sensitive than the testing machine itself.

Ray was able to hear all frequencies and at even the lowest volumes the machine could produce. How much more sensitive his hearing might be was anyone's guess until more sophisticated testing could be done. And after I studied the CDC report, I was curious to find out if there might be more that Ray was capable of doing.

"I brought in some crayons. Dr. Martin says you're good at colors." I waited to see if Ray would respond. He didn't.

I continued, "I'll pick a crayon and draw something with it behind you. Here's a box for you with all the same colors. All I want you to do is pick the same color I'm using here behind you. Okay?" There was still no response from Ray.

"Okay." I took his silence as a 'yes', and picked a green crayon and made a scribble on a note pad. "Can you show me which crayon I'm using?

Ray lifted the new box of sixty-four colors I had set it down in from of him. He moved it close to his face and rotated the box slowly a full 360 degrees before setting it down.

He selected a crayon and said, "Green." He returned to twiddling the green pen and his expression remained blank.

"That's right! Green." I reached around Ray's shoulder to retrieve the crayon I compared mine with the one Ray had given me. The labels both read Asparagus. "Very good!"

Next, I selected a blue crayon. This time I noted the label, Midnight Blue, before making a scribble on the note pad. "Now which color am I using?"

"Blue." Ray said as he pulled the Midnight Blue crayon out of the box.

I took the crayon from Ray and read the label. He could have picked one of several shades of blue, but he picked the exact same one. "Wow! That's exactly right."

I looked around the room to make sure a mirror wasn't conveniently placed allowing Ray to see which crayon I was using. There wasn't one, but just in case, this time I put my left hand over the top of the box and blindly selected two crayons at random with my right hand. Keeping them both concealed under my left hand, I used both crayons simultaneously to make a double scribble on the note pad. "Okay, let's see if you can tell me which crayon I'm using now."

Ray hesitated a second, then said, "Orange."

I looked at the crayons I was using for the first time. One was labeled Laser Lemon. The other one was Scarlet. "No Ray, that's wrong."

"Orange." Ray said without changing his tone. I thought I saw the hint of a smile on his lips as he held up two crayons he had taken from the box.

I felt a chill run down my spine. I didn't need to read the labels on the crayons Ray was holding. I could see they were the same crayons I held in my own hand. I looked at the note pad where I made the scribble with the red and yellow crayons. The two colors had overlapped sufficiently to form the color orange.

I couldn't believe it. There must be some kind of trick. *How did he do that?* "How did you know that, Ray?"

Ray remained silent. I moved my chair around in front of Ray so that I could look him in the eye and repeated the question with emphasis. "*How* did you *know*?"

Ray looked directly back into my eyes. There was something malevolent in Ray's gaze that I couldn't quite put my finger on. Ray's eyes were brown, but there was a threatening darkness that seemed to be hidden behind them. It reminded me of Limpy. I felt queasy.

"Julia." The name seemed to crawl out of Ray's mouth, like the rattlesnake I once saw crawl out from under a rock in the desert, slowly, and with menace.

"Julia? How did Julia…?" I thought that Ray might not have fully come to grips with his wife's death. I switched to a softer tone. "I'm sorry about Julia, Ray. She died from the virus."

"*They* killed her." Ray said almost under his breath. It was the first time I had heard Ray say a complete sentence containing more than two words.

"Ray, Julia died from the virus. No one killed her." I wanted to get back on subject. "We can talk about that later. I just want to know *how* you can tell what crayons I'm using?"

"Julia helps me." Another full sentence, this time I thought I heard reverence in his voice.

"How does Julia help you Ray?" *Could he be hearing voices?*

"Hate." Ray's tone was cold, almost sterile.

"What do you mean, Ray?" I knew Ray had loved his late wife. "Hate from whom, toward whom?"

Ray did not respond. He stood up and took a step toward his bed. Almost as an afterthought, Ray stopped momentarily and flipped his hand toward the crayon box, releasing the last two crayons he had been holding. The crayons arced and flipped across the four feet from where Ray was now standing. Each slipped easily into their respective slots in the crayon box.

I blinked twice. I couldn't believe what I had just seen. I simply could not have seen what I just saw! Maybe I didn't. I turned to say something to Ray as he walked toward his bed, but nothing came out. I just watched Ray with my mouth open.

Ray sat down and lay back on his bed. He closed his eyes and folded his hands across his belly. Ray had done this before. I knew it meant that Ray was not going to be responsive any more that day. He had simply tuned me out.

###

"No, I'm not kidding. He knew what color crayons I was using." I had just sat down in a recliner by my freshly decorated Christmas tree with a glass of eggnog spiked with cherry flavored brandy.

"That's pretty weird. And, you're sure he couldn't see you? What about smell?" Tom was stretched out on the couch.

"They're not scented crayons. They just smell like wax to me. I don't know. They use different dyes to color the wax. I suppose a very sensitive sniffer might be able to detect the different dyes."

"Maybe his smell is just as sensitive as his hearing. You said that it's off the chart, right."

"Right. Huh, maybe. But there's something else."

"What?"

"I can't quite put my finger on it. I told you about him knowing about my broken ribs. He just seems to know things. Jan said he gives her the creeps. I guess he gives me the creeps too." I chuckled at my use of that word.

Tom tilted his head to the side, directing his gaze toward the hallway. "Speaking of creeps. I see someone creeping down the hall." He laughed.

I sat my drink down and hauled myself stiffly out of the recliner. "Tyler, this is the third time. I told you, it's bed time now." My tone gave me away. I could not be angry with him on Christmas Eve, and he knew it.

Tyler giggled and ran back to his room and jumped onto his bed.

"Give me a few minutes, Tom. I'll try and get him to stay in bed this time." The grin on my face belied my exasperated tone.

Tom chuckled. "Take your time. I need to call Starla and find out exactly what time she's going to show up for Christmas dinner tomorrow."

"I hope it's early. I think we could probably use a little female help here." I said over my shoulder as I headed for Tyler's room.

Tom had only been dating Starla for a couple weeks. It was long enough for a Christmas dinner together with me and Tyler, but apparently not long enough for a Christmas Eve sleepover, and certainly not long enough for a Christmas dinner with her parents.

Tom usually ended his relationships before they got to the meet-the-parents stage anyway. His last girlfriend, Lacy, had found that out the hard way when she invited him to Thanksgiving dinner with her parents. *Only a month. That's Tom.*

"Okay you little monkey, it's sack time!" I expected Tyler to resist going to sleep. Any change in his environment would keep him awake. At least he wasn't upset and throwing a fit as he often did when there was a change in his routine.

I knew it would be stressful to break Tyler's routine, but I thought it would be good for him in the long run. It would help him to learn how to handle new situations. At least, that's what I told myself.

The truth was that Tyler was probably never going to be able to deal with anything close to a normal family environment. But I would not, could not, let go of the goal that someday he would be *normal*, or at least independently functional. I wasn't going to be around forever. He needed to at least learn to take care of his basic needs.

"Here's your car, and here's your blankie. I'll wind up moo-cow for you." I brought home some of Tyler's favorite things. The red metal car with half of its paint chipped off and only two wheels, remained his favorite. The baby blanket, that he had had since he was born, he carried with him everywhere. It was faded and tattered, and it had to be secretly confiscated periodically for washing while he was asleep.

I wound up the musical cow-jumped-over-the-moon mobile suspended over his bed. "Look at your moo-cow."

Tyler was rocking his head back and forth on his pillow. "Cukie. Cukie. Cukie."

"You already had a cookie. It's time to go to sleep now." I sat down beside him and gently held Tyler's head, helping it rock back and forth. Gradually he slowed the rocking until Tyler focused his attention on the mobile turning overhead.

After a few minutes he stopped rocking his head and stared blankly at the mobile. I stayed with him until his eyes closed and his breathing became heavier. I gently kissed him on the forehead, and cautiously got up and left the room.

He would sleep through the night. But I knew that tomorrow would be a very challenging day for Tyler, new toys, new people, and new food. *It's worth it.*

Tom was just concluding his conversation with Starla when I returned to the living room. Tom's tone suddenly became more guarded. "Okay, ah, me too... I can't wait 'til next year either… Yeah, aha… Okay, see ya tomorrow around one o'clock… Okay, yeah… I know. Me too… Okay, bye ah, bye… No, don't worry about it… That's right… Alright…Okay, bye now."

Tom hung up the phone and let out a long sigh. I looked at him with a knowing smirk. "Remind me not to ever call her on Christmas Eve again. She's like a little kid. I couldn't get her to hang up." Unlike my earlier comments about Tyler, Tom's exasperation was real.

"And, if she says one more word about *next* Christmas while she's here tomorrow, please just shoot me in the head! Jeez!"

"I don't know how you put up with women like that." I said with mock sympathy.

"I don't know either." Tom missed my sarcasm.

"Yeah, it must be tough. Big tits, tight ass, long silky hair, legs like Barbie, and she wants to spend *next* Christmas with you *too*, I don't know how you can take it." I added extra emphasis to make sure Tom would catch the sarcasm this time.

"Ha ha. Okay, so she's a knockout. That doesn't mean I want to spend the rest of my life with her."

"She's just not the right one, huh?"

"Ah well, I don't know yet."

"How many women have you gone through in the last year? Eight? Ten?"

"Who's counting? Like my Dad used to tell me, I'm just a son-of-a-Birch." Tom laughed.

I wouldn't let him deflect the conversation. "It's not the quantity, Tom. I've met most of those women. And besides all of them being knockouts, a few of them actually seem to have pretty level heads on their shoulders too. Do you think there's ever going to be a *right one?"*

"What, you mean like Wendy?" Tom was feeling threatened, and that automatically put him on the offense.

"Ouch! That's a low blow. Okay, maybe I deserve it. It's none of my business how many women you date. I just think you might try having a long-term relationship for a change. Who knows, you might even *like* spending two holidays in a row with the same woman."

"I know I'm sitting on your couch, big brother, but do you think maybe you can just drink your eggnog and save the psychoanalysis for the Institute?"

"Fair enough." I knew I had gotten as far as I was going to get into Tom's personal business. Although I was genuinely concerned about the parade of women that came and went through Tom's life, I knew it was time to change the subject.

Besides, I didn't want the conversation to shift onto my own dismal social life. Since the separation and divorce, I could count the women I had dated on one finger. Her name was Maureen. I went out with her a couple times. She wasn't stunning, or brilliant. The word that popped into my head is, "pleasant." Tom would never have dated her, too bland for his taste.

She met Tyler on our third date. I asked her out again, but she suddenly seemed to be too "busy," and then stopped returning my calls. After the second "busy" and the second unreturned voicemail, I stopped calling. You don't have to hit me over the head. I got the message.

I didn't blame her, really. Not many women would *volunteer* for mom duty with Tyler. After that, I sort of gave up on dating. I told myself, *later.*

Yes, it was best to end this conversation while I was ahead.

"Thanks for coming over and helping us put up the tree." I said.

"No problem. I haven't had one at my place in years, but I do like the smell of fresh cut pine." Tom took a deep breath.

We both stared blankly at the tree. My mind wandered across the many Christmases I had known. There was the Christmas I got that new bike. Other Christmases had not been so happy, like the Christmas after Nan died, or the one just before Mom died, the same one I opted *not* to spend with her and Dad, the last Christmas they would ever have.

I pushed these darker thoughts out of my head and turned to that magical Christmas before Tyler was *officially* diagnosed with autism. I guess I knew, but I hadn't yet allowed myself to see the signs.

Wendy and I, and baby Tyler, were the picture-perfect family. In fact, we had a Christmas portrait taken that we sent out with our Christmas cards that year. The future we saw then was bright and promising. Like that family portrait, it was only a snapshot in time, a time that spoke only of Christmas bliss, but said nothing of future changes that were just over the horizon.

Was the future already written for us, waiting for us to read the next word? Or, was the future a blank page waiting for us to *write* the next word. Fate or free will?

"Hey Tom."

"Huh?" The brandy was having its effect on him.

"Do you believe in fate?"

"Huh? What do you mean?" Drowsy, his brain was searching for first gear.

"I was just thinking about how things change, and how it all seems so unpredictable. Do we really have any control, or is it all predestined."

"Whoa! Where the hell did that come from? You need another brandy-eggnog." Tom was not exactly the philosophical type.

"Some people think that everything is a matter of fate. Some people think that there is no fate, but that we determine our own future through the decisions we make."

"Okay. I don't know. I guess I don't believe in fate, because that would mean that no one has any choice, that we are all slaves to some cosmic script writer." He was hoping that would end the conversation.

"I remember reading that Albert Einstein once said that 'God does not play dice with his universe.' He believed that everything could be foretold with mathematical certainty, if only we knew the formula, and had enough computing power."

"Why did he think that?" He didn't care. He was humoring me.

"He was responding to a quantum physicists that subscribed to the Heisenberg Uncertainty Principle. Don't ask me to get into the details, but…"

"I won't." Tom interjected.

"The way I understand it, on a sub-atomic level, there is a built in randomness. Things can only be predicted as a probability, but not with any exact certainty."

"Okay, okay, you lost me. I don't know if you're trying to screw with my head or just put me to sleep, but you're succeeding at both. Christ, where's Billy. You should be talking to him."

"Stick with me. If Einstein was right, fate rules the universe. If Heisenberg is right, there's the possibility that we can load the dice, so to speak. In other words, we can influence the outcome. It opens the door for free choice to determine the future of the universe."

"Sure, whatever you say. Where the hell is Billy anyway? When's the last time you talked to him?"

"I haven't seen him since Dad's funeral, but he called me when I was in the hospital in Anchorage."

"So, what's he up to these days. He's the one you need to be talking to about this shit. You guys used to do this to me when we were kids too. Remember that time we went camping with Billy and his family. You two kept me up all night talking about how to make a real Spiderman web gun, and how Superman could really have x-ray eyes. Who the hell gives a flyin' frog fart!"

I was laughing out loud by this point in Tom's rant. "Yeah, how does Superman do that?"

"Don't get me started. I need another eggnog." He slumped back in his chair shaking his head in frustration.

"Okay, I'll quit. But, that's a good question about what Billy is up to. We ought to invite him out here, have a reunion. What do you think?"

"That would be great, if you can get him to come. Last I heard, he was pretty busy being the big wig, William G. Olsen, professor of physics at Cornell."

"That's why we might be able to talk him into coming out. He's published all kinds of papers, and got himself a pretty good reputation. He makes the university look good and brings in a lot of grant money for them. I think they'd cut him some slack if he asked for some time off."

"So, call him. Tell him I need a break from *you*. You guys can philosophize to your heart's content."

"Okay, I will." To tell the truth, I was getting too tired to continue with any more deep thinking anyway. My thoughts were starting to wander off the trail and into the woods.

What if? What if I had chosen to stay at Cornell like Billy, instead of coming back to Seattle? I wouldn't have met Wendy. Tyler would not exist. I probably would have met someone else, and there would be another child or maybe children. What if I had come back to Seattle sooner, before Mom died? Maybe Dad would still be alive. Maybe. What if? Free choice? Fate? Who rolls the dice?

I shook my head to dispel these heavyweight questions. I was too tired.

"You know, you're welcome to sleep on the couch, Tom. You've got to be here early anyway to help me get stuff ready. You promised you'd help me fix a *real* Christmas dinner this year, with all the trimmings, remember?"

"I'm hoping Starla will try to impress me with her culinary skills so I can sit back and watch the parade on TV." He chuckled while he considered my invitation. "Yeah, okay. But it's too early for me. I want to sit here for a while and watch the lights on the tree, maybe watch some TV, while I sip on my eggnog."

"Well, unlike you, I need my beauty sleep. You know where the blankets and pillows are. Try not to scare Santa away." I was filled with Christmas spirit as I always was on Christmas Eve, but decorating the tree with Tyler had been an ordeal. And, the thought of dealing with Tyler, and at the same time, trying to produce a *real* Christmas dinner, made me yearn for bed.

I still had a lot of physical recuperating to do, I reminded myself, and a good night's sleep was the best medicine.

I stripped off my clothes and let them drop on the floor next to the bed. I was just too tired to put them away properly. *I'll pick them up in the morning.* I pulled back the blankets and sat down heavily on the edge of the bed.

I checked the clock on my nightstand. It was only 9:30, but it felt like in it should be much later. I knew I would sleep very soundly tonight. To insure that I wouldn't sleep too late, I set the alarm for 7:00.

I slid between the sheets and pulled the blankets up under my chin. A wave of relief swept over my body. I took in a deep breath and let it out slowly. Yes, it had been a long day. I knew I would be asleep in minutes. I reached over to turn off the lamp on the nightstand.

As my hand touched the lamp switch, the phone rang. The thought crossed my mind to just let it ring. Voicemail would pick up after a couple rings. But then I thought that Tom might try to answer it, to keep the ringing from waking up Tyler. No, I'd better answer it. *Who could be calling this late on Christmas Eve, an elfin telemarketer perhaps?*

I picked up the receiver before it could ring a second time. "Hello?"

"Heck? This is Jan."

"Jan, shouldn't you be dreaming about sugar…?" I was trying not to sound like I was about to go to sleep, but she cut me off before I finished the sentence.

"Heck, I know it's Christmas Eve, but I need you to come down to the Institute." I could hear that she was fighting to keep control. There was urgency in her voice, but also something else. *Fear?*

"Now? Jan, tell me what's going on." The last thing I wanted to do was to get dressed and go down to the Institute in the middle of the night. But I knew Jan well enough to know it must be important. Her voice was trembling. She was trying to hide it, but I could tell that she was under a lot of stress.

"It's Ted. He's dead!" I could hear Jan's voice break. The immediate crisis was over. She had taken charge and did what she had to do. Now her reserve of cool-headed control was drained. She began to cry.

"Oh my God! Ted Wheatly, the janitor?" I had talked with Ted briefly the day before when I picked up Tyler. He was as jovial as usual, and he looked like he might have put on a few extra pounds in preparation for his yearly roll as Santa impersonator.

"Yes…" She tried to control her sobs. "The ambulance just left to take him to the hospital, but he's dead. I know he's dead!" The weeping overcame her again.

"What happened?"

"There was no pulse! I tried to give him CPR, but… Heck, I tried to save him! I tried!" Her sobs became muffled. She had covered the receiver while another bout of crying temporarily took over.

"Jan, breath, calm down!" She had either not heard me, or was unable to comply.

I tried again. "Jan, listen to me! Calm down and tell me what happened."

"Okay, just give me a…" I waited as she regained her composure. "It was… an accident. Everyone was in the dayroom. Ted was playing Santa, like he does every year for the Christmas Eve party. We were singing carols, then… it just happened!"

"What?"

"Oh my God! The blood! It's all over me! It's all over the floor!" She had just allowed herself to become aware of her blood-soaked clothes. She sounded on the verge of becoming hysterical.

Although Jan was a medical doctor, she had gone directly into psychiatry after her residency, in no small part because she had discovered she had a strong aversion to blood.

"Blood? Jan! What happened?" I spoke slower and louder, enunciating each syllable.

"Heck, I need you to come down here, now!" She was pleading. There was a note of desperation in her voice. Something was terribly wrong.

"Okay, okay! I'll be there in fifteen minutes."

"Please hurry, Heck!" She lowered her voice to almost a whisper. "It's Ray. I don't know how. I think he… I don't know, but he did something. I saw him just before it happened. Heck, he knew! He was smiling! He never smiles! And he kept smiling while I was trying to save Ted. I saw him, Heck. His eyes were… weird. And he saw me looking at him! I think he knows that I know he did something. He was smiling at me the same way a minute ago! Heck, I'm afraid of him!"

"I'm on my way!" I was already getting dressed. Tom would look after Tyler 'til I could sort out what was going on at the Institute.

"I don't know where he is now. I've got to go!" She hung up the phone abruptly.

I had never seen Jan in any situation where she was not in complete control. And I had never known her to be prone to hysterics.

She's afraid!

It had been only a minute since I was ready to turn off the light and fall asleep. Now, I was wide awake. I had to get down there!

She's afraid! Of Ray?

CHAPTER 22
RAY

I could hear him coming from the far end of the main hallway. Ted was wearing those old Santa boots that were two sizes too large. *Unmistakable.*

People had been trickling in and out of the Rec room. I had my favorite Pacific Blue crayon, and a number-two pencil newly sharpened. I was twiddling the crayon between my thumb and index finger in my left hand, and the pencil in my right hand. *Synchronized. Calming.*

He was getting closer. He will walk across the room to my left. He won't get very close, maybe ten feet away. I scanned the area where he would walk noting every imperfection in the linoleum floor.

He should have worn cotton socks, or even wool. The thin nylon socks he was wearing only made the oversized Santa boots flop around even more. *Smooth leather soles. No traction.*

Jake Hanson was sitting five feet away on my right. He cradled his personal box of crayons, as he always did. Jake was twelve years old, and very possessive of his "stuff," especially his crayons.

The phrase, "my stuff" was one of the few he had mastered. Sharing was a concept he did not grasp, and probably never would. I had listened to him say "my stuff" at least ten times a day, every day since I had arrived. This was usually followed by some kind of verbal or physical altercation, whereupon Jake would get "his stuff."

Almost to the door now. Timing. I concentrated. *Focus. The feeling.* I tuned into the flow of the moment. I was feeling acute intensity, but not what you could call excitement. I felt anger, but I was under precise control. The ebb and flow of my surroundings came to me as a single consciousness, a oneness, the "Now." Jake blinked. His stomach growled. A small dust bunny rolled slowly along the baseboard near the door. A lone ant had somehow managed to invade the far side of the room. Its random journey was intimately connected to the oneness that was "Now."

Ted's hand touched the door. The door opened. Ted took his first step into the room.

"Crayon." I said, and offered the Pacific Blue crayon to Jake. He turned. His eyes opened wide, and he stood up.

Ted took his second steep into the room, exactly on the path I expected. *Timing. The flow.*

I motioned to Jake, offering him the crayon and saying, "Your stuff."

Jake hesitated a second. *Timing.* I could feel it now. *The Now.*

Ted took his third step. *Timing. Yes!*

Jake bolted toward me, his right hand extended, his left hand holding his personal box of crayons. *Timing.* Jake would arrive in two and a half quick steps.

Ted was just completing four and one third steps into the room, when Jake arrived.

There it was. I could see it all happening before it happened. There was no doubt about it now. *Timing. Power.*

My right knee snapped and my foot shot straight out, kicking Jake's left toe as it swung forward, driving it behind his right heel. He toppled forward instantly, reflexively extending his hands to catch himself. His crayon box hit the floor. Crayons exploded from the box directly at Ted.

At that exact instant, I threw my Pacific Blue crayon at Ted's left foot just as his heel hit the floor. Only not "threw." "Placed" would be a more accurate description.

The pencil followed an instant later. It was aimed, or placed, at a spot just behind Ted's center of gravity. The crayon and the pencil tumbled through the air like a juggler's bowling pins I had once seen used at a circus. It was a symphony of motion and I was the conductor. *Precision. Timing. Power.*

As the splash of Jake's crayons arrived in front of Ted, my Pacific Blue crayon landed under the ball of Ted's left foot. His foot rolled forward as Ted's weight came down on the crayon. Ted's left foot shot out in front of him, letting gravity pull him backwards toward the floor at the gravitational acceleration rate of thirty-two-point-two feet per second squared. I didn't need the mathematical formula. I knew. I felt. *Timing.*

Ted's butt hit the floor first, followed by his elbows, and finally his back in quick succession. As his back came down, my newly sharpened number two pencil landed, eraser end down, under and between Ted's shoulder blades. The pencil bounced once, then tilted to exactly vertical just as Ted's full weight touched the newly sharpened tip. It plunged full length through his chest, traveling through the center of his heart.

The tip of the pencil stopped just short of piercing the skin to the left of Ted's sternum. Blood would collect under the skin in a minute, making it look like a big pimple on his chest.

"Eight ball in the side pocket!" I whispered to myself. I didn't want to draw attention to myself, but I couldn't help smiling. I'm sure champion golfers feel some small portion of what I was feeling when they sink a fifty-foot putt for an eagle, but certainly not like this. *Power.*

Ted's mouth gapped open, like a roast pig waiting for the apple. He made no sound. His wide open eyes blinked twice, then closed forever.

The righteous will rejoice when he sees the vengeance; he will bathe his feet in the blood of the wicked. Psalm 58:10.

Yes, I hear you God. But, why did You take Julia from me? She was not 'wicked.'

Jake was crawling on the floor around Ted on his hands and knees, picking up his crayons, repeatedly saying "my stuff, my stuff." Jake didn't know or care what had happened to Ted, nor why. It did not occur to him that he should be concerned about the man in red lying in the middle of "his stuff."

Dr. Martin heard Ted fall, and saw the spilled crayons. She came to help, but it was too late. Ted was unresponsive. By the time she understood that he was dead, everyone had gathered around. Santa lay motionless on the floor on top of a growing pool of blood.

So, Ted was the star of the Christmas Eve party after all. Ho-Ho-Ho!

Dr. Martin noticed me smiling. I couldn't help it. My eyes met hers. Hers said, "Fear." Smart woman, but not smart enough.

CHAPTER 23
HECK

By the time I reached the Institute, the ambulance had already arrived at the hospital. They got there with somewhat less speed than might be expected. The lights were flashing, but the life-saving speed was noticeably missing.

The paramedics knew there was no hope for Ted, even though he would not be pronounced officially dead until a doctor examined him. Despite this, they did all they could, a pressure bandage on the wound, a saline drip, adrenaline injection, a ventilator. They were prevented from doing heart compressions because of the location of the imbedded pencil.

"Heck!" Jan was outside the front entrance smoking a cigarette. It was her first in twenty years.

"Jan, what happened? Are you okay?" She looked better than she sounded on the phone, but not by much.

"Come inside. I need to sit down. I need some coffee." She put out her cigarette, and led the way inside to her office.

I let her settle down until she was ready to talk.

"Heck, I need to call the police. I want this handled like a possible homicide." She grabbed her phone before I could rally my thoughts to comment. She was routed to a Lieutenant Boswick in the Seattle P.D. Homicide division. He told her not to touch anything, he would radio for uniformed officers to get there first to guard the scene, and then he and a forensic team would be there in less than thirty minutes.

Jan hung up the phone and then jumped up and rushed to her office doorway calling to the front desk. "Sue, find a couple people to stand guard at the Rec room entrances. The police are coming, and I don't want anyone to go in there until they get here."

"Okay, Dr. Martin, I'll get Joe and Teri." Sue was showing herself to be a good person to have around in a crisis. No questions, just action.

Jan returned to her desk and plopped into her chair with a loud exhale. She took a couple of cleansing breaths. I let her.

"Heck, I think he did it."

"Ray? How? What exactly did he do?"

"I don't know *exactly* what he did. No one really was paying any attention. But it looked like little Jake Hanson tripped and spilled his crayons in front of Ted. Ted stepped on a crayon and fell. At least that's what it looked like. Ted was somehow stabbed in the back with a pencil when he fell.

"A pencil? How the hell does that happen?"

"I don't think it does, not by accident anyway. Jake doesn't even use pencils. He doesn't like them. He prefers colors." She said.

"So what, do you think Ray stabbed Ted with a pencil?"

"I don't know. He was sitting at least ten feet away when I heard the noise and looked over. It couldn't have been more that a second. He was just sitting there, smiling!"

"That's not much to go on." Maybe she was displaying a touch of delusion brought on by the trauma of the tragic event. People naturally look for a cause, even when shear chance is the only logical cause there can be.

"Yeah, I know. But I've been in the people reading business for a long time now. And that Cheshire cat smile of his said to me, 'I did it, and I'm proud of it.' "

"Okay. We'll let the police look into it. In the meantime, we'll just have to keep a close watch on Ray."

The police came, took a lot of pictures, and asked a lot of questions. Lt. Boswick seemed to have a permanently raised left eyebrow. It raised a little more at each answer he was given. An occupational idiosyncrasy I guessed.

Two days later, Lt. Boswick called to schedule a meeting with Jan and myself at her office.

Lt. Boswick was a direct, even a blunt man. That was the charitable assessment of his personality.

He started by saying, "I don't have anything to go on."

"But…" Jan started, but was stopped by Lt. Boswick's raised hand.

"Let me tell you what we do have. We have a crushed crayon and a sharpened number 2 lead pencil. Cause of death: a punctured heart."

"Any fingerprints?" I asked.

"No. If there were any on the pencil, they were washed away by the blood. And the crayon wrapper was too waxy and torn up to get anything."

"What about Jake? Why did he trip?" Jan was still looking for a connection.

"Well, it looks like he just tripped. All Ray had to say about it was, 'He tripped.' and not another word. I understand that low verbalization is a symptom of his condition. Is that right Dr. Beckman?"

"Yes. And it's quite typical of other patients we have with Autistic Spectrum Disorders."

"Yeah, I know. Jake doesn't say much either. 'My stuff' seemed to be about it."

"So that's it? You couldn't find anything? I know that a smile isn't much to go on, but I'll bet my PhD that he did it. I don't know how, but I *know!*"

"I didn't say I didn't have *anything* exactly. I said I didn't have anything to go on."

"Okay, so what have you got? I've got something too." I said.

"First, you said that Jake never plays with pencils. So, where did the pencil come from? It's an important question, since it killed Mr. Wheatly. Second, there were two Pacific Blue crayons in Jake's box. One was normal looking, and the other was partially crushed, presumably the one that Ted stepped on. So, we have another unanswered question. I guess the Crayola company could have made a packaging mistake. If not, where did the second, and apparently fatal, Pacific Blue crayon come from?" There was a pause while Jan and I considered the possibilities.

"And last, we have a witness that saw Ray shortly before the incident playing with something in his hand that might have been a pencil or a pen."

"Okay, here's what I've got." I said. "I don't know that it's anything except weird. I didn't say anything before because it was, well, too weird. It was weeks ago when I was visiting Ray, he tossed two crayons at once, and they both landed perfectly in their respective slots in the crayon box from about four feet away. I know what I saw, but it was just too weird to acknowledge as real. You know, like a magic trick or something." Lt. Boswick did the eyebrow thing again combined with a dismissive shrug.

"Hum. Interesting." Lt. Boswick did not seem very interested.

"But that's not all. We've been keeping an eye on Ray. Yesterday he was in the Rec room by himself. I was watching him from the hallway through the door hinge crack. He was playing pool by himself. He carefully racked the balls and pointed at a pocket. When he broke the balls, the eight ball dropped into the pocket he had pointed at. I heard him say, 'Eight ball in the corner pocket.' "

"So you're saying he's good at pool. I don't see how…"

"No, wait. That's not all. I continued watching him. He racked up the balls, and did it again on the next clockwise pocket. Then he did it again! And again! He dropped six eight balls in six sequential pockets, on six breaks, in a row." He had to be impressed with that.

Lt. Boswick did the eyebrow thing along with another shrug. "Okay, I correct myself. He's one *hell* of a pool player. I still don't see where that gets us." He was looking for bricks and mortar, not clouds and shadows.

"Just this, if he can toss crayons precisely into a crayon box from four feet away, and drop six eight balls into six selected pockets in a row, maybe he can throw a pencil so that it lands behind Ted's shoulder blades at exactly the right angle, at exactly the right time."

"Sure, and maybe he sprinkled fairy dust on the floor." Lt. Boswick was not above sarcasm. Indeed, he was proud of it. I was certain that his ex-wife would attest to this.

He wasn't even going to give me a courtesy eyebrow and a shrug. He just scoffed and shook his head. "You're supposed to be a professor, aren't you? How much did you say you paid for that PhD?" He chuckled at his own sardonic comment. Lt. Boswick did not have a college degree, and his ego made him question the intelligence of anyone who did.

"Alright. I know it would never fly in court, but it's something to consider, isn't it?"

"It wouldn't fly in a nut house, much less in a court house." This was not the first time he'd used this particular metaphor. He had stolen it from someone years ago, and kept it in his shirt pocket for easy access.

"Okay, here's how it's going in my report. Jake Hanson tripped and spilled his crayons and a pencil. He probably got the pencil from the Day Room supplies. At some point in time, he also acquired a second Pacific Blue crayon, probably also from the Day Room. We found seven sets of

Crayola crayons in the Day Room in various states of wear and completeness.

"Ray was seen sitting at least ten feet from Ted when the accident occurred. He was seen in the Rec room diddling with a pen or pencil. The object is thought to have been one of your green retractable pens, with the Institute's name and phone number stamped on it. Ray has often been observed playing with it before.

"Mr. Wheatly stepped and slipped on one of the crayons. He then fell backwards onto the pencil in such a way as to push the pencil into his back and through his heart, resulting in his immediate death.

"With all due respect for your *suspicions*, Dr. Martin, unless you show me some solid evidence to the contrary, I'm calling this an accident. An unusual accident, sure, but just an accident none the less." There was no "due respect" at all in his sarcastic tone.

"So, that's it? That's all you're going to do?" It was a rhetorical question on my part. I knew the answer.

Lt. Boswick didn't think I needed an answer. He chuckled again as he got up and took a step toward the door. "I've got to get back to the office. You've got my number. Call me if you come up with anything, ah, useful?" He left shaking his head.

"What an asshole!" That word, coming from Jan, surprised me. I hadn't notice that she had been quietly steaming for the last couple of minutes. "I don't care what *he* thinks. I think you're onto something. I don't know what exactly, but something."

"Yeah, maybe, but he's got a point. We don't have anything solid. We'll just need to keep a real close eye on Ray. Beyond that, I don't know what else we can do."

CHAPTER 24
SAL

Christmas at the Donaldson's had been idyllic, just like an old Saturday Evening Post magazine, complete with Norman Rockwell images of the season. We all sat around the fireplace on Christmas Eve, drinking eggnog, and telling stories of Christmases past, while we listened to classic Christmas songs.

We all got up way too early on Christmas morning, thanks to Becky. We exchanged gifts, but we shared much more than just trinkets. The real gift, we gave to each other, was love.

I was home. Despite all that may have happened, or all that would happen, we were family. I glowed from within, like Rudolph's nose, with the warmth of that knowledge.

The next morning, we were packed and on our way to Florida.

Our arrival at Tampa International Airport was uneventful. Becky had arranged for a moving company to meet us at the storage locker tomorrow afternoon giving her some time to sort and pack all of her stuff. First, we rented a car and checked into a nearby motel.

The first thing on Becky's agenda was to go to Chuck's attorney's office to take care of the divorce paperwork. Barclay & Barclay was the name on door, husband and wife, I found out later.

A husband and wife divorce attorney team seemed somewhat ironic to me. I wondered if witnessing the ugly side of failed marriages on a daily basis would serve to undermine, or to strengthen their own marriage vows.

I waited in the lobby while Becky went into the office. She emerged in only minutes. She wasn't smiling, but she wasn't crying either. I don't know what made me think of it, but she looked like someone leaving a restroom, business done, time to move on.

"Let's go." She said flatly.

"Everything taken care of?" I sent up a weather balloon.

Becky answered me indirectly. "Are you ready for lunch? I am. Let's go somewhere they have booze, okay?"

"Sounds good to me. How about that sports bar we passed down the road?"

"Sounds greasy, but I don't feel like a salad. Let's do it."

The menu was as greasy as Becky predicted. And, nachos was the closest thing to a salad that they offered. Burgers and fries seemed like the safest item, and hardest to screw up.

Becky ordered a beer with her burger. I ordered ice water. Grease and alcohol did not sit well on my stomach.

Besides, I would have ordered a more feminine mixed drink, if I ordered anything. Becky was the beer connoisseur and always had been. I never developed a taste for beer. I stuck mostly with what Becky referred to mockingly as "girly drinks."

Becky stayed mostly quiet until she finished her first beer just as our burgers arrived. She ordered a second beer, and dove into her meal.

The burgers were surprisingly good. They were perfectly grilled, seared on the outside, tender in the middle, not too thick, not too thin, on a fresh Kaiser roll, with all fresh toppings.

The fries were cut thin and deep fried in very hot oil, making them come out crispy and nearly dry of grease. Nothing special really, but it showed a level of pride that I didn't expect from what looked like a shoestring mom and pop establishment.

"Well, it's done." Becky started.

"Yup." I wanted her to let it out, whatever 'it' was.

She chewed quietly for a minute. "It's just hard. It's hard to say it, ya know. But, it's even harder to feel it. I mean, I know it's done. It's over! Signed, sealed and delivered, almost like it never happened. But I just don't feel it!" She took a big bite, chewed quickly, swallowed hard, and then washed it down with a big swig of beer.

It didn't work. She couldn't swallow her tears. Both eyes sprouted rivulets down each cheek. She *was* feeling it.

I wanted to say something, but what? I felt like I did when Robbie died, helplessly watching her pain. My own tears welled up.

She sat with her head in her hands for a minute. Then like she had flipped a switch, she quickly dried her eyes with her napkin. She took a deep breath and let it out forcefully, throwing her napkin on table.

"No! I'm not going to give him one more tear. He doesn't deserve it! I know I ain't perfect, but it wasn't *my* fault!

"They say it takes two to make a marriage. That's true. But ya know Sal, it only takes *one* to screw it up!" She downed the last of her second beer, and set the glass down hard on the table.

Like a judge with his gavel, pronouncing the end to any further dispute over the verdict. "It's done!" She said.

"That's right. He screwed it up. It's his fault. His loss." My voice was shaking more than hers.

"Let's talk about something else, anything." Becky raised her glass toward the passing waiter signaling that she needed another one. She caught his eye, and he acknowledged her request with a node.

"Okay." I said. She was waiting for me to come up with a subject. "I'm a little anxious about visiting Mr. Atkins, the last Bangkok virus victim."

"And…?"

"He's in an extended care facility not far from here. I still feel like I'm the one who put him there. I don't know what I'm going to say to him. I guess I could use a little moral support. Will you come in with me?"

"Sure." The waiter placed a fresh glass of beer in front of her and hurried off. "But, I disagree that it was your fault. I'll go if you promise you're going to try to find a way to help him, and *not* just to apologize. Where's the place? What's the number? Let's go there now."

"Well, ah, I thought I would go tomorrow, and…"

"No, you're stalling. We'll go today. Besides, I need your help packing tomorrow morning. Now, make the call." She took a swallow of beer, but kept her eyes on me.

She was right, I was stalling. "Okay. Okay. I'll call. Finish your beer."

The call was mostly a courtesy. I could have just stopped in unannounced. It's not like Leonard Atkins had any other plans.

We arrived at Reflections Extended Care Center thirty minutes later. It was a one story rambling building bordering a quiet residential neighborhood. The grounds were heavily wooded with one-hundred year old live oaks that were generously festooned with Spanish moss. It looked more like a southern style plantation than a medical facility.

I made Becky chew on a breath mint before we went in. I signed in using my official CDC credentials, and naming Becky as my "Assistant."

There was a release already on file for the CDC, so I was given full access to all of Mr. Atkins' files.

He had spent only a week in a coma before awakening. He had shown the same initial symptoms as the Miller and Grant cases in Seattle.

The registered nurse and Director of Patient Care for the facility, Linda Baird, explained that Mr. Atkins' condition had steadily improved since coming out of his coma. He continued to be non-verbal, but was able to write short notes, albeit notes that were often unreadable and/or incomprehensible. Ms. Baird said that Leonard spent most of his day rocking and painting.

"He started showing his artistic talents the first day we took him to the Day Room and gave him crayons and paper. His first work is there in his file." Ms. Baird opened the file and pulled out a finely detailed crayon rendering of herself.

"Wow! That looks just like you." The detail was amazing. She was a woman pushing sixty, and Leonard had not spared even her tiniest wrinkle or blemish. An eighth inch of untinted gray roots was faithfully depicted as well.

But beyond the vivid detail, she had been captured in a thoughtful pose that displayed her as a calm and caring professional. The essence of her personality seemed to almost waft from the paper, not unlike the light perfume she wore.

"I was reviewing some files when he drew it. It only took him about fifteen minutes. Pretty impressive for a first effort, huh?" She apparently did not mind the brutal honesty of the image. She even sounded a little flattered.

"I'll say. You said he paints too?" I asked.

"When we saw his talent, we gave him access to other mediums: charcoal, pastels, oils, and clay. But it's the Tempera watercolors that he likes best. His sister bought him a full set of supplies. He's recently started using some Indian ink accents too. Wait 'til you see his room. It's covered with his artwork.

"He's in our Day Room now, but I'll show you his room first. It's on the way. There's a local gallery that wants to have a showing." We walked toward Leonard's room while we continued talking.

"Did he have any artistic talent before the coma?"

"No. His sister says he wasn't even very talented at painting his house." She unlocked Leonard's door and opened it. The room was large. Except for one wall with a four foot square window, and a bathroom door, all available space was covered with watercolor paintings.

"Wow!" Becky's mouth was hanging open. "There's so many."

"There's a lot more, but we ran out of space. A few we display in the Day Room, but the rest we keep in his storage locker. He doesn't really seem to care if we hang them up or not. When he's done with a painting, he's done. He immediately starts working on another one."

I scanned the dozens of images, mostly facial portraits. "It's like I can feel what the person is feeling."

"Yeah, it's uncanny, isn't it?" There was a note of pride in her voice, as if he was her son.

"Are these all people at this facility?" I wanted to know if he was simply capturing the image, or creating it from scratch.

"Mostly, but not all. See these two here. His sister said they're of their deceased parents. And this one is his son Daryl, who lives in Oklahoma.

"Daryl hasn't been here to visit. Apparently, they haven't spoken for years. There's a divorced wife somewhere, but his sister's family, who live in the area, are the only close relatives he has." Yes, there was a tone of sadness there. She was one of those rare senior medical administrators who really did care, and one who had survived becoming jaded and cynical from years of seeing human pain and hopelessness buried under mountains of governmental regulation and bureaucracy. I hoped people could say the same about me in twenty years.

"Well, I think these should sell very well in a gallery." I'd seen a lot worse.

"The gallery Director, Mr. Hyatt, says that Leonard's work is quite sophisticated, but at same time "primal and elemental," whatever that means. He said his use of color and balance, and his background treatment is very advanced." Now, she was bragging.

Maybe it's not so bad. Maybe I've given him a new career. Maybe I didn't screw up his life that badly.

Nurse Baird locked Leonard's door as we left. I noticed that all the other rooms were locked as well. The doors could be easily opened from the inside. It was a policy intended to insure security while preserving residents' freedom to move about as they wished. But locked doors always made me feel confined, especially in a long hallway full of them.

Leonard was sitting in front of an easel next to several large windows. He was working quickly, intently, almost feverishly. There were three completed paintings drying on a nearby table.

Nurse Baird introduced us. Leonard looked up and glanced at me first, then Becky, and then back to his work. There was no change in his expression. No smile. Nothing.

Linda explained. "Dr. Salinger and Ms. Becky are from The Centers for Disease Control. They want to see how you are doing. They like your paintings very much."

Leonard again glanced from me to Becky. This time he nodded in the affirmative, and looked back to his work. No smile. We were clearly an unwelcome distraction.

"Well, I can see that Leonard is busy right now. Perhaps you can come back at dinner time." Ms. Baird took a few steps away, shooting me a look that invited us to follow.

She whispered, "He doesn't like to be interrupted while he's working. His psychiatrist says it's OCD, Obsessive Compulsive Disorder. He really *can't* stop painting unless he needs to go to the bathroom, or when he's too hungry or too tired to continue." I didn't need to be told what OCD was.

I felt sick. "That's okay. We just wanted to meet him and see his new-found talent." I just wanted to leave.

"We could come back later Sal, if you want." Becky didn't get it. I wanted to get out of there before I lost it. The air suddenly felt depleted of oxygen, like I was breathing into a paper bag.

"Maybe we can come back another day. We've got a very busy schedule today." We had absolutely nothing on our schedule for the rest of the day.

Only Becky could hear the slight quaver in my voice. She got it. "Oh, yeah. Okay, That's right. We can come back another day… when we're not so busy." Only I could hear the question mark in her voice.

Director Baird looked a little puzzled at my sudden rush. "Anytime. You really don't need to call. I'll give you a copy of his file. If there is anything else the CDC needs, or if you have any questions, just let me know. You have my card."

We signed out and I hurried to the car.

"What's wrong?" Becky knew my moods, sometimes better than I wanted her to.

"He's a cripple, and I made him that way!"

"Oh Christ! Are we gonna do this again? He's an artistic genius is what he is. Isn't that a good thing? What's the problem?" A short deliberate sigh punctuated her exasperation.

"Look Becky." I needed to take a deep breath. *I screwed up. Knowing what I did is one thing. Seeing it is something else.*

"That man creates some really nice paintings. Hell, he might even end up making a bunch of money off his paintings. But the thing is… he doesn't have a *choice!* You heard her, OCD. I took that choice away from him. He doesn't even look like he's having fun. Not to mention he can't talk and he can't live on his own. His life, as he knew it, is over!" I pulled a tissue from my purse and dabbed my eyes before they could overflow.

Becky was quiet for a minute. She instinctively understood the power of timing. She should have gone into sales. "Okay, so what are you going to do about it?"

I shook my head. "I don't think there *is* anything I can do about it."

"Maybe you can't fix Mr. Atkins back there, but what about the next one?"

"'The next one' what?"

"The next victim of the Bangkok flu, or whatever the next bug of the month is."

"What do you mean? I'll do my job the best I can, I guess."

"Will you? Are you now? I don't think giving up when things go wrong is part of your job description. Do you know *everything* there is to know about this bug? Are you as ready as you can be to do *everything* possible, if this virus, or something like it, pops up again? Why are you doing this working-off-the-clock thing anyway? Just so that you can make a self-pity stop? Or, are you really gonna try to *do something* to help Mr. Atkins?

"And, what about all the other people who might need an over-educated Blondie Girl who might just save their lives? *If*, she can get over whatever she thinks she didn't do before, and can concentrate on what she *can* do *now*?"

I was quiet, thinking. She was quiet, letting me think. Timing, logic, *and* silence, a born salesman for sure.

Becky had a sometimes irritating way of seeing the heart of things, and laying it out with just the right words. Becky's reference to "Blondie Girl" was intended to remind me of my daddy. It did. Daddy also used to be able say the right things whenever I needed someone who I trusted to tell me what I didn't want to hear.

A friend is someone who can tell you you're wrong, and still be your friend. *Damn it, she's right. I have to DO something!*

"Okay." I took a deep cleansing breath. "I'm ready now. Thanks." I dug my phone out of my purse, pulled up my contacts list, and hit the speed dial button next to "Rose – Cell.'

CHAPTER 25
RAY

I was lying on my bed at the Institute taking in all the voices, sounds, vibrations and smells that came into my room through the partially open door. I was practicing at directing my focus. That was the key.

An image of Julie popped into my head, as it often did. Usually, I would struggle to push thoughts of Julia out of my mind. It was far too distracting when I was trying to concentrate. But this time I embrace the memory of *her*. It was like a dam breaking, flooding me with everything Julia. I let her memory wash over me like warm waves on a tropical beach.

We had a discussion one evening during our trip to Japan. We had talked about the future. We decided we would have two children, boys or girls. It didn't matter.

We would work hard and save our money. I worked as software programmer then. She worked as teacher for an Eastside elementary school. It seemed so long ago, but so vivid, like it was yesterday.

We would buy a house, and move out of that cramped apartment on Bel-Red Road. The Eastgate area was okay, but we had our eye on the more upscale neighborhoods overlooking Lake Washington: Yarrow Point, Meydenbauer Bay, or maybe even Medina, Bill Gates' neighborhood.

We knew we probably wouldn't be able to afford our ultimate dream house right away. We figured we might have to buy two or three stepping-stone houses first. We had gone to a couple Open House's, in those neighborhoods, just for fun. We got to look at a couple one-million-dollar-plus lake-front properties. As long as we had each other, anything was possible.

At one point in our conversation Julia had said, "Okay, so we work, we bring up some great kids, we make lots of money, then we retire comfortably and play with the grandkids. Is that it?"

"Yup! Sounds good to me."

"No, I mean, isn't there more? Shouldn't there be more?"

"More? Yes, then we'll live happily ever after. Isn't that what it's all about, the pursuit of happiness?"

"I don't know. Is it? I mean, don't you think we should try to leave something more than money and kids behind when we're gone?"

"Like what?"

"Like, I don't know, something."

"Give me a hint."

"Okay, well like Alexander Graham Bell. He gave us the telephone. Where would we be without that?"

"We'd have cell phones." I chuckled.

"No, I'm serious. I mean maybe like Abraham Lincoln, the Emancipation Proclamation and all that. Even Herman Melville gave us Moby Dick." She giggled. "But, you know, something to make the world a better place."

"How old are you? Are you sure you didn't grow up in the sixties, peace and love and all that?" I laughed as I made the two-fingered peace salute.

"Ha ha. I don't think so. I don't even like paisley. But, wouldn't it be great for our grandkids to be able to say, 'Yup, old grandpa and grandma, they made the world a better place?'"

"Alright. I agree. That *would* be nice, but just how do you propose we do that?"

"I don't know. There's so much evil and so many bad things that happen in the world. There's plenty of room for improvement, that's for sure. We don't have to know yet. We just need to have it as a goal and keep our eyes open for an opportunity."

"Okay, we'll grab the first opportunity that we see *to make the world a better place."* I laughed. "I love you."

"I'm not kidding!" I could see that she was not kidding. "Promise me we'll at least try."

"I promise. I will try to find a way to make the world a better place. And, I still love you!"

###

It was a promise that I could not, and would not forget. But, there is so much bad in the world. Where do I start?

Does it matter? Ted was bad and stupid too. The world was a better place without him. All the people connected to that flu on the plane were bad. If they contributed to Julia's death in any way, they were bad. Certainly, I could eliminate them from the world.

What about Dr. Martin and Dr. Beckman. They want to stop me. They want to stop me from eliminating bad people.

They didn't know I could hear them talking to Lt. Boswick. "Weird," they said. They're going to keep "a close eye" on me. I needed to leave soon. But first I needed to wrap things up. *That's right. I just need to wrap up a little business.*

I became aware of a faint smell, similar to flatulence, but not quite. It's amazing how often people fart. It permeated all of the indoor air. I had gotten used to the smell and just ignored it.

But this was different. It was purer, artificial. It took me a second to identify it. It had to be natural gas laced with methyl mercaptan, to make the otherwise odorless methane easier to detect. I remember reading about this somewhere. The level was very faint, even for me. I was sure no one else could smell it.

I decided to track down its source. I ambled down the long west wing residential hallway, through the dayroom, past the Rec room, and into the large dining room. No one was in the dining room at the time. It was past breakfast, and lunch preparation wouldn't begin for another hour.

The smell was coming from the kitchen. The kitchen door was open. As I approached, I could hear a faint hissing, very faint. I held my breath and focused on the sound. I could almost see it. It was the main shutoff valve.

At this distance, I could smell the brass fitting. The pilot lights were lit, but had a different sound and smell.

No one was in the dining room or the kitchen. I could hear no one in the hallway or anywhere nearby. I ducked quickly into the kitchen through the open door. It took me only a second to find the faulty valve. *There it is.*

The valve was cracked. The crack went through the entire body of the valve. An x-ray would have revealed the crack, but I was sure it was invisible to anyone else's visual inspection. I could see it.

The crack looked like it had been there since it was originally cast, but it had gone unnoticed for years, and probably would continue to go harmlessly unnoticed. *Unless.* The dust on the valve handle showed that it had not been touched in a very long time. *I can change that.*

I left the kitchen as quickly as I had entered. Only seconds had passed. I was sure no one had seen me. I had touched nothing, nor did I need to.

People are things too, things that I can control. Cause and effect.

CHAPTER 26
SAL

"I called my Momma while you were in the restroom, and let her know that we're taking a little detour to Seattle. I told her to expect my stuff to arrive in a couple days." Becky said.

We were waiting in the airport concourse to board the fight to Seattle.

"Was she surprised?"

"Not as much as I expected. She told us to have fun and to send her a postcard. A postcard? I think she thinks we're going on a sightseeing tour, or something."

"Maybe she's just tired of you moping around the house, and would be glad to see you go anywhere but home." I grinned to let her know I was just ribbing her. She wasn't moping today. She was excited about going on an "adventure," as she called it.

She ignored the jab. Another thought had taken priority. "Hey, maybe we *can* do a little sightseeing, if we get some free time. Ya think?"

"Sure, *if* we get…" My phone rang.

"It's Rose. She said she'd call me when she got all the files together."

I touched the talk button. "Hi Rose! Did you get everything?"

"Hi! Yes, I encrypted everything like you said, and sent all the files to your private email. How are you doing?"

"Becky and I are doing fine. We took care of her business in Tampa. I visited Mr. Atkins. We should be in Seattle by six this evening local time."

"Dr. Edelman hasn't gotten wind about what you're doing for me, has he?"

"No. I'm only gonna work on your stuff while he's out of the office, just to be safe. Oh, I just got an update on Mr. Miller from Dr. Martin at the Behavioral Health Institute in Seattle."

"I thought she knew I was going to Seattle?"

"Yes, she does. I left her a message. She called me back to confirm. She says that there have been some *developments,* as she put it, with his case."

"What kind of *developments?*"

"She wouldn't get specific. She said she would give you all the details when you get there. She mentioned something about the death of one of her janitors. She didn't say specifically, but I got the impression that she thinks Mr. Miller had something to do with it." Rose's impressions were usually ninety-nine percent accurate. She had often demonstrated her gift for hearing what wasn't said.

"Really! Now, that's interesting. Anything else?"

"She said that you need to meet with both her and the psychologist who's been working with Mr. Miller. His name is Dr. Hector C. Beckman. He's also is a professor at Washington State University. I sent you his info and phone number."

"Okay, great! I'll call them tomorrow morning. Thanks a bunch! You're the best!"

"Damn straight, girl! An' don' you fuget'at. You go'a buy me a big juzzy steak 'en you get back'n town." Rose let some of her at-home hood slang slip in, just to let me know that she was having fun being my "girl frien' " and co-conspirator.

"You're on! I'll keep you updated." I hung up with a chuckle. She reminded me that I missed being around the office. I missed the action, the people.

Becky's curiosity was piqued by the half of the conversation that she could hear. "What's going on? What *developments?* What's *interesting?*"

"We may be dealing with a murder." I said dramatically with an artificially sinister smile. Becky saw through my semi-playful facade, and her eyes widened.

Maybe it would turn out to be nothing. But something told me, *maybe not.*

CHAPTER 27
HECK

Jan called me while I was on my way driving to the Institute.

I wanted to spend some quality time with Tyler. I had planned a day out together. First, I thought I'd take him to a local park playground. Then, we could go to the local fast food joint and get him a Kids Meal with a toy. I'd probably break down and get him an ice cream too. He'd usually get about half way through his meal before he would start chanting, "'ceam, 'ceam." This was one of the few words he used on a regular basis.

Tyler loved the swings at the playground, and would stay on them all day if I didn't get tired of pushing him. I encouraged him to play on other playground equipment too, like the slide and the playhouse.

The playhouse was an environment where he could interact with other children. They would often try to interact with him, but he would mostly ignore them. Although on a few occasions, I had observed him acknowledging other children and having minimal exchanges. It was a start. Baby steps, I told myself. Maybe, with time and persistence he could gain some social skills that would make his life easier and more fulfilling.

I hit the talk button on my cell phone. "Hey, Jan."

"Hello, Heck. I wanted to catch you before you got here to pick up Tyler."

"Well, you caught me. What's up?"

"I have a new prospective patient, Anna Grant. She's here for a tour and initial interview. Remember, we talked about her?"

"Yes, I do. She's the other surviving Bangkok flu victim here in Seattle, like Ray Miller."

"I'd like you to meet her today so that you can give me your assessment. Like we discussed, she'll be your case while she's here." She said.

"I've been looking forward to meeting her. I want to see how alike, or different, her case is from Ray's. But I wanted to get going early with Tyler. How long a meeting did you have in mind?"

"Well, I can do the tour part without you. I just wanted you to be here for the interview. It shouldn't take more than a half an hour, or so."

"Okay. How'd she get there? I didn't think she was able to drive."

"She has a caregiver who drove her from West Seattle."

I arrived at the Institute shortly after Jan had completed her tour of the facilities.

"Go right in Dr. Beckman, they're in her office."

The receptionist was new. I had been introduced, but I couldn't remember her name. Was it Linda, or Lindsey, or maybe Lacy? I didn't want to guess wrong, so I just said, "Thank you."

Jan glanced up as I entered the open door of her office. "Oh, Dr. Beckman, come in please and join us." I noted the somewhat formal greeting and took it to mean that she wanted to keep things on a professional note. I was instantly self-conscious of my casual attire, consisting of a short sleeve print shirt and jeans with beat up hiking boots.

Jan provided the visitors with an explanation. "Dr. Beckman is picking up his son who is also a resident here. He wasn't expecting to meet with you today, but I asked him to stop in for a moment. Dr. Beckman is our staff psychologist, specializing in Autism Spectrum Disorders."

There were two fiftyish women seated in front of Jan's desk. One was in a wheelchair. I assumed she must be Ms. Grant. I nodded. Both women were waiting for Jan's introduction.

"This is Anna Grant, and this is Karen Wilson, Anna's caregiver."

I shook both their hands in turn. "I'm very glad to meet you." They both smiled their acknowledgment.

I immediately noted two differences between Anna and Ray. Ray rarely smiled, especially not when greeting someone. And, he would never voluntarily shake anyone's hand.

Jan took the lead. "I'd like to start by bringing everyone up to speed. First, Dr. Beckman has been working with Ray the other surviving case of the Bangkok Flu who is also a resident here. I didn't see him on our tour, but I'm sure you will meet him at some point.

"Ms. Grant, can you please tell us about your experience and about your current condition?" Jan wanted to see a demonstration of Anna's verbal ability. At the same time, Jan wanted to avoid a discussion *about* Anna's condition, preferring a discussion *with* her about it. She wanted to get right to business, but to set the right tone. The corners of my mouth turned up slightly with my admiration of Jan's skills as a therapist.

Psychologist and psychiatrist can sometimes be skeptical of each other's different patient perspectives. Psychologists are sometimes thought to be too touchy feely and not sufficiently schooled in the physiological causes of psychosis. But, psychologists sometimes distrust psychiatrists' understanding of the human side of psychological abnormalities. Jan was an expert in both fields.

Anna was caught a little off balance by Jan's question. "Well, I don't know what you need to know."

"Just start at the beginning. What happened on the plane?"

"I don't remember everything. It was terrible. Everyone was getting sick. We did the best we could, but people were..." She trailed off, starring at remembered visions of the events on the plane. Her verbal faculties seemed to have escaped any obvious damage.

"And then, you got sick too. Is that right?"

"I tried to help everyone. My head was throbbing, and everything was spinning."

She paused, reliving the haunting events in her mind's eye. She shook her head quickly as she said, "That's all I can remember."

I had observed other patients who unconsciously used a physical action to symbolically rid their minds of a painful thought or memory. Sometimes it was just a head shake, like Anna's, sometimes a shrug. Sometimes it was a whole-body shake or shiver.

Jan picked up on this too. "Okay. We know there were a lot of people suffering on that plane. And, a lot of people would die. But, you helped those people too, for as long as you could. You did the best you could under the circumstances, and you made it better for everyone.

"What about in the hospital? What was it like when you woke up from the coma?"

"I don't remember much when I first woke up. I remember screaming. I was tied up. I remember the nurse giving me a shot. Then, I remember dreaming. Only, it wasn't a dream. It was… how can I explain it? It was sort of like shaking a large jar half filled with pennies. Only, the jar was my head, and the pennies were words and letters. It wouldn't stop. It just kept going and going." Her eyes glassed over in a stare.

"Anna, I'm just trying to understand. The words and letters, were they images? Could you see them? Can you tell us any more about that part of your experience?" I asked. This was something that was completely new to anything I had ever heard or read about.

"I've tried to explain it to people. It's just too *big*. I guess that's one word. Maybe *infinite* is a better one. It was like I was in a universe of darkness being bombarded by words and letters. But they weren't anything I could see exactly, I felt them."

"You say it was dark. Do you mean like someone turned off the lights?" I remembered a terrifying darkness too. Was her darkness the same one I had experienced?

"No. It was dark and light at the same time. It was dark like a sort of nothingness, but the nothingness was everything too. I know that sounds crazy. I think maybe I was crazy."

"How did it stop? You're not having those *visions,* or whatever, now are you?" I had taken control of the discussion. Jan had no objection to the transfer of leadership.

"I think the drugs have helped. I still see flashes of letters and words, but now it's only when I want to see them."

"Why would you *want* to see the flashes?"

Her answer was slow in coming. "They tell me things." It was something she hadn't planned to talk about.

"I don't understand. Do they talk to you? What *things* do they tell you?

"No. They don't talk to me. I don't hear voices or anything like that. I just know things." She seemed uncomfortable with where the discussion had gone, embarrassed even.

"I'm sorry. I don't want to upset you. But the more I know about your condition, the more I will be able to help you." Well, maybe. But my motivation at that moment was sheer professional curiosity. For anyone who studies the workings of the human brain, this was fascinating.

Karen spoke up. "She doesn't want you to think she's a psychic or some kind of mystic or anything. She doesn't like to brag, but she can tell you things that nobody else knows. And she's always right!" Anna had turned a half shade redder.

"Really? Are you saying she's a fortune teller?" I smiled like it might be a joke.

Anna was quick to speak for herself. "No, I'm not a *fortune teller*. I just see words that tell me about people."

"She reads people. Just like a palm reader, except she uses letters. I brought them along. I thought you might want to see. She unscrambles letters, sorta like an anagram."

Karen leaned toward Jan and I, cupping her hand beside her mouth, and said in a semi-hushed tone, "Please don't call her… ah... *that* name. She hates it." It took me a second to fill in the blank. Jan smiled slightly. She got it a half a second before I did. I nodded my head once to assure Karen that we would not make that particular faux pas.

Anna pretended not to have heard Karen. "I told you to leave those letters at the house." Anna was more self-conscious than angry, like a young girl who's shy about wearing that tiny bikini in public for the first time.

It was too late. "Show them, Anna." Karen said. Emboldened now, she reached into her handbag. It was an oversized purse almost the size of a diaper bag that held a host of womanly items. She pulled out a quart-sized leather bag with a draw string, and set it on the small coffee table between the two visitor chairs.

I said, "I'd like to see how it works, if it's okay with you. Maybe you can just do the short version for us." I didn't believe in psychic readers of any kind. This sounded like a new twist on the old delusional pursuit of fortune telling.

"Okay, okay. Just a quick look." She had a coy smile. She was like a child prodigy violinist, who had to be coaxed into doing a private recital, but who was secretly thrilled to have an audience.

She moved her wheelchair closer to the table and picked up the bag. "I have four sets of Scrabble letter tiles. I need to get all the letters of your name. Can you write down your full name just the way you spell it, please." She looked at me.

"Oh! You want me to do it." I wrote H-e-c-t-o-r-C-l-i-n-t-o-n-B-e-c-k-m-a-n on a piece of note paper and gave it to her.

"I'll help." Karen dumped a couple hands full of letters onto the table and began to sort through them picking out the letters of my name.

When all the letters had been found, Karen scooped up the remainder and dumped them back into the leather bag.

I glanced at Jan. She sat expectantly wide-eyed. She had nothing to say.

Working with Jan had been educational as well as enjoyable. She seemed to always know what *not* to say, and when *not* to say it. This was a talent I admired, and one I hoped to improve on. I took Jan's lead and let Anna proceed unquestioningly.

"Dr. Beckman, I need you to hold all the letters of your name in your hand." I extended my open hand, and she deposited the letters carefully.

"First, I want you to think about events in your past. Anything at all.

"While you're thinking about your past, cup the letter tiles with your other hand and shake them up." I complied.

I didn't know what to think about, so I just let my mind wander.

"Now, hold the letters with your right hand and hold my hand with your left." Her hands were cold, small and frail.

"Okay, give me a second. When I say, dump the letters onto the table." She closed her eyes and inhaled.

She exhaled slowly and said, "Now."

I dropped the tiles onto the table from about six inches. They bounced and clattered, and finally came to rest in a rough circle about a foot in diameter.

Approximately half of the tiles had landed letter-side down. Anna carefully turned each of these over, leaving them in their same location and orientation. She did not attempt to turn the letters in any one direction.

She studied the letters for a few seconds, then finally said, "H-E-R-O, H-I-K-E."

She pointed at the letters. "See, right here." Indeed, the letters she indicated did read, "HERO HIKE.'

"Do you know what that means?" She asked as she glanced squarely into my eyes. There was something deeply penetrating, something knowing in her gaze.

"I have no idea." I lied and shrugged. It had to be just a coincidence.

"Let's see if there's more to see. Toss the letters again."

I picked up the letters and we repeated the process. I shook the letters. She took my hand. She closed her eyes. There was another pause before she gave the word. The letters clattered. She carefully turned over a few. It all seemed a bit too theatrical to me.

I looked at the letters. I saw nothing at first. I waited for her.

"There it is, see. A-N-K-L-E, T-O-M, and B-R-O-K-E-N. Do know anyone named Tom?" She caught my eye with that deep gaze again.

"Well yes, I have a friend named Tom." Jan had met Tom, but I couldn't remember if I had told her about the Mt. Rainier incident. I told very few people about it, and only when it came up. It just came up.

"And, did he ever have a broken ankle?"

"Yes, he did." I was determined not to volunteer anything.

I had read about cold reading techniques where a so called "psychic reader" could infer information with only small clues, deductive reasoning, and cleverly worded questions. The target, or mark, is lead to think that the reader has access to secret information, when in fact the target is unknowingly supplying the reader with all the clues he needs.

"*Now,* do you understand how the HERO HIKE ties in?" It sounded like she already knew the answer and was challenging me to admit it.

"We went for a hike on Mt. Rainier. Tom fell and broke his ankle. I helped him get back. The newspaper exaggerated the story and called me a *hero.*" I was feeling a little uncomfortable, like the room temperature had just gone up five degrees.

I wanted to stop. But before I could find a plausible reason to stop, we were repeating the process. It was just a game, I told myself. I remembered my friends and me playing a similar game with an Ouija board when I was a kid. We wouldn't let Nan play because she was too little, she laughed too much, and she pushed the pointer around like it was a toy car. But, she hung around bugging us anyway.

I tossed the letters.

"Oh my. B-L-A-M-E, N-O-T, and T-O. Who's *not to blame,* and for what? Oh wait, is that a name, N-A-N, crossing the A? Maybe a nickname? See?"

"I had a sister, Nancy. We called her Nan for short. She died in an accident when I was a kid. I blamed myself for a while. That could be it." I must have given her a clue, but what?

"Yes, I'm sure that's it." I watched her eyes. She flashed me that look of hers. It said that she was sure.

"You are a very good subject, Dr. Beckman. I can see more than usual. Do you want to continue?" Was that another challenge?

"Ah, okay. Sure." I told myself that this exercise was a way of building rapport with the patient. I've played cards or other games with patients before as an evaluation tool. This was just another game. Besides, I wanted to figure out what the trick was. Of course, there must be a trick of some kind.

"Think of another event in your past." Anna was confident now. She was giving a show. Karen looked on with a smug expression. She had seen the show before.

We went through exactly the same process again. She studied the letters and said, "B-L-A-C-K, C-H-O-I-C-E. What does that mean?"

"I'm not sure." I didn't want to be sure.

"It sometimes takes a few tosses to fill in the gaps."

I tossed the letters again. She studied them and said, "N-O-T, C-H-A-N-C-E. And here crossing the A again, like a crossword. B-E-A-R. Did you have a Teddy bear?" She smiled ruefully. She knew. I could see in her eyes that she knew that it was not about a stuffed toy.

I glanced at Jan. Of course, she knew all about the bear in my past, but his name was not Teddy.

"I had a run-in with a bear in Alaska. Maybe that's it. I don't know about the rest." I knew all about the rest. For an instant, I was there again, floating in the blackness, my whimsical choice to live or die. Was it chance that I lived? *Was it fate?*

"That's okay. Sometimes the meaning is not clear until later."

"Read some of his future." Karen chimed in like a cheerleader from the sidelines.

"No. I'm sure Dr. Beckman has had enough for now. Do you want to go on?" She had an odd way of asking a question that seemed like a challenge. There was something almost mocking in her tone, but nothing specific I could pin down. Maybe it was only my interpretation. On the surface she sounded only cordial and polite.

"Please continue. This is very interesting." This was from Jan. It may have been directed at Anna, but she was looking at me. I felt like I was being stripped naked, one piece of clothing at a time.

"Okay." I said with less enthusiasm than Jan showed. I didn't want to seem like a party pooper, and quit now.

"This time, I want you to try to think of nothing at all. Just let your mind drift." Her tone was soothing now, like a hypnotist."

The first toss brought a broad smile from Anna. I saw it too this time. C-H-E-C-K, L-O-T-T-O, and I-N-C-O-M-E.

"This is a very strong reading. It looks like you're going to come into some money." She looked like she believed it. I didn't. This had to be the number one fortune she told to everyone. I didn't know how she made the letters line up like that, but it was all too convenient.

"I'll bet you say that to all the boy's." I said with a crooked grin. Anna laughed openly at my joke, and gave me that knowing glance of hers that made me feel even more naked.

Jan was writing. Anna noticed her, and said, "Yes, you should write everything down. The trouble with the future is that you can't prove it until it's the past. You can't be sure of the future, and you can't be sure of what the words that I see will mean. It could be years. And memory being what it is, you should write down everything.

The tosses came in quick succession now, since there was no point in discussing what words meant. Nothing seemed to make any sense. It's like Nostradamus' quatrains, general enough to mean anything, or nothing, but specific enough to make it seem like it means something important.

The longest string was, L-I-N-K, T-O, T-H-E, C-R-E-A-T-O-R. Huh? Followed by: T-A-K-E, H-E-R, H-A-N-D, and M-A-L-E, H-E-I-R, B-O-R-N.

The last three seemed like warnings: K-I-N, I-N, H-E-A-T. N-O, T-I-M-E, and B-R-A-K-E, H-I-M.

"Notice that word is "brake, as in stop, not "break" as in separate. I think that's important somehow." She was obviously ready and willing to continue.

I wasn't. "Okay, I think that's enough for now. Thank you very much Anna. That was, ah, fun! But, I'm going to need to get going. Tyler is waiting for me."

Jan raised her hand with her index finger extended. "Just one other thing, Anna. I see that you're using a wheelchair. Are you able to walk at all? We have wheelchair accessible rooms of course, but I want to know if we will need to make other accommodations for you."

"Well yes, I can walk, but I fall a lot. The doctors call it pre…or pri…something. Here, I wrote it down." She fumbled for her purse.

"Propioception." Karen volunteered, before Anna could locate her notes from the hospital.

"Oh yes, I remember reading about that in JAMA a while back. I don't have any experience with it though." Jan looked at me to see if I knew anything. I had heard of it somewhere, but had forgotten the details.

Seeing that I wasn't going to be any help, Jan continued reviewing her understanding of the condition for my benefit, if not for Anna's. "It's a type of SPD, Sensory Processing Disorder. SPD's are like traffic jams in the brain causing a person to inappropriately respond to stimuli.

"Proprioception, a form of SPD, is when you have trouble correctly perceiving your body position in space. It's rare, but it can be caused by brain trauma.

"Do you have trouble walking when you're not looking at your feet?" Jan asked.

"As long as I don't take my eyes off my feet, I can walk okay. But if I look up to see where I'm going, I fall down."

"How about your hands?"

"It's the same thing, except I don't fall down. I just drop things, if I'm not watching my hands."

"I believe there are specific therapies for this condition. Did the hospital refer you to anyone?"

"No. They mentioned something about therapy, but I didn't get a referral." Anna said.

"I'll look into it for you. We should be able to arrange for a physical therapist, trained in this area, to see you on a regular basis."

"I'm sorry I have to run, but Tyler gets cranky if he's expecting me and has to wait too long. It was nice to meet you, and I'm looking forward to seeing you after you move in."

"Don't forget your reading notes." Jan said, and handed me a piece of note paper. I folded it and stuck it in my shirt pocket. I shook hands with Anna and Karen and left.

I grabbed Tyler's "go bag" from his closet, containing extra clothes, road toys, snacks, water, medications, diapers, and miscellaneous items such as wipes, tissues, safety pins, bandages, etc. Many things I rarely, or never, had occasion to used. But, you never know.

Better to take it and not need it, than to need it and not have it. I learned that lesson the hard way. Tyler was fully capable of creating an unpleasant situation of the worst kind, in the worst place, and at the worst time.

I had tossed out the baby blue pastel flowered diaper bag that Wendy had bought when Tyler was a newborn. I picked this one out myself. It was made of a plain brown fake leather vinyl material. It looked like it could be a professional satchel of some kind, or a piece of carry-on luggage. I didn't like to *call* it a diaper bag, but that's what it was.

Changing diapers? No problem. Hey, if you've got kids, you do what you have to do. But carrying a baby-style bag around, that *looks* like a diaper bag, I saw that as a wholly unnecessary degradation of my manliness.

That was the down side of having a kid. On the upside, was seeing the world fresh through your kid's eyes. Tyler's somewhat skewed and but innocent view of the world was a joy to see. He loved sitting on my lap while I read stories to him. It was one of the few times I could get him to sit on my lap for more than a few seconds. One book about a wayward fire-breathing dragon was his favorite, I think more for the illustrations than anything. He made me read it over and over. Sometimes I would add sound effects and act out the scene to make it less repetitive.

As I took Tyler out the front door of the Institute, he reached for me to pick him up. I carried him to the car. I normally made him walk. My leg was still not one-hundred percent, and he was no longer a light-weight. He was usually not the most affectionate kid, but today he seemed more willing than usual to be carried and hugged. So despite the extra pain in my leg, carrying him was a pleasure.

When we got to the park, Tyler ran ahead of me, straight to the swings. It took him a few seconds to clamor into the sling-style seat. When I caught up with him, he was rocking back and forth grunting, waiting for a push. He had not yet learned how to pump his legs like the other kids.

"Alright buddy. Are you ready?" I pulled him backward to my chest level and then pushed him forward. He let out a squeal as he reached the swing's apogee, hovering for an instant before returning for the next push.

I knew from many previous visits to the playground that he would continue to let out a squeal on every cycle of the swing until he became tired or bored. When the squeals stopped, it was my signal that he was ready to stop swinging and do something else. But, this could take quite a while.

When I pushed him in the swing, I would talk to him, sometimes just a word or exclamation. Sometimes, I would make comments about other kids, squirrels, the weather, anything. It didn't really matter. He understood very little of what I said, but he understood that I was talking to him. That was what was important. Like any baby, if he was to learn language, he needed to hear language. Tyler was just going to take a little longer than most.

Nan liked to swing too. Maybe that's why I thought of her just then. My thoughts of her had become less frequent over the years. The words that Anna had *seen* spurred more memories of my long gone sister. *Not to blame.*

###

She was not much older than Tyler when she died. I was only fourteen. Mom thought I was old enough to be left in charge of Nan from time to time.

"Hector, look after your sister." This dreaded order was like a jail sentence that I didn't deserve, complete with shackles, and a ball and chain.

I saw the world through a boy's eyes then. It wasn't fair that I couldn't go play with my friends. It wasn't fair that I had to make excuses for her when my friends came by.

I loved her then. I know that now. But it took her death and years of growing up, to make me realize it. At the time, I thought of her only as a chore, a nuisance, and an embarrassment.

Today, she would be diagnosed as autistic, or more properly with Autistic Spectrum Disorder. Back then, a lot less was known about autism. Most people lumped her condition in with others children with developmental disabilities, and simply called her "retarded."

Unlike Tyler, Nan was more verbal, more affectionate, and she smiled all the time. I remember that innocent exuberant smile of hers. It was a smile that proclaimed a joyous world, one that she alone inhabited. In fact, it was her smiling for no apparent reason, and talking to herself while she played alone, that was embarrassing to me when my friends were around.

To add to my embarrassment, Nan was more than a little plump. Her sweet tooth knew no limit. Mom tried to hide the goodies, but Nan could sniff out a cookie at fifty yards.

To add to her weight problem, she had been put on Depakote to treat her epileptic seizures. It was effective. She was having grand mal seizures once or twice a week until she started on the medication. They went down to one only every few months, but in her case the drug benefits came with a side effect, a significant weight gain.

I should have defended her from the cruel and ignorant names the other kids called her. Their favorite was, Lardo Tardo. This was deemed by the hecklers as a more eloquent insult than the previous, Fatso Retard.

The kid who invented this new insult was duly acclaimed by his fellow antagonists. I had imagined he might have grown up to be a great poet. He might have gone into advertising. Or, my favorite fantasy was that he died in a bar fight at the hands of the unappreciative target of his sardonically poetic skills. One can only hope that karma had the final word.

For my part, I'd either say nothing, or worse, I'd sometimes throw in my own slurs. Albeit, nothing quite so catchy.

My egocentric childhood mind rationalized my childish attitudes. To defend her, would have been an endorsement of her afflictions. And by association, they would become mine. Her shame would be my shame. Thus, is the rationale of a young teenage boy.

But then, she was never ashamed. She was blessed with the inability to be shamed. The slurs and insults thrown at her never hurt her. Instead, they only secretly hurt me.

As I matured, I eventually realized that it had always been *my* shame that was the problem−first, my misplaced shame of her, then later, my shame of myself. Would karma someday knock on my door, too?

Of course, kids will be kids, and I was just a kid. You can't blame me, right? It was a question I had asked myself for a long time. I never got an answer I liked, so I stopped asking, until today.

Not To Blame.

CHAPTER 28
RAY

I met Oscar, the Kitchen Manager, in the hallway on his way to begin lunch preparations.

"I shouldn't eat the beans today, they'll give me gas." I said with no introduction.

He gave me a peculiar look, smiled awkwardly and said, "Yeah," and continued on his way. Oscar was apparently used to residents saying odd things at odd times. He must think that it's best to just humor us, and let the medical staff deal with the *crazies*.

I understood Oscar. I had been watching him for days. He was a simple man in many ways. Suggestible. Pliable. Steerable.

My comment that morning was specifically designed for his ears: the exact words, the exact cadence, the exact tone. I had been prepping him for days with small comments and actions, not overtly directed at him, but that were designed to register in his subconsciousness.

The human mind is not as complicated as some believe. Most people spend most of their time on mental autopilot. They act and react predictably to stimuli, simple minds, even more so, like rats in a maze. If you know how to build the right maze, for the right rat, and put the right bait in the right place, at the right time, the rat's actions are predictable. He will follow the course you define for him. Cause and effect. Action and reaction. Humans are no different than any other machine, except there are more moving parts.

To others, understanding and controlling long and complex cause-and-effect sequences, was impossible. Not for me, not anymore. Most people think that, if a thing is impossible for them to control, it must be a matter of chance or luck.

If a golf player shoots a hole-in-one, he's thought to be lucky. Likewise, if a pool player sinks the eight ball on the break. Just luck, right. But I had done it six times in a row, and in deliberately successive pockets.

I did not need to prove to myself that I could sink those eight-balls that day. I did it only to show off to Dr. Beckman who thought he was hiding behind the door, *keeping an eye on me.* Why not give him a show. No one would believe him anyway.

Luck did not rule my world as it did others. I ruled luck. My certainty of this fact grew each day, and with it, my feeling of power. Power to do good, *to make the world a better place.* One day, the Master of luck Himself will come to envy me. Is there room in heaven for two Gods?

I had one last string to pull on my puppet, Oscar. I went into the dining room and selected a table in front of the serving area. Not too close, not too far. The serving area was the only place where the kitchen had an open connection to the dining room. I had earlier downloaded a song from the library computer, and burned a CD. I took my old CD player/AM/FM radio, the one that Ken had brought to me along with my other things. I also came supplied with crayons and paper.

I inserted the CD and put the player in the repeat mode. I hit play button and quickly adjusted the volume. Too loud, and Oscar would hear it on a conscious level. Too many variables to control there, even for me. Too low, and he couldn't hear it. It needed to be just high enough to register at a subconscious level.

The song I had selected was the '70's pop tune, *Jumping Jack Flash* by The Rolling Stones. It's a catchy tune with a hook line that includes the phase, *"It's a gas, gas, gas."* I adjusted the tone to heavy bass. Bass travels further than treble, and is received at a more visceral level.

Ever get a tune stuck in your head? That was the effect I controlled now, but at a subconscious level. Music sinks into a deeper part of the human brain. Taking a different route, it bypasses the normal cognitive speech center, and goes directly to the primitive and emotional hypothalamus.

The message of "gas" would permeate his subconscious mind. It would become an itch he couldn't scratch. The message would not be received in the same way by others. The stimuli were designed specifically for Oscar, on that day, at that time, in that place.

I stayed there at that table playing that CD at a low bass volume through lunch and dinner. I pretended to be involved in coloring. Strange thing, if an adult uses crayons in a facility with mentally impaired people, he's assumed to be retarded by most of the staff. It worked effectively as a cover. No one bothered me or attempted to make me leave.

By the end of the day, Oscar was tired. I could hear it in his footsteps and in his breathing. It was as I had planned. Now he was most vulnerable to suggestion.

At ten minutes until the end of Oscar's shift, I turned off the CD player and left the dining room. The sudden silence was like a clap of thunder to Oscar's subconscious mind. The void needed to be filled. The itch became unbearable. His subconscious mind hungered.

"Do you smell gas?" He asked Mike, one of the kitchen staff who was just getting ready to leave for the evening. Oscar could not smell the minuscule amount of gas like I could, but his subconscious mind told him he did.

"No. I don't smell anything." He sniffed around the stove area. "Are all the pilots lit?"

"Yeah, I checked. They're on." Scratch it.

"Huh. I dunno. I don't smell anything but my own BO. I gotta go. George is waiting for me. We're carpooling today." Mike said as he headed toward the back door.

"Okay. I think it's my imagination. I'm going to turn off the gas, just in case." The itch must be scratched.

Oscar was tired. Just this one more thing before he could leave. In a little while, he could kick back with a cold one, turn on the auto-recorded game, and zone out. He could see himself relaxed in his recliner at home, an image I helped to create.

Oscar reached up to close the main gas valve. It was stiff from years of disuse. *Okay, it's off, he thought. Or, maybe it isn't.* He turned the valve back on, then off again hard. The itch was still there. Oscar turned the valve on and off four more times, until the itch finally subsided.

Now it's off. I can go home. I'm so tired. Who are the Hawks playing? I'm really tired.

If Oscar had not been in a hurry to leave, he might have smelled the *non-imaginary* gas. The microscopic flaw in the gas valve had grown to one-sixteenth of an inch at its widest point. Not a full and obvious break, but it was more than enough.

Gas was now escaping at a significant rate. Room temperature methane would normally rise to the ceiling, but the gas line ran underground, and the gas was cold. It was cold enough to spill into the kitchen, filling it to waist level in two hours. It then spilled over the serving counter into the dining room. The dining room doors were closed as usual, trapping the gas.

By 2:00 a.m., most of the gas had warmed and was diffused throughout the kitchen and dining room. The gas density increased by the minute.

The kitchen and connecting dining room stayed warmer than other areas in the building, due to latent heat from the oven and stove, and from the warm exhaust from the refrigerators. It was a cold night, and the thermostat was set to sixty-eight to save energy.

At 3:06 am, the dining room thermostat reached sixty-seven degrees and switch on, ordering the furnace to supply heat. There would be more heat delivered than intended, and not from the furnace.

I had detected the slight smell of ozone weeks ago, and I understood that the thermostat was an old bi-metal open contact design. It generated a small spark when the desired trigger temperature had been reached.

The air had attained a sufficient gas to oxygen density. The thermostat contacts closed. The gas was ignited by the spark.

The slow explosion took the better part of a second to fully ignite the gas and blow the roof off the building. The whole end of the building was leveled. And what remained quickly sprouted flames.

I was awake, of course, counting the seconds. My calculations were a little off. I had not anticipated the one degree inaccuracy of the thermostat. It was a silly mistake on my part, and I promised myself that such an oversight would not happen again.

None the less, I was not surprised by the explosion that shook the entire building. In fact, I was dressed and packed. I had put my clothes and other items into a small duffle bag. I would be leaving the Institute permanently that night.

If anyone's work is burned up, he will suffer loss, though he himself will be saved, but only as through fire. 2nd Corinthians 3:15.

They won't be able to *keep an eye on me* anymore, unless I want them to.

They should be glad that I didn't need to kill anyone to make my point. All the residents were housed at the other end of the building. Even the dimwitted night time staff should be able to call the fire department and get all the residents out. I am merciful, like that other Guy up there *says* He is. I found this thought amusing and left my room smiling.

I walked into chaos. I should say, chaos by anyone else's definition. Staff were running down the hallways unlocking doors and yelling at residents to wake up. People who were up, were half awake, coughing and confused.

I saw only order. The universe was working as expected, like a finely made clock. Tick tock. Cause and effect.

I walked out of the building unnoticed by anyone. A calm and orderly person in a sea of chaos and hysteria becomes invisible. I took a last look over my shoulder. The flames seemed to be licking at the clouds, at heaven itself. God must be happy.

For our God is a consuming fire. Hebrews 12:29

There was a lot of smoke. The insulation, the carpets, and the foam furniture cushions were on fire. *Better hold your breath until you get outside. That smoke can kill you.*

I know I could have predicted the exact actions of each staff and of each resident. But, I was tired. It would take too much mental energy. And for what, to verify that people will do what they can to save their lives? Where's the challenge in that?

I will execute great vengeance on them with wrathful rebukes. They will know that I am the Lord, when I lay my vengeance upon them. Ezekiel 25:17.

It is my "purpose" to make the world a better place. I am the Lord of Julia's vengeance.

CHAPTER 29
TYLER

Tyler was awakened by the earth-shaking boom, like everyone else. He was afraid. Had a giant monster stepped on the building? Was the monster coming for him? First, he hid under his blankets. Then, he heard people yelling in the hallway.

He got out of bed and peaked out of the door. He saw fear and confusion on the faces of people in the hallway. This scared him even more. They had seen the terrible monster that must be after them.

Run or hide were Tyler's only choices. A big monster was a fast monster. It would catch him. His father and he had played hide and seek many times. He was a good hider. His Dad had said so. Tyler chose to hide in his small closet.

He did not think to close his room door. He ran to the closet as fast as he could. He closed the closet door behind him and wiggled behind some boxes and his imitation leather diaper bag.

It was dark. Tyler could hear voices in the hallway, fearful voices. But he was safe. The monster would not find him here.

After a while the voices lowered and stopped. Maybe the monster was gone. Or, maybe he had caught them and ate them. But he was safe here, in the dark, alone.

Then he heard the monster breathing in the hallway. It started as a low rumble. It grew into a growl, and then a roar. It was in his room, outside the closet door. Tyler could smell the monster's smoky breath. A dragon who breathed fire, like in the story his Dad read to him.

It became stronger and stronger, and hotter and hotter. He couldn't breathe. He coughed. He gagged. The monster was going to get him. *Hide!* He pulled the diaper bag over his head.

It was 3:46 a.m.

CHAPTER 30
HECK

I woke for no apparent reason. My eyes just popped open, and I was wide awake. I looked at the soft glow of my digital alarm clock on the nightstand next to my bed, and noted the time. It was 3:53 a.m.

I sometimes woke in the middle of the night when there was something bothering me, an unsolved problem of some kind, or an unresolved personal issue. When Wendy and I were in the throes of our breakup, I woke up several nights after only a couple hours, unable to go back to sleep.

But, there were no immediate problems or issues that I was aware of. I laid there in bed for several minutes. I thought that maybe I'd fall back to sleep. I closed my eyes, but sleep did not come. I had that nagging feeling you get when you've forgotten something important, but you can't remember what it is.

There was something I had left unfinished. It was almost tangible, like the awaited sound of the proverbial second shoe dropping. The sound didn't come, but my expectation of its impending arrival gnawed at me.

It's nothing. I tried to go back to sleep. My thoughts wandered. Images fluttered randomly across my mind's eye, benign at first. Then, more disturbing images began to creep in from the shadows. Tom's broken leg. Wendy, shouting at me, inches from my face. Limpy, roaring at me, inches from my face. Tyler's bloody forehead. Nan, face down in the creek.

I sat up quickly, my eyes wide open in the dark. *Where did that come from?*

It had been years since I had been haunted by dreams of the accident. I thought that episode in my life had been safely stowed away on a dusty back shelf in my mind. *Maybe not.*

It was apparent to me that I would get no more sleep tonight. I hopped into the shower and adjusted the water to extra hot.

I stood leaning on the small chest-high window sill shelf, the hot water on my back. I had opened the window. The hot moist air mixing with the cold outside air created thick clouds of steam that blurred my vision. That unsettling feeling of something unremembered persisted. I pushed it away, but it remained, a presence floating in the steam.

I toweled off and wiped the condensed steam from a head-sized spot on the vanity mirror. I still had the beard I had grown in Alaska. I was going to trim it, but then I decided to cut it off entirely.

The jagged red scar started at my left temple, extended past my ear, and ended under my jaw. It was not as red as it had once been, but without the beard to hide it, it was now prominently displayed.

I studied my newly denuded face in the mirror. If I turned my head just a little to the left, I could hardly see the scar. I decided to own my scar. It was mine. For better or for worse it was me. I never cared much about what others thought of my looks. That part of me was certainly not going to change now. People would just have to accept it, like I accepted it. Anyway, being self conscious about it was the surest way to draw attention to it.

The surgeon had done a good job stitching it back together. The scar would lighten over time, and would eventually become almost invisible.

I noticed other features that had been disguised by the beard too. I had aged some. My skin had taken on a slightly leathery look. There were lines around my eyes and mouth that hadn't been there a year ago.

Also, there was a certain toughness that had crept into my overall appearance. I decided that I liked it. Perhaps it was my weight loss that made my eyes just a little darker, and my cheeks just a little more hollow. *Oh well, there goes my boyish good looks.* I grinned at myself in the mirror.

The phone rang at 5:28. It was Jan.

"Heck, there's been a fire at the Institute. We can't find Tyler! One of the staff thought they saw him outside, but when we took a head count, he was missing. No one knows where he is." She sounded worried, but not afraid.

"Okay. I'm leaving right now." *Tyler is hiding.* "You can fill me in when I get there. Is everyone else okay?"

"They got the fire out. Ray Miller is missing too, but everyone else is accounted for. It's crazy here. I really need your help. Come as quick as you can."

"I'm sure Tyler is just hiding somewhere. You know how he hates crowds and confusion. Check the bushes. I'm on my way." I was worried, but not afraid.

I finished getting dressed, and was out the door in two minutes flat. *He's hiding.*

Once I was in the car and heading down the road, I keyed my cell phone on and hit the speed dial for Tom.

The phone rang several times before a groggy Starla answered. "Hello, this is the Tom Birch residence?" Her tone carried a question. *Who is calling so early, and why did I answer the phone?*

"Hey Starla. This is Heck. Sorry to call so early. Is Tom there? It's important."

"Oh Heck, yeah, he's here give me a minute to wake him up." She must have laid the phone down on the bed. Muffled voices in the background confirmed that Tom was being woke up. Then, the sounds of blankets rustling, a bed spring squeaked, and Tom picking up the phone.

"Heck. What the hell? What's up?" He sounded like he had just gargled with cat litter.

"Listen, Tom, can you meet me over at the Institute right away? They had a fire. No one was hurt, but there's a lot of confusion, and Tyler is missing. I think he's probably hiding somewhere. You know how he is. We could really use your help over there. Sorry, I got you up so early. I'm on my way there now." I didn't have any doubt that Tom would hop out of bed to help, no matter *what* he was doing.

"Sure. I'm on my way." I heard him yawn. "Give me a minute to get my pants on." Starla said something from the other side of the room. I couldn't make it out, but it sounded like a complaint. Men learn quickly to recognize that tone, the one that communicates a woman's dissatisfaction, without the need for specific words.

"Okay. See ya in a few." I hung up the phone, and concentrated on getting there.

As I crested a hill, the dawn's early light illuminated a semi-dispersed cloud of smoke over Mercer Island.

He's hiding. I was worried, but not afraid.

CHAPTER 31
TOM

It took me a few minutes to splash some water on my face and find my clothes, all the while dealing with Starla's whining.

"Do you really have to go so fast? Let me make you some coffee. How about a bagel with some cream cheese? You can eat it in the car." She had thrown on a robe and was sitting on the edge of the bed.

"I don't have time. Heck needs me. He's worried. I could hear it in his voice." She shot one of those little-girl disappointed looks at me.

"Where the hell did my other shoe go?" I said, more to myself than to her as I scrounged around the bedroom. "Oh, there it is."

"We were going to sleep in this morning. I was going to fix you breakfast in bed." Yes, she was pouting. Pouting!

Really? Cute, but childish. I liked the cute part, but not the childish part.

"You can go back to sleep. I'll probably be back by noon. I'll call you. Maybe you can fix me *lunch* in bed instead." I flashed her the best devilish smirk that I could muster this early in the morning.

"Ooo! That sounds good! I'll fix a *hot* lunch just for you. Maybe we can take a *nap* together. *After*."

She turned toward me, leaning on one arm, deliberately letting her robe fall open a few inches. Her breasts were perfect in every way, just perfect, and so was the rest of her. If I understood the innuendo correctly, I'd be *needing* that nap. *Whatever stops the whining.*

I hopped into Heck's Bimmer, fired her up, released the brake, stomped the clutch, slapped her into first gear, and launched out of the driveway. I squeaked the tires a little on the dew-glazed pavement as I popped it into second. It definitely did not have the raw muscle of my Mustang, but it was a fun little rag top.

I figured that Heck would get there about ten or fifteen minutes ahead of me. As I drove Eastward crossed the I-90 bridge to Mercer Island, I noted an ambulance racing in the opposite direction on the westbound side of the divided floating bridge.

Heck said that no one had been hurt from the fire. It was possible that one of the elderly retirees who lived on the island was having a heart attack. If it had been someone from the Bellevue side of Lake Washington, the ambulance most likely would have gone to a Bellevue area hospital instead of crossing the lake to Seattle.

I thought of calling ahead on my cell phone, but thought better of it. Heck probably had his hands full right about now, and I'd be there in a couple of minutes anyway.

The immediate area around The Mercer Residential Rehabilitation Institute had been cordoned off by the fire department. I parked a block up the street and half-ran the rest of the way. Four fire trucks and about a dozen yellow-coated firemen surrounded the building. Hoses had been deployed and were dousing the still smoldering embers.

Buses had arrived to take residents to other temporary facilities. Staff personnel were busy collecting and organizing residents into small groups for transport to specific locations. Several staff had obviously been called out of bed, as was evidenced by their casual clothing, bed-head hairdos, morning stubble on the men, and lack of makeup on the women.

I began looking for Heck. I figured he was busy helping the other staff, but I didn't see him. I spotted Dr. Martin sitting on a low decorative landscape wall at the driveway entrance. She should know where Heck was, and she was the one to ask how I could help.

She was hunched over. From behind her, she looked like she was blowing her nose. When I got closer, I could see that she was sobbing. An older staff woman sat next to her with a hand on her shoulder.

The Institute was a mess. Rebuilding would be challenging, expensive, and time consuming. It was "Dr. Martin's baby," as Heck had described it once. I guess maybe I'd be crying too.

"Dr. Martin." She looked up. Her eyes were wet and swollen.

"Yes?" Her voice struggled with this single word. I could tell that she did not recognize me.

"I'm Tom Birch, Heck's friend. We met a few months ago. I picked up Tyler for him once."

"Oh, yes." There was a spark of recognition, but nothing more.

"Heck, asked me to come over to help out. I didn't see him." She didn't respond, but buried her face in the red shop cloth someone had given her and sobbed more.

I was a little confused by her reaction. But then, she was a woman, and she was old, and her "baby" had been hurt. I thought it best to leave her to her anguish, and find something useful to do. "Well okay, I'll find Heck and I'll help him out." I started to turn away.

"No, wait." She grabbed my hand.

She struggle to regain minimal composure. I waited awkwardly. She stopped sobbing and looked at me squarely. At that moment, I knew what she was going to say, but I didn't want to hear it.

"Heck just left in the ambulance with Tyler. They found him in a closet. He wasn't breathing. They were giving him CPR, but…" She couldn't say what she was thinking.

"Oh shit!" It was all I could manage to say. The air had been sucked out of my lungs. My knees felt week.

"They're taking him to Children's Hospital in town. I wanted to go with them, but I have to be here now. You go. Heck will need somebody with him." She stopped talking, but her eyes added, "when he finds out." She released my hand and buried her face in the red shop cloth again. She had nothing more to say, but I wouldn't have heard it, if she had. I was already running back to Heck's BMW. *Heck needs me.*

I negotiated the surface streets semi-legally, and hopped back on I-90 Westbound toward Seattle. I could have called Heck's cell phone. No, I had to be there in person.

I nudged the gas pedal down as I entered the tunnel. Traffic was still light. I scanned front and back for police cars. I hoped they were all changing shift about now.

In the car, I had a moment to think about Dr. Martin's tone, and her half finished sentences. She thought Tyler was dead. I didn't want that thought in my head, but it wouldn't leave.

I knew how this must be affecting Heck. I was there the day he found Nancy in the creek. It wasn't his fault. No one blamed him, not even his parents. He was devastated. He blamed himself for years after. He probably still did on some level.

###

He was just a teen. Yes, he was supposed to be watching her. But Nan was not easy to watch. She was either being a nuisance, or running off somewhere. It was not unusual for her to find a corner and play by herself for long periods.

Billy and I were with Heck in the front yard. I remember Heck asking me if I saw where Nan had gone. I told him that I had seen her go into the back yard. We had been talking about girls. We didn't want Nan around anyway.

Heck had not gone looking for her, for whatever reason. The backyard was a safe place for her to play. He couldn't be expected to watch her every second.

The creek was only a couple hundred feet into the trees behind the back yard. She had played in and around that creek a million times. Not much more than a ditch really, it was less than a yard wide and only inches deep. It would be easier to drown in a bath tub.

They said she must have had a grand mal seizure, fell into the water face down, and drowned. It was thought at first that she might have tripped and hit her head on a rock. But she had no injuries. Although no one saw it happen, a seizure was the most likely explanation.

Heck hadn't been taught proper CPR techniques, but he had seen it done on TV once. He did his best to revive her, but it was probably too late anyway. He sent Billy to get help from a neighbor. I called the police. The number was kept on a sticker by the phone.

The neighbor was a quarter mile away, but wasn't home. The police arrived in less than five minutes. The officer had a CPR certification and took over for Heck.

It was too late. Nan was never revived.

Heck's parents had gone into town. His mom went to the hair salon while his dad went to the hardware store. There were no cell phones then, so they didn't find out what had happened until they got home, just in time to see Nan being loaded into the back of the ambulance.

I remember watching Heck, watching that ambulance leave. The lights were on, but they did not turn on the siren, and they weren't driving fast at all. I knew what that meant, and so did he.

Heck stayed at my house for a couple days while arrangements were made for the funeral. My parents offered, and Heck's parents agreed. They thought he would be better off with his best friend. And they didn't want him to witness his parents grieving.

Maybe it was best for Heck, but it was hard on me. How could I help? My shoulders weren't big enough yet to carry that weight.

Heck's dad came by to check on him while he was at my house. He caught Heck at a bad moment. Heck was crying in my room, his dad was trying to comfort him. The door was open. I was listening from down the hallway.

Heck's dad told him, "Heck, it's not your fault. It was just an accident."

"But why, Dad? Why?" Heck needed an answer. He wasn't going to get one.

"Sometimes, things just happen, Hector. There is no *why*. It is what it is, because it just *is*. That's all." As far as I could tell, his father's rational condolence did not help Heck at all.

That was the worst time that I can remember from my teen years. Heck stayed in my room, and cried on and off all day. I remember feeling totally helpless.

He came out a couple times to eat and go to the bathroom, but he didn't want to talk much. That was okay. I didn't want to talk either. What could I say? What exactly was there to talk about? I didn't even want to look at him. It hurt too much. I never told him this, but I was angry at Nan for a time for hurting Heck. Silly, I know.

###

And now this. My stomach ached, and not because of the skipped breakfast.

I parked by the emergency entrance and went in. Heck was not in the emergency waiting area. I learned at the reception desk that Tyler had been taken to surgery, and that Heck would be in the surgery waiting room. A busty receptionist named Pam with an out-of-place smile gave me a guest sticker and directions.

"Thank you, Pam." I said, without thinking.

Why had I noticed her boobs and bothered to read her name tag at a time like this? Habit? I wasn't exactly looking for a damn date! *You're a sicko, Tom.* If women only knew how right they are when they say, "Men are pigs."

It was a long waiting room with a doorway at either end. I entered through the closest door. Heck was at the far end. I almost didn't recognize him at first without his beard. He was standing with his back toward me at an angle, talking to a doctor in scrubs.

The doctor was slowly shaking his head from side to side as he spoke. I couldn't make out the words, but the tone was low. There was a pained expression on the doctor's face. He was young, probably a new resident. Death had not become routine for him yet. Perhaps, if he was lucky, it never would.

Heck's head dropped, and he crumpled to a half sitting position on the floor as the doctor tried awkwardly to catch him.

I ran to Heck's side. He did not acknowledge me, but I knew he was aware of my presence.

Heck said only one word, "No."

It was not a plea, or a denial, but almost a statement. It was not directed at me, nor at the doctor, but at the world. Somehow, that single word conveyed a universe of hopeless human despair. It entered my ears, penetrated my heart, and sunk deep into the marrow of my bones.

I could say nothing. I could only be there.

CHAPTER 32
SAL

The local time was only 7:00 p.m. when Becky and I got into Seattle. But with the three-hour time difference, my body still felt like it was 10:00. It was a one-stop flight through Houston that took a total of seven hours, including layover time. It was the best flight I could find on short notice. We were both tired.

Becky and I had time for a quick lunch in Houston, but now we were hungry again. We decided to get to the hotel as quickly as possible, have a light dinner at the hotel restaurant, and hit the sack early. We could call The Mercer Residential Rehabilitation Institute in the morning, and make arrangements to meet with Dr. Martin and Dr. Beckman.

It took an hour and a half to get our bags, rent the car, drive to the Seattle Hyatt, dump our bags, and get a table at the Le Maestro restaurant.

It was located inside the hotel, but it was independently owned and operated. Catering to a somewhat upscale clientele, their prices were a bit on the high side. But, they were open late, even on weeknights, and it was an easy walk from our room.

"Whoa! Thirty-five dollars for a burger and fries?" Becky was not used to eating in five-star restaurants.

"Yeah well, I guess they think their version of a burger is a cut above McDonald's. Don't worry about it. I told you, it's on me. This is *my* business trip. But, I'm going to just have something light."

This trip was going to put a big dent in my bank account. Since it was an *unofficial* business trip, I couldn't put it on my CDC expense account. I didn't have anything else planned to do with the money anyway. Why not spend it on a quasi-vacation in Seattle?

"I guess so! Me too." She said.

Traveling for the CDC, I often ended up eating at posh restaurants, either for convenience, like now, or because it was for a work related lunch or dinner meeting with important people. Dr. Edelman once invited me and another associate to join him and three Ivy League university deans for a lunch meeting.

The meeting was ostensibly about summer internships for top medical science students. They spent about five minutes talking about internships, and an hour and half talking about golf, fishing, Caribbean vacations, and New England weather. The meeting was perfunctory, since the important details concerning CDC internships had been worked out months before.

Rose later told me that that particular business lunch for six had totaled over five-hundred dollars, with drinks, tax and tip. Needless to say, that lunch meeting was not at McDonald's. My guess is that most regular McDonald's customers would have had a hard time properly pronouncing the restaurant's French name, much less covering the bill. By comparison, Le Maestro prices were quite reasonable, and the name was semi-manageable too.

"My name is Jon. I'll be your waiter tonight. Have you decided what you would like us to prepare for you?" I can't explain it, he wasn't wearing a name badge, but I'm sure he spelled his name without the "h."

"I'll have the seared lamb chops with the demi-glace." I said to the formal black-and-white garbed middle-aged man.

Becky gave me a "Huh?" look. I completed my order.

"I guess I'll have the burger and fries. And, can I get a beer with that." Becky's tastes were simple and predictable. "That would be our apple wood fire-roasted freshly ground sirloin tip sandwich entrée." There was a not-so-subtle note of condescension, like he was patiently talking to a child. Becky missed it.

"And how would the young lady like that cooked?" He looked at me, like I was the adult who would be answering for the child.

Becky answered. "Just cook it the regular way."

"He ignored her and looked again to me, restating the question. "Ma'am, the young lady has the choice of how well it is cooked. We do not recommend rare, but may I suggest medium or medium-well for maximum flavor." I was a little offended. I'm the "ma'am," and she's the "young lady?'

"Yes, medium-well will be just fine, *sir.*" I deliberately laid a tone of sarcasm onto the "sir.'

He got the point. "Very well." He smiled politely, nodded his head once slightly, and took one step backwards before turning to leave.

"Thanks, I wasn't sure what he meant. Hey, he didn't write anything down. Is he going to get it right?"

"Don't worry, overpaid waiters in overpriced places like this never write it down, and they never get it wrong. It's a thing they do, I guess to prove they deserve a bigger tip."

"Well, he won't get anything extra out'a me. He's kind of a dick. 'Young lady?' " Becky *had* noticed the condescension.

We both laughed in agreement.

"What happened to 'just getting something light?' "

"I know. I guess I'm hungrier than I thought." There was a pause as we sipped our ice water.

"Becky, do you remember Gary Boyle?" *I need to tell her sometime. Maybe now?*

"Oh yeah, Mike's brother. Mike was the older one with the cool van that had the air brushed surfer scene on the side. And, wasn't Gary the football jock? Why?"

"I was just thinking about that van. It was cool on the inside too. It had a sound system and a refrigerator."

"I never saw the inside. Didn't Mike get the van from his rich daddy for his graduation? Why would you be thinking about that?"

"Oh, nothing. Just old times at Fergusons. We'd always get burgers and fries with milk shakes, *not beer.*" *I can't. Change the subject. Not yet. Not now. Not here.*

"Yeah, they were great, and they didn't cost no thirty-five dollars." She laughed. I smiled, but said no more. *Some other time.*

We ate without talking much more. We were both overtired from the trip. The meal was great, but it only served to put an exclamation point on our exhaustion. We were out within three heartbeats of turning off the bedside lamp.

We were up early, refreshed and ready to go. I ordered room service coffee, juice and strudel, and beat Becky into the shower.

When I got out of the shower, room service had already been delivered, and Becky was digging into the strudel. She had the local Seattle morning news on TV.

"Holy crap! It's the Mercer Residential Rehabilitation Institute. It burned down last night."

"What!" I quickly stepped over to the TV and turn up the volume.

"The four alarm fire was quickly extinguished." The news anchor said. The picture showed smoldering debris being doused with water from fire hoses. The scene shifted to a disheveled and tired looking older lady talking to a reporter.

"Dr. Janet Martin, Director of the mental health facility was at the scene." The camera zoomed in on her.

"That's her! That's the Dr. Martin we were going to meet." I blinked reflexively.

She was talking to the reporter, "We were able get almost everyone out." She paused with a pained expression. "One of our young residents was sent to Children's Hospital. And, another resident is still missing."

The scene switched again to the on-scene reporter, apparently now a live shot. "That was earlier this morning. There has been an update on the story. We have just received a statement from Children's Hospital, that eight-year-old Tyler Beckman, the son of one of the Institute's staff psychologists, Dr. Hector Beckman, has been pronounced dead from smoke inhalation. A statement from the hospital said that doctors took exhaustive measures to revive the boy, but they were unsuccessful."

"Oh God, Dr. Beckman's son!" I slumped onto edge of the bed next to Becky while I listened to the rest of the report.

"The search for a still-missing resident is continuing. Searchers are unsure if this resident was trapped in the building too, or if he was able to escape. His name is being withheld, pending notification of family.

"Fire department officials did not comment on the cause of the fire, stating that arson has not been ruled out, and that the circumstances surrounding the fire are under investigation. Staff people, who were working at the time of the fire, said that there was a large explosion from the kitchen and dining room area. Some of the staff suspect that a gas leak may have caused the explosion and subsequent fire.

I continued staring at the screen, even though a commercial for Bob's Plumbing had now started.

"Wow." Becky's eyes were transfixed on the screen, as were mine. She was not referring to Bob's 24-hour on-call service.

"Wow, is right." Neither was I.

"What now?"

"I don't know." I said slowly. *What now?* Becky had no more questions. We sat there in silence, starring at the TV.

Bob's Plumbing gave way to Bentley and Dauber Attorneys at Law. "If you've been injured in an auto accident, don't wait! Call Bentley and Dauber." *What now, Blondie Girl? Who do I call?*

I felt terrible. Even though I didn't know them personally, it was a human tragedy, especial for Dr. Beckman. I felt helpless.

If only there was something I could do to… *Why not?*

"Let's go there! Let's help. I don't know what we can do, but there must be something. I'm sure they can use a couple extra volunteers. Are you up for it?"

"I guess. Sure, let's do it. Give me fifteen minutes to shower. I'll slip into a pair jeans and a flannel shirt, and I'll be ready to go." I never knew Becky to shirk from a challenge. And she was always up for an adventure, one of the many things I loved about her.

CHAPTER 33
HECK

It was a typical winter day. The sky was gray. The air was cold and damp from the intermittent drizzle. There was a steady breeze adding to the chill. *A perfect day for a funeral.*

I sat in the passenger seat of Tom's Mustang. We hadn't said anything since he had picked me up from my place.

###

I can't talk about it. Do not confuse this to mean that I don't want to talk about it. I simply can't, even if I wanted to, which I don't. I lost about 24 hours of memory. It doesn't matter. All I need to know is that Tyler is gone.

It's called dissociative amnesia. It will probably all come back to me, eventually, in a dream perhaps. Or, it might be triggered by something, an object, or an event. I've read all the books. Hell, I've been tested on all those books. I know the science, but knowing the science of a thing is not the same as feeling the reality of a thing.

The last clear memory I have is of being in the ambulance with Tyler. They were working on him. He wasn't breathing. Then, the ambulance went into the I-90 tunnel to Seattle. That's it. I don't remember coming out of the tunnel. I don't remember the hospital, only bits and pieces, fleeting images.

I just can't remember. Or maybe I should say, my subconscious mind doesn't *want me to* remember, if I look at it from a psychologist point of view. But then, I *am* a psychologist. Apparently, dissociative amnesia does not exempt those with college degrees. I can't remember.

Tom told me that he found me in the hospital waiting room when they gave me the bad news. He said I collapsed. I don't know. Sounds about right. I guess I did, if he says so.

Tom handled all the funeral arrangements for me. He asked me about my wishes, but I asked him to make all the decisions. I didn't want to think about it. I guess I'll see what his decisions were today at the funeral. I'm sure it will all be fine.

Tyler's gone.

It doesn't matter to him, so it doesn't matter to me much either. I'm not going to say that to anyone. I can imagine what some people might say. But then, I'm not sure I care too much about that either.

Tyler's gone.

It was an accident. The investigators said that they found no evidence of arson. They said it was a faulty gas shutoff valve. That answers the "how" question.

The "why" questions are harder to answer. Why was it Tyler? Why didn't he leave the building with everyone else? Why couldn't they find him sooner? Why?

In the end, I know there will never be any answers to the "why" questions.

The universe rolled the dice, and Tyler got snake eyes. *It is what it is, because it just is.* This cold and rational assessment does not console me in any way, no more than it did when my Dad said it to me when I was fourteen.

Nan's gone. Tyler's gone.

Role of the dice.

Anna Grant comes to mind. I remember the fortune telling game with Anna. It was the day before the fire. It's a good thing that she hadn't moved into the Institute yet.

Toss of the letters.

"KIN IN HEAT." Did "kin" mean Tyler, and "heat" mean fire? Silly, really. It could mean anything, or nothing. Like the Nostradamus prophesies, you can interpret them in a thousand different ways, depending on your mood. "Kin in heat" could mean my cousin Gloria in Portland is ovulating, if that's what *I want* it to mean. Still, the thought makes me feel even more disconnected from the real world than I already am.

They held a viewing last night. I didn't go. Call me terrible. Tom covered for me. I didn't know how I would react to seeing him in a casket. I didn't want to do it twice. I wanted to *prepare* myself, whatever that means. I guess I'm as prepared now as I ever will be.

People think they know what the loss of a child must feel like to a parent. They're all wrong. I was wrong. No one can know until it happens to them. And once you know, there are no words to communicate to someone else how it feels. It's like trying to explain the color red to someone who was born without sight. Try it sometime, if you ever get the chance.

There is an unquenchable emptiness inside me, a hollowness of the soul. There is a sickening sensation that surrounds me. The world is a blur, yet everything in it is in sharp focus. There is a gray sound that comes from nowhere mixed with a deafening silence that comes from everywhere. I am immersed in a pervasive pain that is not attached to my body at any point. I am here, but I am not here, nor am I anywhere else. I am not sad, not angry, not remorseful, not depressed, not exactly anything, but precisely something.

Like I said, there are no words.

When Nan died, I was a wreck emotionally. I was racked with guilt and self-recrimination. I loved her more than I knew. I missed her more than anything. But, it wasn't the same. Not less, not more, just different. I wasn't the same person then either.

There is a rainbow of pains that have been custom designed for every occasion imaginable and for every individual ever born. If Satan exists, surely the infinite palette of pain that the universe has to offer is some of his most inspired work. If instead that palette was designed by God, I hope He is at least a little embarrassed by the exquisite exuberance of this particular aspect of His creation.

###

Tom pulled me back into this world. "We're almost there. I want to stop at 7-Eleven and get a drink. My mouth is like cotton. Do you want anything?"

"No." I said, without thinking about it. Tom left the car running and got out. But, maybe I *was* thirsty. I changed my mind. I made a different choice on a whim.

"Wait. Get me an orange soda." Tom stopped to poke his head back in the door to confirm my request.

"Just any orange soda?"

"Not diet. Thanks." He closed the car door, and followed another patron into the store.

Tom looked tired, very tired. The last four days had been hard on him. I hadn't even noticed. *Selfish.* Maybe I had a good excuse, but it was still selfish of me to ask him to do so much, and not even acknowledge his efforts. I made a mental note to make it up to him somehow.

Tom told me that Wendy had been there for the viewing last night. She was alone. She didn't stay long. She didn't talk to Tom or anyone else. No one talked to her. Tom said that she put a small box of crayons and a coloring book in Tyler's coffin, then left.

Nice. I didn't think of that.

I hold no grudges against her. We were happy for a time. We had Tyler for a time. But that was then. Things change. We both made choices that lead us down different paths. She has to live with her own demons now. I hope I can live with mine.

Tom had been in 7-Eleven longer than I expected. Two other people had exited the store since he had gone in.

He was just coming out of the door now.

"Sorry, there was a line." He said as he got in the car and handed me the orange soda.

"That's okay. I was just thinking. Did Wendy say anything *at all* to you?"

"Nope, not a word. I didn't want to talk to her anyway, so that was okay by me. I was afraid I might say something, ah, inappropriate. She kept glancing around, though. I think she was looking for you."

"I don't want to talk to her either. We've got nothing to say that hasn't been said before. She wasn't around for Tyler when he was alive. I don't want anything to do with *her*, now that he's gone.

"Don't worry, I'll keep it together. But I'm hoping she'll keep her distance today."

###

Wendy didn't show up for the funeral. That was okay. No one who knew her, could possibly think anything less of her because of it. Besides, she had made her appearance at the viewing last night. If she was grieving, she was free to do it in her own way. If she wasn't, well either way, it was not my concern now.

I was surprised by my own reaction to seeing Tyler. They did an exceptional job of preparing him. My last memory of Tyler was when they put him into the ambulance. It was a horrible memory. Why hadn't I lost *that* memory? Maybe, because I thought he could be revived then. I know now that he had probably died hours earlier.

So, today was actually the second time I would be seeing him since his death. But, that earlier image of him in the ambulance was all that I had until the funeral.

At the funeral, he was my beautiful boy again. I don't know what I had expected. It was a relief. I said goodbye. I kissed his forehead like I always did when I put him to bed. Only this time, he wasn't going to sleep. He was going somewhere else.

I know a lot about the grieving process. At least, I always thought I did. I can put my psychologist hat on and stand outside myself, and say that my lack of emotional response is only a defense mechanism, and that it will "hit" me later. Maybe it will.

But inside my own skin, I know he's gone. I know my life will move on, because it has to. And, I feel okay with that. Maybe I shouldn't. Maybe I won't later. But, I'm okay with it for now. That's all I've got. It's enough. *Tyler's gone. It was an accident.*

There were a lot of people at the funeral, many I didn't recognize. I didn't realize how many lives that Tyler had touched during his short stay on this planet. Practically the entire staff of The Mercer Residential Rehabilitation Institute and several residents came. There were people we knew from the University. Marta Velazquez, from Little Ones Playland, came.

Surprisingly, some of the children who used to play with Tyler at Little Ones, and their parents, came too. Many parents avoid taking their children to funerals. I would not have taken Tyler to a funeral because I know he would not have understood.

The funeral service was short, thanks to Tom. He knew my limits, and he did his best to pare things down as much as possible. There wasn't enough time to talk with, much less meet, all of the guests.

Tom had rented a banquet room at a nearby motel, not far from the cemetery, and had arranged to have catered finger food and refreshments for the repast. Everyone was invited, but only about a third of the people, who had been at the funeral, attended.

I sat at a table with Tom, sipping another orange soda. Beer would have been better. Tom agreed, but he said some people might think it was appropriate.

"Is Starla coming? I didn't see her at the funeral." Now that I had a moment to think about it, I hadn't heard Tom mention her for the last few days. Too busy, I guessed.

"No, she's not coming." He said flatly.

There it was, that tone. I'd heard that tone coming from Tom several times in the past. "What happened?"

"She just didn't want to come." There was definitely more to that story.

"Okay, *what* happened?" I said, little a more insistently this time. He knew what I meant.

"Nothing happened really. We're just not right for each other."

I waited. I knew there was more.

"Ya know Heck, it's me. With the fire and everything else, I just forgot about her. Zip, she was just out of my mind. I realized, if I can forget about someone at a time like that, she must not mean that much too me. I don't need her, and she certainly doesn't need me."

I waited. It was rare for Tom to talk about his relationships. I didn't want to interrupt the flow.

Tom waited to see if I had something to say. When I didn't, he continued. "I guess that's the point, isn't it. I want to need someone, someone special, ya know. Starla's a real sweetheart, but she's just not the one."

I waited some more, but Tom had nothing more to say. He was having a heart-to-heart talk with himself right then, and I didn't need to be part of it. I said nothing.

Tyler's death was painful for Tom too. It was a different pain than mine, but it was there, and he was dealing with it. Evaluating his own life was Tom's way of putting Tyler's death into perspective, and to maybe give it some meaning.

My stomach was angrily talking to me about the pigs-in-a-blanket. Two and a half still remained on my paper plate. I was debating on whether to take another bite, or to toss them.

It was then that Jan came over to our table with two women I had seen at the funeral, but had not met.

"Dr. Beckman, I want you to meet some people who have been helping me out with the clean up over at the Institute. This is Dr. Sally Salinger, and Ms. Becky Donaldson." Jan never used the Dr. title unless she wanted to keep things formal. *Why,* I thought.

"And this is Dr. Beckman's friend, Tom Birch." Tom nodded his head, smiled, and extended his hand, but said nothing.

"Pleased to meet you both. Ah, Dr. Salinger? I'm sorry, have we met before? Your name sounds very familiar, but I can't place you." I said, as I shook their hands in turn after Tom.

Dr. Salinger opened her mouth to respond, but Jan beat her to it. "Dr. Salinger is with the CDC. She is working on the Bangkok virus case, and was scheduled to meet with us on the day of the fire to talk about Ray and Anna.

"Since things have been turned upside down for us, she and her friend Becky volunteered to help out for a few days until things settle down." Jan's smile was a tiny bit too big, always putting forth her best face for the Institute.

"Oh yeah, that's right. Now I remember. Thank you for helping us out and for coming to the funeral. Sorry I didn't get a chance to meet you earlier."

Dr. Salinger spoke a little too quickly, glancing at Jan. "Dr. Beckman, first I want to say how sorry we are about your son. We heard about it on the news, and we just wanted to help out in any way we could. I only wish we had had the chance to meet him." There was a little choke in her voice. I caught her eye for a second. She seemed uncomfortable and looked away quickly.

"Thank you. I know you must have a lot of things to do back in Atlanta. I'm very glad you could stay."

Becky was about to say something, but Jan was a little faster. "They have been such a big help too. The cleanup crews are doing most of the hard work, but we have boxes and boxes of wet files to dry out and reproduce. The computer guys are still working on recovering our data from the wet computers. Residents have personal items that need to be gathered up, cleaned up and delivered to their temporary housing locations. And there's just a lot of miscellaneous work that's got to be organized by someone. Heaven knows, I can't do it all.

"Heck, ah, Dr. Beckman, it's really killing me. I'd have had a heart attack by now, if it wasn't for these two running around for me." Jan was a little out of breath just talking about it.

Becky chimed in quickly, "Me too, Dr. Beckman. I'm so sorry about Tyler. I'm really glad we could help out. I'm just tagging along with Sal. We're sorta on vacation, so we've got some extra time anyway. We got to do a little sightseeing yesterday too! We went up on the Space Needle and took some pictures."

"Please, just call me Heck, everyone does." I looked at Dr. Salinger when I said it. There was something about her, kind of a glow, a sparkle, but on a solid foundation of intelligence. It's funny how I could see something as nebulous as intelligence so quickly. I decided I liked her.

Jan had a hint of a scowl that was only evidenced by a slight and momentary decrease in the width of her smile.

Dr. Salinger's smile broadened, and her eyes widened. "Thank you. And you can just call me Sal. I'll take your word that you went to college, if you'll take mine. Then we can drop the doctor thing." She laughed. It was a lilting and unguarded laugh, almost musical. It reminded me of something that might come from a song bird.

I unconsciously looked at Jan, not really intending to put her on the spot. She didn't seem happy about it, but she *was* the only *other* doctor around. After a pause, she said, "Oh, yes. Please, just call me Jan."

Becky said, "And, you can call me Becky." She looked down immediately, embarrassed, realizing that there was no danger that she would be called "doctor." No one said anything.

Becky recovered quickly, displaying her irreverent brand of wit. "Unless you wish to address me as Ms. Donaldson of course." She said this with her best highbrow British accent, adding a curtsy. A curtsy! Who does that anymore? Funny woman.

We all laughed loudly. I didn't realize how much I needed to laugh at something, anything. It was a welcome release. It felt like a breath of fresh air. I breathed it in deeply.

Taking Becky's lead, I turned to Tom. "Mr. Birch?" I said with a smirk. Everyone looked at him.

He did not expect the question, or the attention. His eyes popped open. You'd have thought I had slapped him.

"Ah yeah, right. If anyone calls me anything but Tom, we're gonna have a problem." Everyone laughed loudly again.

"Others in the oversized room, who had kept a hushed tone out of respect, heard the laughter, and saw that I had joined in. It was the permission they needed to relax. The tone in the room became noticeably lighter, louder and more animated.

I noticed that other people in the room kept glancing my way. I got it. They were waiting for an opportunity to talk with me.

"Can we all meet somewhere tomorrow for lunch. I really want to talk to you about Ray and Anna. Tom, can you set something up for us? I want you to come too. I need to say hi to a few people here."

"Sure, Heck. No problem. Save some time tomorrow to read all the cards from the funeral too. I'll take care of sending out the thank-you's, if you're not up to it."

"Thank you Tom. Sal and Becky, I'm happy to meet you both, and thank you for coming. We'll get a chance to talk more tomorrow."

I excused myself, and made my rounds to acknowledge and thank others who had attended. I didn't mean to cut it short. I really did appreciate their coming, but I just wanted to go home. It had been a long day, not in hours, but in emotional strain.

It was over. *Tyler is gone. What about tomorrow?*

CHAPTER 34
RAY

No one paid much attention to the average looking guy standing at the corner of Madison Street and 3rd Avenue. There was no reason to give me a second look. I wore a green plaid flannel shirt under a tan canvas jacket, jeans, and hiking boots. Probably every third person, male or female, in Seattle that day was dressed roughly the same. I probably appeared to be deciding which direction to take as I stood there, looking back and forth.

It was a typical winter day. The sky was gray. The air was cold and damp from the intermittent drizzle. A steady breeze coming off Elliot Bay added to the chill and carried with it the scent of seawater.

I had been following the man for the last couple of hours. Stalking him I guess, but from a distance. I wanted it to be at a distance. It needed to come out of the blue, like Julia's death was to me. It would be an insult to my abilities and to the sanctity of my mission, if I did it the easy way. No, it required finesse and artistry.

It's surprising what information you can get about someone, if you say the right things to the right people at the right time in the right ways, especially when they think you are someone else.

I should say that "others" would be surprised. I was not. People are trusting, too trusting, and stupid. You can rely on it. Con men have always understood this side of human nature.

I knew where my target would be and when he would be there. I knew that he planned to meet an old friend later. I knew the old friend too, only she wasn't *my* friend. Another target, but for later. Right now, focus was the key.

I held a non-functioning green plastic retractable pen in my right hand with the words *Mercer Residential Rehabilitation Institute* stamped in gold letters. I absently twiddled it rapidly back and forth between my thumb and forefinger. It helped to focus my thoughts.

I had spotted my well-dressed target a second ago as he weaved his way through other pedestrians down the steep hill near 2nd Avenue. The well-dress man had a name of course, but I needed to keep my anger in check. I needed him to remain anonymous for now, so that my brain would be free to do what it did, without any unnecessary clutter. I needed to reach a state of calm intensity. The full furry of my hatred could wait. I willed myself to block the man's name from my consciousness. I thought of him only as *the eight ball.*

A pedestrian moved out of my line of sight. *There he is.* The well-dressed man had stopped to talk with someone. *I've been following you long enough. It's time.*

Near me in the gutter, lay a recently lost hubcap. *Ford*, I thought, not that it mattered. I picked it up and turned it over several times studying its smallest details, its weight, its balance, logging all this and more in my mind.

I looked down at the sidewalk. Starting at my feet, I let my gaze systematically roll down the sidewalk between myself and the well-dressed man. I let my eyes scan the same length of sidewalk again, but this time from the bottom of the hill up to where I stood.

There was no hurry. Slowly every detail, every imperfection in the concrete, every piece of discarded chewing gum and miscellaneous piece of street debris was recorded in my mind in hyper-high resolution, until I could *feel* the texture.

I scanned the scene around me once more in all directions. People scurried about on the busy downtown street corner. Cars and trucks maneuvered for position, coming and going. A businessman in an overcoat placed his foot atop a fire hydrant to tie his shoelace. A woman with a child entered a shop. A seagull hopped from his rooftop perch and swooped into an alleyway to inspect the contents of a dumpster. I swallowed the entirety of my surroundings in one gulp.

One block down the street the well-dressed man stopped to talk to a vagrant who was asking for handouts. I'm sure he was hoping the well-dress man would be the generous type.

I overheard the locals call the vagrant, Whiff. I figured it was a nickname he had earned from his obvious lack of personal hygiene. Even from this distance, I could see his greasy hair, 7-day beard, and stained pants.

It looked like it had been a slow morning for Whiff. Everyone was ignoring his pleas for, "…a little change for a hot cup of coffee." *Right.* He probably preferred a bottle of fortified wine to warm his belly on cold days like this.

I recorded it all in my mind in infinite detail. *There he is.* I closed my eyes and inhaled deeply, taking in the smells and sounds of the city. I let the knowing, the *feeling*, begin to grow within me.

In the beginning, I couldn't control it and it had terrified me. I had started once to explain it to Dr. Beckman, but he couldn't understand, no one could. And, no one could tell me how I could *feel* what I did, but "how" didn't matter. Now at least, I understood "why."

"To make the world a better place." I whispered to myself.

I held my breath for a moment as I focused my concentration. "Ah, there it is." I said aloud to no one.

I paused a moment. Timing is everything. Then, I casually crouched down and rolled the hubcap down the steep hill. It rolled slowly at first, but rapidly picked up speed. "Yes! That's it."

I *knew* it was right. I *felt* it in a place I could not describe. I couldn't help but smile impishly, like a school boy who had just planted a tack on his teacher's seat.

An eye for an eye, tooth for tooth, foot for foot, burn for burn, wound for wound, stripe for stripe. Exodus 21:24. A life for a life.

I started walking down the steep incline of Madison Street. I paused briefly and turned around just as a man with a black scarf began to cross the street at 3th.

"Hi!" I called out loudly as I waved my arm broadly.

The man with the black scarf glanced my way and paused only a half a second, long enough to see that I was not anyone he knew, and to decide that I must be waving at someone else. But, he would remember me. Insurance.

I turned back and chuckled out loud and continued walking down the hill. None of the people on the street who might have been a witness seemed to notice me. *This is too easy.*

By this time the hubcap had traveled more than half the distance and had reached a lethal speed. The hubcap was no longer rolling but now bounding crazily six feet into the air with giant leaps covering 20 feet per jump before it would briefly touch the sidewalk, and rebound instantly into the air again. I leaned back against the building to watch.

"Now for the fun." I said under my breath, just as a woman noticed something flash past a foot from her head and jerked away reflexively, probably thinking it was a street bird. Pigeons and gulls were always flitting this way and that, contemptuous of pedestrians.

"Hah! Not even close lady." Oddly, no one else seemed to notice this instrument of imminent death as it streaked past them. Maybe there were too many people milling around, too much ambient noise and movement. Or maybe, it was just too bizarre to be noticed. I read somewhere that people tend to ignore things that are either too ordinary, or too extraordinary.

I could hear Whiff starting to give his standard pitch to the well-dressed man. Whiff looked surprised that the man had actually stopped and reached into his pocket.

"I'll tell ya what, buddy, I'll give ya whatever I got in my pocket, but you gotta promise me ya won't spend it on booze, okay." The well-dress man had a distinct Texas accent.

"No way, man. Not me." Whiff assured the man as he extended his hand accompanied by his tobacco-stained smile.

One block down the steep hill from me on Madison near 2nd Avenue, Whiff and the well-dressed man with the Texas accent were just concluding their transaction.

"Thank you, man." Whiff was showing the man that he had not forgotten his manners?

"Any time." The man started to turn away to continue on his way. The inflection in his voice said, *Right. Any time you need a chump to buy you a drink.*

Whatever he was thinking, it was the last coherent thought Captain Marcus John McKenzie would ever have. The blow struck him on the back of the neck, smashing into his third vertebra, cracking the bone like a walnut, and instantly severing his spinal cord. It was a satisfying sound when it reached me a fraction of a second later. Captain McKenzie collapsed like a wet washcloth. He did not hear the tinkle of coins as they fell from Whiff's startled hand onto the sidewalk.

"Woo-ha! Eight ball in the side pocket." I said aloud with a satisfied grin.

No more Captain McKenzie. Now, that *makes the world a better place!* I thought of how proud Julia would be of me at this moment. I could see her smiling at me. I thought of our wedding, as I often did.

I continued leisurely down the hill, absently twiddling the green plastic pen between my right thumb and forefinger, as I watched people gather around the fallen airline pilot.

I began to whistle Neil Young's *After the Gold Rush.* I was just a kid when I had first heard it. I can't remember all the words, but I still like the tune.

I hung around the scene for a while, just another curious bystander. The police and ambulance showed up. I heard witnesses tell police that the hubcap "just came out of the blue." That's what I wanted to hear.

On page three of the Seattle Times the next day they reported that the *accident* victim was a pilot for United Airlines on a layover killing some time doing a little downtown shopping.

What God has created, let no man put asunder. I could hear my old preacher Dobson's words. *Hah! We'll see about that. Maybe He will have to pay too. Surely, He must take some of the blame. But first, the others.*

It had been over four months since I had seen her smile, but to me it seemed like only yesterday. The realization that I would never see her smile again had, for a while, stripped my life of all meaning. But, now there was something else that gave my life meaning again.

You made the world a better place for me. I'll do it. I'll make the world a better place. I'll do it for you. I smiled at the thought that I could now fulfill my promise to her.

Yes, I was certain she would be proud of me if she were still alive. But if she were still alive, there would be no need to build my *Memorial of Vengeance* in her honor. *I like the sound of that.*

CHAPTER 35
TOM

I buzzed Heck's doorbell. I was early. We were supposed to meet at the restaurant later. I was afraid he might not be up and ready yet. Heck opened the door after only a few seconds. He was dressed.

"Hey, Tom. Why are you here?" He raised an eyebrow and looked at his watch. "Weren't we supposed to meet at the restaurant at 11:30? It's only 10:00."

"I know. I've got a surprise for you."

"What?" Heck looked perplexed. Then Billy Olsen stuck his head out from behind the corner of the entry alcove.

"Hi, Heck. It's been a long time. You're look'n good." He held out his arms for a hug.

Heck just stared. Then, recognition spread across his face. "Billy!"

They hugged, quick and manly, nothing to too long or too hard. "I picked him up at the airport a little while ago. I didn't tell you yesterday, 'cuz you had enough going on. Besides, I wanted it to be a surprise."

"Holy crap! I'm surprised alright."

"Sorry I couldn't make it to the funeral. Tom called me, but I had a lecture commitment. I couldn't get out of it on short notice. I figured, better late than never. So, here I am. I'm really sorry about Tyler."

Billy was about an inch shorter than me and probably weighed an extra eighty pounds. He was on the chunky side when we were teens, but now he was a little beyond chunky. He had always wore glasses and he still did, the simple black, old-man type.

With all this, and his receding hair line extending well behind his ears, you might conclude that he was five or ten years older than he was. But there was never any dispute, Billy was the smartest one in our little clique.

"Come on in. I just put on some coffee."

Billy and I sat down at the kitchen table while Heck got the cups, creamer, sugar, and spoons and brought them over to the table, before going back for the coffee pot.

"So, tell us about what you've been up to at Cornell. Are you still hanging out at Clark Hall? Are you Dean yet?" Heck knew he wasn't the Dean.

"Still at Clark Hall. No, I'm not Dean yet. Still just a professor in the Physical Sciences department. At least I'm tenured now. Who knows, I've got my eye on the Physics Department Head job, maybe a few years down the road."

"I saw a paper you wrote a while back, something about quantum probabilities? I got about two paragraphs into it before I was completely lost." If Heck was lost, I didn't have a chance. But then, I didn't want one. You couldn't pay me to read that stuff.

"Yeah, that's the area I've been working in for the last couple years."

"A *couple years?* Really? A cure for cancer, I could understand, but quantum probabilities?" Heck was dangling the bait in front of Billy's nose. Billy loved a challenge. Here we go. That's all I needed.

"So, tell me, Professor of Cognition and Perception, what have *you* been working on for the last couple years? A cure for cancer perhaps?" Billy said. Challenge accepted.

"You know I've been working on building a better understanding of Autistic Spectrum Disorders these last few years. It has real-world benefits for real people with autism. Who's going to benefit from knowing more about quantum probabilities?" I could see that this was going to be a Superman, x-ray vision, kind of discussion. I put my elbows on the table, and covered my face with both hands. They ignored me, just like the old days.

"Don't get me wrong. You do some great work with autistic people. And I've read a couple of your papers too. But, let's say you find a cure, or you find out how to prevent autism, or at least how to effectively treat it. It could help tens of thousands of people. That would be great! Right?"

"Right. That's what I'm saying."

"So, that would be great. But, what if you discovered something that would benefit all of humanity? That's what *I'm* saying."

"Okay, how the hell is *quantum probabilities* going to do that?"

"I'm glad you asked." Ugh! I leaned back and crossed my arms while letting out an exaggerated sigh. This was not going to end anytime soon. They ignored my exaggerated sigh.

Billy continued. "Do you believe in God?"

"Maybe. But what's that got to do with anything?"

"Well, I do. And, I believe God created quantum probability."

"I know you used to go to that Baptist church every Sunday with your family. So okay, nothing new, you're a believer. Again, what's that got to do with the price of beans in Siberia?"

"I don't exactly call myself a Baptist any more. But, you should have gone to church with me. You might a have learned a thing or two.

"Wouldn't you like to know with a *mathematical certainty* that there is a God, or that there is *no* God? Either way, wouldn't that be a monumental achievement for humanity?"

"There was way too much singing at that church for me. But, now you're off the subject. You're talking about religion, not physics."

"If you want to understand the mind of God, you have to understand the physical laws of the universe that He created, don't you? If we understand God, or at least His physical laws of the universe, we might understand not only the question of *how* the universe was created, but the question of *why* it was created."

"I'm sure you've heard of Albert Einstein, a pretty notable physicist, right. Didn't he say that, 'God does not play dice with His universe.' He was talking about probabilities, wasn't he? If he was right, how can probabilities be the key to understanding God?"

"The short answer is *free will.* You see, Einstein believed in the existence of God. And like me, he thought he could understand God through physics. But his work was clouded by his belief that God would not create an "accidental" universe. He believed God must be in total control of the universe, and Einstein's quest was to prove it mathematically.

"That's backward science. You don't start with a conclusion then go out to prove it. You gather all the facts first, only *then* do you come to a conclusion based on the facts. That's science."

"So you're saying Einstein was wrong?"

"No. I'm saying that he was asking the wrong questions, and that he let his personal beliefs interfere with his science.

"You've heard of Steven Hawking, another notable physicist. Back a few years ago he said, 'All the evidence points to Him being an inveterate gambler, who throws the dice on every possible occasion.' That's not an opinion, that's an observation. The math backs him up."

"Okay, so let's say the universe is based on quantum uncertainty, what's that got to do with *free will?*"

"Now, this is just my hypothesis. Let's say you're God. You can create anything, any way you want it. You have a choice. You can create a determinate universe where everything is totally predictable. Fate is inflexible. In the fate universe, there can be no free will. You don't have a choice because every event has been cast in stone since the beginning of time."

"Tom and I were talking about this." I rolled my eyes with no effect.

"Your other choice, as God, is to create a universe with free will. But how do you do that, and not have chaos? Probabilities. Casinos don't know the outcome of every roll of the dice. But they do know that they are going to come out ahead in the end. How? Because they know the odds, and they know that, with thousands of throws of the dice, they'll win more often than they lose.

"By defining the probabilities on a quantum level, God does not need to know the outcome of every roll of the dice. You can make your own choices, but in the end, the universe will come out as God planned."

"You're saying that God does *not* know it all?"

"I'm saying that God does not *want* to know it all. If you know everything that's going to happen, how boring is that? If you were God, wouldn't you want to be surprised a little once in a while? But if God is omnipotent, how can He surprise Himself? Probabilities. And with probabilities, uncertainty is built into the design of the universe at its most basic quantum level."

"Then, how does uncertainty on a quantum level give us free will?"

"Okay, this is where it gets a little weird. It seems that probability itself can be indeterminate, and can be influence by our collective consciousness. There are experiments that demonstrate this, like the famous "Double Slit" experiment. Apparently, *all* possibilities exist simultaneously until we become conscious of it. In other words, we collectively decide what reality is."

"That's a very big bite you're asking me to swallow."

"I know, it's counter intuitive, but all the evidence points in that direction. I'd like to be the one who mathematically proves it, or at least the one to document the reality that human consciousness does determine reality."

"I hope you don't talk about this too much on the campus at Cornell. They'll think you're loony."

"Well no, I don't talk too loudly about it. Even though Cornell has got its share of mavericks, they're not the ones that get the plum assignments. But that's my problem, how can I work on it, and how can I get grant money, if I don't state my hypothesis?"

"Sounds like a problem, yours, not mine. I keep my feet on the ground."

"But you know, it's not just me. There are a lot of distinguished people working on this idea. But that's why they get to work on it in the open, because they *are* distinguished. Us grunts have to toe the line."

"Tom, you've been pretty quiet. What do you think?" Heck knew what I thought. He just wanted to give me a poke in the ribs.

"I think we should get down to the restaurant before my head explodes. Jeez, you guys do this to me every time you're together! Let's just go." If we didn't leave then, I was fully prepared to put a double dose of Drain-Fast clog remover in my coffee.

"Billy, I don't know if you have any plans, but I assume you're coming along." Heck said. I prayed to God that they weren't going to continue this conversation about God at the restaurant.

"I could only get away for a couple days. My only plans are to see you and Tom. I don't know if I can be any help, but sure, let's go. It's still a little early for lunch, but I might be able to force myself to eat a little pie." I smiled. Same old Billy. He always had a healthy sweet tooth. I didn't expect that any "force" would be needed.

CHAPTER 36
SAL

I was working on my laptop at the small snack table provide in the Hotel room. Becky was taking her time getting ready for our 11:00 brunch meeting with Drs. Beckman and Martin from the Mercer Residential Rehabilitation Institute.

I smiled thinking about Becky's curtsy. I must remember to address them by their first names, Heck and Jan.

"Oh, oh." I was looking at the results of the genetic sequencing for the three surviving Bangkok Virus victims that Rose had sent me. I had gotten blood samples from all three sent to the CDC before I went on leave. I ordered the genetic sequencing at the same time. I gave it a low priority, no-rush, status. It was more to complete our records, than for anything else.

" 'Oh, oh' what?" Becky said.

"I think we may have a problem with the virus."

"What kind of a problem." I liked Becky's curiosity, especially on subjects that she had little knowledge. She was never afraid to ask a "stupid question," a prerequisite for true intelligence.

"We might see it again. That's 'what kind of problem.' " It could be a very big problem.

"Why? How?"

"It's part of their DNA. This virus is apparently like some other viruses that incorporate themselves into our human DNA sequence and lie dormant. Like gonorrhea for example, you've heard that people can have flare ups. That's because the virus is hiding dormant inside of their cells. When you have a weakened immune system, like when you get a cold, the virus breaks out and is then contagious."

"I didn't know viruses could do that. That's kinda scary."

"It's been studied. Apparently, 7-8% of the human genome is made up of foreign viral DNA that we picked up sometime during our human evolutionary history. Some scientists believe that this mechanism may be responsible for a large part of human evolution."

"8% isn't enough to change us into a lizard or anything, is it?"

"Well, considering that only 1.8% separates human DNA from chimpanzee DNA, I'd say 8% could potentially have a pretty big effect."

"Can you stop it? What are you going to do?"

"There's no way that the corrupted DNA can be fixed. It will be with them their whole lives, and will most likely be inherited by any children they have.

"As for the breakouts, we can monitor their health. And if they get into an immune compromising situation, we can isolate them and treat the symptoms. We may be able to develop a vaccine, like we have with shingles, another dormant virus."

"So, are you going to let them know at the CDC?"

"I guess I have to, don't I. But that's another problem."

"Why? Can't you send them a report or something?"

"I can, and I will, but it'll probably be the last thing I ever do for the CDC."

"Oh that's right, you said you were ordered not to work, 'or else.' "

"Dr. Edelman was very clear, 'Take off work until the first of February, or you're fired.'"

"Couldn't you just hold off a few weeks, then turn in your report?" She knew the answer.

"What, and put people at risk by not notifying them of the threat as soon as possible? I don't think so."

Do what you know to be right, Blondie Girl. Regardless of the cost?

###

Becky and I were a few minutes early, but we arrived at the restaurant at the same time Heck and Tom got there. They were just getting out of their car. They were with a short, stout, balding black man wearing Buddy Holly glasses.

"Hi. Dr. Beckman, I mean Heck. Tom." *Green eyes.* I felt a chill, but forced a smile.

"Sal, Becky. I'd like you to meet Billy, or Dr. William Olsen, if you prefer." Heck winked at Becky as he said the last. She blushed. I smiled.

"Good to meet you, Billy." Becky and I shook his hand.

"Billy is an old friend of ours. He couldn't make it to Tyler's funeral because of work commitments at Cornell University. He just got in today."

We went in and got a table for six. Jan had not arrived yet, so we ordered drinks while we waited.

"Billy, Heck said you work at Cornell. What do you do there?" Small talk, the grease of verbal communication, especially for work.

"I'm a professor in the physics department. And, Heck said you work for the CDC."

"Applied physics or theoretical physics?" I'd be talking more about what *I do* in a few minutes. I wanted to learn more about Billy. He seemed at first to be an unlikely friend to Heck, but then so did Tom.

"Theoretical. I work with quantum mechanics mostly. Heck and I started college there together. He came back to Seattle. I stayed in Ithica."

Becky was talking to Tom. "It's so beautiful out here. Do you and Heck live near the Space Needle, or near that Pike Place Market place? We went to the Space Needle, but we haven't been to that market yet." I noticed that she had been looking at Tom a lot since we sat down.

"That's more downtown. Heck lives in Montlake, up toward the university district. I live in the Ballard area, North of Seattle."

"Oh." Becky had no idea where these places were, but she didn't want to show it.

"Heck and Billy and I grew up in Monroe, it's a little town about a half hour Northeast of Seattle, sorta out in the sticks." Tom looked like a "sticks" kind of guy, a little rough around the edges, like Becky in a way.

I looked up and saw Jan coming our way. She seemed in a hurry.

"Sorry everyone. I wanted to get here early. Heck, your phone is not working. I've been trying to get a hold of you." Heck checked his phone.

"Crap. I must have accidentally turned it off somehow."

"We're going to have company in a few minutes. I wanted to tell you." Jan sat down, but did not acknowledge Billy.

"Jan, this is Billy, an old friend of Tom and I."

"Glad to meet you." She gave him a perfunctory smile.

"Nice to meet you too." Billy didn't smile.

Jan looked toward the door. "Oh, here he is now." She stood up and waved at Lt. Boswick.

"What's *he* want?" Heck was obviously not happy to see this man.

Jan didn't seem happy about it either. "He'll fill you in." She pulled up a chair from another empty table and slid it to the head of our table, but he didn't sit down.

He introduced himself, but didn't bother to get anyone's name. He apparently knew Jan and Heck.

"Jan told me that you all would be meeting here today. I thought it would be good chance to ask a few questions.

"First, let me tell you why I wanted to talk to you. There was an accidental death yesterday in downtown Seattle. The man's name was Mark McKenzie. Captain McKenzie was a pilot for United Airlines. Does that ring a bell for anyone?"

Everyone looked at each other. No one recognized the name. I probably should have.

"He was the pilot on the flight that had that Bangkok flu outbreak. Does *that* ring a bell?" Impatient, sarcastic, arrogant, all seemed to be easily displayed aspects of Lt. Boswick's character. He was making no attempt to hide them.

Even Billy had heard about the Bangkok flu outbreak.

"I'm from the CDC. I'm in charge of the Bangkok flu case. I am very familiar with the case. I didn't recognize Mark McKenzie's name because he did not contract the virus." I felt that I should establish my credentials.

"Okay, whatever. Do you believe in coincidence?" It was a rhetorical question. He wasn't waiting for an answer.

He continued, "Well I don't! First we have poor Mr. Wheatly who dies from a tragic *accident,* at the Mercer Institute. Ray Miller is accused of playing a part in that *accident,* but there's no hard evidence. Then, the Institute has an *accidental* fire that killed that little boy, and Ray Miller mysteriously goes missing. Finally, we have Captain McKenzie *accidentally* killed by a flying hubcap in downtown Seattle, and Ray Miller is in the vicinity. Are we starting to see a connection here?"

He was acting the professor, challenging his slow-witted students. Did he know that "that little boy" was Heck's son? Did he care?

"You found Ray? I submitted a missing persons report, but haven't heard anything from the police." Jan said.

"*Yes,* we found Ray Miller. He wasn't that hard to find. I got a hunch when I found out that McKenzie was flying the plane that Miller and his late wife were on. As you know the lease on Ray's apartment lapsed while he was in the hospital. His in-laws put his things in storage. He's not staying with them. I checked.

"So, where could he be living? I ran a check on Miller's credit card receipts. He's staying in at the Executive Hotel on Spring Street, a few blocks away from where Captain McKenzie met his *accidental* demise."

"I didn't think he had credit cards. Did you talk to him?" Heck was obviously surprised by the news.

"No, you didn't *think*. And *yes,* I talked to him." I added condescension to Lt. Boswick's list of charms.

"He admits to being in the area where McKenzie was killed, but says he saw nothing until afterwards when the ambulance showed up.

"I also asked him why he disappeared after the fire. He said he thought it was time to leave, just that. Hey, it's a free country. He hasn't been judged legally incompetent. He can live wherever he wants.

"Oh, and he had a message for you *Mr.* Beckman. He said, 'You won't have to keep an eye on me anymore.' What do you think he meant by that?" He gave the "Mr." a deliberate emphasis. What an ass.

Heck ignored the slight. "I don't know for sure. Dr. Martin and I decided it would be a good idea to watch him after Ted Wheatly was killed…er ah, died. But I don't think he *knew* we were watching him. Do you think Ray caused the fire?" Both pain and anger flashed across Heck's face for a second.

"Well *Professor,* I *think* you might be wrong about what Miller knew, and/or didn't know.

"The fire investigators found no evidence of arson, but now, with this latest *accidental* death, I'm not so sure. There's just too many coincidences in too short a time. Does anyone know anything that might be helpful, either that implicates Miller, or that clears him?"

No one said anything. We were all taking in this new information. Heck's eyebrows were pinched in thought.

I hadn't noticed before, but there seemed to be a lot more to Heck than I had thought, an unseen depth that lay just beneath the surface. There was gentleness there, but it was combined with a kind of stoic toughness.

I dared to look directly into his emerald green eyes for a moment. I did not feel the chill that I had when we met after the funeral, and again in the restaurant parking lot. There was only warmth now. I wanted to know more about this man.

Lt. Boswick didn't wait long. "Okay listen, I don't have much time to work on a no-evidence case. Hunches don't buy me much slack with my boss. Give me a call, if you think of anything."

He gave out his cards. Actually, he just dropped several on the table in front of Jan, who then distributed them to everyone. His name was written in bold in the center of the card, *Joe Boswick*. And beneath his name, in smaller letters, it said, *Lt. Criminal Investigations.*

Lt. Boswick left as he had arrived, without formalities, without courtesies, without salutations.

Becky studied the card she got like it was a White House invitation. Tom turned his over immediately and asked Becky for our hotel phone number. He didn't ask me, even though I was sitting closer to him, but he did ask to borrow my pen.

When I got the pen back, I took Tom's lead, and asked Heck for his and Tom's numbers. I didn't ask Tom, even though he was sitting closer to me.

The waitress took Lt. Boswick's departure as her cue to ask for our lunch orders. Becky ordered a burger and fries. She did not ask if they served beer, but ordered a shake.

Billy said to me, "Sal, I thought the Bangkok flu outbreak was stopped. Why is the CDC still treating it like an active case?"

Heck raised his eyebrows. He wanted to hear the answer too. "It's not exactly active. We're continuing to monitor it as we do many cases. Nothing is ever really *inactive,* as such."

"So, why are you here? They don't usually send people around the country just to *monitor* cases, do they?"

"No, they don't, but I'm doing some independent work on my own. In fact, I have just made an important discovery that I wanted to share with Heck and Jan." Jan heard her name and looked up from her menu.

It also got everyone else's attention. Becky and Tom had been in a continuous conversation since Lt. Boswick left. They too stopped and looked my way.

"I have just learned that the Bangkok virus is endogenous. I have discovered that it is what we call a HERV, a *Human Endogenous Viral Element,* also called a *provirus.*"

Jan's mouth open a little, and her eyes opened wider. She probably hadn't heard these terms since medical school, but she remembered what they meant. Everyone else just looked puzzled.

I explained, "That's when a virus incorporates itself into the human genome. It becomes part of the subject's DNA, and can be passed on to future generations."

Heck said, "How is that a threat?"

"It *could* be a threat in two ways. The first, it *could* affect the children of any of the victims. Exactly how, is impossible to know. It's not very likely anyway, considering the status of the only three surviving victims.

"I'm more concerned about the second possible threat. The virus is dormant while it's hiding inside the genome. But if one of our victims' immune system becomes weakened for any reason, the virus *could* be reactivated. That person could possibly infect other people."

Jan added, "It's like the herpes virus, or chicken pox, or the human papillomavirus."

"How does that happen?" Heck seemed more troubled than the others.

"It's just chance. As far as we can tell, it's happened many times before, over millions of years of human genetic history. Most of it is just junk DNA, and does nothing. It's a type of parasitic symbiosis. The virus gets a form of immortality. Hypothetically, humans could see some benefits. Some scientists believe it could account for some turning points in human evolution. There can be short term cellular transformations too. These are usually harmful, such as with papillomavirus-caused cervical cancer.

"Our Bangkok virus may be an exception to that rule. It seems to have caused cellular transformations that, arguably, have given our surviving victims some benefits. I've ordered more tests that will show the extent and modality of the cellular-level changes."

"You mentioned *chance*. I consider myself somewhat of an expert on that subject. Can you tell me how you think *chance* has come into play with this virus?" Billy had not said anything for the last few minutes. This seemed like a highly academic subject to me.

I noticed Tom rolling his eyes. Heck noticed too, and smirked.

I thought about his question for a second. "Okay, the virus seems to be the *chance* combination of two unrelated viruses that infected patient number one at the same time. They had a sort of viral *chance* sexual-like encounter inside a cell, and apparently infected each other, resulting in a new hybrid virus having characteristics of both parents, plus a couple of new ones. Chance.

"Most people who were infected, died. The few who didn't die appear to have abilities they didn't have before. *Chance* that they didn't die, and *chance* that they had the outcomes that they did."

"Something is not right about all that. You see, *chance* is not as random as most people believe. It has limits and rules."

"I don't understand." I said.

"Okay, look at it this way. If you went to a casino craps table, and you rolled a seven twenty times in a row, what do you think would happen?"

"I'd be rich?" That caused a few soft chuckles around the table.

"Yes, maybe, but more importantly, the croupier would probably pull those dice off the table. Why? Because, you were being too lucky to be just lucky. He knows, or maybe *feels* is a better word, that something is wrong, and he'd be right."

Billy wrinkled his brow and pinched his chin. "That brings us back to the *chance* accidental events that Lt. Boswick was talking about. My sense is that there is too much *chance* there to be *chance*. I need to think about this some more, run some calculations." Billy seemed to become lost in thought. He had nothing more to say, but started scribbling notes on a napkin.

I changed the subject. "Heck, I've met Leonard Atkins in Florida, the third surviving victim of the virus. I also want to meet Ray, but that might be a problem at this time. Do you think you might be able to introduce me to Anna Grant?"

"Sure, she lives in West Seattle. I'll give her a call. I'm pretty sure she'll be okay with it. When do you want me to set it up, tomorrow?" There was something Heck was not saying, something dark.

"Tom's got our hotel number. Call me when you confirm the time."

The rest of our brunch was filled with small talk. Heck seemed to be not completely connected, and responded in mostly one-word sentences. He must be thinking about his son.

Billy didn't talk at all. His head was full of mental calculations. His mouth was full of a pastrami Rubin on rye, followed by a piece of apple pie.

Tom and Becky had their own conversation going, one that seemed to require a lot of smiling.

Jan and I talked mostly about clinical research topics. Boring to me, but Jan had apparently not had the opportunity to talk shop with anyone for quite a while. I happily obliged.

I was worried about Heck. Funny that. Why would I worry about someone who I barely knew?

Something Daddy said had been bouncing around in my head, for the last couple days. *The right man will come along.*

That was a silly thought. I wasn't looking. And, I certainly didn't think Heck, or anyone else, was the *right* man. How could I? I didn't need any man right now, the right one or any other kind.

But still, there was something. Daddy would have liked Heck, his directness, his stoic-but-sensitive nature. And, there was something else.

I was sitting on Heck's left side. The scare under his chin seemed to glow red, like a neon lightning bolt under heavy smoked glass. I tried not to look at it. It seemed to have an energy of its own, hidden just under the surface. I decided that it added something to his otherwise good looks.

CHAPTER 37
HECK

I picked Sal up at the hotel at 9:00. We agreed that I would drive, since I knew the area.

My clutch leg was still a little stiff, but I was glad to be back in my BMW.

Tom had beaten me to the hotel by about a half hour. He was taking Becky down to Pike Place Market. He had volunteered, and he and Becky weren't very keen on going with us to see Anna Grant anyway.

Billy wanted some time alone. He said he had some theories that he wanted to flesh out.

I decided to take Sal on the scenic route around Alki Point on Alki Avenue SW. I planned to cut back over to SW Admiral Way and circle back to Anna's neighborhood. It wasn't that far out of our way, but it was a clear and sunny day. The view of Seattle from across the bay was inspiring.

I could use some inspiration, I thought. I didn't share my plan with Sal. She wouldn't know the difference in which route I chose anyway, and I wanted to surprise her with the view of Seattle. Funny, I hadn't made an effort to impress a woman for a very long time. Why, now?

"Wow!" Sal was impressed.

"Hey listen, we've got some extra time, if you want me to pull over somewhere so you can take a few pictures."

"That'd be great! I brought my camera, if you're sure we have enough time."

I turned off on California Way SW and went up to Hamilton Viewpoint Park. I hadn't been there since before I went to Alaska with Tom. I took Tyler up there once. He was not impressed with the view. He wanted to swing. The park has no swings, so we didn't stay long.

Sal was much more impressed than Tyler had been.

"It's just beautiful! Look, I can see the Space Needle."

"I don't get over here much, and it's usually raining. I'm glad you like it." I was very glad that she liked it. I hadn't felt like this since my first date with Wendy. I liked the feeling.

My cell phone rang. It was Jan. "I better answer this, it's Jan."

I pushed the button. "Hello Jan. What's up?"

"I just got a call from Lt. Boswick. There's another one."

"Another death? Who?"

At the word "death" Sal turned away from the panoramic view, and her smile disappeared.

"Dr. Stanley Malone. He's a resident doctor at Harborview. He was on the plane. He was the primary medical volunteer on the plane, but he didn't catch the virus."

"What happened?" This is way beyond any possibility of random chance.

"He accidentally took an asthma medicine which caused an arrhythmia, a fibrillation. He must have passed out. He wasn't found until it was too late."

"He was a doctor, for God sake. How does a doctor take the wrong medicine?"

"You know that residents sometimes have to work long shifts. His coworker said that he sometimes took caffeine to stay awake."

"Did anyone tamper with the pills?"

"Apparently not. He had two bottles in his lab coat pocket when they found him. One was marked as caffeine. The other was a prescription for ephedrine. The prescription was written for Tanner Ragan, a patient being treated for acute asthma at the hospital. The correct pills were in the correct bottles."

"Don't the pills look different?"

"I asked that question. The ephedrine comes in a red capsule. Caffeine comes in all kinds of shapes and packages. The ones he had were a time released version, and they also come in a red capsule.

"The timed release feature did not help him. It kept a constant level of caffeine in his bloodstream, in his case, a very high level. Co-workers say they had seen him taking caffeine pills all the time. They said it was probably the combination of both medicines that caused the fibrillation. He was healthy. The ephedrine alone shouldn't have killed him."

"What about suicide?"

"He just got engaged last week to a nurse who works at the hospital. He proposed and gave her the ring while having a romantic dinner at the top of the Space Needle. She accepted his proposal.

"Lt. Boswick said that she is a complete wreck about it, hasn't stopped crying since she found out. 'Check, check, and double check.' Is the way Boswick summed it up."

"What about Ray? Is he connected in any way?"

"No one saw him on the floor where Dr. Malone was working, but several people saw him in the hospital cafeteria that evening. Boswick said that he seemed to be going out of his way to make sure people saw him in the cafeteria. He was wearing a bright purple shirt, and even introduced himself to a couple of the kitchen staff. He dropped a plate, drawing attention with the noise. He dropped several coins on the floor by the cash register, and made a big display of retrieving them. He crawled around on his hands and knees picking them up."

"Did Lt. Boswick question Ray?"

"Yes, as soon as he found out that Dr. Malone was on Boswick's list of people associated with that flight."

"And?"

"And, nothing. Boswick said that Ray was waiting for him in the hotel lobby. Waiting for him! Can you believe it? Anyway, they've got nothing on Ray, no witnesses, no finger prints, nothing but a 'smug mug' is what Boswick called it. I'm sure he was talking about that same Cheshire cat smile Ray had after Ted died."

"But what was he doing at the hospital?"

"Ray said he was simply having dinner. Suspicious? Yes. But apparently, people who have no business at the hospital do it all the time. There's no law against it. It's not too far from Ray's hotel. The food's not too bad. It's pretty reasonably priced. And, they don't expect you to leave a tip."

"Okay. Thanks for calling. Let me know if you hear anything else. Sal and I are on our way to see Anna. I'll keep you updated on what comes of that too." I hung up.

Something was bothering me. I couldn't put my finger on it. It felt like it did the night Tyler died in the fire, an uneasiness.

"Are you okay? What happened?"

I filled her in with what Jan had told me.

"We should be heading over to see Anna." We walked to the car and got in.

That uneasy feeling was persistent. I decided to indulge it for a moment.

"Are you okay?" Sal asked for the second time. I hadn't started the car, and was starring out the windshield. I must have appeared pretty spaced out.

"Yeah, I'm okay. Something about what Jan said is bothering me.

"What?"

"I don't know. Give me a minute. I just want to think about it."

I closed my eyes and let that odd, uncomfortable feeling spread over me. I let go of my rationality. I didn't fight it. I didn't try to control it. I didn't try to understand it. I just let it flow over me.

I remembered being in the void during the grizzly attack. I didn't try to analyze it at the time. I knew I had a choice. I knew. I simply knew. Why, or how, were of no concern.

I let my mind dip a toe into the dark water of that void. For an instant, I touched it. Nothing and everything enveloped me.

Something Jan said. The name Tanner caught my attention. Tanner was the name of my second cousin in Portland. Gloria's kid. Little Tanner, eight years old now. His little sister, Jessica, just four. Little Jess and little Tann Tann. That's what Jess called him at first. It caught on. Everyone called him Tann now. Why am I thinking about him now? Why? Something about that name. It hit me. I knew.

"Do you have a pen and something to write on?" I said with some urgency.

"Ah, sure." She dug in her purse and came up with a pen and small note pad. There was a large question mark on her face. I ignored it for now.

I wrote the patient name that Jan had told me was on the prescription bottle. T-A-N-N-E-R-R-A-G-A-N just the way that Anna Grant had wrote my name when we had first met. Something about that name. It was there somewhere. I knew I was looking at it, but I couldn't see it.

Tanner, Tann Tann, Tann. I scratched off the E-R. It just felt right. Still nothing. What was it? I closed my eyes again, visualizing the letters. I let them float around on their own. Nothing.

There had to be something. I *knew* it. I let go. I let go of rational thought.

We live in a world of rational thought. Without it, we would die, or at least not live as well as we do. Somewhere in our evolutionary history, our brain's ability to think rationally, gave us an edge. We survived and we flourished because of it. Our intuition, our instincts, our feelings, were all given a back seat. Recapturing them is not easy. It's not *rational.*

For a moment I became oblivious to my surroundings. I was no longer in my car, in a park, in West Seattle, with the sun on my head, and with the sea breeze in my face. Sal was not there either. I touched the void again.

"Anna Grant!" I got it. I felt it. It felt right.

"What about her?" Sal was anxious, but patient.

"A-N-N-A-G-R-A-N-T! It's the same letters as Tann Ragan. He's sending *me* a message." I looked Sal in the eye, and only saw confusion.

"I don't understand. Who? What message?" Her eyes were wide, and she leaned away from me a little.

"Ray is letting *me* know that Anna Grant is his next target!" It was clear to me now.

"How can that be? Because the letters are the same? That's just a coincidence, right? How can that be a message from Ray? And, why *you?*" She must have thought I had gone completely over the edge.

I took a deep breath, and let it out slowly. Sal was a rational person. I had to try to explain it to her in a rational way. But, how do you rationally explain the irrational? I needed her to understand. I had to try.

"Okay look, I know how this sounds, but stick with me for a minute, please.

"First of all, nothing with Ray is a *coincidence.* Accidents are not accidents with Ray. I don't know how he does it, but I know he does it. I've seen what he can do, and it's pretty amazing. I can only imagine what he can do that I haven't seen.

"He must have hacked into the hospital computer somehow. He selected a patient that had letters containing the letters of Anna Grant's name. He knows Anna's reputation with words, that's why he chose to use an anagram to transmit the message. It's like he's underlining it with irony. He even directed the message specifically at me. Somehow, he knows I have a second cousin whose nickname is Tann. The extra E-R would have thrown anyone else off. He knew *I* would see it.

"He's being cute. He's showing off. I don't know how he knows that I could figure it out, but this is his way of thumbing his nose at me personally." I hoped I came across to her as something a little less threatening than a foaming-at-the-mouth, raving lunatic.

"So, what you're saying is that Ray is a magical, evil mastermind, and that I should just trust you on that because *you* just know, right?"

She was being a little sarcastic, but that pretty much summed it up. There was something special about this woman, but whatever I had going for me with her, I knew I just blew it.

"Yes, that's about right." I lowered my eyes. Maybe I *was* crazy.

"Okay. I believe you. I don't know why. I must be nuts, but at least I'll come along for the ride."

"Really? Well, we better warn Anna." It felt good using the word 'we.'

I called Anna's home number. Karen Wilson answered the phone.

"Hello, Karen. This is Dr. Beckman. Dr. Salinger and I are on our way over to meet with Anna like we talked about yesterday. We should be there in just a few minutes.

"There've been some developments. I think Anna may be in some danger. I just wanted to tell you to lock the doors, and don't let anyone in until we get there."

"Okay! I will. Anna's Aunt is out for the day. She went into Seattle for a doctor's appointment. What kind of danger?" I think I scared her. She sounded anxious.

"It's probably nothing. I'll explain it when we get there. Okay?"

"Ah, okay, whatever you say." The anxiety was still there.

"Shouldn't we tell Lt. Boswick?" She already had his card out.

I dialed his cell number.

"Boswick here." Not "Hello."

"This is Dr. Beckman, from the Mercer Residential Rehabilitation Institute."

"I know who you are. What do you want?"

"I just talked to Dr. Martin. She told me about Dr. Malone at Harborview."

"Yeah, yeah. Wuda'ya got?" I wondered when the last time was that this guy had experienced a moment of patience.

"I think that Ray's next target is Anna Grant. She was the Senior Flight Attendant on the Bangkok Virus flight."

"What you *think* does not concern me. Why you think it *might*. Give it to me."

"I think there was a message from Ray Miller hidden in the name on the ephedrine prescription that Dr. Malone *accidentally* took."

"Like I said Beckman, I don't give a damn what the hell you *think!* Now, cut the bullshit. What are you talking about?"

"It's an anagram. The letters in the name on the prescription, Tanner Ragan, if you unscramble them, you get the name Anna Grant. He's telling us that she's next." It sounded ridiculous to me now.

"That's *it?* That's *all* you've got?" I could hear him let out a sigh. "Beckman you need to get yourself a laxative, and take a double dose. You're so full of *crap,* I can't believe it!" He hung up without a "Goodbye."

"What did he say?" She had only heard my side of the conversation.

"He gave me some medical advice."

"Huh?" I wasn't going to explain it to her.

"He doesn't believe me. I guess I don't blame him." But, I guess I did blame him, for choosing to be an ignorant ass. Tyler might still be alive if he had believed Jan and I after Ray murdered Ted. He chose to be rational, to do the rational thing. Ignorance is often a choice.

I let it all sink in. The fire was not an accident. It was Ray. I knew that for certain now. That bastard killed Tyler, and the police are *worthless!*

It has to be me. He cannot be allowed to get away with it. He is a clear and present threat. He is a murderer. He is a mutant evil creature that is no longer part of the human race.

Then I made a conscious decision. I *knew* it was *my choice.* I *knew* it was the right one. *I will not allow Ray to live on this planet. Somehow, some way, I will stop him, for Tyler's sake, and for the sake of everyone else who calls themselves human. Ray Miller must die.*

"I guess we're on our own then. We better get over to Anna's as quick as we can." Sal saw my jaw tighten. She was worried, about Ray, and I thought now, about me too.

The clouds had started creeping in from the West.

As I put the car in gear and let out the clutch, the sun went behind a cloud, and everything got darker.

CHAPTER 38
RAY

I sat in my rented Chevrolet Malibu outside of Anna Grant's Aunt's home. I was waiting for Dr. Beckman and Dr. Salinger to arrive. It should be only another three minutes by my calculation.

It was unusually sunny, but the clouds were starting to roll in from the West, promising to make it into a more typical overcast Seattle day.

How lucky it is to have another person from my list of out-of-town murder conspirators here in Seattle. Of course, I knew Salinger would be here. So, maybe "lucky" is the wrong word. "Predictable" is more accurate.

I was finding fewer and fewer things in my world that were truly unpredictable. There were things that I chose not to predict, but those would be in the category of *unpredicted* rather than *unpredictable.*

Humans are, in some ways, more predictable than other things. Like the woman I met in the hospital lobby yesterday on my way out after completing my *chores,* I knew she would go to bed with me that night. I knew her thoughts better than she did. Predictable, and predicted.

Mary was her name, not that it mattered. She was just a thing that I used to satisfy a basic bodily function. She was no more than a tissue, to be discarded when its function was served.

Some might say that I betrayed my beloved Julia by having sex with another woman. That's absurd. First, Julia was much more than the instrument of a simple bodily function. I loved her more than life. Second, she is gone. Any physical commitments I had with her, died with her. Third, if I used a new toilet to perform another bodily function, would this too be a betrayal of Julia? Of course not. Just flush, and walk away.

Predictability. It was exhilarating at first, but it had become almost boring. I found that I needed to continuously increase the complexity of my predictive endeavors, just to keep it interesting.

It took me about three minutes to hack into the Harborview Hospital data base. Passwords only provide the illusion of security for the ignorant. Unauthorized access is, in fact, limited only by the intelligence of the hacker.

With or without access to hospital records, I could see at least a hundred ways to kill Dr. Malone. But, I am becoming a man of high standards. A murder lacking artistry is barbaric. I am above using a blunt club to kill, like some caveman. I am not a common street thug. I am an artist, a master craftsman of death.

Dr. Malone failed to save Julia. He was as responsible as the rest, maybe more. He played his part. There were several things he could have done, but didn't. For example, he could have packed her in ice to get her temperature down. He didn't. Of course, there was not enough ice on the plane to give everyone that treatment, but there was enough for Julia. It might not have worked, but he should have tried.

So whoever knows the right thing to do, and fails to do it, for him it is a sin. James 4:17.

Getting him to take a fatal dose of medication was the easy part. The fun part was finding the right patient who, not only had been prescribed the right medication, but who also had the right letters in his or her name.

I wanted to send Dr. Beckman a message that only he would see. Even though, by the time he saw it, if he saw it, it would be too late. It was enough to know that he would know.

There were exactly 108,364 possible combinations of alternate messages, patient names, and medications. Only three matched my purpose. All three names contained some extra letters, but Tanner was the name of Dr. Beckman's second cousin in Portland, nicknamed Tann.

Dr. Beckman would not remember that he had mentioned his name in passing to Dr. Martin one day during one of their *private* conversations, something about his family's history of autism, and the fact that little Tann did not have it, along with a list of others in his family.

In effect, I put Dr. Beckman's name on the message. He would see it.

Dr. Malone's habit of popping caffeine was a bonus. Oh yes, his medical records were in the hospital data base too, but the caffeine was not mentioned in his medical records. I found it in his personnel records. The hospital kept a list of all medications taken by all licensed staff, containing both prescription and over-the-counter drugs. It was a recent policy designed by hospital lawyers to prevent possible future law suits. Their lawyers could explain their reasoning. I won't.

Once the weapon and method of Dr. Malone's death were decided, the rest was simple. Well, simple for me. Execution of my plan relied mostly on *predictable* human nature.

Yes, I was in the cafeteria. Yes, I was on Dr. Malone's floor. But I was *not* wearing a purple shirt in both places. If you want to be noticed, do something, or wear something that stands out. If you don't want to be noticed, act and appear like everyone else.

People only see what they expect to see ninety percent of the time. A man with a badge and a lab coat acting intent and busy, disappears into a background of other people with badges and a lab coats being intent and busy.

But, Dr. Malone mainly died of his bad habits. Getting overtired and overdosing on caffeine were just two habits that contributed to his death. A third and critical bad habit was keeping his caffeine pills in his left hand lab coat pocket. Taking them had become all too automatic.

Again, people only see what they expect to see. You can rely on it, especially when your target is tired and running on autopilot. Add a conveniently distracting call from his *finance* at exactly the right moment, and he swallows the wrong pill that just happened to be in the wrong pocket.

There was only silence when he answered the call from his finance's cell phone. He may have thought the call had been dropped. In fact, it was the angel of death on the line, and he's not real talkative.

Her phone was off when he called her back. He left her a short voice message. Much later, she would check her messages. It would be the last five seconds of his voice that she would hear.

There they were, coming up the road in Dr. Beckman's black 320i BMW convertible. Right on schedule. Predictable.

I got out of the car and waved at them as they were pulling up.

I could see the recognition in Dr. Beckman's eyes through the wind shield, then the fear, then the anger. Predictable.

"It's him!" I heard him say. The top was up on his convertible, but that did not hinder my hearing.

"Ray?" Dr. Salinger didn't need to ask. Why do people do that, ask questions when they already know the answers?

Dr. Beckman slammed on the brakes, stopping his car in the middle of the road with a loud screech. He didn't get out. He didn't drive away. He was deciding what to do next. Dr. Salinger was not helping him, unless you think that wide eyes and an open mouth is helpful. He needed my help, like I knew he would.

I walked toward his car, smiling a big toothy smile. It was a real smile. I had much to smile about.

This was the motivation needed for Dr. Beckman to get out of his car. He had a woman in the car. Male pride prevented him from running away. Male protective instincts made him defend the woman and his territory, i.e. his car. Predictable.

I extended my hand. I knew he was not going to shake it. More motivation.

"Hello, Dr. Beckman." I said, still wearing that same smile.

"What are you doing here?" His voice was strong and authoritative, but there was a slight tremor in his voice, not fear, but high tension.

"I'm here for the same reason you are, to see Anna Grant." I said honestly.

"Why?" It was a challenge. He had moved closer to a position that was more directly between me and the house. He was in a defensive posture. He expected me to attack him. He could not imagine my true plan.

"I just want to talk to the woman who *didn't save* Julia." She was too busy getting coffee for that arrogant pilot to do more to save my Julia. Sure, she was *helpful* to some, but she didn't help Julia enough.

'Rescue those who are being taken away to death; hold back those who are stumbling to the slaughter. Proverbs 24:11'

"You can't blame her for what happened to your wife." He said. *Yes, I can.*

Anna and her helper had heard the screeching brakes, and had come to the door. They were playing their parts. Anna would be dead soon.

I took a step closer to the house, and to Dr. Beckman. I needed a little more tension.

Dr. Beckman took a step to the side to blockade my path. More tension.

Dr. Salinger got out of the car. Dr. Beckman noticed. It reminded him that she still needed protection. More tension.

"Dr. Beckman, I only want to *talk* to her." I put a measure of menace into my voice, and took a step closer. At the same time I put my right hand into my jacket pocket. More tension.

"Ray, you need to get back in your car and leave, before I call the police." Yes, the tension was building. Almost there.

"Why would you call the police? I haven't done anything illegal, *have I?*" I kept the menace in my voice and my hand in my pocket, and took another step toward the house.

Anna was in her wheelchair with the door partially open, watching the proceedings with obvious fear.

Dr. Beckman took a half step toward me, in a defiant stance. Now he's there.

I took another step, taking me within two feet of Dr. Beckman. I looked him squarely in the eye, and made a threatening move with my right hand inside my jacket pocket.

Dr. Beckman grabbed my right arm and bent it backwards. I pretended to struggle to get my hand out of my pocket.

We wrestled me to the ground. Dr. Beckman pulled my empty hand out of my pocket. He pinned both arms with his knees. His adrenaline was flowing. He was about to punch me in the face, just as I had planned. Predictable.

At that moment Anna yelled, "Stop!" Dr. Beckman stopped to look at her.

She had stood up from her wheelchair. She was looking down at her feet. She walked unsteadily across the porch to the steps.

"Anna, no!" Karen Wilson yelled in protest. But, she didn't try to stop her. She was frozen with fear. She wanted to retreat into the house and hide.

Still looking at her feet, and supporting herself with the handrail, she walked quickly down the steps. She continued to the sidewalk and grabbed a branch on a small bush growing there. Only then did she look up from her feet.

"Let him up." She said to Dr. Beckman. "I want to talk to him." Her voice quavered, but there was confidence and strength in it. Not predicted.

Dr. Beckman did as she commanded. He was as confused. I was confused. It was an unfamiliar feeling for me.

"What do you want, you son-of-a-bitch?!" She was in my face. Her fists were clinched. She was threatening *me!*

I was surprised, another unfamiliar feeling.

When I didn't respond, she said, "I thought so. I know what you've been up to, you snake. Now, get the hell out of here!" She pushed me toward my car.

I got in my car and left. What else could I do at that point? I had lost my focus. I needed to get my balance. I needed to understand.

Dr. Beckman was going to hit me. Anna was going to go back into her house. She was going to lock the door. She was going to call the police. Dr. Beckman and I were going to both be detained. Anna would be questioned in her house. The police would get ice for my injuries from Anna house. All these things would combine and set off a string of events that would culminate in Anna breaking her neck on the stairs to the basement.

It was a symphony. I was the composer and the conductor. But the horn section had decided to play music from a different symphony.

What had happened? It was predictable, but I had not predicted it. I drove slowly down the hill, back toward downtown Seattle.

'Ask, and it will be given to you; seek, and you will find; knock, and it will be opened to you. Matthew 7:7'

I was asking. I was confused. I was frustrated. I was angry.

Be angry and do not sin; do not let the sun go down on your anger. Ephesians 4:26

I did not let the sun go down on my anger. The anger gave me more focus, more balance. I fed the anger more, resulting in even more focus. It became a positive feedback loop of anger-focus, focus-anger, building, expanding until I thought my head would burst.

My mind was a galaxy of stars, each exploding into a shower of a million sparks. The sparks were thoughts. The thoughts were pure energy. My mind was exploding.

The car swerved across the centerline, narrowly missing an oncoming truck. The truck honked its horn. The sound echoed and amplified inside my skull.

I passed out. The doctors later said that I had had a grand mal seizure. Maybe.

The car went off the road and up an embankment. The car slowed a little as it bounced up the embankment. Then, the Malibu came to an instantaneous stop when it met a power pole.

Twenty-four hours later, I opened my eyes. I saw a blurry fluorescent ceiling light. There was someone dressed in white. Was this heaven? It couldn't be. My head was throbbing like hell.

"Just relax Mr. Miller. You've been in an accident. You've been out for a while. Just take it easy." It was a woman's voice. An angel? Julia?

Then I remembered who I was. I knew I was not in heaven.

They must have given me something. I felt extremely drowsy. I went to sleep.

The throbbing pain disappeared. The confusion disappeared. The anger remained.

CHAPTER 39
SAL

Anna's lips were tightly pursed. Everyone else's mouth hung open as we watched Ray drive away.

Heck noticed Anna wobbling first, and grabbed her arm to steady her. I noticed the way he touched her, confident and strong, but gentle.

"Are you okay." Heck was talking about more than her wobbling.

"I'm fine. I just need to sit down." The commanding tone had left her voice.

"Hang on to her for a minute. I'll get her wheelchair." I ran up the steps to the front door where Karen still stood unmoving.

She awoke from her semi-hypnotic state just as I got there. "Oh, I'll get it. There's a ramp on the other side of the porch." She hurriedly pushed the wheelchair down the ramp, down the driveway on the other side of the lawn, and back across on the sidewalk. It would have been quicker just to carry it down the steps, as I had planned.

We got Anna back into the house and parked her at the kitchen table. Anna seemed out of breath.

"I'll make some coffee." Karen busied herself with the chore.

Heck and I pulled up chairs on either side of Anna.

I didn't want to rush her, she seemed so frail, but I couldn't wait any longer. "Anna, let me introduce myself. My name is Dr. Salinger from the CDC, Sal, if you like."

"How do you do. I'm very pleased to meet you." She seemed to have regained some of her composure.

"Anna, *what* was that all about?" Heck beat me to the question. We both wanted to hear the answer.

"I'm not sure I know exactly. I mean, I was afraid. I wanted to get into the house, bolt the door and call the police."

"So then, why did you confront him like that?" That's not what I would have done." I said.

"I know he's evil, not just by what I've heard about him, but because of his eyes. I know how this sounds, but he has evil eyes." She shuddered at the mental image.

"If you know he's evil, why did you confront him like that? Who knows what he's capable of doing." This was from Heck.

She closed her eyes and shook her head. We let her gather her thoughts.

"When I was eight years old we inherited a cat from my aunt after she passed away. It was a big yellow tabby tomcat. Bigelow was his name.

"He was an *evil* cat. He had evil eyes. He hated everyone. He wouldn't let anyone pet him. If anyone tried, he would hiss at them and scratch them. He mostly just hid from people.

"I was the littlest person in the house. He wasn't afraid of me. But I was afraid of him, and he knew it.

"He would ambush me when I wasn't watching out for him. I'm sure he enjoyed terrorizing me. He would jump out from behind a chair when I was least expecting it. My legs were constantly covered in scratches that summer when we first got him.

"I was afraid of him, but I was angry at him too. I hated that cat." Where was this going?

"Anna, we were talking about Ray. Why did you threaten him?" I thought that maybe she had gotten side tracked.

"I *am* talking about Ray. Evil is evil, whether it's a cat or a man. I know something about evil, and if I may continue, I'll tell you what I know."

"I'm sorry. Of course, go ahead." Her physical frailty belied her inner mental strength.

"Thank you. As I was saying, I hated that cat. One day I caught sight of Bigelow crouching behind the sofa, about to pounce on me.

"I pretended not to see him. When I got close to the sofa, I let out the loudest roar that an eight-year-old could muster, and I pounced on *him*.

"I'm sure I scared the cat crap out of him. He never bothered me again." She laughed at the memory.

"So you were treating Ray like Bigelow?" Heck was a trained listener.

"Yes, that's right. You see, cats, and some people, are predators. What do predators do? They attack their prey. And what does the prey do? If they're rational, they are afraid of the predator, and they try to run away. And, *that's* what the predator *expects.*"

"I get it. You did the unexpected. You were the prey that acted like a predator." I guess I've always known this, but I've never put it to practice."

"Yes. If there is one thing that predators hate, it's being the prey." Anna was proving to be, not only brave, but street-smart as well.

"I had to deal with a bully in grade school once. I must have been in fourth or fifth grade." Heck said.

"We called him Big Larry. He had been held back a couple years and was older, and bigger than anyone else in my grade.

"I was afraid of him, and just like with your Bigelow, he knew it. He'd pick on me all the time. He liked to do things like snap me behind the ear with a rubber band. Or, step on my toes. Oh, and he loved giving wedgies too."

"Sounds like a real sweetheart." Anna and I laughed. Heck didn't.

"He made the mistake of snapping me behind the ear while I was carrying my lunch tray in the cafeteria. I knew it was him. I was pissed.

"I spun around with the tray so fast that he couldn't get out of the way. The edge of the tray caught him right in the kisser. My food went flying all over the cafeteria, and so did three of his teeth. *He* didn't expect it either." Heck looked pleased with himself.

"Then what?"

Heck shrugged. "I got suspended for a week. He got a fat lip and a trip to the dentist. My Mom cried when she came to pick me up from school, but Dad understood.

"I thought Big Larry would retaliate. He talked about it, but he never did. He left *me* alone, but he kept picking on some of the other kids."

Karen began serving coffee to everyone.

Anna continued, "That's exactly what I'm talking about. Predators don't expect to have the tables turned. They don't expect their prey to act irrationally. And that's why it's the most rational thing you can do." She had regained some of her previous strength.

We all stopped talking while we doctored our coffee, except Heck. He drank his black.

"Anna, Heck, ah… Dr. Beckman, told me about your abilities with words and letters. He told me about the process, but I'm very interested in what goes on inside your head when you're doing it."

"I wish I knew what goes on in my head. I see words, and the words make sense to people. Some call it fortune telling. I don't like that. I prefer the word *divining,* because I believe I am able to divine information that is unseen by others, and that it comes from a *Divine* source."

"Do you believe that God is giving you this information?" Is she a religious zealot of some kind, or a charlatan perhaps?

"No, not exactly. I don't think God has chosen me as His messenger or anything like that. I think I might have somehow accidentally tapped into a leak in God's universal knowledge."

"You think that you can see the future?" It was a direct question from Heck. He was testing her.

"No. As I said, I'm *not* a fortune teller. I see bits of information. Sometimes it's relevant to future events, but you have to interpret the information yourself. I don't get exact information. At best, all I can give you are hints about the future, but the interpretation of those hints is always personal. Unlike a fortune teller, I can't tell you what your future will be."

"I don't want to put you on the spot, but Heck has told me so much. I'd love to see a little demonstration, if that's okay."

Karen stood up and left the kitchen.

"Sure, I'd be glad to. We can just do a quickie, so that you can see how it works. I haven't had a chance to practice lately anyway. I don't know if this kind of thing can get rusty, but I don't want to take the chance." It was obvious that it was *fun* for her.

Karen returned to the kitchen with a bag filled with Scrabble letter tiles, and carefully dumped them onto the table.

"We need to pick out the letters of your full name. Can you write them down for me so I get the spelling right, and I don't miss any letters?"

I spelled out S-A-L-L-Y-S-U-E-S-A-L-I-N-G-E-R. Heck had a subdued smile.

I knew why he was smiling. Everyone has the same reaction when they first see my *full* name. "I know, funny, huh? I don't use the whole thing very often. My daddy was the only one who ever actually called me Sally Sue."

Heck's smile was a little less subdued, but he made no comment. Good for him, a man who knows when to keep his mouth shut, a rare quality. But, I didn't feel embarrassed with Heck, like I sometimes did with other people, especially men who found my name humorous.

His smile was not threatening, but comforting in a way. Something about him made me feel safe. Maybe it was the way he had reacted to the unexpected threat from Ray a few minutes ago.

Anna explained the process she used. She started by asking me to think about the past.

On her signal, I released the scrambled tiles onto the table with one hand while holding her hand with the other.

She turned over all the face-down tiles, and studied them for a few seconds. "Nothing. Do it again. Really *try* to think about your past this time."

This time, after studying the tiles for a few seconds, she said, "All I see is E-R-A-S-E. See, right here."

She studied the tiles for a few more seconds. "Did you know anyone named G-A-R-Y? I just saw that. And, it crosses at the "R', a strong connection."

"I've known a lot of people named Gary." I lied. "What does that mean?"

"That's a question only you can answer. All I can say is that those two words are connected in some way."

"But, 'erase Gary' makes no sense." It made all kinds of sense, but I was not going to talk about it here. The message was clear to me, because it was the same thing I had been telling myself for the last fifteen years. *Forget the past. Forget about Gary. Erase the whole thing from my life, and move on.*

"Remember, we're not using all the letters in the alphabet, so I can never see every possible word in the dictionary. You have to think about it tangentially. A word may have several meanings, and dozens of connotations. "Erase" might mean ignore, or forget, or kill, or disregard, or maybe undo. It's up to you to decide what the meaning is, or if it has any meaning at all."

"That brings up a question, why *don't* you use all the letters in the alphabet?" Heck asked.

"I tried that, but it doesn't work. I need to have a specific personal connection. Maybe it works like Google. If you're not specific enough, you get all kinds of irrelevant information.

"Okay, now think about the present. Think about your feelings, your state of mind, your circumstances."

On cue, I released the tiles. She studied them intently, as before.

"Well now, there's a word you don't see every day. S-A-N-G-U-I-N-E."

"I've never seen that word at all. What does it mean?" This was Karen. She had been very attentive, but quiet.

"I think it usually means hopeful or optimistic." Anna apparently had a better vocabulary than me. I didn't know what it meant either, but I didn't admit it.

"Wait there's more, L-E-E-R-Y. That's interesting. They're definitely connected, but they seem to be opposites in a way. Like I said, that's for you to figure out."

"I don't know if I feel either of those." I felt more "leery" than "sanguine" at that moment.

"Okay now, the future is a little more difficult. I need you to try to empty your mind." I released the tiles on cue again.

"Oh my, G-E-N-E-S-I-S. A new beginning? A new creation? A fresh start maybe? What do you think?"

"I have no idea." I really had no idea how that might relate to my future, if at all.

Heck said, "You know that my son died in that fire at the Institute?"

"Yes, I'm very sorry for you." She looked genuinely pained.

"Thank you. But, I wanted to remind you of the reading you did for me on the day before the fire. Reading my future, do you remember what you told me?"

"That's *divining* your future, please. And no, my memory is not so great these days."

"You got KIN IN HEAT, and NO TIME. I believe now that it was about my son, the fire, and that it was going to happen that night."

"Unfortunately, hindsight is always twenty-twenty. Too bad, it wasn't more useful for you."

"That's my fault. I didn't believe there was anything real to your abilities. I have changed my mind." Heck was having a hard time revealing his guilt. I could see his anguish.

"It wasn't your fault. Even if you had believed, you would not have known the specifics. You would not have been able to prevent it." Anna seemed to have rehearsed this condolence before with others who had not heeded her warnings.

"Yes, thank you, but I'll never know for sure." He gathered himself. "There was one more thing. It was BRAKE HIM, remember?"

"Yes. I remember pointing out that it was the *brake* that means *stop* and not spelled like the other kind, like a coffee *break.*"

"That's right. I believe now that message was about Ray Miller. I believe he was responsible for the fire and my son's death. I believe I am now responsible for stopping him before he can hurt anyone else. We stopped him today, but I'm sure that's just temporary. I need to stop him for good." He sounded resolute.

"Do you think he killed Mark McKenzie too?"

"Yes, I do. I believe he killed Ted Wheatly and Dr. Stanley Malone too. And *you* were next on his list." Heck let that sink in.

"You know, Mark and I worked together for a long time. He was in town. We were going to meet for lunch, to catch up on things." Anna said. A tear formed at the corner of her eye.

"That bastard." She shook her head. "Can I help you stop him?" Her eyes narrowed.

"Maybe you can. Can you do a reading for Ray?" There was a cold, almost icy, tone to Heck's voice.

Anna didn't say anything for a few seconds. "I don't know, maybe. I touched him out by the street. That might be enough. I can try." She did not have the enthusiasm that she did when she was reading me, but determination took its place.

"Do you need his middle name?" Heck asked.

"It would be helpful."

"I know it starts with an 'S.' " He thought for a second. "I believe I saw 'Steven' on his chart at the Institute."

We all sorted through the letter tiles until they were all found. Anna started with the present. She said that the present would be easiest to see if she could get anything at all.

She held the scrambled letters in her cupped hands, and closed her eyes. She seemed hesitant, but she released them onto the table.

When they had been reversed and studied, she said, "I see two words. First a name, M-A-R-Y. Does anyone know anyone named Mary who is connected with Ray?" Heck and I shook our heads.

The second is N-E-O-N-A-T-E. There's another word you don't see every day."

Karen raised her hand excitedly, as if she was in a classroom. "I know that one. It's a baby. I used to work in a hospital cafeteria. The obstetrics staff used it all the time."

I said, "Very good, I believe you're right." I thought her ego might need a little lift, and I felt a little guilty for not admitting that I had not known what sanguine meant.

"Now, I'll do one for the future. This is not easy for me. I feel too close to him, like I'm breathing in as he breathes out. It's sickening."

She shook the tiles in her hands for several seconds with her eyes closed, before releasing them onto the table.

She turned over the reversed tiles slowly one by one, being careful to keep them in their same position and orientation. She then studied them for a full thirty seconds.

"E-V-I-L and S-I-R-E, crossing at the 'I'." She let out the breath she had been holding.

"That's it. I can't do any more." She slumped back in her wheelchair rubbing her temples.

"Can I touch the tiles now?" I asked Anna.

"It doesn't matter. Do what you want." She had closed her eyes, and continued rubbing her temples.

"There's something odd about how the tiles are arranged." I carefully removed all the extra tiles, without disturbing the ones containing the message. "Does anyone else see what I see?"

Everyone, including Anna, took another look at the letters.

Heck volunteered, "It's a cross?"

"Yes, but see how the letters are spaced, it's almost a perfectly proportioned Christian cross. Anything else?"

Everyone leaned and twisted their heads to see it from my angle.

Anna said, "I see it. I see what you mean." Her eyes widened.

It was Karen who said what we were now all thinking. "It's an *upside down* cross."

CHAPTER 40
TOM

Becky and I had had a wonderful morning wandering around Pike Place Market. Of course we had to watch them throw some fish around at the fish market, but we tired of that soon enough. We investigated all the street level vender booths before going to all the shops on the lower level for the rest of the morning.

I had made a small business out of selling some of my framed prints from a booth in the Crafts Market area for a while. But with the National Geographic projects, I hadn't had time lately, and I didn't really need the money now either.

We walked down the hill from the Market to the Seattle waterfront to have lunch at a popular seafood restaurant. The plan was to go to the Seattle Aquarium after lunch. She didn't know it yet, but if our schedule worked out, I was planning on inviting her to join me for a ferryboat ride across Eliot Bay to have dinner at the Seacrest Landing Restaurant, Heck's favorite place on Alki Point.

It was fun playing tour guide, and Becky was the perfect tourist to guide. She was bright and funny and unabashed. She said whatever popped into her head, no pretense, no games, no holding back. She was who she was, and you could take her or leave her. I found that refreshing.

Seeing Seattle again for the first time through her eyes was a joy. I had lived in the area for so long that I had come to take it all for granted. Seattle is a very beautiful and interesting city. I had forgotten that. Her wide-eyed exuberance reminded me again.

This was not a date exactly, and Becky was not the type of woman I usually dated. She was short. She carried a few extra pounds, not that much, but she carried it all in the wrong places, too much on the hips, not enough on the boobs. She was not going to win any beauty contests, nor was she going to win any Halloween contests. She was not bad looking, but she was not exceptionally good looking either, just normal, whatever that is.

Most of the other women I had dated might very well have been able to win beauty contests. I didn't date them if they weren't beauty contest material. Why shouldn't I date the best looking women? A lot of great looking women seemed to be attracted to me. So, I could pick and choose, and I did. What's wrong with that?

The fact that I was asking myself the question meant that there *was* something wrong with that. Becky might be showing me the answer. She was not a PhotoShopped Cosmopolitan magazine cover girl. She was real, tangible on a granular level. Not that the other women I dated weren't *real.* But, it was the way I saw them.

I was attracted to Becky in a non-physical way. Was that what I had missed? Had it been a blind spot for me, something that was always there, but that I hadn't been aware of?

I thought of my photography. Many people had told me that my photos were unique. My work had been praised for my "ability to see the world from a new perspective." That's what one photo contest judge had said about my work. Maybe that's what I needed, to see my relationships with women from a new perspective, a Becky perspective.

"Oh look, there's a cruise ship coming in!" Becky was excited about everything she saw. Her excitement was like caffeine, it opened my eyes.

"We can walk down and watch them dock if you want. It's amazing how they can maneuver a big ship like that, as easy as a row boat."

"Okay, let me finish these clams first. They're great."

"Do you like carousels?"

"Why, is there one on the ship?" She giggled. In that moment, with that giggle, I could have believed she was a teenager.

"No. You're funny. They have one down here though, if you'd like to have a ride."

"Does it have horses and music? I haven't been on a carousel since I was about twelve at a carnival. That would be fun." There it was again, that wide-eyed exuberance. She probably had that same look on her face when she was twelve at the carnival.

My phone rang. The caller ID said, Janet Martin. It was her personal phone. "Hello."

"Hello, Tom. This is Jan Martin. I can't get a hold of Heck. Do you know where he is?"

"He and Dr. Salinger were going over to West Seattle to meet with Anna Grant, weren't they?"

"Yes, but I need to talk with him, and he's not answering his phone. I thought you might know something."

"We're supposed to connect up later. If you'd like, I can give him a message when I see him."

"Okay. Lt. Boswick called me. He says he's been keeping tabs on Ray Miller, and he just got a report that Ray was in some kind of a car accident, and is in the hospital. I'll try to get more information, but if you talk to Heck, tell him to call me."

"Huh, that's interesting. Okay, I'll let him know." I hung up.

"Who was that?" Becky's mouth was full of clams.

"That was Dr. Martin. She wants me to tell Heck to call her. He's not answering his phone. She said that Ray Miller was in a car accident, and is in the hospital."

"Isn't Heck with Sal?" She already knew she was.

"Yeah?"

"Well, I mean, why don't *we* call *her?*" Duh! Good question. I hadn't thought of it.

"Here, I have her number on my phone. I'll call her. She can give the phone to Heck."

Becky touched three spots on the cell phone, put the phone to her ear, and waited for an answer.

"Hello, Sal. Is Heck there? Dr. Martin has been trying to call him. She called Tom instead." She paused to listen to Sal. "Okay, put him on. I'll give the phone to Tom."

She handed me her phone. There were muffled voices and other miscellaneous sounds of a phone being handled. "Tom?"

I repeated the information that Jan had given me, and told Heck that Jan had asked him to call.

"I guess I must have left my phone in the car. There's been a little excitement here, I wasn't thinking about it."

"What excitement?"

"Ray was here, just a little while ago. He was trying to get at Anna. I'll fill you in later. He must have gotten into an accident just after he left."

"Huh. Okay, I'll let you go so that you can call Dr. Martin. She said she was going to try to get more information about Ray. Keep us posted. We'll see you later." We had planned to meet later at the hotel.

Heck hung up, and I filled Becky in.

"I thought Ray made *other* people have accidents, not himself." She said.

"I don't know. I guess he's just *accident prone.*" Becky smiled at my weak pun.

I liked her smile. It was infectious, and I had been infected.

CHAPTER 41
HECK

We all met up at the hotel early that evening.

Tom had picked up Billy who was excited about some calculations he had been working on. He had started to tell Tom all about it, but Tom stopped him, telling Billy, "Heck will want to hear this. Why don't you save it until later, so that you don't have to explain it twice?" Billy would have been glad to explain it twice, but he knew Tom, and took the hint.

I had touched bases with Jan before we left Anna's home. Jan said that she had found out that Ray had head injuries. He was stable, but unconscious.

This news was a great relief for Anna. It was a great relief for me too. For the moment at least, I wouldn't have to worry about the safety of Anna, or Sal, or anyone else that Ray might have been considering going after.

The bad news was that Ray was still alive. And as long as he was alive, I had to consider him a threat. Besides being a threat, I wanted him dead for my own reasons.

He killed my son. I would not give up, until his soul was safely locked away behind the gates of hell. But for now, I was content to put him on a back burner.

We had decided to have dinner at the Seacrest Restaurant, and take the water taxi over. It would be well after dark when we returned. I convinced Sal, Becky, and Billy that the nighttime view of Seattle was worth the small fare.

For most of the way over, Billy stood out on the rear deck looking at the Seattle skyline with the wind at his back. He didn't seem to mind the cold. The rest of us stayed inside.

Tom told me a little about his day with Becky. His words told me the facts of where they went and what they did. But his voice, his eyes, and his body language told me a lot more. It was obvious that he liked Becky, maybe more than he knew he liked her. And judging by Becky's body language, the feeling was mutual.

Becky and Tom were effervescent, Becky was the bubbles and Tom was the fizz. They had settled into a corner, and were in an animated discussion that seemed to involve a lot of laughter.

Sal and I had been talking about Ray, and the events of our day. Although our discussion did not initiate any laughter, there were some smiles. Despite everything, it had been a pleasure to spend the day with her.

In the car, her smell, her close proximity, were more than a little stimulating. How could I not like her, brains and beauty in one package? That, plus her unassuming nature, gave her three solid stars.

But under all that, there was something else with Sal, a certain barely perceptible, insecurity. Tom would say that it was just the psychologist in me working overtime. She was outwardly self-confident. There was nothing I could point at, just a feeling. I know that almost everyone has some hidden insecurities. If I knew her long enough, I would eventually see them.

After we ordered our drinks at the restaurant, Billy could not remain silent any longer.

"It's not chance, and I can prove it."

"Are we talking about Ray?" If I didn't keep him on track, he would start to ramble.

"Yes. I'm talking about what we suspect he may be doing. I've done some calculations." He pulled out a small pocket notebook, and displayed a couple of facing pages filled with numbers and symbols. It might as well have been hieroglyphics for as much as any of us understood it.

"We're not your physics students, so translate that into English for us, please."

"Okay, fine. I gathered as much information as I could about the *accidental* deaths surrounding Ray: Ted Wheatly, the Institute fire, Mark McKenzie, and just today, Stanley Malone.

I then looked at all the variables that were in play at the time from a quantum perspective. I reduced the exponents to their prime roots to get their base line coefficients, and then..." He was seeing multiple eyes starting to glaze over. "Okay, bottom line. Those deaths could not have happened by chance."

"Do you mean that that the odds are just too great against it?"

"No, I mean it's impossible. It could not have happened without some conscious intervention at a quantum level."

"Thanks, but I already knew he did it, I just didn't know how."

"Yes, but what you know by intuition, I can prove with mathematics." He crossed his arms and leaned back in his chair, looking quite smug.

"Okay, so how does that help us?"

"I'm a *theoretical* physicist. I don't concern myself with practical applications. I leave that to the engineers.

When I get back to Cornell tomorrow, I'm going to clean this up a little and publish a paper." He raised a finger, indicating that we should wait for a forthcoming pronouncement. "I think I'll title it *Quantifying Quantum Consciousness.*"

"Great. I hope you get an A-plus. Now, can we talk about what we are going to actually do about Ray?" Tom had heard enough of Billy's scientific *mumbo-jumbo.*

Billy did not change his smug expression.

"I've told you all about what Anna got when she did a reading on Ray. Does anyone have any ideas on what it might mean, or how it could help to stop him? Of course, I'm assuming he's going to need stopping, if or when, he gets out of the hospital."

"Usually, the simplest answer is the correct one." Billy had not retired yet.

"And the simplest answer is what?" Tom was being especially confrontational with Billy tonight. He may have been getting tired of playing host to an out-of-town guest staying at his apartment.

"That, somebody named 'Mary' is pregnant with Ray's 'neonate,' and it's going to be an 'evil sire.' Is that simple enough for you?"

Sal raised a finger. "That's the obvious meaning, but there could be several less obvious meanings and connotation, like Anna said. How can we know? And even if we think we know, how does that help us?"

"We don't *know*. But, maybe a hint is all we'll need." I said.

Tom added, "Does anyone know if Ray even has a girl friend?" Everyone shook their head, no.

"So we've got nothing tangible to go on, just hints. Maybe that will be enough, maybe not." I was thinking of Tyler. The *hints* I had gotten were not enough. *Did I let my son die, when I could have prevented it?*

"One other thing," Sal said. "I called Lt. Boswick to report Ray showing up at Anna's. He said that it sounded like Ray did not do anything illegal, however suspicious it might have been. He said he'll monitor Ray's condition in the hospital. If anything develops, he said he would call Jan.

"He didn't sound like he was very interested in doing much of anything. I think we are on our own." She said.

I had let her call Boswick because I thought he might just hang up on me again, if I called him twice in one day.

I liked the way she looked at me when she used the word "we."

The waitress brought our drinks and started taking our orders. Our discussion about Ray seemed to be over. We took turns discussing the menu with the waiter, and making our choices.

It was Becky's turn to give her order to the waiter. She was taking longer to decide than everyone else. Sal said to Becky, "I think they have hamburgers here." Apparently, it was an inside joke, because Sal laughed.

Becky apparently got the joke, but she didn't laugh. She looked at Sal with an impish grin.

She said, "Okay smarty pants, since you volunteered to pick up my tab, I think I'm going to have *both,* the filet mignon and the king crab legs. I'll bet they can make it a combo for me. I'm feeling adventurous tonight. And, hungry." She glanced at Tom.

Sal raised her eye brows theatrically and said, "Well, maybe *I* better get a hamburger then." She laughed, but not quite as loud as before. She stopped laughing completely when it was apparent that Becky was not joking. Sal ordered the baked salmon after rechecking the price.

Tom said to me under his breath with a smile. "You should have seen her at lunch."

Then louder, he said to me, "Have you opened all the cards from the funeral? My offer still stands. I'll send out the thank-you's for you. I thought I'd get some reprints made of that really good picture of Tyler I took at Christmas, and send them out to everyone too."

"Okay, I will. Thanks, Tom. That's a good idea." I didn't want to think about it. That's why I had put it off. Better to get it done, and put it behind me.

The ten minute water taxi return trip across Elliot Bay to Seattle was as advertised. A full moon had risen over the city, and the stars had come out. Both added to the dramatic effect of the city lights reflecting off the water at night.

We all stood shoulder to shoulder looking out the front window of the water taxi. From left to right, it was Tom, Becky, Sal, me, and Billy. Funny how much you can tell about relationships simply by how people line themselves up. Tom and Becky were together, maybe a couple. Sal and I were together. A couple? I didn't think so. Billy was separate, the single guy.

I suppose that we might have lined up the same way if Sal were the single member of our group, but then that would imply that Billy and I were a couple.

Billy said to me, "It's beautiful. You were right. Too bad that Eric couldn't get away from work and come with me."

"Eric?" I was a little confused. "I thought he flew the coup six months ago."

"Oh yeah, I forgot to tell you. We got back together last month. I guess he needed to *spread his wings*, or some crap like that. Anyway, he's back in the *coup* for now."

"I'm glad to hear it. Do you think it will work out this time?" I was honestly glad, and honestly concerned.

"Ya know Heck, I really don't know. Relationships are tough. I don't have to tell *you* that."

"Yeah. Unfortunately, I know all about it."

Tom and I knew Billy was gay since we were sixteen. He really didn't have to tell us, but he did. It was a few years later that he came out to his parents. His relationship with them was never the same. But for us, nothing really changed.

As far as Tom and I were concerned, it was just another *thing* about Billy that was different from us. He was black.

He was short and chubby. He was a wiz at math. He studied harder than any of us. He was a Baptist. And, he wasn't interested in girls. Billy was Billy. It was nothing more than that.

Sal must have overheard part of my conversation with Billy. There was a mild look of surprise on her face, but she said nothing.

I said to her, "You don't get to see this kind of view in Atlanta, or in Tennessee for that matter."

"No, we don't. I'm glad you talked us into going this way." She looked up at me with those baby blue eyes. Suddenly, I felt like maybe I had had one too many glasses of merlot.

Just then the water taxi hit the wake of another boat broadside, causing it to rock from side to side. Sal grabbed my arm to keep her balance. She kept holding my arm for several seconds, long after the boat had steadied. It felt good.

CHAPTER 42
SAL

We slept in and had a leisurely breakfast in our room. I had just put our dishes outside the door. I made sure the "Do Not Disturb" sign was out so that maid service did not try to come in while we were getting dressed.

It was Becky's turn to use the shower first. I busied myself by tidying up the room while I waited for her to finish her shower.

My cell phone rang. It was Rose. It was 10:05 a.m. in Seattle, but 1:05 in Atlanta. It must be something about my report.

"Good morning, Rose." I said, as nonchalantly as I could.

"Sal, Dr. Edelman wanted me to get you on the phone for him first thing after lunch." No "Good morning," or "How are you doing?" All business, not good. Her tone was neutral, no hints there.

"Okay." It was time to face the music. It was time to have my last dance as an employee of the CDC.

There was a click, and I was forced to listen to the cheesy music on hold for what seemed like a very long time. "Dr. Salinger, this is Dr. Edelman." Not "Sal." Not "Albert."

"Good morning." Why not be polite to your executioner, before he chops off your head?

"Is it? You know why I'm calling you, right?"

"Is it about the report I sent in?" I knew that it wasn't.

"Nice try. Try again." Was he toying with me? I might as well get it over with.

"You're calling to fire me because I've been working off the clock when I was ordered not to return to work until the first of February." I tried to keep my voice steady, but failed.

"So, you *did* hear me when I told you that I would fire you if you returned to work before February. I'll get to that in a minute. But first, I want to understand *why* you would deliberately jeopardize your career by disobeying my order, and then you send in a report knowing that it would let me *know for sure* that you were disobeying my order." He was incredulous.

I felt like a school girl called into the Principals office. How could I answer? I couldn't say that it was because of my long-dead daddy's advice to "do the right thing" whatever that meant. What have I got to lose?

"I wanted to do something to…"

"To make up for what you *think* was your mistake, right?"

"Yeah, I guess. I couldn't just forget about it. I wanted to make up for it… if I could."

"So, you sneak around the country, interviewing victims, ordering lab work and downloading files through Rose, your *undercover* cohort."

"Please don't blame Rose. It was all my idea; she didn't really know what I was doing." I lied.

"Don't lie, it's beneath you. I know that Rose knew *everything* you were doing." How did he know?

He somehow could see the question on my face. "That's right, I knew everything you were doing. Rose kept me updated."

He might as well have hit me with a sucker punch to the gut. Rose betrayed me! I felt a stab at the pit of my stomach. I couldn't breathe, much less talk. I thought she was my friend.

"What did you think would happen when you sent in that report?"

"That, I would be fired." I squeaked out the words.

"And you still sent it in! Why would you do that, if you thought it would get you fired? Don't you care about your job, your career?"

It was a damn good question. Why *did* I do it? My career was over. Was it worth it?

Tears ran down both cheeks. I gathered enough air to talk. "I had to let people know what we're dealing with. If I waited, more people could be in danger." I took a breath. "I guess… I did it because I wanted to *do* my job, more than I wanted to *have* my job." My voice was tiny.

There was a pause. I could imagine him tugging on his left earlobe.

"There it is. That's what I wanted to hear you say." He let out a long sigh. "Sal, I'm sorry I put you though this, but I had to know."

"I don't understand. You had to know what?" *He called me Sal.*

"I had to know if you had what it takes to handle more authority. I'm creating a new department that will focus research on evolving and emergent viral strains. I want us to get ahead of the ball, so that we can better *anticipate* outbreaks, so we don't have to just *react* to them. I want you to head it up."

"You were testing me? How did you know what I… Why did Rose…" I felt like some kind of lab rat in a controlled experiment.

"I didn't really think you could leave the job alone for that long, but you did need a rest. I figured you'd do something. I just didn't know what.

"I told Rose to expect a call from you. I told her to play along, and pretend that I knew nothing about it. She knew about the new department I was planning. And, she knew I had you in mind to be in charge of it. Sometimes I think that woman knows what I'm thinking before I do.

"So, do you want the job?"

"I don't know. I didn't expect anything like this. Why me? There's a ton of people with more experience."

"Simple. It's not about experience. It's about attitude. You've proven to me that the goals of the job mean more to you than anything, even your career.

"You could have done nothing, like I told you to, but you didn't. You could have held on to that report until after you came back, but you didn't. By the way, if you had delayed that report, I would have fired your butt on the spot. But, you stuck your neck out for the job. I needed to know that about you before I stuck my neck out promoting you.

"There's a lot riding on this project. You'll be in charge of dozens of people and millions of dollars, not to mention thousands of lives of possible outbreak victims. I have a boss too, ya know, and believe me, he's watching."

"Are you up to it?" I could hear the familiar squeak of his old leather swivel chair as he leaned back.

"Yes. If you think I can do it. When do I start? Where do I start?"

"Take off the rest of the month. Finish what you're doing in Seattle. Oh and, since you've been *sorta* working and *sorta* vacationing, CDC will split all your travel expenses. Of course, there'll be a nice raise in it for you too. We'll talk about all the details when you get back. You'll need to start building your staff right away. Be thinking about that."

"Thank you, Albert, for believing in me. I won't let you down." Now I was crying again, but for a different reason.

"Damn right, you won't! Now, I gotta go. *Some* of us have to work for a living." His voice cracked a little.

I hung up the phone and stood up. My knees were a little wobbly. I had just taken a wild emotional rollercoaster ride. It was going to take me a minute to regain my balance.

Becky stepped out of the bathroom wrapped in a towel. It only took her one glance to know that something was up. "What?"

"Dr. Edelman called." I didn't smile.

"Oh Sal, is it going to be right away, or are they going to let you stay to wrap things up before…" She assumed the worst, just as I had.

I couldn't hold my smile any longer. "I got a promotion, and a raise!"

"Are you serious? Wow! That's so great!" She hugged me with only one arm, because the other arm was on towel retention duty.

I told her everything that Dr. Edelman had said.

When you're expecting a beheading, and the executioner gives you a kiss and a gold coin, you see the world in a fresh new way. It had started raining outside, but the sun was going to be shining on *my* parade today.

We were planning on having a lazy day in Seattle. Now that I no longer had an axe hanging over my head, it was also going to be a *fun*, lazy day in Seattle. The steady drizzle would keep us mostly indoors, but there we lots of indoor things we could do. We thought we might do a little shopping downtown, or maybe go on the Underground Seattle tour that Heck had suggested.

We took our time getting dressed and ready to go out. We had no specific schedule to keep. Tom and Heck were taking Billy to the airport today. Heck had suggested that we get together for dinner later this evening. The prospect of spending more time with Heck elevated my spirits even more than they already were.

Last night on the water taxi, I took Heck's arm when the boat started to rock. I was pretty sure that I would *not* have fallen without holding on to him, but it felt good. I could feel his muscles under his jacket. He was not any kind of showy gym jockey, like some guys I've known. He was naturally fit and well toned. Despite the slight limp, he was no couch potato. He had the kind of strength that is not for display, but that you know is there when you need it.

Heck was right, the lights of the city reflecting off the water, the full moon perched above the skyline, and the stars twinkling in the clear sky, were well worth the modest water taxi fare. The sight took my breath away.

It was a storybook moment for me when I looked up into his eyes for just a second while I was holding his arm. Those deep green eyes of his talked to me in a way that words could not. They were gentle and kind, but strong and resilient. They said that this was a man I could trust.

Heck looked nothing like Daddy, but I could see something of Daddy behind those eyes, the wisdom, the goodness, the resolute character.

Maybe it was the sparkling city at night, the spectacular dinner, the wine, and the chilled ocean air. All I know is that I felt good being with Heck. He made me feel good about myself, more confident, even when I had thought that my career with CDC was going to end. Standing there, holding Heck's arm, I felt like no hardship could diminish me. I didn't want to let go. Maybe I shouldn't have.

I hadn't been aware of it until last night, but Heck had started to occupy a lot more of my thoughts. I felt safe when I was around him, less self conscious. I could relax and be myself, and I liked that other self.

Tom seemed to be having a similar effect on Becky. This seemed to be a good time for a little *subtle* probing.

"So, what's up with Tom? When are you getting married?" I smiled to make sure she knew I was just kidding. Subtlety takes too much patience, besides good friends don't need to be subtle.

I caught her off guard. Her eyes popped open. It took a second for her to read my playful smile. "We're planning to elope tomorrow. Didn't I tell you? We thought we'd tie the knot in Vegas, then it's off to Bora Bora for our honeymoon." Becky was always quick with a snappy comeback. We laughed together.

She continued, "What do you mean, 'what's up with Tom?' Nothing is *up* with Tom." She was not being completely honest, and she knew that I knew it.

"Come on, I saw the way you looked at him. And last night, you two were practically glued together at the hip."

"Me? Look who's talking, Ms. puppy-eyed 'I'll have whatever Heck is drinking.' " Yes, sometimes a good offense is the best defense. We laughed some more. Now it was time for honesty.

"Okay, Heck and I get along very well. Okay, better than very well. He's... well, he's different than other men. And, Tom?" I had her cornered now.

"Alright, Tom is Tom. He's fun. And, have you looked at him? He's a cross between Brad Pitt and Matt Damen. What's not to like?"

"And, he seems to like you too."

"Yeah, he does, doesn't he? That's nice too." No modesty there.

"So, how do you feel about him?" Becky's feelings about men were not always easy to read.

"I don't know. It's been a while since I've been out there. Sal, it's so nice to be with someone who isn't a butthead, ya know. It feels good to have a guy notice that I'm a woman.

And, it's flattering when it's a guy like Tom." Her eyes rolled the same way they did last Christmas when I watched her bite into that brandy truffle.

"Yeah, I know. There's been a couple of guys from work that have shown some interest, but none of them were really my type. I haven't been with a man since Bruce. Heck is different."

"You can't compare Heck with Mr. Ass Wipe. Heck is a man."

It's time.

"Becky, don't blame Bruce. It was me."

"What do you mean? He's the one who dumped *you*." Becky scowled.

"He had a good reason."

"To dump you? I don't think so."

"No, it *was* me. I wouldn't… I wouldn't let him touch me."

"Huh? I saw him hug you. I saw him kiss you. I saw you holding his hand. What?" Then her expression changed. She knew what I meant.

"I wouldn't let him have *sex* with me." I felt like I had just vomited. It spewed out of me with all the ugliness of a bad lasagna dinner mixed with eight tequila shooters. I know, because it happened once when I was in college.

"Why? What was wrong with him?" Her tone had changed to sympathetic, but she still didn't get it.

"There was nothing wrong with *him*. It was *me!*" Becky waited for me. Timing was a sixth sense for her.

"Becky, you remember I mentioned Gary Boyle?" She nodded, waiting.

"He raped me when I was fifteen." More vomit. I could taste the bile.

"Oh Sal, you never told me. Why didn't you tell me?" She moved over and sat by my side on the bed and put her arm gently around my shoulder.

"I don't know. I was so ashamed. I screwed up. I shouldn't have gone into his brother's van with him. But, he was so nice. I screwed up."

"It wasn't your fault, honey."

"Yes it was. I didn't tell him to stop when he kissed me. It felt so good. I didn't tell him to stop when he unbuttoned my blouse and started feeling me up. It was exciting. I was floating. I couldn't stop him." I wasn't crying. I don't know why. Maybe, I had cried about it too many times before.

"Then he put his hand in my pants. I didn't stop him. It felt so good. I didn't want it to stop.

"I didn't really know what he was doing. He started to put his finger inside. It hurt. I told him to stop then, but he didn't. He shoved his thump inside me. It really hurt bad. I screamed.

"I think I scared him. He let me up. I got out of the van and ran home. I was bleeding. By the time I got home the bleeding stopped. I washed my bloody underwear in the bathroom. I did all the laundry back then for Daddy and I anyway. He never found out that I lost my virginity in that way.

"I was so ashamed. I didn't want anyone to ever know, not even you. I screwed up. It was my fault. I didn't stop him soon enough. I couldn't let Daddy find out. I didn't know what he would do, or what he would think of me."

Once I got started, it all spilled out in one big gush. Like vomit, there was no stopping it mid-stream. Also like vomiting, I felt unexpectedly relieved. A weight had been removed.

"After that, I just couldn't trust a man to touch me in that way. Bruce didn't understand. I don't blame him. I never told him about it. I should have. Maybe... things might have been different.

"Wait a minute. Sal, you didn't lose your virginity. You lost your hymen. There's a big difference between a thumb and a penis." Becky still had her arm around me, but sounded less sympathetic.

"The law says that unwilling penetration of any kind is rape." I looked it up once.

"Yeah, maybe it was *legally* rape. But you weren't *spoiled* as they used to say. Hell, girls lose their hymens riding bicycles all the time. That doesn't mean they're not still virgins. Look it up, *doctor.* You're considered a virgin until you've had sexual intercourse. Penetration with a thumb is *not* sexual intercourse."

"But, I didn't tell him to stop until it was too late. It was sex, and it was my fault."

"It was some heavy petting that went a little too far. But you *did* stop before it was too late.

"I'll make it simple for you. Did he put his prick in you? Hell, did he even pull it out of his pants?"

"Well, no, but he..."

"Then it wasn't *sex,* and you did *not* lose your virginity." She said it with a note of finality.

She knew when to stop talking. I had nothing more to say, but a lot to think about. She knew me. She was counting on that, a born salesman.

Had I been beating myself over the head all these years, stewing in false guilt, sabotaging my relationships with men, because I thought that one incident had *spoiled* me? Was it men I couldn't trust, or was it myself I didn't trust?

I made a mistake. I screwed up. Is it time for me to forgive myself? I didn't have the answers yet, but I felt like I was asking the right questions.

Becky finished getting ready, and tidied up the room for several minutes in silence.

Finally, Becky figured I had chewed on it long enough. "Are you ready? Let's go have some fun! We need to celebrate your promotion. You look like you could use a new pair of shoes, and maybe a purse to match?"

CHAPTER 43
BECKY

Sal and I had the day totally free together. I showed Sal around Pike Place Market. We didn't go down to the waterfront like Tom and I had. Instead, we spent most of our time browsing downtown shops and boutiques. We decided to go on foot. We had considered taking the rental car, but we didn't plan on going far, and we didn't want the hassle of finding a place to park for every stop.

Pike Place Market was several blocks down Pine Street from our hotel. It was a cool and drizzly day, not the best window shopping weather. Fortunately, we had bought small collapsible umbrellas at an airport souvenir shop after we landed. Seattle has a well-earned reputation for rain. We wanted to be prepared.

We took a hint from other people on the street and got coffees to go. It was like carrying a hand warmer, and it tasted so good. Seattleites sure know how to make coffee. I can see why. On a day like this, it's almost a basic necessity of life.

Our spirits were up, despite the rain. Sal had plenty of dress shoes of all descriptions, but except for one pair of sneakers, she was woefully lacking in casual shoes. I promised her we would fix that today. We were on an adventure, in search of the illusive perfect pair of ankle boots, for starters.

I wanted her to have some fun. She needed to forget about everything, for a few hours at least. I know the good news about work was a load off her shoulders, but I also knew it would soon become the next thing for Sal to worry about.

Her revelation about Gary Boyle was a shocker. I never had a clue. But it did answer a few questions, like why she hadn't had any boy friends since Bruce. She'd been hiding it for all these years, blaming herself. She had always been too self-critical.

Her daddy loved her, but he put her on a pretty high pedestal. I know that she loved him so much that letting him down would have killed her. I wished she had talked to me a lot sooner.

What was more shocking to me, was that she was still a virgin. I wasn't going to let her know I thought it was a big deal, but wow! I didn't want her to see that I thought it was anything more than a minor curiosity. She needed to realize that all the fears that prevented her from revealing her "screw up" were imaginary, and now she could let it go. She could let it go, and get laid already for heaven's sake!

I wanted her to trust herself with men, but I wasn't sure I was ready for that one myself. My breakup with Chuck had cut me deeper than I let anyone know. I had been bitten hard, and I wasn't sure I could pet that dog again, not yet, maybe not for a very long time.

When Robbie died, it hurt, but at least he didn't dump me like Chuck did. There was less blood, but the pain went deeper with Chuck. The wound from Robbie's death hadn't healed completely yet, and Chuck's stab wound was still fresh.

Time heals all wounds, they say. I hoped I'd live long enough to find out.

My stomach growled.

"Let's have lunch before we go on the Seattle Underground Tour." It hadn't been that long since we ate breakfast, but all the walking in that chilly, damp air had given me an appetite.

"Sounds good to me. Can we have something *other* than seafood?"

"I was thinking the same thing."

We ducked into a little sports bar. Except for all of the Seahawks and Mariner memorabilia, it looked like my kind of place. I'm a Titans and Blue Jays fan, but a good burger has no team affiliation.

The burger was great, way above average. It was thick, and hot, and juicy, and I washed it down with some really cold beer. I'll drink beer just about anytime, but it always tastes better to me on a cold day. I had two.

The underground tour was interesting and fun, but it was clearly designed for tourists. It was not the kind of thing you'd want to do twice if you were a local.

When we finished the tour, we were getting tired, and we didn't want to walk all the way back to the hotel carrying shopping bags. Sal had scored a pair of tan leather ankle boots and a small matching tan leather shoulder bag. She also got a cute pair of comfortable cranberry suede espadrilles for traveling. I just got a new wallet and a couple of silk scarves. We took a taxi.

On the short ride to the hotel I said, "Heck said that he and Tom would call us today to set something up for dinner tonight, right?" How should I put this?

"Yeah, that's what he said. Why?"

"I was just thinking, Tom told me about his photography portfolio. His pictures have been published in the National Geographic. They've got to be pretty good. He asked if I wanted to see his portfolio sometime. I do. I really do, but we might not be in Seattle for much longer." I wasn't good at nibbling around the edges of things. I liked to take big bites and get right to middle. But, I didn't want to put her on the spot.

"Yeah, and what?" She wasn't going to connect the dots for me.

"Well, I thought that, if it was okay with you, Tom and I could do our own thing for dinner tonight, and he could show me his work at his place later." Sal smiled. She could see where I was going. Was that where I was going?

"I don't know. We'll have to ask Heck if he has other plans. What did you say you wanted to see, Tom's what, *portfolio?*" She giggled.

"No, *that's* not what I meant. I just don't want to miss the chance to see his…" I shouldn't have paused.

"Portfolio?" She suggested, still smiling. She wasn't buying it.

"Okay, I admit it. I like Tom a lot. He's... interesting. I want to spend some more time with him before we have to leave Seattle. I just don't want to leave you hangin'. I don't know if you're comfortable having dinner alone with Heck, or what."

"Comfortable? Yeah, I'd say I'm *comfortable* having dinner with Heck. I think he's *interesting* too. But, I don't know how he feels about it.

"I'll tell you what. When we meet, if you bring up the portfolio thing, I'll act like I'm not interested. That will leave the door open for Heck to suggest we go our own way tonight. If he doesn't, well then, he doesn't."

"Yeah." I said hesitantly. "But you know how dense men can be. Do you think he'll take the hint?"

"Heck is not someone I would classify as 'dense.' But, I guess we'll see."

###

Heck called Sal to ask about dinner. He said he wanted a chance to talk with her more about Ray Miller, and how to proceed if, and when, he recovered. Sal told him they should wait until everyone was together to decide on dinner.

We met in the hotel lobby at 6:00. It was getting dark outside. Or maybe I should say, it was getting *darker* outside. The sun had not been shining all day. It was no longer drizzling. Now it was misting. Still wet. Still cold.

"When is it going to stop raining? It's been nasty all day." It was more of a rhetorical question. Tom and Heck both smiled.

Tom looked at his watch, and said, "I'd say it should definitely stop raining sometime around *June.*" Tom and Heck laughed. Sal and I didn't.

Heck said, "We were lucky last night. Sometimes we can go months without seeing the moon, or the sun for that matter."

Sal said to Heck, "Where would you recommend for dinner?"

"Depends on what you feel like, and how hungry you are."

Here's my chance. I said, "I was hoping we'd have time after dinner to stop over to Tom's. He offered to show me his photography work."

All of us looked to Tom. He looked a little uncomfortable. "Okay, sure. There's that seafood place over by me. We could go there."

Sal said, "I don't think I can take any more seafood. It's all been great, but I'm starting to overdose on it. And, we did a lot of walking today. I don't know if I'm going to have much energy left after dinner." She looked to Heck, so did Tom and I.

"Okay, there are a couple places in town we can go that have a mixed menu, so everyone can have what they want. We can stop by Tom's on another day before you leave town." No one said anything, but Sal and Tom looked disappointed. I wasn't too happy either. Heck didn't get the hint. Men are dense.

Heck looked a little confused by our collective reaction. Then after a second, he said, "Or… Tom, if you and Becky want to go out to that place by you, Sal and I can have dinner here at the hotel. I hear they have some pretty good steaks. That way, Sal and I can take it easy.

"And Tom, since we took your car, you can just pick me up when you bring Becky back later." He got it. I smiled and looked at Tom.

Tom saw my smile. "That's okay with me, if that's okay with you girls." I think he knew the answer.

Everyone agreed. I caught Sal's eye to acknowledge her part in orchestrating our plan. In a few minutes I was in Tom's Mustang heading toward his end of town, Ballard he said.

The stereo was set to a modern country rock FM station. It was a little too loud. Tom reached over and turned it off. The car suddenly shrunk to a much more intimate space.

We rode in silence for a few minutes. I didn't know what to say. Should I talk about current events, politics, religion, the weather, the rising price of women's underwear? I've never been good at girly small talk with guys. I'm usually better off keeping my mouth shut, so I can't accidently stick my foot in it. But if I said nothing, what message would that send?

I didn't remember feeling this awkward since my first school dance. Why did I feel this way? I was no little girl. There was nothing going on between us. Or, was there?

I was going to say something, just to break the silence. I turned toward him, started to open my mouth, but I chickened out, and just smiled.

He turned and saw my awkward smile. He smiled back with an understanding look and said, "Yeah, me too. I don't know what to talk about either." We both laughed.

It was an ice breaking moment. We both relaxed and started talking about all kinds of stuff. We told funny stories about things in our childhood. We talked about Heck, and about Sal. We talked about Seattle. We talked about Tom's work with National Geographic.

Tom told me about their trip to Kodiak Island last fall, and the bear attacking Heck. He only gave me the Cliff Notes. It had to be very traumatic for him to see his friend near death and not be able to do anything about it, but Tom stayed away from the emotional part of the story.

I told him about Robbie. I don't know why exactly. It couldn't compare to Tom's bear story, but it was traumatic to me. I guess I was trying to draw him out a little, to make him feel more comfortable talking about his feelings. No luck. Guys just don't do that.

The truth is, I don't really like guys who do talk about their feelings too much, even if they're not gay. It makes them seem vulnerable. I guess for me, vulnerability is not all that attractive in a man. I dropped it.

We got back to talking about positive and fun things. The drinks with our dinner helped loosen the conversation even more. We lingered over some chocolate mousse and Amaretto coffee.

"So, what happen with your ex?" He paused, and shifted gears. "You know, it's none of my business, really. You don't have to tell me. I shouldn't have asked." It didn't seem like an inappropriate question to me.

"No, that's okay. I haven't really talked about it much to anyone, not even Sal. Maybe I should.

"He dumped me for another woman. That's about it." Of course there was more to it. He waited. "I guess we just grew apart. Something was missing for him. I guess something was missing for me too. I don't know what it was.

"It was great for a while. Then, it was okay for a while. Then, it was nothing for a while. Then, it was just too late. I didn't see it in time. I can't explain it. I wish I could. I don't know if I could have changed anything."

"I'm afraid I wouldn't know about that. I've never really let any of my relationships get past the 'great' stage." Wow, what an honest revelation. He didn't seem ashamed of it, maybe a little regretful though.

"Really? Never married? You're the love 'em and leave 'em type, huh?" I forced a giggle to let him know I wasn't being judgmental.

"See, that's what I mean. I look at people who get married, and it all just falls apart after a while. Heck, you, even Billy. It always goes south." He thought about it for a second, then said lower, "Except, when it doesn't."

"Billy? Was he married?" Somehow, I couldn't picture him married.

"Not exactly. It's a long story. Anyway, I see other people who make it work. Maybe that's it. They *work* at it. Maybe, I don't want to do the work."

I was seeing another side of Tom, a more introspective side, perhaps a more sensitive side, but a side that had some issues.

"So, what happened with your last girl friend?" Fair is fair. He started it.

"Starla? It didn't work out." That was a cop out, and he knew it. I raised my eyebrows in a question mark. "Okay, that's my way of saying I dumped her. She was great. I had no complaints. She was just perfect, in every way I can think of."

"Apparently, there must have been *something* wrong. You dumped her."

"Yeah, there was *something* wrong, something wrong with me. I guess I can't handle too much perfection." He laughed self-consciously. He took a drink so that he didn't have to look me in the eye.

"I understand. You just didn't want to make a commitment. You wanted to play house, but you didn't want to do the house work. But sooner or later, every relationship requires some work, doesn't it?

"I guess I didn't want to do the work either. Ya know, you only get out what you put in. I didn't put in enough. You didn't put in anything at all." I snorted a laugh when I caught my accidental double entendre. It took him a second, but Tom laughed too.

It was a good thing that Tom didn't have to drive too far. We were both getting a little giddy from the drink, and the good humor.

When we got to Tom's he made us some non-alcoholic coffee before he showed me his work. He had a studio set up in one of the bedrooms. Several of his best photos were blown up to poster size on the walls. A cabinet held several large binders with hundreds of eight by ten and larger sized prints. Another larger set of shelves held what looked like catalog index boxes containing negatives, all labeled. On one wall, he had hung several awards. In the center, there was a framed copy of the National Geographic cover that had used his photo.

He pulled out a couple of the large albums and laid them on a small work table. He leafed through them slowly, describing each one. They were all stunning. Several were awe inspiring. Many pulled you into the action. But a few, especially the ones containing people, stirred the emotions. Those pictures seemed to talk to me.

Tom definitely had a talent for seeing the world, and framing it in a way that revealed the previously unseen. In addition to showing a new view of the world, his pictures showed me a new side of Tom. There was a sensitivity there that I had not seen before in a straight guy. He might not talk about his feelings much, but they were imbedded in his work.

I looked into his eyes. "They're beautiful." I was talking about more than his photos.

"I try." he said and shrugged his shoulders.

"You do more than try." I took a step closer to him. "I'm very impressed, and a little surprised."

"Why surprised."

"I think these pictures show me the real Tom Birch. You put yourself into your work, and it shows who you are." I moved a little closer.

First kisses are supposed to be awkward. This one was not. Our lips did not exactly touch, they seemed to flow into each other. I felt like my whole body flowed into his. We were one for a few seconds. I was floating off the floor.

The kiss ended after what seemed like a very long time. I have no idea how long it really was. It could have been seconds. It could have been minutes.

He held me back a few inches, and took a breath without taking his eye off of mine, holding me away, but keeping me close.

We kissed again. It was impossible that it could be any better than the first, but it was. His arms held me firmly, but gently. Without his embrace, my knees would have failed me.

I wanted to go to bed with him right then. I wanted to feel him. I wanted to be part of him. At that moment, I wanted him more than any other man that I have ever known, even Chuck that first time.

The bedroom was only a few steps away. I found my feet moving in that direction. We were not walking exactly. Tom was not leading me there, nor was he carrying me there. We just seemed to arrive there, on the bed.

We tugging at our clothes with no real plan of how to get them off, we just wanted them out of the way. He was touching my breast and kissing me.

But something was wrong. He had stopped. Tom suddenly sat up on the bed and said, "No!"

I felt like I had been plunged into a pool of ice water. It took my breath away. I couldn't talk. I just stared at him.

"It's not you." He said. "You're beautiful. I didn't plan this. I didn't want this to happen." I was limp. He pulled me to a sitting position next to him and hugged me.

Slowly, I found my arms again and hugged him back. We sat like that for a long minute. I didn't understand what had happened. I didn't feel insulted, or embarrassed, or put off in any way, just confused.

When I was younger, I know I would have thought it was about me. Now, I knew that it wasn't. He would tell me what it was. He was wrestling with himself. He needed a little time. Timing is everything. I only needed to be there and to be patient.

He said softly. "I'm sorry."

"It's okay." I said, just as softly.

He gently stood up and let go of me and said, "Give me a minute." He went into the bathroom. I heard the water running. Was he washing his face? I was still where he left me when he returned.

"I'm really sorry." He said. I gave him a soft hug when he sat down, but said nothing.

"It's just too easy. No, I don't mean that *you're* too easy. I mean I always get things too easily. I never have to work for it. But, then I lose it just as easy. I *want* to do the work this time."

"What work? It's not work to be with you. I want to be with you."

"That's what I mean. Things are always easy for me at first, too easy. But you're special. You're not like the other women I've known. Believe me, that's a very good thing. I want to earn it for once, especially with you. You deserve it. I've never felt like this with anyone, and I've been with enough to know. I don't want to jinx it. I want it to be something that lasts."

No one, other than my folks, had ever exactly called me "special." I didn't know if I should be flattered or offended.

"I don't think I'm very special. You're the one with all the talent, not to mention the looks."

"No, you *are* special. You're real. You're not just a retouched cover girl illusion. Don't take this the wrong way. I love that you're not perfect that way. No one is perfect, really. They only look perfect. That's why I think you could be perfect *for me*. Do you understand?" I had no clue.

"No, I don't understand. Are you saying that because I'm not perfect like Starla, I *am* perfect for you?" Did I just say that?

"I'm sorry. I'm not making any sense. I *love* that you're you. I *love* your little imperfections, like those freckles. They're what make you, you. I want something real for a change. I don't want another playboy toy." Did he just use the word "love" twice?

"Maybe sometimes, I'd like being a playboy toy." I giggled, and then got serious. "But, I think I understand. And I think that I *love* that you think I might be *imperfectly* perfect for you." I can say it too.

"I want to get to know you. I want you to get to know me. I want to do the whole dating thing. I want to do the *work* to build a foundation that has a chance of lasting.

"I know it might not work out. I know there are no guarantees with any relationship. I just want a chance to try to make it something more. Will you give me that chance?"

"Do you think I'm worth it? I mean, I can be a bitch sometimes, really, ask Sal."

"I really *don't* know if you're worth it. That's the point. I want to find out. I feel something special for you. Don't you feel something too, something more than just hormones?"

"Yes, I think I do. I didn't think I could. I was afraid to try. I'm still a woman on the rebound, ya know. But, I think you're pretty *special* too. And yes, I want to give it a shot."

"Do you want to spend the night, I mean to talk. I just want to be with you, if that's okay."

"What about Heck?" I wanted to stay in a big way.

"Oh, that's right. I guess I'll have to go pick him up." His disappointment was tangible.

"Wait, let me call Sal. We have our rental car at the hotel. We can let Heck borrow it until tomorrow."

Sal and Heck were expecting us to return to the hotel when I called. Sal had no problem letting Heck borrow the rental car, but Heck may have had an issue with it. I heard his voice in the background. I couldn't make out the words, but the tone did not sound happy. I didn't care, as long as the answer wasn't "no," we could sort it out later.

We spent the night with our clothes on in Tom's bed. It was the most wonderful night I can remember ever spending with a man, including the nights when I *did* have sex.

We talked. We cuddled. We kissed, and finally we fell asleep in each other's arms.

CHAPTER 44
HECK

Sal and I had finished our dinner, and were sipping on coffee in the bar when Becky called.

After a short one-sided conversation, Sal turned to me and said, "It's Becky. She wants to know if it's okay if you take our rental car to get home tonight. It's apparently taking them longer than expected at Tom's." *That son-of-a-Birch.*

"Sure, I can borrow your car, if that's what you want. If that's what *they* want."

She hung up the phone and looked at me, puzzled by my tone.

"Ya know, Tom's a great guy. Hell, he's my best friend. But he's got this thing with women. I guess it's none of my business." I couldn't help but sound exasperated.

"Becky's my best friend too. What kind of 'thing' are you talking about? Is it something I should be worried about?"

"Don't worry, he not some kind of pervert or anything. He just has a history of chewing up women and spitting them out."

"What do you mean?"

"It's not his fault, at least not completely. Women think he's a good looking guy. And he's got that bad boy thing going for him too. I just think he takes advantage of that. But the thing is, none of his relationships go anywhere. He dumps them before they've had a chance.

"Look, I love him like a brother, but I wish he'd settle down. I hope Becky knows what she getting into. But hey, like I said, it's none of my business."

"I disagree. I think it is your business, and mine too. What's a friend for, if not to tell you where you're going wrong? I'll have a talk with Becky, and you should have a talk with Tom."

"Yeah. You're right, I guess. I *have* tried to talk to him, but he doesn't like to talk about his relationships."

"I guess it's different with women. Becky and I talk all the time." She paused. "Well, maybe not as much as we should."

"Tom accuses me of psychoanalyzing him, and he's probably right. Hey, I'm a psychologist." I laughed. She laughed with me. It was a non-judgmental laugh.

"Becky is the only one who tells me what I need to hear, but not always what I want to hear. If it was coming from anyone else, I wouldn't listen. I trust her. I'll bet it's the same with Tom. He trusts you, doesn't he?"

"So, what you're telling me is that constructive criticism coming from someone you trust is most effective. Good point. I'll write that down. Now who's playing psychologist?" I was kidding, and she knew it. She laughed at herself with such ease.

"The car keys are in the room. You can follow me up if you'd like." There was something in her voice, something cautious. I hoped I had not given her any reason to be fearful of me.

"Sure, I'll walk up with you."

We had been talking continuously all evening. But now, on our way to her room, we seemed to have nothing to say.

The elevator ride to the eighth floor was quiet. The elevator smelled slightly of stainless steel polish. But behind that was Sal's perfume. It was the same perfume she was wearing when she rode in my car to see Anna. I hadn't noticed it in the restaurant earlier. It was light and flowery, with a subtle earthy hint that reminded me of a damp forest. It suited her personality, I thought.

There's something about being in an elevator alone with an attractive woman. It's the intimacy of a closed, private space. Nothing ever really happens in an elevator, except in cheap romance novels, but it could. I thought of that moment on the water taxi when she held my arm. We were not touching now, but I was acutely aware that she stood only inches away.

The door of the elevator opened onto the eighth floor. Sal led the way out of the elevator to the left down the hallway.

She glanced at me momentarily as she unlocked the door to her room. It was an odd look, not fearful, certainly not suggestive, maybe curious, but curious about what.

"The keys are in my other bag. I'll get them." She walked to the other side of the large executive suite. It was more spacious than I was accustomed to on my travels. The rooms I stayed in for conventions and other business trips never include a living room area like this one.

She walked back across the room with the keys. Again there was that odd look, this time with a smile. "Here's the keys. You can bring it back whenever. We don't have any plans, at least I don't. I've got some computer work to do. Just give me a call tomorrow sometime."

"Thanks, I'll call you when I get up. I'm sure it'll be after you." I turned to go.

"Are you in a hurry? I mean, it's still early. I feel like raiding the mini bar. Becky's not here. Do you want to join me for a night cap before you go?" Now, that was unexpected.

"You read my mind." I had nothing of the sort on my mind.

"Great! Help yourself. Give me a minute, I'll be right back." I could hear the water running in the bathroom as I picked out a couple of miniature bottles of vodka and a half-pint carton of orange juice.

I left a twenty dollar bill on the mini bar, because I know those items are not cheap. I felt funny about mooching off a woman. She insisted on putting her own dinner on her room bill, but this was different.

I found a glass, but I discovered that there was no ice. I called through the bathroom door. "I'm going down the hallway to get some ice. I'm leaving the door propped open for a minute."

"Okay. I'll be out in a second." I heard her say from behind the closed door. There was a definite lilt in her voice.

The ice machine was on the other side of the elevator that we had just left.

She was still in the bathroom when I got back. I prepared my drink and sat it on the coffee table next to the small sofa in the living room area.

She seemed to be taking a very long time. A "second" of bathroom time for a woman is apparently much longer than it is for a man. I was sure I could have showered, shaved and dressed in less time, if I wanted to.

"Can I get a drink for you?" I called again through the bathroom door.

"Thanks. I was going to have a rum and Coke. Thank you. I'll be out in a second." Where have I heard that one before?

I made her drink using only half of the miniature bottle of rum. I sat the remainder next to her glass on the coffee table next to mine. I sat down on the far end of the sofa and sipped on my drink while I waited. And then, I sipped on my drink some more while I waited some more.

The bathroom door finally opened. "Sorry I took so long. I just wanted to get comfortable. Is that okay?" Did she need my permission?

She was dressed in heavy plaid flannel pajamas, but you'd have thought she was wearing a skimpy lace negligee, as self-conscience as she seemed to be.

"It's okay with me. It's your room. You can check with the front desk, but I think it's a hotel rule. You get to wear whatever you want while you're in your own room." She giggled. It was more than okay with me.

She was beautiful. She had transformed herself from a savvy professional woman, into an all American hometown girl. She had stripped off her makeup. It made her look fresh and sparkly. She had refreshed her perfume, the same one, but now it was no longer subdued. There were also assorted scents from soap, skin lotion, tooth paste and other feminine things that all added up to announce very clearly, "I am a woman." It was intoxicating.

And, she was barefoot too. I don't have a foot fetish, but there's something unexpectedly alluring about a barefooted woman in flannel pajamas.

She sat down Indian style on the other end of the sofa, and took a sip of her drink.

"Thanks for making my drink. It's a little weak though." She poured the remainder of rum from the miniature bottle into her drink and stirred it with her index finger. Then she licked the drips from her finger. "Yum. Just right." This was definitely a side of Sal I had not seen before. She was more relaxed, more earthy, and a lot more sexy. She wasn't trying to be sexy, which in itself, made her even sexier.

We talked about college, where we grew up, her promotion with the CDC. It felt good talking with her, like a sister, not my sister, but somebody's sister. We started our second drink.

There was a lull in the conversation. She said, "I screwed up with the outbreak containment. I was responsible for the man getting infected in Florida. I didn't order the right kind of decontamination procedure for the airplane." Where did that come from? She took a drink and looked me in the eye. What was I supposed to say?

"I'm sure you did your best. Everyone makes mistakes." I just pulled that out of my spare psychologist hat. She could tell.

"That's what everyone says. I guess you're probably right, but I can't stop feeling guilty about it." I know about guilt.

"You wouldn't be human if you could just forget about it. You just live with it. If you need to feel punished for your mistake, *that's* your punishment. You can't forget it, and you're punished every time you think about it. But after a while, you get punished a little less often. Maybe that's all you can expect."

"That's pretty depressing. Is that supposed to make me feel better?" She chuckled to let me know she was not offended.

"I'm sorry. It must be the vodka. At least you *just* made a mistake. It was an oversight, sure, but not a conscious decision that you knew you were making, and that now you know you can never change. You just gotta live with it. Trying *not* to live with it, now that's how you really punish yourself."

"That's the kind of thing my daddy would say. 'Face up to it, bite the bullet,' that sort of thing. Are you talking from experience, or are you reading that from a psych textbook, *professor?*" She smiled.

"I was responsible for my sister's death. I know what I'm talking about." Did I say that out loud, or was I just thinking it?

"No, I don't believe it. You couldn't have killed your sister." I guess I *did* say it out loud.

"No, I didn't *kill* Nan, but I made a conscious decision that resulted in her death. I was fourteen, and I screwed up." A veil of sadness drifted over Sal's face. It was a reflection of my own face.

"I'm sorry. How did it happen? We don't have to talk about it, if you don't want to."

"That's okay, there's not much to tell. I was supposed to be watching her. I chose to shoot the breeze with Tom and Billy in the front yard, while she was playing in the back yard. She wandered off, had a seizure, and drowned in the creek behind our house."

"It was an accident then?"

"It was an accident that I allowed to happen. I made a choice. I knew I was making the wrong choice. I thought I could get away with it. I made a bet, my BS'ing with the guys against her life. I lost. Nan lost. That's the part that I have to live with.

"What would your daddy have to say about that?" I said.

I didn't really expect an answer, but I could see that she was trying to think of one.

"Well I guess, if he was talking to me, he would tell me, 'Sally Sue, you made a mistake. Accept it. Apologize for it. Make it right if you can. Learn from it. Don't make the same mistake again. And, move on.' "

"He sounds like he was a real down to Earth kind of guy. Good advice, hard to always follow though. Do you think he would forgive you if you consciously made a wrong choice, and knew it was wrong when you made it?"

She thought about that for a minute. Then her face scrunched up and she started to cry. I didn't expect that at all. I moved over to her on the sofa and gently put my arm around her, because... well, because that's what you do with a crying woman, right?

"Don't cry. I'm sure it's not that bad." I just wanted her to stop crying. Nothing can make a man feel more helpless.

She took my other hand and held it in both of hers. Her hands were soft and warm, and seemed delicate and fragile. I gave her time to cry it out. It doesn't take a psychologist to know that there's a time to talk, and a time to shut up.

"Heck, my daddy was the kindest, most loving man I have ever known. I know he would forgive me no matter what I did… if I gave him the chance." She had something specific in mind.

"I made a mistake when I was fifteen. I made the wrong choice, and I knew it was wrong, but I was too ashamed to tell Daddy about it. Now, I wish I had. I've felt guilty about it ever since. He died, and I never told him. Now I can't."

"Yes, you can." I said it softly, but in a confident, soothing tone. I had used this technique before with good success. Of course, I couldn't tell her that I was using any kind of "technique" on her.

"What do you mean? He's dead." That started a new round of sobs.

I waited. "I know he's dead, but even if you don't believe his spirit is listening, *you* will hear it. *You* will know it. Just get it out. You can pretend I'm your daddy if it helps." I kept the same soothing, confident tone.

"I don't understand. How will that do any good?" She said hopefully.

"I know you're not Catholic, neither am I, but that confession thing they do really works, whether you believe you're talking to God or not. Try it. What do you have to lose?" Soothing. Confident.

"I guess. Okay." She turned so that she could look directly into my eyes. "Daddy, I'm sorry. I got into the wrong van, at the wrong time, with the wrong guy. I screwed up. I knew it was wrong. He… violated me. I didn't stop him when I should have. I knew I was doing the wrong thing. I lied to you about why Bruce and I broke up. It was me. I wouldn't let him… touch me that way. I felt like I was soiled somehow, and I couldn't let myself trust him. I haven't let myself trust any man. I'm sorry Daddy. Please forgive me." She looked down into her lap.

I hadn't expected anything like that. I felt ashamed that I had asked her to bare her soul that way. I had no right. It made me feel almost perverted in a way.

"Look Sal, I'm sorry for making you tell me all that. I didn't know. I didn't think it was… I just didn't think." I just blew it, and I knew it.

She continued holding my hand. Now, was another time to shut up. She had every right to throw me out, and that was what I expected.

But at that moment, I reveled in being next to her, her smell, her warmth, her slow breathing. I was holding a precious jewel that I knew I had no right to be holding. Still, I didn't want it to end, but I knew it would.

She slowly turned her head up and looked again into my eyes. Her eyes captured me. I wanted to look away in shame, but I couldn't.

"Thank you Heck. I feel a little better. I think it helped. I'm sorry I made you hear that, but I needed to say it. I needed to say it to Daddy. Thank you for listening *for* him." She laid her head onto my shoulder and wrapped her arm around my chest.

That simple move felt so natural. Of course, it wasn't natural at all. I had only known her a few days. Now, we were sitting in an easy embrace, on her sofa, in her hotel room. We had told each other intimate things that we hid from everyone else. I couldn't explain it, but it felt so right.

I was reprieved, forgiven, cleansed of my sin of psycho-analytical impropriety. Maybe there is a God. I promised myself, and Him, if He was there, that I would never try anything like that with her again. She was not one of my patients. I hoped she could become more than that.

It didn't feel like I was with a sister anymore.

CHAPTER 45
RAY

I had been awake for the last hour. I had been orienting myself to my new-found environment, the sounds, the smells. I inventoried all of the items in my room, their spatial relationships, and their physical qualities. It was like studying the pool balls on an unfamiliar pool table.

It was raining softly, but steadily outside. I knew this without looking. The blinds had been shut, but the sound that penetrated the double glazed windows was all I needed.

They had attached me to an intravenous saline drip. They had also inserted a urinary catheter. I was naked except for a skimpy hospital gown and a sheet. This was all too familiar. I had been here before, in this same hospital.

I listened to the chatter coming from the nurse's station twenty yards down the hallway. I realized that they were talking about me.

"Was Lt. Boswick at the police station notified that Mr. Miller is conscious, as he requested?" It was a doctor. I could tell by the tone of her voice. She was someone with authority.

"Yes, I left him a message. He called back a few minutes ago to tell us that he is on his way up. He told me to 'keep an eye on him' until he gets here. He hung up on me before I could ask what he meant. What a butthead." It was the head nurse. I knew this with a certainty that no one would understand.

"I don't know. Maybe they think he's going to try to escape or something."

"This is not a prison. If they're worried about an escape, why didn't they send someone down here to guard him? I've got better things to do. I don't have time to be a turnkey too. Besides, he's on a drip and a catheter, and he's wearing a hospital gown. How far is he going to get?"

I started to gather items within reach that I could use, a spoon left with some jello that was supposed to be my lunch, a straw left for my ice water, and a retractable pen left by a nurse no doubt.

I pushed the nurse call button. When they came, I asked for a bedpan. I acted like it was an urgent request. The entry level nurse did not want to have to clean up a mess, so she brought me a bedpan quickly.

I had discovered upon waking that my reaction speed had increased. More precisely, from my perspective, I noticed that everything was moving more slowly than before. I didn't have to test myself. I knew my capabilities. I felt them. I calibrated them in my mind.

I restudied the tiniest details of every item in the room. It would be easy. I was ready. *They think they can keep an eye on me.*

It had been an embarrassment. I was too confident. I overlooked a small detail. It wouldn't happen again. They were all going to die. But first, I need to clear the way. Lt. Joe Boswick was going to be in my way. He knew too much, or thought he did.

Next, I wanted that blond bitch from the CDC. When she dies, Dr. Beckman will be there, and he'll die. I know about them too. The pheromones wafting off of them told me everything I needed to know. But there were other things too, subtle things.

Most people don't know that your iris will expand when you are talking to, or looking at, people you like a lot, and it will contract when you look at people you dislike or are afraid of. I could spot that from a hundred yards, if I wanted to.

Oh yes, they've got a thing for one another. They probably don't even know it yet themselves. They will be together alright. He will be protective. They will both die. How tragically romantic it will be.

Then, there will be no one to stop me from going back for that witch in West Seattle. She was special. I wanted to make that one slow and painful.

You shall not permit a sorceress to live. Exodus 22:18.

I didn't have to wait long. I followed his progress through the front door. He double checked the room number at the information desk. He got on the elevator with one other rider, female. He got off the elevator. He stopped at the nurse's station, and asked a nurse to accompany him, *in case he needs something.*

Then he was entering the room. "Well, hello Joe. Wud'ya know. I've been expecting you." That will throw him off balance.

"Mr. Miller, I have some questions for you about a couple of recent deaths. First, I want to know why you visited Anna Grant in West Seattle yesterday." Right to the point. I like that. I'll do the same.

"I have a question for you Joe. Do you want to shoot yourself in your right ear or your left ear? Which one do you think your ex, Linda, would choose?" I knew everything about him. I mentioned his wife just to rattle his confidence.

"Look here asshole, I can be nice, or I can be not so nice. How would you like me to handcuff you to your bed?" He was becoming rattled. Anger now, the fear will come soon.

I raised my knees, and rustled around under my sheet for a second for effect. Then, I racked an imaginary round into my imaginary twenty-five automatic, and flicked off the imaginary safety. I said, "If you try to do that, I would have to shoot you."

"He's got a gun!" He yelled to the nurse that had accompanied him. Now the fear. Joe pulled his thirty-eight special revolver, pointed it at me as he dropped to one knee behind the foot of my bed. At the same time with his free hand, he pushed the nurse who was behind his left shoulder out of the door.

Quick fellow. Old school weapon though. He really should get himself a more modern firearm, not that it matters now.

"What makes you think I have a gun?" I was calm. Tone was important here. He needed to know that I knew that I was in control. For a control freak like Joe, this would be intolerable.

"You said you had a gun! I heard the action. Show me your hands, now! Don't make me shoot you!" Oh yeah, the adrenaline was flowing now. He had both hands on the gun. He was shaking a little, not bad though. He'd been in a fire fight once or twice before.

"Did I say I had a gun? I think I said I would have to 'shoot' you. I could have a camera. You can't be sure, can you Joe." Calm, in control. I moved slowly under the sheet between my knees. The sheet traced my menacing movement. "Wow, what pheromones you have, Joe—pure fear."

"Show me your hands, asshole!" He was almost screaming. You'd think he could come up with a more imaginative insult with all that cop experience of his.

"I'll give you one more chance to answer my question, or I'm going to have to decide for you. Right ear, or left ear?

"Of course, you *could* choose to shoot yourself between your eyes, but that would be bad for Jimmy to see at your funeral, wouldn't it? He must be, what, nine-years-old now? You really should have picked him up last weekend, ya know. He was expecting you, but you didn't show up, did you? Now you'll *never* show up again." Truth hurts. That was the point.

"This is your last chance, asshole!" Yes, there it was, the micro-quavers in his voice, his needle-point sized pupils, his fear-laced sweat. He believed that he was going to die.

"Your personal life is miserable, isn't it Joe? So, what's the point? Let's just end it. Now, *where* would you like to shoot yourself?" Low and slow, and very calm. *I'm in charge.*

"Drop it!" Now he was definitely screaming. I could see the blood pumping in the tiny blood vessels in his eyes, one-hundred-thirty-three beats per minute. His blood pressure was two-hundred-five. He was ready.

I flinched under the sheet. That was all it took. I watched his painfully slow finger pull the trigger on his thirty-eight. I had plenty of time. I recalculated the angles, no different than pool really.

I watched the bullet exiting the barrel of his gun. I reached over and pulled the I.V. pole three inches closer. At the same time, I positioned the bedpan exactly where I wanted it. Then I waited for the bullet to arrive.

I had decided on the left ear. Hey, I gave him a chance to decide for himself, but he didn't take it.

The bullet hit the bedpan at an obtuse angle. A direct hit would have allowed the bullet to penetrate the thin stainless steel. It bounced off, traveling to the left side of my bed, striking the I.V. pole. No chance of penetration there. It was made of a much heavier steel. Since the pole was round, it gave me a full range of deflection angles to use. By moving the pole only a millimeter one way or the other, I could cover the whole room.

The bullet then traveled all the way across the room to a cabinet door pull that was made of chrome plated steel. It was a nice half-inch wide flat surface, not much calculation needed there.

Unfortunately, the bullet had lost much of its energy by this point it its journey. When it finally entered Joe's left ear, it was only able to penetrate half way though his brain.

Joe crumbled to the floor. His breathing stopped a moment later.

"Eight ball in the side pocket!" It wasn't all that fancy, but it got the job done. I had decided that fancy was just for my ego. I knew what I could do. I didn't need to prove it to myself, or to anyone else.

There was all kinds of commotion in the hallway, women screaming, someone barking orders. Someone was calling the police from the nurse's station. They were telling them that I had a gun, and that I had shot the officer. I wouldn't do that. Their forensics people would eventually figure that out.

I carefully disconnected my catheter and I.V. I found my clothes in the closet in a paper bag. I could smell them there. I got dressed without any hurry. It would take the police a while to get organized. I left Joe's gun where it had landed. I wasn't going to need it. I took the retractable pen with me.

I walked casually out of the room to be greeted by more screams from down the hall. People were hiding, from what, me?

I said loudly and slowly, so that even the most panicked person would understand, "Tell Sal she's next." All I needed to do was to plant that seed. It would grow.

I walked around a corner and disappeared, at least that's what they would tell the police.

CHAPTER 46
SAL

What was I doing? It was crazy, but it was wonderful. I was in the arms of a man I didn't know until a few days ago. I had just confessed my deepest secrets to this man. How could I trust him as if I had known him all my life?

Is it possible to know someone who you don't know? Is there a difference between knowing, and knowing? If you can know the facts about someone without knowing their heart, can you also know their heart without knowing all the facts?

I knew this man, somehow. That made no sense. It went against every rational fiber of my body. I was a woman of science, not emotion, or so I thought.

Heck was not my daddy. I was not confused about that, even though I had confessed to him as if he was my daddy. Although, for just a second, when I looked into his deep green eyes and spoke to him, I felt like my daddy was listening.

Heck was right. It did make me feel better, like a weight had been lifted. I still felt guilt, but it was mostly guilt that I hadn't trusted Daddy enough to tell him while he was alive.

I felt safe with Heck. There was something about him that said to me, "You can trust me. I won't hurt you, and I won't let you be hurt." I felt it when we first met, when my hand first touched his. I couldn't know it was true, but I could feel the truth of it. Right then, the feeling part of me was in charge.

My head was nestled on his shoulder. His arm was around my shoulder. My arm was wrapped around his chest. I held his other hand in mine. It felt natural. It felt wonderful. Words were not needed. We sat like that for minutes without talking.

It wasn't normal. It wasn't right. It felt too good. Was I screwing up?

The rational part of me took over.

"I'm sorry." I sat up and put my arm back where it belonged. I let go of his hand. "I'm not like this. I don't know what got into me." I was talking as my much to myself as I was to him.

"No, no, that's okay. I understand." He took his arm off of my shoulder and move away a couple inches.

"It's just… talking about Daddy, gets me emotional. I'm really sorry. I don't want you to think…" What *did* he think?

"Me too. I mean, talking about Nan. I get a little emotional too. I haven't talked about her to anyone for a long time. It felt good. And, I don't get many hugs these days either. Thank you.

"I don't want you to think that I was taking advantage of you or anything." He was embarrassed by what *he* did, but he didn't do anything.

"It was time for me to unpack some of my baggage. I've been carrying it around for a long time. Thank you for letting me dump it on you. I know you're a psychologist, but this isn't your office, and I'm not your patient." I felt a little exposed.

"No, you're not my patient. But, sometimes it's better to talk to a friend anyway. I hope you can think of me like a friend." Those eyes expressed such sincerity.

"Yes, I do. You feel like a friend to me, maybe more like the brother I never had."

"Thank you. And you feel a little like the sister I wish I had." I knew he meant it. This man would never hurt me. I knew it. Was I screwing up? Or, was I still afraid of my own judgment.

"It's like I've known you for a long time. It's weird, I know. I can't explain it." The feeling part of me overruled the rational side.

I reached over and took his hand. "Maybe it's the rum, maybe it's something else. I don't know. I just know I feel safe with you. I haven't felt safe with a man in a long time. Thank you for listening to me. Thank you for being here." I said.

I looked down at his hand in mine. I couldn't look directly into his eyes anymore. It was like he was looking straight into my soul. I didn't want him to see that my soul was saying, *I want you.*

We sat like that for a minute without talking, but it seemed longer. I couldn't see his eyes, but I could feel them.

They seemed to envelop me with respect, with admiration, and maybe even reverence.

This was silly, I thought. Here was a perfect man, a man who I trusted, a man who I was sure wanted me, but a man who respected me too much to make any sort of move on me. I made a decision, an irrational decision, a crazy decision, a decision I might regret. I raised my head, looked into his eyes and kissed him.

It was only a little kiss. I gently touched my lips with his. I knew it was the right decision instantly.

I looked into his eyes again. They were open much wider now. There was surprise there, but beyond that, there was adoration. It reminded me of the look on Becky's face when she got Robbie that Christmas. It was gratitude, combined with excitement, combined with awe.

I kissed him again. This time it was longer. Not passionate, but tender. We lingered. He rapped his arm around me. I put my free hand on his chest. I felt him breath. I felt his heart beat. I felt the rough stubble of his whiskers on my skin. I breathed in his distinctively male scent. Yes, he wanted me, and I wanted him. I made another decision.

I stood up still holding his hand. I coaxed him to a standing position facing me. We kissed again. This time we hugged with both arms. It was a full body kiss. It was deep and passionate. It stirred feelings that I remembered from that night in Gary's brother's van.

A jolt of fear ran through me. Then, I felt Heck's strong arms around me, firm, gentle, protecting. The fear dissolved.

I lead him to my bed. He started to object.

"Are you sure? I don't want to…" I put a finger to his lips.

"No, don't say anything. This is all me. I want this. I know I won't regret it. Please."

He made no further objections. It was selfishly all about me at that moment. He sensed that I needed to lead him. He let me do what I wanted, at my pace. I lead, but he showed me the way.

There was no hurry. We took time to explore each other. When I finally guided him inside of me, there was no pain. It felt so right, like he had been made for me, and I had been made for him.

All that guilt and all that fear, for all those years, and this is what awaited me. I paid a steep price, but it was worth it, because Heck was worth it.

He was a giving lover. He took what he wanted, but in ways that gave me more in return. He showed me things about my body that I had not known. He showed me the beauty I had only read about before. I gave myself to him completely.

CHAPTER 47
HECK

First-time sex is always exciting. But, our first night together transcended exciting. It was magical. It bordered on the divine.

Her body was beautiful. But it wasn't about her body, and it wasn't about my body. Our bodies were only the instruments of our spiritual ecstasy.

There was none of the awkwardness that usually accompanies first encounters. There was a familiarity usually experienced with long-time couples, without sacrificing any of the freshness of new love.

I did feel love, but I wasn't going to say it, not yet. I didn't want to scare her away. I wanted a very long future with this woman. Beginnings can be very fragile things. Best not to build the house until the concrete foundation had solidified.

I had been sleeping for less than four hours when I woke up. I got up carefully and sat on the edge of the bed next to her. It was 7:15 by the nightstand clock. The night's emotional and physical demands had depleted my energy reserves. In other words, I was hungry.

Sal was still sleeping. The light was dim, but I didn't want to turn on more lights and wake her. My eyes were adjusted to the dark. I could see her well enough. She was naked under the sheet. She had not bothered to put her flannel pajamas back on. I did not have to pull back the sheet to know every perfect nuance of the body hidden there.

I studied her head poking out of the sheet, her hair tangled across her face, her mouth askew against the pillow. She looked beautiful to me. I watched her breath softly for several minutes. In a way, they were the most intimate minutes I had spent with a woman in a very long time.

I decided to let her sleep a little longer and take a shower. I made the water hot. You never have to worry about running out of hot water in a good hotel. I had closed the door, and turned on the exhaust fan, but the small bathroom quickly filled up with steam.

I could not have imagined a more perfect night, or a more promising morning after. But, something was wrong. I had that nagging feeling again, like I had forgotten something important, but couldn't remember what it was.

I remembered the night of the fire, the night Tyler died, when I woke up early and took a shower. I had that same ominous feeling then. I thought it was just one of those things, one of those things that have no explanation, an odd coincidence, a meaningless feeling. Probably nothing. I tried to put it out of my head and finished my shower.

I toweled off and got dressed in the dim light. I thought I would write Sal a note just in case she woke up, and then run downstairs to a bagel shop I had seen. Coffee, and toasted bagels with creamed cheese sounded good. I could bring hers up, so that it would be waiting for her when she woke up.

I got back to the room in less than fifteen minutes. I had my hands full with two coffees and a bag containing two large toasted bagels with all the fixings. I put them down on the small desk beside the beds.

Sal was already up. I could hear the shower running. I called to her behind the closed door.

"I'm back with coffee and bagels."

"Okay. Thanks! I'll be out in minute." Right. I chuckled to myself.

I turned on some lights and set about doctoring my bagel. I took a sip of coffee, and was about to take a bite of my bagel and creamed cheese, when my cell phone rang. It was Jan.

"Good morning Jan, what's up?"

"Heck, are you near a TV. Turn on the news."

"Okay, what's going on?" I found the remote. I knew this was not going to be good.

"Lt. Boswick was murdered yesterday afternoon. They're saying Ray did it. There were witnesses."

"Okay, I've got the TV on. I'm looking for the news. What happened?"

"They said Ray shot Lt. Boswick at the hospital with his own gun."

"That doesn't sound like Ray. There must be more to the story."

"Heck, can you call Sal. I can't find her card. Everything is such a mess. I can't find anything. They say that Ray said that 'Sal's next.' Several people at the hospital heard him say it. The police didn't know who he meant. That's why they called me."

"Yes, I can call Sal. Do they know where Ray is? Did they arrest him?" I didn't want to tell Jan that I was in Sal's room, and that she was in the shower. I didn't want her to find out about *us* that way.

"They don't know where he is. The people at the hospital said that he just disappeared." That sounds more like Ray.

"Thanks, Jan. I'll tell Sal. I'll call the police too, so they can get an officer out to guard her." I hung up the phone just as a picture of Ray came on the TV screen. I turned up the volume.

The reporter was saying, "…was shot in the head when he was visiting the suspect in his hospital room. The alleged gunman, Raymond Miller, was heard threatening to kill another individual who has not yet been identified. Police say that Miller only used the intended target's first name, Sal. Anyone knowing the whereabouts of Raymond Miller, or who has any information about this person named Sal, should contact the Seattle Police Department immediately at this number." A large phone number was put on the screen beneath Ray's picture. I grabbed the pen and note pad I had used earlier to write the note for Sal, and I quickly wrote down the number.

I called Tom first. I woke him up.

"Heck? What?"

"Tom, this is serious. Ray Miller is out of the hospital and he's killing people. He shot Lt. Boswick. He said he's coming after Sal. I need to keep her safe until the police can stop him. I need your help."

"Sure Heck. What?" He was still groggy, but the news had woke him up.

"Come down to the hotel. We need to make sure Sal is safe. Can you pick up the Berretta and the clips from my place? You know where the key is. I think Becky would be safer if she stayed at your place."

There was a discussion in the background. Tom explained the situation to Becky. Then, I heard Becky say, "No way. I'm going with you."

"Sure, I'll meet you there in about twenty minutes. Becky wants to come too."

"Look Tom, we don't have time to argue about it, but I think bringing her with you is a bad idea. Try to talk her out of it, but get down here as quick as you can. Call me when you get close." I hung up.

Sal had just stepped out of the bathroom wrapped in a towel. "Try to talk who, out of what?"

"Sal, I'll fill you in on the details later. Right now, you need to get dressed as fast as you can."

"Tell me what's going on." She was not the kind of person who was going to take blind orders. I should have known that.

"Okay. Ray's out. He killed Lt. Boswick. He says he's coming after you. The police don't know where he is. And, all this happened yesterday afternoon. He's got a head start. He could be outside the door, for all we know. Now please, get dressed fast. We need to get out of here." She didn't ask any more questions.

Her hair was wet, and she had no makeup, but she was dressed in two minutes. I wouldn't have believed it possible.

During that two minutes, I called the Seattle Police. I told them who 'Sal' was, her connection to Ray, where we were, and that we were going to hide until an officer arrived. A rookie cop had been assigned to take the calls.

"Okay sir, we'll send an officer over there as soon as we can." I am a professional reader of tone and inflection. The police were going to take their sweet time to follow up on my call. They probably had gotten dozens of calls, mostly from old busy bodies who thought they saw someone who looked like the photo. And, most of those people probably had a hard time seeing if their shoes were tied.

Maybe I was wrong, but I wasn't going to wait around for them to show up like the cavalry, just in the nick of time.

"We need to hide as best we can until the police get here." We needed a plan. I didn't have one.

"Where do we hide where he won't be able to find us?" Sal asked.

"I don't know. We need to try to do the unexpected. Remember what Anna said. He's a predator. We're the prey. We can't act like the prey, or he'll be able to predict what we are going to do."

"So, what? Do we go knock on his door?"

"If we knew where the door was, maybe. But for now, we try to hide. There is nothing else we can do. When Tom get's here with my gun, I'm going to be the predator. Tom can take you and Becky somewhere safe. I'm going after him."

"Tom's bringing a gun! Heck, this isn't the old west. You're not the police." She wasn't criticizing me, she was trying to reason with me. She was afraid, and that made me even angrier at Ray.

"Sal, right now you're being threatened. You're afraid. I can't stand seeing you afraid. I have to stop him. He expects us to run away. I'm deciding to do the unexpected. I'm going to kill him, if I can." I wanted her to understand that I was not crazy. I was only being rational in an irrational way.

"I'm afraid for you too. He's dangerous. He can do things. He'll kill you Heck if you get in his way." I could see the shadow of my death in her eyes, the sorrow, the regret, the tears.

"I'm definitely going to get in his way. You're right, he might kill me, but I can't let anything happen to you. That would kill me for sure. Whatever I do, it's my choice, and I'll have to live or die with the consequences. Whatever happens, *I'm* responsible. This is *my* choice, Sal." I said softly. I hoped she could see my resolve too.

Something in her eyes touched my heart. "I trust you, Heck." She leaned over on her tip toes and kissed me. "You have to do what you think is right. I'm with you. That's *my* choice."

I poked my head out of the door cautiously. Nobody was in the hallway in either direction.

I put the Do Not Disturb sign on the door. It couldn't hurt. Maybe he'd get there and think we were still in the room.

I decided to take the stairs instead of the elevator, less confining, maybe less predictable. The problem with trying to be unpredictable is the fact that everything you do is predictable from your own perspective. If someone is able to get inside your head, and see things from your perspective, your every move can be predicted. In order to be truly unpredictable, you have to surprise yourself. Not easy.

We took the stairs to the basement level. Then we made our way to the back of the hotel and took the service elevator up to the kitchen.

We told a confused kitchen staff person that we had to talk to the hotel manager immediately. Fortunately, he didn't want to deal with us, and just handed me a house phone and dialed the manager's extension, then took off.

"Hello, Sykes here."

"My name is Hector Beckman. One of your guests has been threatened. I have notified the police. They are on their way. I am hiding her in your hotel until they arrive. Please tell the police when they get here to call me at my cell number."

"What are you talking about? Where are you? I'm calling the police." He was used to prank callers.

"I can't tell you where we are for security reasons. Please call the police, and give them this number." I gave him my cell number, and hung up.

I didn't know where we were going. I was making it up as we went along. I was trying to surprise myself.

I spotted what looked like a dressing area for kitchen and wait staff. There were uniforms and aprons hanging up. I took two aprons that looked like they'd fit us. I rolled them up and put them under my arm.

There was a doorway that led to a hallway. The hallway was used only by hotel staff. It was empty.

I tried doors that looked like they might be closets. I found one on my third try. It contained cleaning supplies.

We stepped in, found a light switch, and closed the door behind us.

"We can hide out here for now. Tom should get here any minute. Put the apron on. It's not much of a disguise, but it can't hurt.

"If someone comes in, we can pretend we were caught philandering on company time." I grinned at her. She smiled back. It carried a warmth that I hadn't seen yesterday.

"Maybe we should try to be more convincing." She leaned into me, and put her arm around me. It felt good. It felt like we were a couple. I guess we were, but I hadn't really thought about it until just then.

My phone rang. It was Tom.

"Heck, I'm almost there. Where do you want to meet?"

"There is an alley behind the hotel. Meet us there."

I knew there had to be a back door to that alley. I had a sense of where it should be, but we had to look around a little. We met other staff people, but no one gave us a second look. The disguise worked.

It only took a couple minutes to find the alley. We just beat Tom to it.

There was Tom. He was turning his Mustang into the alley. Becky was with him.

I waved. He pulled up. He and Becky were getting out of the car, when Ray stepped out from behind a nearby trash bin. Tom saw him at the same time I did.

Sal let out a surprised scream. The sharp sound bypassed my ears and stabbed directly into my heart.

Ray spoke first. " 'I came to cast fire on the Earth, and would that it were already kindled.' Luke, 12:49.

"Sally Sue Salinger, you are responsible for killing my Julia. You failed to prevent her death. That was your job. You 'screwed up,' didn't you Sal?

"Oh yes, I know about poor Leonard too." Ray pulled out a hunting knife with a heavy ten-inch blade.

"Ray, she did everything she could. It's not her fault." I wasn't unpredictable enough. *It's my fault if she dies.*

"Don't worry professor, you're all going to die with her. You're in my way. Step aside, and let me kill the bitch quickly." He took a step forward.

Tom had the Berretta in his hand. He had put in a full clip earlier. He racked the action and pointed the muzzle at Ray.

"Okay asshole, you brought a knife to a gun fight. You lose. Put it down." Tom's voice was as unsteady as his hand.

"Oh, it's the son-of-a-Birch right on time. Sometimes, Mr. Birch, it's better to bring a knife to a gun fight. And, why can't anyone think of an original insult?" He took a couple steps toward Sal and I. He was less than eight feet away.

"Stop or I'll shoot." Tom's voice was a little higher.

"Tom, don't shoot! That's what he wants." Tom glanced at me. He didn't understand. Ray took another step.

Tom fired. Ray moved the knife at lightning speed. The bullet hit the blade and ricocheted back at me, grazing my right temple. It knocked me out, but it couldn't have been for more than a second, long enough to not remember hitting the pavement.

I could hear Sal screaming. She was on her knees next to me. Tom had moved closer to me too, in a defensive position. Things were fuzzy, but I was still in this world.

"See what you did Birch. You shot the professor. And now I'm going to take care of Sally Sue too." He moved toward us.

Tom fired again. The knife flashed. The bullet bounced off the blade and returned into Tom's midsection. He dropped. The gun fell out of his hand near me. Becky screamed and ran to Tom's side.

Ray instantly lunged at Sal. He grabbed her around the neck and dragged her across to the other side of the alley. She struggled at first, but stopped when Ray put the knife to her throat.

"Okay Hector, it's your turn. I like you, so I'm giving you a choice. You can either watch me cut your little Blondie Girl's throat, or you can shoot her yourself. Go ahead, pick up the gun. I put it there for you. That's why I didn't kill you a minute ago."

"You're crazy! Let her go!" I picked up the gun, but I didn't have much of a shot at this range, from my position.

My vision was blurry. Ray crouched down and held Sal in front of him, like a shield. Even if I did see an opening, and even if I were an expert shot, which I'm not, he would simply move out of the way. Or worse, he'd bounce the bullet back at me off of his knife. He had just done it twice. I had no doubt that he could do it again.

"Yes, I suppose I am crazy by your definition. But mostly, I'm just different. The world has never seen anyone like me. God, in His *wisdom,* put me here. He made me in His image. So, I guess I'm only as crazy as He is.

"My purpose is His purpose, to make the world a better place. That's what Julia wanted. I promised her. When the bungling bug doctor here is dead, the world will be a better place. But, *my* work is only beginning.

"So what's it going to be, Hecky? You shoot her, or I cut her throat. Don't worry, you won't have much time to feel guilty about it. You'll die five seconds after her, just enough time for you to know that it was *your* fault."

I knew that his promise to kill Sal and I was more than a promise. It was more than a prediction. It was a fact. It was a mathematic certainty. Ray had predicted every possibility, and calculated every contingency. Unless there was something he hadn't thought of, and something that I could see in time, we were as good as dead. I knew it.

The blood had started to build up inside of my skull. The bullet had caused a concussion. My vision became more blurry. I felt dizzy. I knew I was going to lose consciousness in a minute. *Do something. She will die. Decide now!*

"I've got things to do, other people need to die too, you know. I can't wait forever for you to make up your mind. I'll give you to the count of three to decide. One."

I could feel the void creeping toward me. Things were getting darker. That ominous nothingness was calling, threatening, yet comforting.

The void was telling me something, not in words, or sights, or sounds, but through some other sense.

I can't do anything he would expect, I told myself. I must also not do anything he would expect me to do, that I thought he *wouldn't* expect me to do. If I thought of it, he had probably thought of it too. What would I *never* do? It has to be something that there is zero possibility of me doing.

"Two." He was relaxed, casual, no hurry, no worry.

I would never shoot Sal! I wouldn't even shoot near her, in my condition. I was lying on the pavement, nearly unconscious. I had no chance of shooting him without a virtual certainty of hitting her. That would be irrational.

That *is* irrational! Therefore, I wouldn't do it. Therefore, he doesn't expect it. Therefore, he hasn't predicted it. He *knows* I won't shoot her. *I have to shoot Sal. No, I can't! But I must.*

The darkness began to envelop me like a cloak. The gun was still in my hand, but I could no longer see it. The void was telling me to wait. *Wait for what?*

I forced myself to let go of all rational thought and surrender to just my feelings. My consciousness diffused itself into the darkness.

Suddenly, I could see. I could see myself lying below me. I could see Ray and Sal from a position somewhere above the scene. Ray was holding Sal with the knife at her throat. I was holding the gun limply in my hand. My head was on the pavement. Blood was dripping off of my right ear. My eyes were closed.

"Three." Ray said with a note of finality.

Then, Sal did something I never expected. Neither did Ray. She grabbed Ray's crotch. It was not a crushing grip meant to inflict pain, but a tender caressing grope. She was feeling him up!

Ray was not only surprised, he was momentarily paralyzed with confusion. Sal had managed to do something he never expected, he never planned for.

The voice that was not a voice said, "Now!" I pulled the trigger without thinking, without questioning, and without aiming, but with the absolute certain knowledge that it was right.

From my unique vantage point, I saw the muzzle flash from the Berretta. I saw Ray and Sal fall together. I saw blood oozing from Sal's blouse. I saw blood oozing from Ray's shirt. Becky was screaming next to Tom. Sal did not move.

Ray was talking, low and labored.

"'The dead do not praise the Lord, nor do any go down into silence.' Psalm one…"

His voice faded. He did not complete the reference.

I slipped completely into the darkness of the void. It was my mother's womb, warm and comforting. I heard a siren from somewhere. The sound was blue tinged with bright silver.

Then there was nothing.

CHAPTER 48
SAL

Heck moved his foot under the sheets in his hospital bed. I came over to the side of the bed. His eyelids were closed, but his eyes were moving behind them.

"Heck, are you awake?" I said softly, and leaned over and kissed him on the cheek.

He opened his eyes and blinked. "Sal?" His voice was weak and rough.

I pushed the nurse's call button.

"Heck, don't talk. I'll get you some water." I raised the head of his bed until he was in a semi-sitting position. I held the straw for his ice water next to his mouth. He took a sip.

The nurse came in. I said, "He's awake. The doctor told me to let you know when he woke up."

The nurse checked his pulse and blood pressure on the bedside monitor. She checked his I.V. "Well okay, good morning. How are we feeling?" she asked.

"My head hurts." Still raspy, but not as weak. He reached up and touched the bandage on his head.

"It should. We had to drill a hole in it to relieve the pressure. I know, that's all you needed was another hole in your head, right?" She laughed. I didn't, but Heck managed a half smile.

"It looks like you're doing fine. I'll tell the doctor that you're ready to dance." She left the room with a smile on her face. She had a job to do, but it obviously wasn't work for her.

Happiness is a choice. Daddy used to say.

"Sal, what happened? I thought I shot you. I saw you fall." His voice grated across course sandpaper, not much more than a loud whisper.

"You did shoot me! Well, a little. I guess I fainted. The bullet barely broke the skin though. See." I lifted my blouse and showed him the small bandage on the side of my left breast under my arm. It was going to get in the way of my bra until it healed. Then I showed him the other small bandage under my left arm, directly across from the other wound.

"I'm sorry. I didn't want to hurt you. I didn't mean to shoot you." I could see that he was taking it far more seriously that it deserved.

"Heck, it's okay, really. I don't know how you did it, but you did what you had to do, and so did I. Did you see me grab him in his *delicate* area?" I smirked. "I was trying to distract him somehow. I guess it worked.

"They put two stitches on my side, and three on my arm. I won't even notice it in a week." He looked a little less pained.

"I was trying to shoot Ray. I think I hit him. Where is he?" He didn't know.

"I guess he's at the morgue. You shot him in the heart. He's dead."

"Thank God." He was relieved. Then, the pain on his face returned. "Tom! How's Tom?

"He's fine. He's doing fine." I tried to sound as reassuring as possible.

"I saw him get shot?"

"He was shot, but he's doing okay. The bullet went all the way through. It damaged his liver. They had to operate to stop the internal bleeding. They said that nothing else was damaged. He's okay, he's been awake and talking. Becky is with him.

"They've got him on strong pain medication, so he's been sleeping a lot. As soon as you're fit for a wheelchair, you can go see him."

"Is Becky okay? Was she hurt?"

"No, she's okay. She stayed with us the whole time. She called 911 and got three ambulances on the way before the police had time to even think about it.

"She might have saved Tom's life too. She kept pressure on his wound until the paramedics got there. It slowed the internal bleeding. The doctor said that it was probably what kept him from bleeding out before the paramedics could get him to the hospital.

"We're all going to be okay, Heck." I leaned over and kissed him on the lips this time. "Thank you." I said.

Life is a gift. Daddy was right about that too, and here was that gift right in front of me. I kissed him again, and hugged him the best I could from the bedside.

"What about the police?" I killed a man.

"They're calling it *self defense.* He had a knife, and was threatening to use it. Besides, Lt. Boswick was one of theirs. They didn't say as much, but they made it clear that they wanted him dead. They're not going to give you any trouble."

Jan walked into the room.

"Heck, you're awake. Sal called me. She said you would be okay, but I was still worried."

"Jan, thanks for coming to see me. The nurse said I'm ready to dance." She gave him a hug.

"Don't even think about it. Thank God, you're okay. I'm going to see how Tom is doing before I leave. Sal told me *everything.*"

"How are *you* doing?" I said. "I know you've been killing yourself trying to get the Institute opened up again."

"I'm okay. It's been a struggle. I'm trying to pace myself. I'm hoping we can reopen the undamaged wing in a couple months. The big issue there is a getting a working kitchen up and running. It will probably be another year before everything is back to the way it was."

Heck said, "I'm sorry I haven't been more help. I promise I'll do anything I can to help when I get out of here." Heck was sorry? Hadn't he done enough? He had saved me, and who knows how many others.

"One thing you can do is help me deal with the bank. They're burying me in paperwork. The insurance will be coming through, but I need a short term loan. And the insurance is not going to cover everything. I'm also going to need a long term loan to carry the Institute until revenues start to cover expenses again. I thought maybe we could build a new wing too while we're at it, but the bankers are making that look impossible for now."

"Sure, I can deal with paperwork. I didn't go to college for nothin'." He grinned. Heck was looking more like himself. I smiled at him like I imagine a mother would smile at her baby whose fever had broken. Maybe someday I would know that feeling for sure. For now, I could only imagine.

"Sal, don't you have to start that new job next week. Jan, did she tell you that she's getting a promotion?"

"No, she didn't. Congratulations, Sal."

"Thanks. I called my boss and told him everything. He gave me another week off."

"That was nice of him. Tell me if he has any openings. Maybe I'll go work for him. I'm tired of being the boss." Jan's laugh made it clear that she was just joking. But then, 'Many a truth is said in jest' according to Shakespeare.

After several more minutes of chatting, Jan left the room to go see Tom.

I was alone again with Heck. I liked having him all to myself.

"Heck, I'm sorry if I sound a little selfish. But if I'm going to be here another week, I don't want to spend the whole time watching you do paperwork for Jan. Do you think maybe you can get better fast and get out of here, so that we can have a little time… together?" I gave him my best conspiratorial smile, and leaned over to kiss him again. He knew exactly what I meant, and reached over to hug me.

"Sounds good to me. We can start now if you want." He returned the same smile. I giggled. I don't giggle that often, but this moment called for it.

I kissed Heck again, this time more passionately. Daddy told me this day would come. I doubted it for a while. It was another of Daddy's truisms that was being proven true today, '*Tomorrow is a promise.*'

CHAPTER 49
TOM

I was sleeping when I heard Becky talking quietly to my nurse. She was here early this morning. Today was the day they said I could go home, pending a final okay from the doctor.

I had been sleeping normally for the past few days, if you can call being woke up in the middle of the night to have your blood drawn, normal. I was still pretty sore, but my pain medication had been reduced. It was tolerable.

They encouraged me to take short walks a couple times a day. It was painful, and I felt weak. I would rather have stayed in bed, but Becky wouldn't have it. She practically forced me to get up and move around. She wanted me to get better, and she wanted it yesterday.

Becky had been at my bedside almost continuously for the last week since the shootout. She attended to all of my needs that she could, and made sure the nursing staff took care of the ones she couldn't.

Starla would never have been so diligent about supervising my care and recovery. Starla was mostly about taking care of Starla.

Mostly we talked. We talked about everything. We talked about things I had never talked about with any of my previous girlfriends. It wasn't so much that I didn't want to have long in-depth discussions with them, which I really didn't, but it was more that they would not have be capable of it.

Becky was easy to talk with. She was one of the few women I've known who actually wanted to talk about me. Most pretended to be interested in me, but only long to give them an excuse to list all of their own wants and needs.

Becky visibly drank up every word I told her about myself, my past, my work, even about some of the other women I had known. I even found my feelings sneaking into the conversation with her. Feelings had always been very uncomfortable ground for me, but it felt okay with Becky.

"Good morning." She had just come to my bedside, and saw that I was awake.

"Good morning, Freckles." She smiled that beautiful 'good morning' smile of hers and kissed me.

She had called herself that name a couple days ago. I had told her that her freckles were beautiful. I told her that they complemented her strawberry blonde hair perfectly, and they made her face seem to explode with joy when she smiled. She wasn't so sure.

She told me that she had tried unsuccessfully once to get rid of them. "…So, I gave up. Just call me Freckles I guess."

I did, and it stuck. It had become my private term of endearment for her.

"Today's the day. The nurse said the doctor would be in later this morning to give his seal of approval."

"It will be so good to be in my own bed with no one waking me up in the middle of the night to poke needles in me."

"I want to get you settled in, and make sure you have everything you need before Sal and I fly out tomorrow." Her smile disappeared.

My smile had disappeared too. "Becky, I was thinking. Could you stay in Seattle for a while? I don't want you to go." It actually hurt to imagine her so far away. That was a new feeling for me, one of many since I had met Becky.

"Tom, I don't want to go either, but I have too. Sal already paid for the ticket. She asked me to come to Atlanta with her. Maybe I can get a job there and make it a long term thing. I can't live with Momma and Daddy forever."

"Okay, I'm not asking you to move in or anything. I'll pay for your hotel. Maybe you could get a place closer to me. You can cancel the darn ticket. I'll pay Sal back. And you know, with Sal's new job, she's going to be doing nothing but working and sleeping twenty-four seven. You know how she is. She's not going to have much time left over." I wasn't begging exactly. I was emphatically asking. There's a difference.

She smiled, but with an anguished look. A tear formed in one eye.

"Tom, I want to stay. I really do. I wish you had said something before. I promised Sal. I thought you would say something, but when you didn't I thought that was that. I thought maybe it was time for you to move on." The single tear became a trickle.

I took her hand and pulled her closer to me. "Becky, I want you to understand one thing for sure. I *have* moved on, and *you* are who I've moved on to. I've never met anyone like you. I can't bear to think of you out of my life." I took a deep breath.

"Becky, I think I'm in love with you. I don't know how it's supposed to feel. You know how hard it is for me to say… things." I didn't truly know what my feelings were until the moment I put them into words. Now there was a tear in my eye too. The dry hospital air sometimes made my eyes water a little.

She hugged me and began to convulsively cry on my shoulder. It's hard to tell sometimes about a woman's cry. It could be good, or it could be bad. I wasn't sure.

After a minute, the sobs stopped. She stood up and reached for a tissue and for her cell phone at the same time. She didn't look at me, she just hit the autodial. She dabbed her eyes while she waited for an answer.

"Sal, I'm staying in Seattle. I'll talk to you about it later." She disconnected the call. Then she looked at me for the first time since I said… those words. She didn't smile she just looked at me for a long moment. I could do nothing but look back at her. I was afraid to smile. All I could think of was how beautiful she was at that moment, and how lucky I was to be with her.

"I'll stay in Seattle, at least for a while, but you have to let me get a job and get my own place. I want to be here because I *want* to be here, not because you're paying my bills."

"Okay." She could have asked me to stand on my head and whistle Dixie every hour, and I would have gladly agreed.

Then she smiled, and her freckles exploded across her face like the Fourth of July.

CHAPTER 50
HECK

"What was that about?" I said when Sal hung up the phone. She was sitting in my kitchen wearing nothing but a bath robe having a cup of coffee with me.

"It was Becky. She says she's staying in Seattle."

"What? Why?"

"She didn't say. She said we'd talk about it later, but I already know why. She's staying for Tom."

"Does she know what she's getting in to?"

"I think she does. We talked about it the other day. She was waiting for him to ask her to stay. She wasn't sure if Tom wanted anything long term, or if it would be over when we flew out tomorrow. He must have asked."

"I hope he wants her to stay to be more than his bed warmer."

"I think he does. She told me that they didn't have sex, even though they spent that night together."

"That's new for Tom. That must have been Becky's idea, right?"

"No. She said she wanted to, but Tom said 'no.' She said he wants to 'date' first.

"That's a first for Tom.

"Wait a minute. Becky told you all this about her and Tom? What did you tell her about us?"

"Nothing. Well, mostly nothing. She guessed. She said I had 'the glow.' I didn't deny it. I am glowing." She took my hand and squeezed it. I felt the warmth of that glow. I was glowing too.

"Speaking of dating, I don't want you to fly out of my life tomorrow. I know you're going to be working a lot, but I plan to make regular trips to Atlanta. Maybe you can find the time to come out here too. I'd go with you to Atlanta, but I have obligations here, the Institute, the University." I sounded like I was trying to make excuses. I wasn't.

"It'll only be for a little while. We'll work something out. We have to, don't we Heck?"

"Yes, we just have to find a way. Maybe I can get a professorship at Georgia State or another university around Atlanta."

"I trust you Heck. We'll find a way. I know you'll find a way for us to be together."

"I promise you, I will. We've just got to hold on for a little while."

"I don't want to talk about leaving. I don't want to think about it. Becky is driving Tom home. We planned to get together with them later today. But right now, it's just you and me, okay."

She pulled the tie lose from my robe, and reached her hands inside to caressed my bare chest. I pulled her close and kissed her head.

We had made love last night, but I couldn't seem to get enough of her. Apparently, she felt the same. We had made love every chance we had after I got out of the hospital five days ago.

She was inexperienced and a little awkward like you might expect from a much younger virgin, but she had the patience and intelligence of a fully mature woman. Making love with her was more than pleasure, more than excitement. It was as spiritually fulfilling as it was physically fulfilling.

She was sensitive to my needs, and I was sensitive to hers. We were like a dance team, each sensing the other's desires, and choreographing our dance moves to achieve a sort of artistic perfection.

We went back to bed. After the music of our dance had reached its final crescendo, we napped in each other's arms.

We got up for the second time. It was late morning. We showered together.

A couple showering together is about much more than getting clean. It's a pair bonding ritual that may or may not have anything to do with sex. Sal understood this intuitively.

We scrubbed each other's backs. I massaged shampoo into her hair. We hugged and kissed while the hot water splashed on our naked bodies. It was a deeply intimate experience for both of us. Regardless of where our relationship might eventually lead, we would always have these sparkling jewel-like moments to remember.

Since I completed my morning routine much sooner than Sal, I decided to make us a simple breakfast of eggs and bacon. Toasted bagels, fresh coffee, and orange juice completed the spread. It was ready by the time Sal emerged from the bedroom, dressed but still brushing out her hair.

"Smells fantastic. I'm starved." She sat down and immediately started eating. I sat down with her.

"Me too. I think we've burned up a lot of calories." I said. She attempted to laugh with a full mouth. This made me laugh too.

"You said you sent in another report to the CDC yesterday. I thought your work with the case was pretty much done." Breakfast is not the same without a little small talk.

"It is, mostly. Rose sent me the results on some post mortem tests that I ordered on Ray."

"What more do we need to know? He's dead. That's all *I* need to know."

"There's only so much you can tell from a blood sample, genetic information yes, but not a lot more. I asked the Seattle Coroner to get me some tissue samples from Ray when they did the autopsy. I was especially interested in brain and nerve tissues. I express-shipped them to our lab in Atlanta. I wanted to know more about how Ray was able to do the things he did."

"Okay, how did he do it? He was awfully fast with that knife, deflecting those bullets."

"I won't bore you with the whole report. I'll give you the summary.

"You know how nerve cells communicate with each other, right?"

"It's been a while. Refresh my memory." I said.

"The electrolytic properties of sodium and potassium ions generate currents across the cell membranes in two ways, a passive movement of ions across the cell membranes, and an electrical charge differential. You can think of nerve cells as tiny batteries of sorts. They charge and discharge from one cell to the next, like a bucket brigade. That's why it takes about two-tenths of a second for a signal to travel from your brain to your hand, for example. For comparison a hard-wired electrical signal travels at the speed of light, millions of times faster than a nerve signal. That relatively slow reaction time delay is a factor in almost everything we do. It controls not only how fast we can move, but how fast we can think too."

"It's coming back." It wasn't coming back at all.

"That's how it works for normal people. But, Ray was not normal. The chemical analysis of his nerve cells showed that he had a very high concentration of sodium that made his cells much more conductive. Plus, there was much more copper than normal. It's usually just a trace element, but Ray's was 500 times the normal level. Instead of a bucket brigade, his cells were more like a telegraph line, transmitting signals at least hundreds of times faster than normal.

"Do you know if Ray ate a lot of salt?"

"Jan mentioned that he liked to put salt on everything. I didn't think anything of it. Just a quirk, I thought. Hey I'm a little quirky with salt too. I can't get out of the habit of putting salt on my fries before I've tasted them."

"I'll bet he was eating a lot of shell fish too. They're high in copper. But everybody eats a lot of seafood out here don't they?"

"I guess some people do."

"Anyway, that's probably why his abilities increased with time. He was building up his sodium and copper concentrations."

"I could use a little more speed. Pass the clams and the salt, please."

"Sorry, it doesn't work that way. You'd just pee out the excess. Ray's genetic structure made his cells change so that the extra sodium and copper could be retained in his nervous system. Good thing he wasn't born with those genes."

"Why?"

"You could compare Ray, before he got the virus, to say a Volkswagen Beetle. When the virus changed his genetic structure, it was trying to turn him into a Cadillac Escalade. That's pretty hard to do. There's only so much you can change. But if you're born with Cadillac Escalade genes, it's much easier to build from scratch.

If you bake a chocolate cake, and then decide you want vanilla, you don't try to change the existing cake, you start from scratch and bake a new one. Same thing."

"I love it when you talk science to me, Sal. It turns me on. But then, you turn me on without saying anything at all." She laughed, but I meant every word.

"Okay, maybe later. Right now you have to go through those cards from Tyler's funeral. I'll help. You just open them, and I'll write down the names. You've got the Thank You cards. You've got the funeral attendee register. We got back the photos of Tyler. I'll match up names and addresses, and stuff the envelopes. It should only take us an hour or so."

"You're right, I should get them out." She knew that I needed a little push. She put the shoe box with all the cards in front of me. She got a notebook and a pen for herself. I had been dreading this. I didn't want to face it, to be forced to relive the funeral. Sal made it bearable.

When I got to the card from Tom, I was surprised to see twenty dollars in lottery tickets. The note he wrote said. 'Sorry I didn't get any flowers. I'm here for you, Tom.' "

I learned later that he had picked them up at the 7-Eleven where we had stopped when we were on our way to the funeral. He had been so busy with funeral arrangement, he hadn't thought about ordering flowers from himself. It was a last minute impulse, a symbolic sentiment. That's Tom.

I set the tickets aside. I'd check the numbers later, when I got time.

###

It had been one year now since I killed Ray. He was responsible for many changes in my life, some bad, but some good changes too. Decisions and consequences. Things happen because people make them happen, even when they don't know it.

I understand now that you can't get out of making choices, the universe won't allow it. When you don't make a choice, that is also a choice. And, *all* choices have consequences.

Three months after I opened the card from Tom containing the lotto tickets, I got the time to check the numbers. I had an eighty-million dollar jackpot winner. My luck had changed, but it was going to get even better.

I made Tom sign the ticket with me. After all, he bought the ticket. He argued that my orange soda request had delayed him long enough for another customer to enter the 7-Eleven before him, and to buy a lottery ticket before Tom purchased his twenty dollars worth of quick-picks. True, but I argued that it was both of our individual decisions combined that won the jackpot.

We took the forty-million cash option. After taxes, we each got a check for fourteen-million dollars.

It was Tom's idea to make a joint donation to the Mercer Residential Rehabilitation Institute. There had been talk of a new children's wing sometime in the future. Why not now? We decide to donate four-million dollars each for the *Tyler Clinton Beckman Memorial Children's Wing.*

Jan was thrilled, but she insisted that Tom and I be on the board of directors of the Institute, and that I play a significant role in the management and operation of the new wing. We all agreed, and work began within a month.

Most of the restoration of the old structure was complete now. The Children's wing is set to open in a few months.

Anna was one of the first to move into the Institute when it reopened four months ago. I see her on a regular basis.

She has gotten quite a reputation, through no effort of her own, just word of mouth. People travel from across the country to have her do a reading for them. She refuses most requests, and she refuses any payment for those that she accepts. I help run interference for her.

I asked her how she decides who to do a reading for, and who to refuse. She said, "I don't know. I just decide. It works out better, if I don't think about why."

I resigned my position with the University of Washington. I agreed to give guest lectures from time to time, but I spend most of my time at the Institute.

I'm not going to say that Sal and I fell in love. That would be too cliché, and it wouldn't be exactly accurate. We did not fall into anything. Our love for each other was revealed to us. It was as if it was always there, from the day we were born.

I've often heard the term 'soul mates' to describe relationships like ours. Maybe that's what we are to each other, but I never really understood the full meaning of that term until I met Sal.

Before I met her, I was a jigsaw puzzle with one piece missing. In retrospect, my life had always been a quest to find that piece. When that final piece of my being finally slid effortlessly into place, I knew I was complete.

Wendy was never that missing piece, only one that sort of fit, but it had to be forced. I don't regret my time with Wendy. It produced Tyler. I will always be thankful to her for that.

Oh, I should mention, Sal and I were married three months ago. We were shuttling back and forth between Atlanta and Seattle. It wasn't working for either of us. It was obvious to both of us that we needed to be married and living together, and soon.

We agonized over it, but Sal decided she would have to resign her position with the CDC, and try to find another job in the Seattle area. It made sense, but it wasn't an easy decision.

When Sal's boss got the news, he was not at all happy about it. Sal's performance at her new job had been outstanding. The new department was fully staffed and up and running. He did not want to see her leave. No one there wanted to see Sal leave, least of which, Rose.

A week later, he called Sal into his office and gave her our wedding present. He had an old college buddy who was now the CEO at the Mantelle Corporation in Seattle, a private research firm. It turns out they needed a Research Scientist with a background in epidemiology. Dr. Edelman gave Sal such a glowing recommendation that the interview a week later was almost a formality. She got the job.

We had a small wedding in Tennessee at the Donaldson farm. Sal insisted that her Uncle Ben be the one to walk her down the aisle and give her away. Of course, Tom was my Best Man, and Becky was Sal's Maid of Honor.

'Small' turned out to be over one-hundred-fifty guests. A three-thousand square foot tool shed that Ben had recently built was emptied out and decorated for the occasion. It all worked out okay. It was what Sal said she had always wanted. She was happy, so I was happy.

Sal only had a couple weeks off between jobs, so we had to shorten our honeymoon to just five days. We decided to stay at an upscale resort in the San Juan Islands, not far from Seattle. It was beautiful, but we didn't get a chance to see much more than the inside of our room.

Last month, we confirmed that Sal is pregnant. It's too early to tell the sex, but we agreed that if it's a boy, we'll name him Samuel after her father. And if it's a girl, we'll name her Nancy, after my sister.

We paid five-million dollars for a condo on Alki Point near Seacrest Landing. It overlooks Elliot bay and downtown Seattle. The view from our fifth floor patio is spectacular.

Becky went to work for a Ford dealership. She had to first convince the sales manager of her car-selling abilities, even though she had no experience selling cars, or anything else. She talked him into hiring her on a commission-only trial basis.

She was salesman of the month for her first six months running. When the sales manager had to leave for health reasons, Becky got his job.

Becky's now living in a duplex in Bellevue on the Eastside. She got a puppy shortly after she moved in. Her duplex neighbor, a retired widow, looks after the dog during the day when she's at work. It's a beagle. She named him Robbie.

We have a pet now too. Sal adopted a stray cat that had been hit by a car. Someone rescued it from the street and left it with the vet where Becky takes Robbie for his shots. His left front paw had to be amputated. The vet had him in a cage in his lobby with a sign that read "Free to good home."

Sal was with Becky when she dropped off Robbie at the vet. They were on a girl's-only last-minute Christmas shopping marathon last December. Sal saw the crippled cat and her heart went out to it.

The *free* cat cost fifty dollars for shots. It cost us another three-hundred dollars to have the vet take care of the cat for another two weeks until we got back from Christmas in Tennessee with Becky's folks.

Sal named the cat Ferguson. She said, it was because he likes fried hamburger. I just call him Limpy. I like him okay, but he sits only on her lap. Cats just know things.

Tom decided to publish a new monthly magazine. He's calling it *Expedition America.* He's put up a million dollars to get it off the ground. It's modeled after National Geographic Magazine. It's stuffed with high resolution photos, but it will focus on real-life American adventures and the people who live them.

Tom and Becky have been 'dating' for a year now, an all time record for Tom. Sal and I predict that their relationship will soon be moving past the dating stage.

Billy recently published a paper titled *Quantum Consciousness.* It created quite a stir in the physics community. In the paper, he postulates that there is no objective single reality, and that every individual constructs his own reality with each quantum decision. Effectively, everyone lives in a private universe of their own creation.

It sounds a little out in left field, but Billy backed it up with some pretty convincing mathematics. Convincing that is, if you're a quantum physicist. The math is the part that's caused the stir.

I gave Tom a copy of Billy's paper. I think he must be still studying it, because he hasn't gotten back with me yet to talk about it.

I visit Tyler's grave every week or so, sometimes with Sal, but usually by myself. I don't blame myself for his death.

Yes, my decisions, or lack of decisions, contributed to his death. But, I'm only human. Humans make mistakes.

Sometimes we don't know we're making a mistake, sometimes we do. I trust my intuition more now. It seems that the more I think about a difficult decision, the more often I'm wrong.

When I think about it, which is not very often, I thank God, if there is one, for my ability to make mistakes. The freedom to make a wrong decision comes with the ability to make any decision at all. I've made some bad ones, but I think I've made a few good ones too.

I accept responsibility for the consequences of my decisions, whatever they are.

CHAPTER 51
MARY

This last year had been hard for me. I lost my job and Mom died in the same month. Then, I found out I was pregnant the same week I got the eviction notice.

I had to move in with Dad. I didn't want to do it, but I had no choice. No one wanted to hire a pregnant girl.

Dad drank a lot. He always was a drinker, but when Mom died it got worse. I put up with his abusive language. He wanted me to do all the housework and cooking like Mom had done. I was effectively his house slave. I didn't complain though. I had a roof over my head, and food on the table. His house, his rules, but that would change.

Dad didn't accept that I had gotten pregnant by a stranger. He referred to the baby as 'The Bastard,' both before he was born and after. He wanted me to abort it, but I couldn't do that.

After Jeremiah was born, Dad wanted me to go after the father for support. All I knew about the father was that his name was Ray. I didn't know anything else. He came out of nowhere, he was there when I needed someone, then he disappeared.

He listened to me. He understood me. I had had a few drinks, but I was far from drunk that night when I left the hospital after Mom died. I can't explain it, but he seemed to know what I was thinking, what I was feeling. Before I knew it, we were in bed together. I have never done that kind of thing before, but I did it with him. It felt okay. He made it feel okay.

The next morning, he was just gone. I never saw him again. The one thing that stuck in my memory of that night with him is what he said after we had finished having sex, a Bible quote of all things. He looked at my belly when he said it. It was weird. I guess that's why I remembered it.

He said, "'Before I formed you in the womb I knew you, and before you were born I consecrated you; I appointed you a prophet to the nations.' Jeremiah 1:5." Funny, but I think now, that he knew I was pregnant.

I looked it up. It was in the Bible all right. He must have been some kind of holy roller or something.

Anyway, I decided to name my son, Jeremiah. I wished I had gotten Ray's last name. Then I wouldn't have had to give him my last name, which was also my father's last name, Morgan.

My father suggested that I give him his middle name too, Harold. I told my father that I had decided not to give him a middle name at all. What I didn't tell him was that I had just made that decision because of his suggestion.

Jeremiah, or Jerry as I sometimes called him, had been doing very well. He was three months old now. He was strong, and the doctor said he was developing at an above normal rate. He could sit by himself when he was one month old. He could crawl at two months. He watched me closely when I talked. He seemed to know what I was saying, just a mother's imagination, I thought.

He had been sleeping, but I thought I heard him stirring that morning. He would make noises, but he never cried. I started giving him a bottle filled with water when I put him to bed. He slept better.

I went into his room to check on him. He was standing in his crib holding on to the railing with one hand. With is other hand, he was holding his bottle. No, not *holding*, he was *twirling* his bottle balanced on one finger, like I've seen basketball players do with a basketball.

I stopped in the doorway, startled at what I was seeing. He heard me. He looked at me and smiled.

He said, "Goo momin mama."

I fainted.

THE END

About the Author

R. Roy Lutz has worked closely with developmentally disabled adults with various impairments, including autistic spectrum disorders. He has had a diverse career in real estate, manufacturing, military, electronics, business, and social services.

Roy has known the joy of holding his new child for the first time, and the grief of saying goodbye to a loved one for the last time. He has viewed the world through many eyes, from a minimum-wage parent struggling to pay the rent, to a business owner struggling to make payroll, to a courageous soul with an imperfect body struggling to live on his own.

Roy is a life-long reader of fiction, and an avid collector of scientific and historical trivia. When he's not working on a novel, he enjoys pondering the riddles of the universe and poking fun at the absurdities of the human condition.

Roy is a father of four and a grandfather of seven. He lives with his devoted wife Christine, and their talking cat Gizzy in New Port Richey, Florida.